The Concierge

Martin Fallon

This book, and everything, is for Gretchen.

ACKNOWLEDGMENTS

I'm grateful to Iris and Dennis Sullivan who remain inspirational. Rebeccah Beegle was a supportive and insightful editorial presence. Jordan Kayser was always ready with the latest hospitality insights. And I'm thankful that there is a real John Friday sharing his music from Nashville to Key West. Thanks also to my Southwest Florida family and friends who never said: "Whaddya, crazy??" They were remained in my corner long after I passed the ten-year mark. And to my daughter Christina, the universal muse, role reversals are hard work but have never been more appreciated.

Chapter I

FEBRUARY, NAPLES, FLORIDA

Dale glided the front seat as far back as his big car allowed, thankful that the vintage Camaro outsized most modern GM models. He slid over to get closer to his "date" and crooned in his best husky come hither voice, " Closer, darlin'..."

The girl closed her eyes and prayed he was a good kisser. Shannon had let herself be picked up by this guy, it being late on Saturday night. Now, getting more sober by the second, she was beginning to suspect Dale was less of a playboy and more of a dreaded local cracker on a weekend sex hunt.

Dale had started his prowl much earlier in the day at Pelican Perch Country Club a quaint bar in southern Lee County. The joint was old, with knotty pine walls left over from whenever knotty pine was considered fashionable. What drew people here was the pleasant ruse of a bar being called a country club when it was clearly a dive. One need only witness the patrons drinking beer with their breakfasts at seven in the morning. The affordable suds made the PPCC popular among both young adults and older cheapskates.

His cheap buzz clearly on, Dale left the joint for Yeti's on Fifth Avenue, in the heart of downtown Naples. Most of its patrons could afford the ten dollar drinks and the expensive rents in an area famous for high rollers. It was eleven when he strolled in and immediately spotted Shannon and her empty glass. Dale grabbed the open seat next to her, wondering why the place was not spilling out onto the sidewalk. One week before, the establishment had been packed, but he felt so outclassed that he retreated back to Bonita, resolving to buy some better clothes before trying to mix with the rich folks again. His price tags removed, and feeling fortified by the earlier beers, Dale asked the pretty girl what her name was and what she was drinking.

"Shannon", she answered quietly.

"Why is she alone.", Dale thought. Tall, blonde and young, with her skirt way up on those impossible legs, her recent arrival had brought about a temporary social vacuum. This was an older crowd on a slow evening, guys with girls that now seemed somewhat lacking. It all screamed for realignment. Or maybe it was just the incomprehensibility of a supermodel unaccompanied on a Saturday night. The consensus was that she was waiting for someone. Her high status alpha male was parking the car. Whatever the astrophysical blip in the social firmament, Shannon pointed to her glass while eyeing Dale. But being a little out of focus herself, she was not able to guess his social standing.

"Dirty martini," Shannon informed him when he asked and the little slur in "dirty" told Dale that she might have already downed two (or more) before he arrived to rescue her. When she asked, he told her not entirely truthfully that he owned a service station in Estero. Yeti's was clearly dead, or dying, so when he suggested going to the hottest dance place in the area, Shannon accepted. The truth was that she was probably not the sharpest knife in the drawer, as if that excuse was any apology for foolhardiness. But Shannon, by all visual accounts, filled the description of a big girl, even if her actual maturity was still up for grabs. His vintage car looked old, but when Dale punched it, the absence of pollution controls and that big four-barrel carb pushed Shannon back in the seat and she felt the surge between her legs.

Swings nightclub was throbbing with excitement, though Shannon was a little put off when Dale offered a gift certificate to get in, effectively avoiding the twenty dollar cover charge. She ordered a Long Island Ice Tea, a stiff favorite featuring gin, vodka, tequila and triple sec with a little cola and lime juice. Two of those, on top of however many dirty martinis she'd had at Yeti's, fogged her headlights just enough so that when Dale suggested they leave, Shannon could think of no reason not to go.

Instead of heading to a cushy condo or hotel, he parked on the access road to Rookery Bay on the way to Marco Island. This unfortunate surprise became impossible for Shannon to let slide. She questioned his choice of spots.

Dale answered, sounding quite macho, "My roommate's shacked up in our one bedroom apartment."

However, by then Shannon was nursing some serious misgivings. When Dale compounded this growing list of indignities by not being a good kisser after all, Shannon suddenly remembered that she had to get home, "NOW!" because she had an early shift at the Hotel Sherill.

Steaming, Dale fired the big engine and fish-tailed a half circle on the rough limestone road, almost running into the canal. This specific maneuver caused him to have to brake hard to a stop. There, in the echoing expletives, night mist and stone dust, they both saw the partially submerged bodies of what looked like two men. Dale, his night already in the toilet, wanted to drive away, so it was Shannon who dialed 911 on her cell phone.

Detective Daniel Logan sat with his fiancée, Corporal Veronica Menendez, at the Parma Hotel bar in Estero. As couples go, they were of the striking variety. Dan stood six-four and close to two hundred and fifty pounds. Roni was tall but Dan still dwarfed her. She, at twenty-eight, was a stunning woman with skin much darker than her redhead Irish fiancé's, and big beautiful eyes accompanying a full head of long, lustrous black hair. She was dressed to dance and have fun, and the two had elicited a lot of attention from the other hotel guests. Dan and Roni were catching a breather and watching the swimmers still trying to navigate the "river" current that ran from the waterfall in the hotel's huge swimming pool. As a betrothed couple, hotel hopping had become one of their routines while they searched for the perfect spot for their wedding reception, just a few weeks away.

A dance combo was still playing, and Roni used the excuse of their future festivities to get Dan out of his comfort zone and back onto the hardwood floor.

"Nice dancing, big boy," she whispered to him, not wanting to dampen any of her lover's enthusiasm for the salsa rhythms pulsating from the bandstand.

"You're not so bad yourself." Dan pretended that it was his girl's lack of coordination that caused them to stumble into an older couple.

Roni giggled at his exaggeration and stood back to show him some fancy steps. He noticed other patrons turning to look at his spectacular date and reached out to grab Roni and pull her onto his lap, ending the free floorshow. She burrowed into his chest, kissing his neck, then his ears, and he shivered as an erotic jolt ran through him. But they were in a public place and his phone was ringing, the screen reading 'headquarters'.

Still grinning at the good-natured ribbing, Dan flipped on his vibrating phone and got the message about the bodies in a canal near Marco Island. Ordinarily, he would have let Corporal Brady lead the initial investigation on a routine 911 call. He would much prefer to keep his mind on his beautiful date and later try to coax her into bed. They both had enjoyed some wonderful trysts at his house in their time, but ever since their engagement, Roni had chosen to remain celibate until after the wedding. Now this call suggested the possibility of a gang hit – no car in the drink, so no accident. He guessed this was the real thing. Dan would have to go, freeing Roni from his ongoing seduction for one night. Business was business. But on the ride back to Roni's house, they had a little time to talk about their latest resort research.

"What'd you think of the hotel?", he asked her.

Roni was not at all impressed. "You heard the night manager. He said we'd have to use one of the side banquet rooms. Those spaces were shabby"

"You're right," Dan had to agree. Compared to the showy common areas, the hotel's back selections looked second class.

Dan had acknowledged that his fiancée was able to see beyond his misty-eyed response to these places. All he wanted was to be married to this woman. And *soon!* When the hotel official dropped the ballpark estimate on the per-person costs, the decision to reject this place became an easy one.

"Okay, we've looked at six possibilities," Dan added, "and we're running out of time!"

Roni could hear his frustration. She knew that he was *not* on the same fun ride that she was enjoying. She could've gone on forever this way, having dinner here, a fancy drink at a stylish joint there. Just one special date after another.

They pulled up to her home and Roni made sure he had the small chance to begin to undress her before she bolted from the car, running to the front door and leaving Dan ready for a different type of excitement. This one was nowhere near so sweet. This being among the first police officers to arrive on a new crime scene.

Dan met Corporal Gary Ritter at the substation. Ordinarily, Sean Brady was Dan's partner, but Sean was driving his mother for a cancer consult in Gainesville. This corporal was there with the rest of the team, major crimes requiring high ranking officers to be present, and the chief was on board. Gary raised an eyebrow and mumbled a greeting, any familiarity blunted, glancing over his shoulder at the presence of so much brass.

Chief Jerry Kelly was glad to get out of the bridge game his wife Margaret had scheduled. He sucked in the rich tropical night, stretching his back to ease the pressure of too much time in a hard backed chair, playing badly. When her action addicted husband ran toward his first love, Margaret always sighed with relief. She was tired of losing at cards.

Chief Kelly clapped Dan on the back, his joviality a little forced but the gratitude sincere. Dan could see the chief was excited too. It had been some time since their last murder.

"Sorry to get you out on your weekend off." The chief was only now noticing Dan's tropical shirt and creased dress pants. He got a whiff of a perfume that was not Bay Rum, and guessed with whom his favorite detective had been consorting. But that was not any of his business, as he could only look at Corporal Menendez from afar, Dan having won *that* lottery.

The Medical Examiner, old Doc Weeks, was also on his way, a man who had been on the job for as long as anyone could remember. He was always full of crusty stories of the "good ole days" when all he had for forensics was a scalpel and thermometer. Now, the lab had a guy who studied insects so they could judge the time of death from the size of the maggots. The dive team would meet them at Rookery Bay.

The bodies had been in the water long enough to make the faces difficult to recognize. Tied together, the single Danforth anchor had not been heavy enough to keep them underwater after the body gases increased their buoyancy. The wind, tide, and a recent storm had combined to push the men close to shore. The six foot rope tying them to the weight had ceased to be an effective deterrent to disclosure. The whole area was now closed to the public, yellow crime scene tape across the road. The local kayakers would have to find another access point to Rookery Bay. The tech team hadn't found anything on the ground, leaving Dan to be convinced the crime had been committed elsewhere. He didn't want to waste too much time on site until they got more data from the Medical Examiner. He had more important things to do. Doc Weeks supervised the bagging, promising to call as soon as he had anything beyond the probable causes of death, which for these two appeared to be multiple bullet holes.

By the time Dan and Gary finished questioning the temporary couple, the witnesses were sober, cold, and ready to go home. Dan thought the girl looked familiar to him, but couldn't place her. He felt she was too young and too much the looker for the guy in the old car, the two of them acting like they couldn't wait to have the evening end so they could separate. The team had their phone numbers and addresses.

Shannon was trying not to shiver. Her little blouse and short skirt were poor protection for the damp night that was getting colder.

Dan checked his notes. "Where did you say you worked?"

The girl blurted, "I work at the Spa in the Hotel Sherill. I just started last month."

"Ah", Dan thought. He'd been there just this week, investigating several off site robberies of guests.

Then, he double-checked the cracker. Dale was standing far from his date and mumbled a response that Dan couldn't quite hear. The cop demanded, and got, a louder response.

"I work at the Grease and Tire in Bonita."

Shannon spun around, not believing her ears. "What'd you just say?" That was her last straw, and she stomped farther from the man's slumping disappointment.

Sensing the estrangement, Dan asked, "Are you guys okay? Does anybody need a ride back?"

Shannon interrupted Dale's refusal, saying quickly, "Yes, please! I need a ride. To *my* car."

They let the vintage vehicle go first. Gary and Dan put Shannon in the back seat of the cruiser for the trip back to downtown Naples. The town was buttoned up by the time they reached Third Street. Very early Sunday morning was a time of sleep in this community. Sensing Shannon's vulnerability, Dan and Gary checked to see if Dale or anyone had followed them.

Still rubbing her arms to get warm, Shannon whispered a quiet, but still sexy, "Thank you," got out of the cruiser and unlocked her car. It was difficult not to look when she had to hike her skirt even higher to squeeze in behind the wheel of her little Tercel. All lights operational and heading in the direction of the young woman's stated place of residence, the police turned their Crown Victoria toward Bonita and the police substation.

TWO MONTHS EARLIER

Two phones rang simultaneously. "Hotel Sherill. This is Richard at the concierge desk. Please allow me to put your call on first response." Then, almost repeating himself, he said to that client, "Hotel Sherill. Richard speaking. Please allow me to put your call on first response. I will be with you in a moment." His deep baritone and aristocratic accent were persuasive elements in the creation of all the clients' beliefs that their call were about to receive immediate exemplary service.

The excited patrons were correct. At the Hotel Sherill, or "The Sherill" as the insiders referred to that venerable property, service was their primary commodity. There were newer facilities in town. In fact, most of the hospitality centers in and around the Naples area had been conceived and built long after (Sir) George Sherill brought his unique performance philosophy to Southwest Florida. However, none of the newcomers had the Sherill's record of guest satisfaction and customer loyalty. And the prices at the more recent facilities were not even close to the exorbitant bills the well-heeled guests at the Sherill were grateful to pay for the opportunity to be a part of this mystical heritage of ambiance and exclusivity.

Richard went back to his first caller. "Again, this is Richard. Please accept my apology for the wait." (The wait was never more than twenty seconds.) "How may I be of assistance?"

"My name is Myra Frothingham, calling from Manhattan. My husband Albert and I are arriving for the holidays."

"Yes, Mrs. Frothingham, please allow me to check your reservation." Richard punched in the name on his computer, revealing the news that they were VIP guests, occupying a suite that would house them and their grown children and grandchildren through Christmas, New Year's celebrations and beyond. This had apparently been a Frothingham tradition going back to the hotel's earlier days, the family's *olde* money unaffected by bear markets and other cycles that inhibited mere mortal folks' travel plans. The total cost of the visit was going to exceed fifty thousand dollars, not including extras. It was for these a la carte items that Mrs. Frothingham needed assistance. The list would be long.

Richard begged Mrs. Frothingham for a micro-interruption with the realization that all of her lengthy requests might take more than the "moment" he had quoted to the person on the other line. He promised that second patron a quick return call before reconnecting to the first high roller. Richard could have pushed another button alerting a backup employee, but Richard was greedy. He wanted both clients to know that it was he, Richard Smythe, who had turned over heaven and earth to meet their outrageous demands and more. Before these two guests left the hotel, they would regard "their Richard" as a devoted family friend, knowing it had been *his* particular pleasure to serve them. They would know of his welcoming smile that greeted them each time they walked through the lobby on their way to breakfast or through the big gold doors to their waiting limo. On their return, it would be Richard's sincere inquiry as to the progress of their special visit that first addressed them.

Their personal Concierge would be there for these guests throughout their stay, and he would be the last in-house staff member they would thank on their final exit, the gratuity stuffed into a diminutive envelope passed discretely, so as not to give too much notice to this small token of their appreciation for Richard's selfless performance. Of course, it was understood that dear Richard (what was his last name?, they would later wonder) was not welcome at their home on New York's Upper West Side, or their places on the Cape or in Palm Beach. That was the deal. But Richard has no desire for tea and conversation. He wanted cold hard cash. Last year, the Sherill had paid him thirty-five thousand, and he had pocketed close to fifty K in handshake tips, reporting only eight thousand of the latter to the IRS. That take home would have been enough for most service personnel, but not for Richard. His retirement plans required much more. He was in a hurry. A childhood of poverty had combined with an exposure to wealth which created a hunger that mere employment could not hope to satisfy.

Early on, Sir George Sherill had recognized the potential market in Southwest Florida. Already a hotel magnate on the east coast, Sir George had predicted the population change in the Naples area. Even he, however, had been surprised by the amount of growth. In 1980, Collier County was just beginning the transformation from a sleepy coastal village to an eventual haven for the rich, with one of the highest per capita incomes in Florida. The hotelier had built a solid reputation for service delivery in Palm Beach and wanted to be on the ground floor of a similar facility in a county eager for growth, and willing to make accommodations to those proposing to invest in the area. He wisely chose beachfront property just north of the Naples city limits where zoning laws were fluid and tax breaks the order of the day. Sir George bought land in large clumps with the future growth clear in his mind. There was enough acreage for two golf courses and parking for guests and employees. The main building would be eighteen stories, four more than the previous height allowances, housing six hundred and twenty guests through the first seventeen floors, the top level reserved for twenty suites with space for personal servants and/or penthouse concierges. The property fronted the Gulf of Mexico continuing across Gulfshore Boulevard all the way to the Tamiami Trail, Florida's old road from Tampa to Miami, thus the name. Future developers could only turn green with envy at the tax abatements with environmental and impact fee relief that Sir George demanded and received as a condition of his "bringing civilization" to this new frontier of opportunistic acquiescence.

East of the main building was a low rise structure holding administrative offices which were connected to the hotel with an underground tunnel, computers, and closed-circuit TV's. The managers had all public areas under 24-hour surveillance, including the restaurants, main lobby, swimming pools, and meeting rooms. Only the eighteenth floor was free from observation, the on-site staff being sufficient security, allowing those most expensive areas a certain degree of privacy. No cameras were allowed in the guest rooms and bath areas. Patrons had to be assured that no one would be intruding as they went about their most fundamental business. And, of course, there was the Spa. It was also off limits to cameras. The guests who arrived there had little to hide, covered up with towels on massage tables, or soaking nude in saunas and aromatic pools. No one but the Spa staff had to know who had what reminders of which cosmetic surgeries.

The hotel employees punched in, showered, dressed, and ate in the administration building. The only time workers mingled with guests was in the completion of their hospitality duties. Their facility commute was underground, a lit tunnel to the employee locker rooms and the laundry facilities. The pro shops for golf and tennis were next to the administration building, and there was an informal restaurant where the athletes could get food and enjoy nineteenth-hole libations before going back to the more formal setting across the street at the grande olde hotel.

But, it was from the beach that the hotel was the most impressive. The prescient planners had brought in enough fill to raise the structure. This made walking to the gulf waters a downward series of paths and boardwalks that looked out on nature pools filled with multi-colored fish while the sand dunes were perfectly netted for protection of the exotic wildlife. Guests could marvel at mini-eco-friendly areas with gopher tortoises, snowy egrets, herons of all colors, roseate spoonbills, and other birds whose real habitat had, long since, been gobbled up by development. This particular area provided guilt free viewing for patrons lulled into a sense that nature had been somehow temporarily appeased. For a significant fee, some guests could enjoy a sunset wedding, followed by drinks at the several tiki bars, and a torch lit return to the Grande Salon for pictures and a private reception to follow in one of the many elegant party rooms.

Sir George had sequestered one hundred yards of priority beach, along which hotel patrons could enjoy the breezes under green canopies while resting on gold loungers. These amenities were provided by special staff, dressed in gold shirts and green shorts, strong enough to lift and carry the heavy equipment and still be able to bring drinks from the bars. These tiki bars were scattered at intervals and allowed the thirsty the chance, if they so desired, to sit or lean and swig down a Heinekin, margarita, mai tai, or pina colada. There were kayaks, canoes, and catamarans for rent, all a la carte items showing up on the remarkable bill presented at the end of the exclusive vacation.

Twenty-seven years after the first ceremonial shovel of sand, the Hotel Sherill was still the local luxury leader.

There was competition. The Ritz-Carlton maintained their excellent tradition of service in their beach and golf centers farther to the North, and the Regency had arrived with great fanfare. That facility, less than two miles from the Sherill had a long copper roof that angled down. The progressive architectural sight gleamed in the late afternoon sun. The Parma on the bay in Estero, was the most recent competitor. They had stayed afloat as the neighboring pastures were graded for their first Walgreen's, getting ready for high-end shopping and the ensuing golf course communities that had to follow. Estero and Bonita Springs' booms looked great enough to keep the Parma going, just as long as the population and job growth didn't suffer a downturn.

The Sherill was not going anywhere. Their clientele remained unaffected by volatility. And that is why Richard chose it. He was a thief, and thieves go where the money is.

Palm Springs had been his last hunting ground, and it had been looking good until some brainy cop had pressured Richard's accomplice into parting with some incriminating details concerning missing diamonds. Then it was time to go. It had taken three years and moving across the country for Richard and his new identity to feel less paranoid. Naples became his choice by sheer chance. Richard had picked up a trade magazine in California that extolled the virtues of a Palm-Springs type venue on the "Florida Southwest Gulf Coast". The glossy pictures and promised luxuries seemed endless. To read the brochure, in this part of sunny Florida, the streets were paved with gold.

He'd found reality less consistent. Naples had pockets of poverty to the east and south. Whole villages of migrant workers were just getting by, complaining of the need for a one-cent increase in the price of the tomatoes they picked. Some communities were incomplete, the builders going belly up, filing for bankruptcy, leaving many new owners high and dry.

Richard started work in Naples in restaurants, waiting on tables, doing prep work, and hosting. He would change jobs at the end of each season, moving to more prestigious settings, getting more experience and always leaving with excellent recommendations. He found that the easiest labor was acting as a host, helping to organize equitable seating, keeping the wait staff happy, the patrons satisfied. It was not long before he recognized the Hotel Sherill as *the* local, high-end destination for the well-to-do.

Richard continued to peruse the want ads daily while he built his local resume, waiting for his chance. It came in the form of a job fair, the Sherill's recent expansions requiring a jump start of employees to keep pace for the added accommodations and the new tourist season. He chose the laundry department, believing that section required the least accountability and background checks, hoping his recent employment history sufficient when compared to the Hispanics and Haitians who made up most of that unit's staff. He knew that these recent arrivals to the United States had little history beyond the willingness to do this hot, back breaking work. And they would not be making regular contact with the guests. The minorities were kept as far from the clientele as possible. The management didn't want their employees to be embarrassed by the color discrepancy and language difficulties, a labor arrangement that seemed eminently suitable for workers and guests alike.

Richard made an immediate positive impact. His language skills made interpreters unnecessary for communication with the house staff. He got a quick raise and more responsibility. It was not long before he moved into housekeeping, and then to final room inspections, white gloves running along all the horizontal surfaces before the space could be declared habitable. Richard was regularly prostrate, on the floor, under beds and around toilets looking for any reminders of the previous guests. It was he who arranged the hospitality bags, loaded with Sherill-signature shampoos, conditioners, soaps, body washes, and lotions. There were complimentary razors, and even the toothbrushes and toothpastes carried the hotel's logo. He made sure the luxurious bathrobes were hung neatly and that gold-wrapped, imported chocolates appeared on every pillow. Richard insisted that his name accompany those of the maids' on the gratuity envelopes placed strategically on the hall tables. The tips were good. He bought a used red Mercedes Coupe. In Naples, second-hand luxury cars outnumbered Chevrolets. The *Daily News* devoted half a page to that popular German model.

Richard's move to concierge was so gradual, no one saw it coming. He had timed his room- inspector lunch breaks so they paralleled the shift changes at the front desk, giving him the chance to buddy up with whichever concierge was going off duty. Since one concierge, at least, had to be present at all times in the lobby, Richard was regularly able to be one-on-one with a member of the hotel's most visible, albeit smallest, department. Because of their importance and employee rank, plus that intimidating tuxedo uniform, *les portieres solitaires* (the lonely concierges) regularly ate by themselves, other staff members feeling uncomfortable in their presence. They welcomed the companionship Richard offered and the chance to talk to him of their complicated jobs. In these little chats, Richard reinforced the concierges' opinions that theirs were the most difficult and sensitive of hospitality positions. Richard would cluck sympathetically over the lengths to which the front staff went to satisfy the volume of excessive demands the guests routinely required. He was glad to play the straight man in the "Ain't It Awful?" game, incredulous at the latest outlandish request from Mrs. Van So-and-So's supercilious mouth. By doing this with each of the three day concierges, Richard learned the breadth of their collective responsibilities and the skill required to meet an endless array of wants. If anyone could do three jobs at once it was these multi-task warriors. And always, of course, with a smile and the added, "It is my particular pleasure!" This sounded a lot better than "You've *got* to be kidding!" which was what the concierge was most usually thinking.

Per usual, with this amount of job stress came absenteeism, illness (real and imagined) and, ultimately, staff turnover. It was at one of these pressure confluences that Richard got the big chance he was waiting for. At the Sherill, there was an assumed overlap of responsibilities. A bell boy could park a car, a valet carry a suitcase inside, a maid usher a guest to the right conference room, servers could bus tables. It was all to provide seamless service. If someone dropped the ball, another was supposed to catch it before it hit the floor. The guests were never to know that a staff member had been unable or unwilling to carry out his or her tasks. The uniforms were supposed to dictate responsibility areas, all green and gold, the doormen wearing spats. The chefs kept their traditional white coats and toques, usually invisible to the clientele, seen only when called out for applause, bowing at the tables' accolades. This was, after all, food and service, second to none. Five stars all the way!

But it was difficult to replace the concierge people, the only ones in dark blue tuxedos, their unique garb symbolic of the complexity and importance of their jobs.

One day, as Richard was accompanying Marta, his lunch mate, back to her front desk, they saw the concierge Peter doubled up behind the counter. Gastroenteritis, ulcers, pressure, hypochondria? Down he went. They hustled him through a side door to the infirmary. Peter was done. He had failed one too many times. His superior would have a sad-eyed termination interview suggesting alternative, less stressful employment. Had he thought of the Parma as a possible employer?

Richard quickly stepped behind the desk. Marta soon had her hands full with an irate guest whose dinner reservation in the Saratoga Dining Room had been lost. The phone was ringing.

Without hesitation, Richard answered: "Happy Holidays. The Hotel Sherill. This is Richard at the concierge desk. How may I be of assistance?" While listening to his callers, Richard also showed some guests the map and pointed directions to Fifth Avenue South. Then he gestured in the direction of the Spa to a young couple with towels and their massage passes. He was in! After two solid hours of consistent phone calls and personal requests, Richard and Marta came up for some well-deserved air.

"Have you done this before?", she gushed with admiration. Marta didn't remember that she and the other front desk honchos had provided explicit lunchroom details on the workings of their department and all the tricks needed to stay one step ahead of the clientele. Richard chose this time to inflate his hospitality experience, highlighting and embellishing those duties that were in any possible way similar to the Sherill's requirements.

Marta was profuse in her praise and gratitude, making sure her supervisor got an earful of how this wonderful man had saved the day. "So much better than poor Peter!", she exclaimed. The boss, given this epiphany, had the brainstorm to solve his nagging personnel problem by moving Richard, provisionally, into the slot pending satisfactory performance. Checking Richard's work history at the Sherill was all that was needed to make the transfer permanent, a tribute to the troubleshooting skills of the front end manager. It was win-win all around, it seemed to all. And so much in the tradition of the hotel to not let the ball capitulate to gravity! The usual extensive background check, devised to limit liability, was lost in the immediacy of a full house and the beginning of the busy season.

At last, Richard was situated and the real work could begin.

Shannon needed this job. Since graduating from high school two years earlier, she had bounced through a series of dead end experiences: waitress, sales clerk, house cleaning, even a short stint as a nanny. Nothing stuck. Never a good student, she had given up early on the college route and the preppies quickly excluded Shannon from their snooty circles. She was too pretty not to be smart, and not smart enough to work being pretty. Her mother kept two jobs, cleaning a local church and waiting tables at Perkins, earning just enough to cover the rent, beer and cigarettes. Tony, her mother's live-in boyfriend, had held a series of construction jobs, but was always laid off, which was fine by him because he was best at lying around the house, watching TV, sucking beer and checking his receding hairline. Shannon's progress through adolescence had not gone unnoticed and when Tony started walking around the house in his underwear, his appreciation of her attractiveness became all too evident. Even Shannon realized then it was time to get a place of her own.

At nineteen, she was now five feet ten inches, and in high heels, although unsteady, was stunning with full breasts and wide athletic shoulders. Shannon wore her naturally curly blonde hair short, accentuating a long neck, as she didn't have the time or money for beauty salon appointments. Her unsatisfactory work history had some regrettable consistency. Her looks would get her in the front door, and then they precipitated unwanted advances in the back rooms and vestibules. The other employees would get jealous at the perceived shifts in the relative power balances, turning on the victim rather than the supervisors. After all, it was the bosses who signed their paychecks.

While living at home, Shannon had saved enough money to take a massage course, advertisements promising untold riches to their graduates. She was in her last two weeks when one of the instructors had taken some liberties during one of his hands-on "demonstrations". Short of a diploma, but not wanting more face down abuse, Shannon applied at the Spa at the Hotel Sherill. The director was impressed by Shannon's physique and rudimentary knowledge, seeing her as a walking advertisement for the virtues of healthy living, and the benefits of her therapeutic a la carte services. She was overjoyed at the ten dollars an hour pay scale and the promised tips were going to be more than enough for her rent and the payments on the used Toyota Tercel.

Richard was so close, in the middle of more wealth than seemed possible, and beginning to formulate plans for getting some for himself. He knew there must be a way because no bank or safe was impregnable. Someone on site was always going to be in a position to profit in ways not possible for outsiders. Trust was the independent variable. Someone could possibly leave something valuable that would only require its being lifted and removed for his safe keeping.

The lost and found kept collecting obscene pieces of odd jewelry, watches, purses, and wallets. Their owners were always abundantly grateful for this level of honesty. Their "thank you so much" tips added to Richard's cash-in-pocket and to his sense that larger hauls were still available. He returned everything, taking cash only from the purses where it had been thrown, not folded, and never more than ten percent of the total. Richard always left the wallets intact. No one questioned his integrity as he grandly handed over the lost material to the relieved owners, most of the women unaware that their six hundred in fifties and twenties was less by three twenties and a ten, the ratio of bills very similar to the previous pile. He was enjoying a steady diet of fastballs, lining them to all fields, when someone threw the change up, and Richard had to step out of the batter's box.

There he was, enjoying a beer with Marta at the end of a busy shift. They had gotten away from the beach resort, going downtown to Tommy Bahamas on Third Street. Marta was married, but she enjoyed Richard's tall good looks, her husband being a mousy CPA, and Richard always took the time to listen to tales of her three-year-old daughter and the ever dirty living room. She had daydreamed of sex with this new co-worker, but Richard wanted to be the one to choose a lover or accomplice, and Marta was too close to home. And too smart, fluent in English and German, having grown up on an army base in Stuttgart.

"Heather cracked her tooth yesterday," Marta recounted, the latest drama her daughter provided the home life.

"She rode her tricycle off the deck! I told her to stay away from the steps, but she never stopped, just went over the edge. Mark was supposed to be watching, but he was cleaning the grill," -- another example of her husband's inadequacy, -- "and the dentist says she may lose that tooth."

Richard tried to console her. "Isn't that a baby tooth?" He felt himself relaxing, and knew that Marta was beginning to unwind, too, and needed this space between the intensity of work and those incessant demands of home. Marta smiled at the encouraging words. Her White Russian was mellowing, and Richard had ordered her another that she wouldn't finish because she still had to drive home to Golden Gate and help Mark make dinner.

"Mrs. Gould almost got to me today." Marta was laughing now, remembering the matriarch's complaint that someone had stolen her mink coat while not being able to recall in which restaurant she was dining when the crime took place. The elderly woman was just finishing her list of likely Hispanic miscreants when Jose had rushed up from the first floor dining area with the missing garment.

"Did you see how red her face got?", Marta asked.

Richard chuckled, "Yeah. I thought she'd never stop tipping everyone. She even tried to give money to that Spanish guy on his way to play tennis!".

Marta was trying to stop giggling. "What'd he say to her?"

"I think it was, *'El dinero no compra clase!'* Something that sounded like money and class didn't always go together."

She was impressed: "I didn't know you spoke Spanish."

He was quick to downplay that facility. "I don't really. Just a few phrases here and there. Certainly not like you know German. That's for sure."

Retelling these stories over alcoholic beverages made the workday humiliations easier to take. Richard ordered another Jim Beam, but Marta pushed her drink away, sliding away from the table.

"Holy Cow! I've gotta go! Mark will be frantic, and Heather will be too tired to eat!" She kissed Richard on the cheek and ran to her car on unsteady legs.

After Marta's departure, Richard swung around on his stool to look at the crowds walking along Third Street, the trendy interloper to Naples' Fifth Avenue South, the original golden street here. This four block section had made a conscious effort to duplicate the opulence that made the original the must-see tourist venue for those wanting to observe the Florida rich in action. There were high end stores, a teddy bear shop, bars and restaurants, the latter requiring reservations from December to May. Then Richard did a double take. In the corner of the bar, shaded by a potted palm tree, were two men, one of them looking familiar and waving lazily, an ambivalent grin on a scarred face.

Chapter III

Jack was not going to be ignored, so Richard froze a smile, grabbed his drink and walked casually to their table.

"Hey, Big man." Jack held out a hand and gestured to his younger, surly looking companion. "This is Louis, my compadre. Grab a chair. Long time, buddy. What've you been doin' with yerself?"

"I was gonna ask you the same thing." Inside, Richard was seething. How had Jack run into him down here? The last he knew, his old "buddy" Jack was spilling his guts to a cop in turn for a plea deal that released him in a case for which the D.A. had little but circumstantial evidence. They found the diamonds in Richard's apartment, his name on the lease, but nothing to implicate Jack beyond their stated acquaintance.

"So, Rick, how long ya been in Naples? And who was that fine lookin' woman? You shackin' up with her?"

Richard was determined to give out as little information as possible. He wouldn't let this unfortunate reunion spoil the plan, so close to execution. "Naw, she's married. Just someone I work with. How 'bout you? I thought you'd still be in LA or San Diego."

Jack relented. "Oh, things were gettin' a little tight off Santa Monica Boulevard. Ya know the score."

"What'd ya do? Knock over an old lady?" Richard wanted to keep the ball in Jack's court, ignoring the sneering "compadre" punk.

Jack's red face indicated that Richard had nearly hit the nail on the head. He knew that Jack was a "snatch and grab" specialist, certain to draw police interest on all such in his geographic area.

"I just needed some new scenery, that's all," was Jack's wounded reply.

"What the hell are ya doin' here, of all places?"

"Aw, Rick. Ain't ya glad to see me, a buddy from the old days?"

By this time Richard knew that this had to be more than a coincidence, his old cell mate, three thousand miles from the California hunting grounds, too slick, wanting some crumbs in a new venue. He had to ask, "How'd you find me?"

Jack, grinning now in a self-congratulatory hug, answered. "Rick, ya know those brochures ya left around when you split in such a hurry? Don't worry. I got rid of 'em before the cops stripped your joint. Well, you'd underlined the Naples part, so I just figured this is the kinda place you like. Ya know, all those rich folks!"

Louis, the younger man, was watching, tongue licking thin lips, a cruel mouth on a face still holding the remnants of adolescent acne.

Richard didn't know how long he could continue the charade, but he wasn't going to tip his hand until he heard Jack's inevitable pitch. He was kicking himself for all those conversations in that lonely cell, showing off, chasing the shadows.

"I've a good job now, Jack. These people throw money at me for just showin' up. No need to steal any more, Jack. I'm gonna settle down. Can I get you boys anything? Beer? Margarita?"

He watched Jack's smile get wider, sure of himself now, not going anywhere soon. Jack shifted back in his seat, getting comfortable. This was going to be a fun trip.

"Louis, you want another Corona? Rick's buyin'! I'll have a Rum Runner. Rick, you? In a job? That doesn't sound like you, man! Too hard. What about that easy street you were always talkin' about?"

Richard tried again. "I'm through with all that crime stuff. The time has come for me to stop runnin' and to settle down. I'm gettin' too old for that game." Richard at thirty, lean and hard, did not look the least bit washed up. That particular fact wasn't lost on Jack, who was far more the worse for wear.

"Sure, sure, Rick. And the sun came up blue this mornin'. If it was bedtime, I'd ask you to tell another story!" The game for him was fun, sticking the knife, twisting it when things slowed down. But then he got more serious. "Listen Rick, don't bullshit us. Me and Louis got bills that need money, and I know you always had a scam goin', so you can tell us all you want, like that ya got religion, or whatever. I'm not buyin' it! What's the deal? Cause we want in!"

This was said with less humor, less of that self-confident smile. Richard's mind was swirling, trying to think of one thing - *any* thing - to throw these dogs off the scent. One thing he was sure of... Richard did not want these two anywhere near the Hotel Sherill, blowing his cover, ruining everything. He was just thankful they hadn't approached Marta, wanting to preserve the secrecy, any clue that he would or could know lowlifes like these two.

Richard changed the subject, knowing full well that they would soon return to the core of this 'less than chance' get-together.

"Where are you boys livin'?", he cheerfully asked.

Jack was happy to take their sweet-ass time. Richard couldn't run from this meeting. "Louis has a place in those apartments on Old 41, near Egret Estates. Ya know it?"

Richard had driven by the apartments, seven miles from the Naples city limits, as close to downtown as any low-income housing was likely to get but closer to Bonita Springs. "Ya got me, Jack. I do have some ideas, but nothin' has fallen into place yet. This new job gets me close to the rich people, but there's security all around and I haven't figured out how to bypass all the surveillance cameras. When I do, you'll be the first ones I'll tell."

"Sure, sure, Rick." Jack wasn't buying it. "You're bidin' your time, just like that diamond caper, and how long did that take? Three months? And how much did you make off that 'little deal'? We need somethin' now, for rent and weed. Things are slow for us." Jack was tightening the screws, not willing to listen to any excuses, thinking that Richard just wanted them to go away and never come back.

That, coincidentally, was exactly what Richard was wishing, knowing full well that any end game he had envisioned was now going to get more complicated, times three. He didn't have to mention the blackmail, that torque wrench already registering two thousand pounds. Richard had no choice now, except how it was going to go down. Whatever the plan, he had to keep these two as far from work as possible.

"Don't worry, old buddy. We won't go near your fancy hotel." Jack was reading his mind. He gestured toward the curb. "I don't think those valets would even park Louis's car!"

Richard then realized that they'd been following him for a while. Jack was pointing to the old Dodge Caravan with the trailer hitch, looking out of place here against the Lexus SUV's and BMW's taking up most of the nearby spaces. He needed time to think and find another meeting location, away from people, away from anyone who could link him to these two and the hotel - an incriminating combination.

"Give me your telephone number and I'll set up a meet. It has to be a private place where we can't be seen talkin'," Richard quietly said.

Louis whispered to Jack and the older man responded, "Louis knows a place, not too far away, and safe."

Richard got Jack's cell phone number and promised to call tomorrow. "Let me go out first. And you guys finish your drinks and leave later."

"Sure, Buddy Boy. But don't forget we know your car and your place in Naples Park, so don't get any ideas of stiffin' us out of our profits!"

Richard controlled his anger at this presumption, Jack implying that they were somehow a team, a gang, ready to cash in on some collegial caper. He smiled. "I wouldn't think of cheatin' you guys. We go way back, Jack, and I haven't forgotten our stay at that LA lockup. Good times." He knocked back his whiskey, almost a toast, but nothing close to the murderous thoughts coursing through his mind. He got up and nodded at Louis. "Call ya tomorrow. What's a good time?'

Jack's grin was gone now, all business. "Call by noon, Rick. We'll be waitin' on ya."

This time it was not a request. It was an order. The tail was beginning to wag the dog. This would not do.

Chapter IV

FEBRUARY

Dan took the call from Doc Weeks. The Medical Examiner had promised a quick response and he did not disappoint. "Cut and dried!" The almost bored voice indicated that his advanced skills were not required, removing for him at least any excitement a forensic ambiguity might have generated. "But those holes in the backs of their heads were not the cause of death."

Dan needed more, but waited. The old pathologist had his own method of unraveling the details.

"They each took shots to the chest, the younger guy getting one in the shoulder, too. The frontal assaults must have immobilized them. The bullets to the craniums were to finish the job. One of the two, the older one, had some salt water in his lungs, so he was still breathing when he hit the water, but he was a goner, with or without drowning. Brain dead and bleeding out, like the younger guy."

Dan broke in, "Find any bullets?"

"We've got two. one from the chest cavity and one from the shoulder, so we should have that info later in the day, and we'll be checking the fingerprints and DNA against the AFIS data base. We'll have to wait at least three weeks for the DNA results, but the fingerprints search should be quick. Right now we're guessing they were in the water five or six days. Mike, our bug guy, said the larvae on the heads means our subjects have been dead maybe a week, so you can start from there. One seems to be Hispanic in his late twenties or early thirties, and the older white guy could be forty, but those are salt water estimates, and best guesses."

Dan was grateful. He knew there was a good chance the missing identification pieces would be provided, perhaps by day's end. "Thanks Doc," he said. "Good job. You're the best!"

"Yeah, yeah," was the old man's crusty reply, but Dan could hear the appreciation for the feedback. The detective knew that Doc Weeks' abrasive manner alienated some of the brass, and for that reason praise was rarely given. They were waiting for Doc's retirement, thinking that a new supervisor would somehow provide instant gratification, but Dan knew that there was no substitute for Doc's experience. Dan let him know that every time they interacted, guaranteeing the old man's maximum efforts.

"And don't forget you're coming to the wedding, old friend."

As Dan left, he turned to see Doc Weeks smile.

There was time for a break, maybe lunch, so Dan looked over the cubicles and saw Roni getting off the phone. She turned in his direction. Now that they were engaged, there was no reason to hide the relationship. As long as he didn't maul her in the equipment room, they could catch a quick meal and share the day every now and then. Roni was on the same wavelength so she grabbed her jacket and headed for the door as Dan maneuvered around a drunk and disorderly to reach the rear entrance to the staff parking lot.

She waited at his Crown Victoria so he could open her door and get the chance for a quick kiss before he shoved her in, taking a look around to see if anyone caught their clinch. They held hands on the way to Taco Mia, one of their favorite spots in Bonita Springs. Dan liked the intimacy of the booths, made to look like adobe with the high backs giving them privacy. The Mexican music made it difficult to eavesdrop.

Roni greeted their server in Spanish and ordered two chicken burritos, taking time to ask her about her family. Roni was well known among the local Hispanic population, regularly taking calls from them, often the first to uncover news of gang activity or human trafficking. Today, however, she was brimming with news, a break in their endless search for a place for their wedding reception.

"Chief Kelly told me about a party house that might cater our wedding. It's called Domenici's near the corner of 41 and Estero Boulevard. The owner sat next to the chief at a Chamber meeting and the boss told him we were looking for a place."

Dan felt a wee bit jealous. What was she doing in the chief's office, bending his ear on their nuptials, while he drooled in four-four time? It was none of Chief Kelly's business. But Dan knew he was wrong about that. Their marriage was everybody's business, as they were all on the invitation list, waiting only for the final details. Roni would not be deterred.

"The chief said he thought the guy would be willing to give it to us for fifty dollars a person, and it would include a thirty minute open bar!" Dan did some quick calculations in his head, figuring one hundred guests, a give-or-take cost of five thousand dollars. It would take most of their savings, but it would be worth it to finally finish the planning.

"Okay," he agreed. "That's the least expensive quote or possible price so far. Let's call the place tomorrow." Roni leaned across the table to grab his hands, finding only one, as Dan's other hand was under the table caressing the inside of her thigh.

Now, however, she was ready to talk cop, telling Dan of her morning and asking about the latest from their favorite Medical Examiner.

"We could have positive I.D.'s by late this afternoon. You may know this Hispanic guy, if he's local. I'll give you the name as soon as they phone it in."

Roni thought out loud: "I don't have any recent reports on missing Hispanic males in that age range, but if he's on the outs with his family, they might not have seen him for months."

Chapter V

JANUARY

Richard was beside himself. He had to think of a way to convince his new "partners in crime" that they could all profit from the potential wealth enshrined within the venerable Hotel Sherill. He needed to plot thefts, taking place offsite, snatches and grabs followed by quick escapes. Absolutely nothing could be connected to a reputable concierge. It was ten-thirty on a humid night, the weather folks promising some rain to mitigate the chronic drought and hold the seasonal brush fires at bay. Richard reluctantly turned on his air-conditioner even though he hated the inflated bills from Florida Power and Light. He tried to avoid the a/c during the winter, but tonight he was sweating as much from his anxiety as he was from the elevated humidity. The hum of the outside compressor would be helpful to muffle any clandestine phone calls he might have to make.

Richard was renting a small ranch house in Naples Park, an affordable neighborhood a fifteen minute drive to the hotel. The cement block house had two bedrooms, one and a half baths and a two car garage. It was short of the square footage most families required, and a little large for a bachelor, but the rental was only $700 a month, enough to pay the owner's taxes until the real estate market improved. The unit was six miles from the Sherill, just outside the higher end communities in Pelican Bay, but still in Collier County.

He didn't have much time, hearing clearly from Jack and Louis their needs for immediate gratification. Richard dialed Jack's number.

"Yeah?" was the answer. Richard could hear music and the clink of glasses.

"Jack, this is Richard. Is this a good time to talk? Is there somebody else there?"

"Naw, Rick. Me and Louis are just kickin' back, after a hard day fishin'! We got all the time in the world."

Richard wasted little time. "I've got some good ideas and we need to set a time to meet. Somewhere private. No outside eyes."

Jack chuckled. "I figured you'd come up with somethin' quick. You always had good plans. We're way ahead of ya, Rick. Louis has a skiff and we could motor out and have our talk without anyone seein' us or overhearin' anything."

Richard saw the value in that setup, needing only the time and the location. "Where and when, Jack?"

"Tomorrow's good for us, Rick. D'ya know the Cocohatchee River Park, near Wiggins Pass?" Richard knew the place, off Vanderbilt Drive, just two miles from his neighborhood, and close to these guys' apartment complex off Old 41.

"What time, Jack?"

"Meet us at seven. The sun'll be down for about thirty minutes. D'ya know the first bridge and the area where they park and launch them canoes and kayaks?"

Richard mentally could see the spot. It was after a half mile stretch between the bay and the backwater, bordered by mangroves, too narrow for development. "I know what you're talkin' about. I drive that route when I wanna get to Bonita."

"Okay, Rick." Jack was pleased Richard didn't need more instruction. "Me n' Louis'll be at the park and we'll put in from their ramp. We'll come around the yacht club docks and pole under the small bridge and pick ya up at the canoe launch."

Richard was seeing the meet in his mind's eye and wanted more protection. "Is that boat legal? Does Louis have lights and a valid sticker?"

"Rick, Rick. Ya worry too much! We got all the right stuff. When ya fish as much as we do, ya gotta have your shit together."

"Glad to hear you've thought of everything," Richard said, giving his old "bud" credit for intelligence he hoped was lacking later on.

"Don't look for my car," Richard continued. "I'm gonna ride my bike and lock it on the racks at the playground. Then I'll walk back over the bridge and meet ya where we agreed."

"Good thinkin', man," Jack clucked appreciably. "You've got it down good! We can't wait to hear about the goodies you've got for us."

"Plenty for all of us," Richard replied good-naturedly, using a voice that he hoped would convey the sense that he was happy for this new diversion. "See you guys tomorrow." Richard hung up gently, not wanting to give in to the urge to slam the receiver down. There would be no hints of his animosity towards these interlopers.

Louis put down his rum and cola. "D'ya think he'll show up tomorrow?"

Jack laughed into his beer. "What choice does he have? We've got old Rick by the short hairs! We're gonna milk that cow until she's dry! I don't buy that 'I'm going straight' bullshit. He's sittin' on a gold mine over there. I feel it. And now's the time to share. D'we need to get gas for the boat?"

Louis shook his head. "Got at least four gallons in the tank. We won't need a pint for our little trip."

Chapter VI

FEBRUARY

Dan and Roni met at the party house to see the facilities first hand. It shared the lot with a dry cleaner and a next-to-new store. Dan thought the place looked a little seedy, the asphalt roadway showing the beginnings of some serious potholes. There was one car parked outside the front door and someone was peering at them through the windows, wondering why two police vehicles were visiting. A slight woman with red hair let them in, Dan asking if there was a manager with whom they could speak. Assured that there was no recent crime her boss had committed, the relieved woman led them to Mr. Domenici's office off the main entrance.

Roni felt better that the interior looked in good repair, the red carpet showing a recent cleaning. Mr. Domenici remembered his conversation with Chief Kelly and adjusted his toupee as he hunted for some contracts. "Sure, sure. Anything for our friends in law enforcement." He hoped, of course, for some breaks on future health inspections.

Roni asked what kinds of meals were offered, the size of the dance floor, all the pertinent information a bride-to-be needs to know. Mr. Domenici took them for a tour, adding "Most people just call me Mr. D."

"Our family used to run a restaurant in Little Silver. That's in New Jersey, not far from the boardwalk.

The parents got too old and my brothers were tired of the hours, so we sold it. We came down here to retire, but I got bored, and this place was for sale. We got it for a good price." He looked around and whispered, "The help is cheaper down here. And I can give you a deal, like I told your boss. Are you gonna have a band or a DJ?"

They had decided on a DJ. Dan's sister recommended one from a recent wedding she'd attended. Roni liked the size of the main room. When she asked about dancing, Mr. D said that he had a portable floor that could be expanded to fit guests and wedding party. "No problem."

Dan wanted to know about the food.

Mr. D was proud of his buffet. "We serve from both sides of the table. That way we can get most of your guests eating in fifteen minutes. There'll be two salads, two hot vegetables, rolls and butter, and four entrees. We have grilled chicken with mango sauce, fish, pulled pork, and at the end, a carver will be cutting from a standing rib roast of beef. Do you want dessert or do you already have a wedding cake? It's cheaper if we don't have to make a dessert, just to let you know."

Roni's mother Carolina had recently contracted with a Cuban bakery in Bonita. She had promised her daughter enough cake to give a small piece to each guest upon their departure. Then Mr. D asked about the size of the guest list. Dan said they thought it would be around a hundred, give or take the usual cancellations. Roni asked about the open bar, a subject about which Mr. D seemed less charitable.

"We'll have an open bar outside the main door for half an hour, until everyone has found their tables and the wedding party has been introduced. After that, it'll be a cash bar, set up in the far end of the room. I can give you the whole package for fifty-five dollars a person." This last sentence was made with an averted gaze.

That didn't last very long. Dan positioned himself directly in front of Mr. Domenici and said, "The chief mentioned that we might qualify for something a little less than that."

Mr. D coughed, remembering his glad-handed conversation. "Oh yeah. I think I remember I told him I could do it for fifty, something like that. I can do it for little, half down two weeks before, the balance the night of the wedding." Then, finally, "We're far cheaper than the hotels."

This was not news for Dan and Roni. It was twenty dollars a person under their best offer so far. And that was a place way out near I-75, Alligator Alley! They went back to the office and signed the contract.

For Roni, this was not the romantic part, doing the nuts and bolts of choosing a less than spectacular party house. This one has none of the ambiance of the big hotels on the water, she was thinking. Dan was also silently unsatisfied at the compromise their budget was forcing on them.

Back in the parking lot he held her, congratulated her on her wise choice, telling her how much everyone would love the place and the food. Roni reminded him of the almost unlimited size of the dance floor and the raised area where the wedding party would sit. They were both showing a lot of teeth, smiling as they got back in their cruisers and waved goodbye, hours before their next reunion.

Chapter VII

JANUARY

     Richard waited until six-thirty before he got on his bike and headed west to the Cocohatchee River park. There was a clear sidewalk all the way with most of the walkers having already retreated to dinner somewhere. There were no serious bikers willing to chance getting creamed on the roadway, the elder drivers here not noted for good night vision. He waited at the light near the mausoleum and continued past the Dunes condominium complex to the elevated bridge over the Cocohatchee. Richard waited at the larger of the two bridges, the engineers not providing more than eighteen inches between the white line and the curb, a small and dangerous refuge for the foot and bike traffic. If a car went over the line, the only escape for the ambulatory was to jump over the guardrail to the river twenty feet below. Most bikers waited for a break in the traffic and then hustled the seventy feet to safety. Richard did the same, jogging his bike across and down the other side to the playground, locking it to the racks there before retracing his steps. He went back over the bridge to the canoe and kayak launch area on the east side of the road. He stood there in the dark looking at the moon. He listened to the night sounds, the lapping of the water, and guessed it looked to be at half tide. Then he saw the red and green lights, seeing someone pole a boat from under the smaller bridge toward the muddy shore. He could barely see Jack's grinning face as the older man grabbed Richard's wrist and helped him step up on the bow. Louis then pushed back, easing the skiff toward the narrow channel. The whole connection took less than twenty seconds. They were then back under the bridge, hugging the mangroves south of the yacht club, it being brightly lit up at close to full occupancy.

Louis had not started the motor, poling the boat between a gap in the shore growth, a place where a small craft could nose in, tie up and fish. But these folks were looking for bigger prey. Louis leaned against the poling platform and Jack and Richard slid into the swivel seats.

Jack was the first to speak. "Well, Rick? What d'ya got for us?"

Richard reached in his pocket and removed two expensive looking watches that had been languishing in lost and found well past the time their owners had ended their stays at the Hotel Sherill. The light glinted off the shiny metal and luminous dials. "Just a small token." Richard watched the two men put the watches on their wrists, moving the time pieces to catch the reflections.

"Real nice, Rick." Jack knew they were being tossed a bone to get them off the scent of a real score. "But these ain't gonna pay our bills, and we're close to empty."

Richard made his pitch to the two men. "Relax. These are just good faith offerings. Here's what I have in mind. I know where the money is. It's in their pockets and purses, and on their wrists and fingers. Every night I send these rich folks out into Naples to go to dinner. I know who they are and where they're going. They're strangers here. They couldn't find their noses without the map I give 'em. Or their GPS systems."

Jack impatiently asked, "Yeah? So? Who cares where the fuck they're goin'?"

Richard was taking his time, waiting for them to catch on to the caper. "There're some places I send 'em that're off the beaten path, quaint, not near lights. Get the picture?" He saw the furrowed brows and decided to fill in the blanks.

"Mr. and Mrs. Richie Rich come out of the restaurant. It's dark out and they've had drinks and wine. He fumbles for his keys, and you boys come out of the shadows and help them to some Naples hospitality. A little duct tape, and you can take your time doing the inventory on cash and jewelry." He could see Jack and Louis looking at each other, putting it together.

Louis, adding his two cents, decided, "We wear masks."

Jack kept it going. "And we walk to our car parked in another lot and drive east, to I-75, get off at the Bonita Beach exit and we're home before these fools have called the cops." He was close to rubbing his hands together, anticipating paying off the Florida Power and Light bill and going to the Bonita Dog Track. "Okay," he came back, wanting more specifics. "What's the name of one of these dark restaurants?"

Richard was ready. "There's this place called La Rive Gauche. It's a French restaurant, very fancy, very expensive. It's down by the city docks."

"I know the city docks." Louis was suspicious. "I don't know what you're talkin' about."

"Of course ya don't know where it is. It's hidden on a little side street that backs up to a canal." Richard was resolved not to lose his temper. What he wanted to say was, "You Goddamn stump brain. You couldn't get out of there for less than two hundred dollars, even if they *would* seat you, which they wouldn't!"

Richard continued. "It's so dark back there, people have trouble finding it in daylight, and after sunset you need a flashlight. And there are no valets to worry about. The place is that small."

"Where would we park down there?" Jack had bought in, but wanted more details.

Richard was way ahead of them. "Ya know the public boat ramp on Tenth Street?"

Louis was on board then. "I've put in there, but the spaces are metered and they want a dollar an hour to park."

"So put in four fuckin' quarters!" Richard was frustrated now but he had to move them along. "And leave the boat and trailer on the back. No one'll think you're anything more than two fishermen back from trolling. You can stash your haul in the tackle boxes or bait buckets until you get home."

"How do we find this place if it's so hidden?" Jack still needed more answers.

"Drive to the city dock tomorrow. Take the boat trailer like you're looking for the public launch. Come in to the circle by the novelty store. Look to your right just past the wooden statue of the sailor and you'll see a side street. It's only a half block long and the restaurant is the last building on the right." Not waiting for more questions, Richard finished the picture. "It'll take you no more than four minutes to cut through the parking lot, past the Dove Inn into the boat launch area. Back from your beer run, you head out to 41, then on to 75, the quickest, but indirect way back to Bonita."

Jack could see it all, but didn't show too much enthusiasm. He didn't want to let Richard off the hook quite yet. "Why would a hotel guest at your snazzy joint wanna go to a small restaurant on a dark street?"

Richard's exasperation came out just a little as he sputtered, "Because they can afford to, and most people can't! That's what makes it exclusive. Rich people spendin' a couple hundred bucks a pop for dinner, plus an eighty dollar bottle of wine, just to eat snails!" He was quiet then, letting them think about how easy this was going to be, and how they were going to spend the money.

Jack was the first to break the spell. "Where and when, Rick?" The alpha male had returned. He wanted Richard to know who was in charge, who was the leader.

"I send people to La Rive Gauche every night the place has an opening. Most of 'em prefer the weekends. I think the best night for this is on Sunday. There's less action at the docks and people are thinkin' about goin' back to work on Monday. There'll be fewer cops on the streets, less kids, stores closing earlier. A whole lot better for getaways."

"How'll we know?" Jack wanted to be absolutely sure about all this stuff.

Richard took a deep breath. "I'll call ya by Friday and set up another meet. By that time I'll have the list of the Rive Gauche's reservations from our hotel. I'll tell ya the year, make and model of the car and its color. You'll have a description of the guests and the time of their reservations. The average dinner lasts about an hour and a half or two. So plan accordingly. It'll be an older couple, people between their mid-sixties and seventies, weaker, quieter, with little resistance. Put 'em in the back seat, hands tied behind their backs, and enough tape on their mouths so they can't rub it off. And make sure ya toss the keys, so nobody can push the alarm button, and you should have at least a twenty minute head start, almost home, if not already there."

Jack needed no further instructions. After all, snatch and grab was his specialty. "Don't worry, Rick. We'll take it from there. And what then? What's next?"

Richard looked at his watch. They'd been out thirty minutes and he was starting to feel the night mist through his sweater. "Let's take it slow. See how this first one goes before we plan number two. I'm afraid we can only hit this restaurant once. Then we'll choose another. The cops'll be all over it after this heist, and we'll have to find another easy spot."

He stopped the directions, knowing, at one time that these two could handle only the immediate details. Richard would try to fine tune them later. But now there was no benefit to repeat instructions, and he turned away from them as Louis moved them back under the small bridge to the canoe strip. The tide had receded making Richard have to jump over mud to get to the higher ground, burying one shoe in the muck. He could hear Jack and Louis laughing at his discomfort as the white stern light disappeared under Vanderbilt Drive.

Chapter VIII

Myra Frothingham wanted to dine away from the hotel. They'd eaten in all the Sherill's bistros, from the beachfront tiki huts to the pool buffet and grill room. She was still waiting to get into the upstairs Saratoga Restaurant, but reservations were backed up, outsiders waiting for years to get a seating. As a preferred customer, Mrs. Frothingham knew she would get the chance for that most exclusive meal far ahead of most ordinary citizens - just not *this* particular weekend. The holidays were over, the kids back north, and all Albert wanted to do was sit and read the *Wall Street Jounal.* She called the concierge desk and asked for Richard. He was on break, so another worker took the request. Mrs. Frothingham *had* to have an eight o'clock reservation at La Rive Gauche. The concierge found only one opening, on a Sunday evening. The Saturday spots were filled well into the late evening. Myra reluctantly accepted the compromise, knowing that even her V.I.P. status could only go just so far in the middle of the high season in Naples -- January through March -- and that impulsive reservations were chancy at best.

"Have them bring the Jaguar at seven-thirty, and make sure that it is clean!", she demanded. With advance warning, the Sherill valets would wash and dry the luxury automobiles preferred customers chose to drive to their fancy destinations, the gleaming cars dropping off guests at the Philharmonic, art galleries, and charity galas. Myra would have preferred the hotel's limousine service but Albert had *insisted* that he drive over from Palm Beach, claiming it was his only fun of the entire trip. This time in Naples was strictly Myra's choice.

She hated that car with its British racing green color, complete with a stick shift guaranteeing that only Albert or their house man could drive it. That left her at home to choose between the Lexus SUV and the Cadillac Sedan de Ville. After the Board of Directors had "suggested" Albert relinquish his chairmanship and take the buyout, Myra's husband had tried a number of hobbies she failed to appreciate. He'd crewed on friends' racing sailboats and even tried sky diving. Then he discovered the car racing club. He threw himself behind the wheel of a variety of high end sports cars, doing well at the competitions until he and his instructor Burt spun out at Watkins Glen, New York, hitting the wall at a hundred and thirty miles an hour. Albert had been lucky to escape with bruises and a limp. Burt, however, after they cut him from the crushed right side, had not been able to walk for a year. This resulted in the rest of the club giving "Lead Foot Al" the cold shoulder from that time on, and he finally gave in, failing to renew the membership. Now seventy-five, and with osteoarthritis in his hip and knees, Myra's husband could only swim. Dancing, never his strong point, was out of the question. He didn't like fashion shows, but still loved to eat, witnessed by the bulging waistline and new suits and tuxedoes.

La Rive Gauche was small, but they had the best French chef in Naples. The Sherill had been trying to woo Henri for years, but the part-ownership in the restaurant gave him a good living and he was in complete control of the menu. There were always at least two apprentice sous chefs on site, eager to pitch in, the patrons being completely unaware how often Henri just sat on his stool drinking wine, glancing at the plates on their way to his discriminating patrons.

Richard made another copy of the reservations print-out, and went to one of the bathrooms off the main hall. He locked the stall door and perused the list. The concierge desk had made three reservations for Sunday night at La Rive Gauche, the earliest at six, one at eight, and the dregs at nine-fifteen. He returned to his post and punched the names into the computer, but unless any of the others were in their eighties, he had already decided the Frothinghams met most of the criteria. They were the only ones over seventy, and the others had chosen the limo option to allow for more wine consumption. The late limo would not be waiting at idle until ten, the six o'clock folks long gone, leaving Mr. and Mrs. Frothingham the only hotel guests who'd be looking in the dark for their car at about nine-thirty. Richard made a copy of the car's picture, including the Florida plate numbers, everything his "accomplices" would need. Now if it had been a white Lincoln, maybe the boys would have had some trouble finding the right one. But the Frothingham's would be the only green Jag in the area.

Chapter IX

FEBRUARY

Dan headed for the Medical Examiner's Office. The new building was on a side street, behind an industrial complex off Airport Pulling Road. The facilities were state of the art, the design a miniature of the Miami complex featured on a hit TV show. The population explosion and growing crime statistics had provided just the impetus the Naples city government needed to float the required multi-million dollar bond issue.

It had been built for the future with all the rooms too big for the current influx. It was, however, ready for the expansions the builders hoped would turn southwest Florida into a concrete and asphalt playground for the rich. The only foliage they envisioned would be from tee to green and all the clubs would have wrought-iron gates. Doc Weeks had decried the waste his new playground demonstrated, but secretly he loved all the toys. And the lights. There were enough fluorescents to make even his weakening vision up to the task.

Dan walked through the main autopsy room on the way to Doc's office. He was glad there were no stiffs out on the gleaming stainless steel tables. Dan always winced at the saws and hammers hanging on the walls, a lot like the tools he kept in his garage to combat the stubborn scrub and palm fronds.

The door was open and the old medical examiner swung around, sliding his illegal ashtray under some files. "Have a chair, Dan!" He pointed to a new computer chair and gestured toward the coffee machine. "It's not good. And it's old. But I can guarantee that it's hot." Dan could tell that the man was ready for a chat and some stories and he didn't want to frustrate this friendly relic, so close to retirement and its inherent irrelevancy. Last month, Dan had stopped by one afternoon to enjoy this jovial cracker and his hospitality and found himself thinking of his deceased father. His dad's alcoholism and early death deprived his son of anything close to the companionship the pathologist and he so easily shared. Dan had been surprised to find tears in his own eyes after that session. The detective could not remember ever crying as an adult.

Doc closed the door, opened the window, looked furtively for prying eyes, and pulled down the shade. He grabbed his pipe and checked the bowl for burnable fragments. He pounded the pipe on the glass, reaching into his desk for the tobacco before thumbing a new smoke. "Well," he remarked to his favorite detective, over white puffs of smoke angling for the outside lawn, "we know who your floaters are, no thanks to DNA. I swear, it takes so long for those labs to respond, we could be into another year before we had a positive match. But AFIS helped. The fingerprints were all we needed. The younger guy is" — he fumbled for his steno pad and adjusted his reading glasses — "Louis Gonzales. He lived in those apartments near the end of Old 41, not far from the intersection with the new road." Doc slid a printout toward Dan.

The details were all too familiar. A local boy in trouble from age eleven, time spent in juvenile detention with arrests for petty theft and assault, one DUI, and a domestic violence intervention, but those last charges had been dropped.

"Nothing recent, Doc. And he's made all his appointments with his parole officer."

"Yeah, I noticed that. I guess the reports that Louis got religion were premature. You think that Roni knows the family?" Both Doc and Dan were aware that someone had to visit the man's relatives. With his fiancée's language skills and community connections, it seemed to make her the obvious envoy.

"What about the other guy?", Dan asked.

"Oh, you mean 'The Traveler'?" Doc Weeks was famous for making up pseudonyms for John Does, and those with colorful M.O.'s. "This one is Jack Burdine, all the way from Los Angeles, California, and, believe you me, he was busy on that coast. There's a name of a police sergeant out there that wanted a call back on anything we had concerning our Mr. Burdine."

Dan could see from the printout that, indeed, the older corpse had a long history of theft, both petty and grand, the latter being equally distributed between jewelry and expensive cars.

"What do you think he was doing here, so far from Santa Monica Boulevard?" Dan was asking himself as much as Doc, looking at the last known California address.

"Oh, I would guess some of the same things, but you'll see he's not been arrested for anything here. Of course, he's not been among their missing for much more than a year, just a parole violator on paper."

Dan continued checking the summary. "There must be a chad still hanging out there if this guy wants a report. More than a parole check, Doc."

The old doctor just rocked and nodded in his swivel chair, puffs of smoke escaping the window, floating to his landscaped courtyard. Soon, all this would be some young hotshot's Shangri-la. The 'powers that be' eagerly awaited the transfer. That way, they could parade the new doctor before the cameras, promising new science that would solve all cases, some even before they were committed. In the meantime, Doc waited them out, withholding even a hint of his timetable to oblivion, happy to chew the fat with his favorites, but making sure he committed the hours needed to complete the required reports in a timely fashion. In truth, Old Doc Weeks was logging almost seventy hours weekly. He had nothing at home as his wife had died several years ago. This was his life, but he was just one stumble away from mandatory retirement.

Dan patted his friend on the back and dumped the old coffee in the sink before he headed back through the gleaming stainless steel to the parking lot. It was now almost eighty degrees. He had the folders on the two murder victims and called Roni from the car. "I need your help."

She was way ahead of him, per usual.

"You found out about our John Does?"

"Can you meet me at Perkins? I'll buy you a donut!"

Roni laughed at their joke. Until she chose a wedding gown, there would be no useless calories consumed. "Ha and double ha, wise guy. I'm closer. I'll get us a spot."

She hung up, and Dan grabbed the left lane and weaved his way to Immokalee Road, dodging the construction to Route 41. So as to not keep his woman waiting, he would test the fifty-five speed limit all the way to the Bonita Beach intersection.

Roni was in a rear booth, near the emergency exit. This gave them the privacy they required. She started to get up, but Dan leaned forward, giving her a quick kiss before sliding in beside her. Roni had two cups of black coffee on the table, a sweet roll for Dan and dry toast for the bride-to-be. Dan grabbed his temptation and surveyed her sandpaper snack. "At least it's not whole wheat." His lips curled in comic distaste, a dollop of icing completing the picture for all to see.

Roni giggled and wiped the sticky stuff from her lover's face, just in time to prevent it from falling on his sport coat. Not an uncommon occurrence, as she so very well knew.

"Okay, what have you got for me? Something that you don't want to do?" Dan handed both files to his girl, the young Hispanic's name on top. She frowned as she glanced at the file. There were many Gonzales's in Bonita, but Roni knew of only one Louis Gonzales who was this approximate age.

"It might be Maria's boy. They live off Dean, across from the new park. Louis was always a problem for her. He was an angry kid, turning into an angry young man. Funny thing, though. Maria did great with the other four, but this one... I just can't quite give you an answer. Maybe his father beat him before he abandoned the family. She stopped me a few months ago. She said he never came around, too old for a missing persons report. Other people told her that they'd seen him. He was definitely avoiding olde Bonita."

Dan said quietly, "Someone has to tell her. And we need all the background she has. You can get that stuff better than anyone else. Friends, enemies, grudges, all she knows. And she may know more than she thinks."

Roni registered mock indignation, turning sideways to him, so he could see her jutting chest. "You mean to tell me that you want me, your fiancée, to make a sympathy call on poor Maria Gonzales, and under the pretext of consoling her, pump the unfortunate woman of all the information she has on her newly deceased eldest child? If you think I'm going to sit here and be manipulated into this kind of subterfuge, you better find another patsy, Buster!"

With that, Roni pretended to try and push by her big boyfriend, only to be wrapped up in a bear hug, while he kissed her ear and whispered, "*Yup!*" He wouldn't let her go then until she squirmed around so she could kiss him into releasing her.

"Okay, okay. I'll do it!" Then she widened her eyes to an innocent look and whispered, "Have you ever considered a career in sales?" This set off more tickling, not dignified at any age, and particularly not so when one of the participants happened to be wearing a too tight police uniform.

They were a team, and they were in love, so there was no use for anyone in the restaurant to register anything more than wishing them well. Dan was amazed at what Roni knew about the Hispanic neighborhoods. Since they'd become an item, she had helped him close more cases in three months than he had completed in the two previous years alone. And she was not snitching on snitches. It was just that she was trusted, and people called her to complain of infractions they would never share with an Anglo cop. Most were afraid that any official contact would set off an INS raid, whole or partial families being sent back to Mexico or wherever. And in some cases, they were right.

What about the other guy?" Roni was curious if he was another local.

"California felon, from LA," Dan summarized. "Lots of priors, nothing really current, beyond parole jumping. There's a cop out there that wants us to call, so there may be more to this guy than meets the eye. I think our 'Traveler,' as Doc Weeks dubbed him, was living with Louis. We'll get a warrant and toss the place. That may give us some clues, but I'm countin' on your visit to Mrs. Gonzales."

Roni quit teasing him. "I'll go this afternoon. What about dinner?"

"How could you think about food after all that delicious toast?" Dan wasn't finished tweaking her.

She was having fun too, but wanted a good report for her man, the lead detective on an important case, with more promotions on the way, more money, a bigger house after they finally were married. She was getting ahead of herself. And she was still hungry.

"I want to try the other Pincher's Crab Shack in Tin City. I hear they have real grouper, not the fake kind. And they have a great singer there." They checked their watches at the same time, getting more and more in sync, finishing each other's sentences, stealing from each other's plates.

Dan loved seafood. "Meet me at my house when you finish your shift. I'll drive us downtown."

Roni could see a trap forming. "Oh, no! I'll get there and you'll want to show me something new in your bedroom and we'll never get out of there. I know you all too well, buddy. Pick me up at Mom and Dad's. I have a new dress you have to see." She slipped by him then, squeezing his side on her way to her cruiser and a bad news interview in Bonita.

Chapter X

JANUARY

The full tide got the bow of the skiff up to the grass and Richard was able to jump in without wet socks. Louis poled backward then turned the bow toward the bridge and the darkening mangroves on the eastern shore.

They went over the plan. Jack liked the Jag. "Man, would I like to open that baby up on Alligator Alley. We could be doin' a hundred 'n twenty between the exits."

Richard knew Jack's history with fast cars and wanted to hear that this was just fantasy. "Take it easy, Jack. Cash, credit cards and jewelry. Keep it simple."

"Yeah, yeah, yeah."

But Richard could hear the excitement in his voice. "What're you two gonna to do with the jewels and credit cards?" He needed to know there'd be no local fences to rat this crew out.

"Don't *worry* so much, Rick. Me and Louis have contacts out of town."

Richard was not satisfied. "This is just between the three of us."

"We got friends, man," said Louis.

Jack supplied the details. "We met some guys in Miami that move stuff offshore. They use mules to carry the jewels on cruise ships headin' for Europe. The credit cards get sold in Miami, but we don't know where the stuff goes after that. They give us a set price, way lower than the jewels are worth, but we don't gotta mess with 'em after that. Louis has a false bottom in one of the boat gas tanks, and after stuff's calmed down, we're gonna take us a little 'fishing trip' to Miami."

Richard was impressed that these boneheads had thought things out that far. He described the marks. "Albert and Myra are in their seventies and slowing down. Albert's getting fat, but the old broad works out and she's wiry. You guys got a gun? Somethin' to scare 'em with?"

Jack reached behind him and pulled a fat forty-five from his waistband. "This good enough for ya, Rick?" He waggled the gun, showing Richard he was not to be trifled with. "And we got the duct tape, enough to wrap 'em completely, and ski masks. So don't be scared. We're not gonna screw this up. We've done this shit before, ya know."

Richard was still not satisfied but he was almost out of questions. "You found the restaurant okay?"

"Yeah. Louis spotted it on our way to the boat ramps. It's small. How much do they charge in that joint, anyway?"

"More than we have in our wallets." For better or worse, it was time to wind this up. "Let's set our next meeting. I think a week from now is good enough, don't you?"

"Sure, Rick, old buddy," Jack replied, in a tone that made Rick's skin crawl. "Me and Louis'll have time to do some serious partyin', if this haul is as good as you say."

Richard stepped off the boat without looking back and headed to the park to retrieve his bike. The next three days would be stressful, waiting to see if these bozos could hit and run without tying the heist to him or the hotel. Now he knew Jack had firepower. Who knew what weapons Louis had squirreled away? So far he had made one phone call, cell to cell, and no one had seen them together, and these river conferences were good for anonymity. It wasn't going to be easy to slip from the box these two had him in. But he liked that they were cocky and would probably get more so.

Richard wanted them to think that he was frightened and intimidated. It was the first step to his escape plan and it had to work. It just *had* to.

Chapter XI

"Hurry up, for goodness sake! Our car will be out front, blocking traffic!" Myra Frothingham was frustrated and excited. They hadn't been to La Rive Gauche since last season, and her husband insisted on fussing over what cuff links to wear with the new tuxedo she had picked out for him. Albert was also having trouble with the cummerbund. While at the store, even though he had been forced to go up a size, the tailor had pronounced it a perfect fit. Now the damned belt cover had to be extended.

"Tell me again why I have to wear this idiot monkey suit?"

Myra sighed, repeating the litany. "Because it is the weekend, and it is after seven, and it is the high season, and we are at the Hotel Sherill, and we have to walk through the Grande Salon to get to the front doors, and everyone there is dressed formally," she again sighed audibly. "Reason enough?" She was tired of keeping him on the right page. Did she have to take care of everything? If it was up to him, they'd be at a hunting lodge somewhere hiking around some godforsaken lake.

She went to him, adjusted his tie, pulled the lapels, brushed off dandruff, and gave him one final look to make sure the old fool was presentable. Myra herself was ready to go. She had taken the diamond necklace and matching earrings from their safe, the ones Albert had given her on their fiftieth wedding anniversary. Her gown was a new Vera Wang purchased in New York City, just before they flew south to Palm Beach.

The Frothinghams made a striking couple as they strode proudly through the throng gathered near the front on their way to a night on the town. The valet was taking a few final swipes with the chamois, removing the last droplet off the hood of the Jaguar. Myra noticed that there were fewer guests leaving for Naples, the majority staying to enjoy the extended social opportunities at the Hotel's six restaurants.

Albert arranged his seatbelt, trying to get comfortable. His tux rode up in the bucket seats.   He wanted to remove his jacket, but his wife's violent shaking of her head told him he must remain sartorially whole as they completed their formal exit.   Albert compensated for his ongoing emasculation by pressing down hard on the accelerator. The Jag's tires made a little squeal when he hit second gear. Gulfshore Boulevard was not a drag strip and this caused Myra to scream as she felt the G-forces of the powerful engine.

"For God's sake, Albert! Don't you see that stop sign up there? SLOW DOWN!"   Albert took his foot off the gas, letting the car engine and the lower gear cut speed as he rolled to the Fifth Avenue four-way stop.   He could have bypassed downtown Naples and found a faster way to the restaurant, skirting the glitz of this famous street, but he knew that Myra liked to crawl the strip.   All the stores and brokerage houses were lit, and people were eating at tables on the sidewalk. Myra was eager for the madding crowd to admire their car and evening dress and she also wanted to observe who else was out and about this warm Sunday evening.

They had a little time until their reservation and needed it because of all the pedestrian traffic cutting across Fifth Avenue - which at times was going faster than the Jag. In Naples, the walkers had the right of way and they abused the privilege by crossing at all points. A few even used the lighted crosswalks designated for that express purpose.

They turned toward the Dove Inn and the circle that ended at the Naples City Docks at Crayton Cove. The space at the end of the street contained the entrance to the public piers and a popular casual eatery named, appropriately, the Pier Restaurant. However, just to the west was a dark alley called Eighth Street, a jog off the main route ending at a little canal. It was here, adjacent to a small parking area, that one could find the five-star gem, La Rive Gauche, having been here as long as anyone could remember, being the local leader in French Cuisine. Albert had to park at the end near the water, backing in carefully as he approached the canal's edge.

"For God's sake, don't run us in the water!" Myra had never forgiven him for buying this car, and used the times she was forced to ride in it as opportunities to criticize his driving. "You know your night vision is terrible."

Albert was aware that if they had taken either of their other vehicles, his wife would have insisted on being behind the wheel. There was method to his madness, but he had to take some crap for the privilege.

They had a short wait for the busboy to finish wiping a small table looking toward the canal. Once the white linen was in place, their server seated them, snapping the napkins and offering an array of wine and appetizer choices. There were still white Christmas lights running along the outside eaves, and they could just see the canal. Everywhere else, it was pitch black. They could have been in Paris. Myra chose champagne.

Louis pulled into a parking space at the public launch area. To be on the safe side, Jack put ten quarters in the meter. It was eight forty-five. They had rehearsed this part. They went back to the boat, going through the motions of checking fishing gear, before removing a dark canvas bag. There were three other vehicles with trailers, the owners out trolling on a cloudy night.

Earlier in the day the area had been overflowing, weekend anglers eager to get their last day on the water before going back to work. Now it was quiet. They walked west, toward the Dove Inn, through the hedges and the parking lots separating them from the public piers. Against the brightness of the city dock it was difficult to see the little side street housing the exclusive restaurant and once in the alley, they waited for their eyes to adjust to the darkness. Then they moved to the end of the parking area.

The Jaguar stood out, more isolated now as customers with earlier reservations headed home. There were no vehicles between the car and the water. Louis and Jack went to the riverbank and hid among the mangroves. Crouched down, they opened the bag, its contents illuminated only by Jack's pencil flashlight. They donned dark ski masks that Louis had found in the free bin at Goodwill. Jack checked his forty-five and Louis flashed his switch blade, all the intimidation they figured would be needed to immobilize the older couple. It was now closing in on nine PM.

"How long'd Rick say it took to eat in that joint?", Louis whispered while scratching his back where a branch was rubbing.

"The man said an hour an' a half, maybe more." He went back into to the bag and pulled out the two big rolls of three-inch duct tape. Louis started his tape and folded it back so it wouldn't stick when he needed his first strip. Jack did the same and they quietly discussed the exit routes. Jack wanted to know why they couldn't go home on the Tamiami Trail, so much closer than Alligator Alley, I-75.

Louis explained, "Yeah, closer. But if they get away, the cops'll look closer. We get on the interstate, get off at the beach road, maybe better at Estero, then come on down to Old 41 from the north, like we've been fishin' on the bay or the Caloosahatchee."

Jack could see that reasoning. "Okay. Anyone closer sees us, thinks we maybe came out on the Imperial River, all in Lee County. I get it. Longer is better."

They'd go south and east, then north again, getting on the Alley at the new entrance on Golden Gate Parkway. They discussed what they were going to do with their soon-to-be newly found wealth. Louis had his eye on a new saltwater pole he'd seen at a bait and tackle shop. "I wanna buy a new poling platform. The whole nine yards."

Jack just chuckled. "You wanna replace that piece of shit? Hell, why not just get a new boat?" He was day-dreaming of a girl he'd met at Bison Chips. She told him she was a server at Bonita Bay, the high-end development west of 41. He figured she was about twenty-two or -three, but he must've bored her early on because she'd moved from the bar to a table to talk with some younger Hispanics she knew. "If I just had some new clothes," he thought. He was hoping that a new wardrobe, and maybe a hot rental car, would move the young lady toward intimacy. Friendship had nothing to do with his objective.

Louis got up slowly, stretching his legs and his back. Jack realized that he was also starting to cramp and repeated the exercise. They had been in the dark long enough that they were able to see detail, all the cars, particularly the one closest to them, now alone in the west end of the parking lot. They were sensitive to all sounds and movement, even hearing the boats on the Gordon River half a mile away. They had no trouble seeing the older couple come out and move hesitantly in their direction.

Louis and Jack looked at each other and nodded. Jack whispered: "You wrap the woman. I'll take the old man." They both now stood up straight in the shadow of the canal mangroves, invisible in dark clothing, masks down, wearing surgical gloves, breathing quietly.

Myra was a little tipsy. They'd ordered the bottle recommended by the maître d', and at ninety dollars she'd been determined not to leave a drop in her glass. The wine, combined with her champagne, had rendered her speech, if not clear, at least loud. "Albert, do you have your keys?" He was fumbling, not familiar with the pockets on his new tux. "They gotta be here somewhere."

His several manhattans hadn't improved Albert's coordination, or his wife's temper.

"For Christ's sake, use mine, if you've lost yours." She came to his side of the car while digging in her evening purse.

Her husband didn't want to give up.. "I've *got* 'em. I put 'em in one of these pockets, in one of these, somewhere in one of these pockets."

They didn't see or hear the men approach or feel their presence on each side of them. Any movement, in their minds, was surely just valets or helpers, not assailants. Within seconds Jack had his gun in Albert's face. The older man's hands rose instinctively into the air.

Louis held his blade to Myra's neck. "Keys, keys!" He whispered in her ear. Myra lifted her set of keys from her purse, looking at them as if they were long lost *objets d'art.*

Louis pushed the unlock button on the key fob. Jack used his first strip of tape to close off Albert's mouth before spinning him to the fender and grabbing his wrist to immobilize them behind his back. Louis was doing the same, taking the roll and running it fully around the woman's head before she could demand of her husband that he do something -- ANYTHING -- to stop this humiliation!

Jack took Albert's watch and wallet. Then he opened the Jag's left side back door and shoved the older man in, face down. Louis walked the unsteady but unresisting matron to same side of the car. He took her purse, ripped the diamond necklace from her neck and pulled off her rings. Then he pushed her in, also face down, toward her husband. They dumped their stash in the canvas bag and completed trussing the couple by wrapping more duct tape around their ankles, effectively immobilizing both from head to toe.

Then they quietly closed the Jag's door but forgot to push the lock button. They threw the keys under the car. No one had left the restaurant. Jack and Louis exited the parking lot at the bay side, and then retraced their steps to the public launch. Jack pulled credit cards and cash from Albert's wallet. Louis went through the old lady's purse and found the earrings -- pricey, but apparently uncomfortable -- credit cards and loose bills. They tossed the wallet and purse in a trash can and put the stash in the false bottom of the gas tank in the boat. The whole operation was done in less than five minutes. It was not strange for a car, boat and trailer to emerge near the Gordon River Bridge, even on a dark Sunday night.

The Limo from the Hotel Sherill pulled up near the walkway to La Rive Gauche. Jorge was early for his carless patrons. They wouldn't be out much before eleven. He turned to the Miami Heat game on the radio. Boy, were they lousy this year. How many games in a row had they lost? He tipped his hat over his eyes, accepting the risk of being seen taking a nap on company time. He had to be alert when they came out, jumping from his seat to open the doors on both sides, inquiring as to their satisfaction. It was this attention that brought in the big tips, usually even more if they were drunk. "Maybe just a quick siesta," he told himself. It would have taken superhuman powers to see the slight vibration of the green car at the far end of the dark parking lot.

Henri held the door for Miguel, his cleaner, as the young man rolled his commercial vacuum through the doorway of the restaurant. It was one-thirty in the morning and Henri had time for one drink with the chef at Virginia's on Fifth, before their bar finished for the night. "See you Tuesday, Miguel." The night man nodded goodbye, the vacuum already on and drowning out all other sounds. He was on contract and wanted to be out of there in three hours, if possible. That way he could help fix his kids' breakfast and get them off to school before getting some of his own hard earned rest.

In fact, he would not get home for another six and half hours.

"WHERE HAVE YOU BEEN???" Miguel's wife was screaming, holding their baby daughter while their son played with his cereal at the kitchen table. Eleana was in her home health uniform, already thirty minutes late for her shift at the assisted living facility. It was seven-thirty, and he was two hours overdue.

"Eleana, I was at a crime scene! They would not let me go! I tried, believe me. I tried!"

Now she wasn't mad any more. Just scared. "Are you okay? Were you hurt? Did you have an accident?"

"No, no. It wasn't me." Miguel took their daughter from her. "Someone robbed these two old people at the restaurant parking lot. I was just packin' up and I saw this green car that just didn't seem right. So when I went over to get a better look, I saw these people all taped up in the back seat."

"What'd you *do*?", Eleana asked.

"What *could* I do? I called 911 and tried to help the old people get the tape off and help 'em sit up." His daughter started to cry so he bobbed her up and down. The movement made him feel how truly exhausted he was.

"Then what happened?"

"The cops were there quick. They put up that yellow crime scene tape, ya know? And wanted to know where I worked, and I said, 'Right here. At La Rive Gauche. This is where I work.' They wanted to talk to Henri, so I guess they woke him up because he came over and showed them through the restaurant. I would still be there if Henri had not told them my schedule. I think they thought I was a suspect."

Eleana was indignant. "You? They thought it was you?"

Miguel shrugged. "I was the only one there. And I heard one of the old customers say the guys that did it were wearing masks."

Eleana had her hands on her hips, tapping one foot. "And they thought it was you. Of course they did. Accuse the first Hispanic they see."

"The old couple helped too." Miguel added, "They said it wasn't me. They said I was too nice. Now you go. I'll get the kids ready. We'll talk when you get home."

Eleana wanted to know more but they needed her paycheck. She was talking to her facility on the phone as she got into her car, explaining her tardiness. Then she thought to herself, "Wait until the girls hear this new story of guilt by ethnicity."

Chapter XII

Jack and Louis were holed up, shades drawn, as they went through the canvas bag.

"I count a little less than fifteen hundred", said Jack while organizing the bills in a stack. There were ten one-hundred dollar bills and the rest in fifties and twenties.

Louis held up the diamond necklace, catching the reflections from the table lamp. "How much do ya think they'll give us for this one?"

Jack wasn't optimistic. "Whatever it is, it won't be close to resale. But I don't think the broken clasp'll hurt us. This watch might be worth more." He was looking at an exquisite Patek Philippe. The inscription on the back read: "To Albert Frothingham, For Years of Exemplary Service. The Executive Board." Jack was disappointed to find identification. "Maybe they can scratch that shit off!"

The men had returned home at ten forty-five in the evening to a quiet parking lot and the hum of air-conditioning units.

"Sunday was a good idea Rick had." That was Jack's grudging compliment to their high and mighty planner. Both crooks had been surprised at how light the traffic had been. There were no late night parties going on, no one to even document their quiet arrival as they backed the boat into their trailer storage spot.

They turned on the eleven-o-clock news, checking all three networks, but luckily there were no late-breaking reports of a robbery.

"D'ya think they're still in there?" Louis felt proud that their tape job could have been so effective.

The next morning the crime got brief comments on the local channels every half hour from seven o'clock on until the stations switched to national programs.

Things were different at the Hotel Sherill. The house staff was buzzing with the news. Two prominent guests were in the hospital having been sent to a restaurant on a referral through the concierge desk! Richard was glad he hadn't been the one to make the reservation. The other two front desk staff had ducked into the back room to watch the sketchy reporting. Richard waited until they returned to get his chance at the coverage.

"The thieves did a pretty good job," he was thinking to himself. Apparently there had been no glaring clues left behind or witnesses to the crime. The victims had remained undiscovered until early in the morning, well past Richard's best guess as to when the police would have become involved. He breathed a sigh of relief and hoped that the haul had been lucrative enough to temporarily whet his "partners" appetites for ill-gotten gains.

But next time, Richard would have to be even more careful.

Upstairs, the executive suite was agitated. Sir George had all the managers collected in the conference room. He wanted the whole story, but more importantly, he wanted damage control. This was not the time of year for Naples' most exclusive resort to experience a public black eye. The souring economy had yet to trickle down to his clients and he wanted no new excuses for cancellations.

"Give it to me straight, boys!" Sir George abandoned his British accent at times like this.

The front end manager gave copies of the reservation sheet to everyone at the table and described what limited information was available. "Marta Shultz made the reservation on Saturday morning. Apparently the initial request was for La Rive Gauche at eight o'clock on Saturday, but they were full. Mrs. Frothingham accepted the Sunday substitute without major complaint, and asked that their car be washed and brought to the front by seven-thirty that evening."

Sir George interrupted, "Why didn't they take the limo? Wasn't one available?"

Stan Merrick was quick with a response. He'd had the concierge staff in his office early, going over all the questions the big boss might ask. "Sir, it seems that Mr. Frothingham prefers his own automobile to the VIP service."

"Okay, okay. So he refused the limo." Sir George was feeling better, thinking that perhaps they were a little less liable. "What do you think, Bob?"

Robert Rosen's days as a Boston corporate attorney were behind him, but he found retirement in Florida so boring that he had offered his services to the hotel for little more than golf course and spa access. He always let Sir George win the last hole. "We can still be sued. Hell, anyone can come after us, but this one seems less a problem. We offered security and they turned it down. They chose the restaurant, but it came off our list of exclusive offerings, so that's a toss-up. This one smells a lot like an 'Act of God, wrong place, wrong time hors d'œuvre.' But let's not make a habit of this kind of thing!"

Yes, Sir George was definitely feeling better. "Okay. So what's their medical status?"

Doctor Weeks, on the payroll, was more respectful with his answer. "They've been moved from ICU to a private room. The physicians wanted to make sure that Mr. Frothingham had not had a heart attack. It appears that they are in excellent condition, mild abrasions from the duct tape, but not much more than that. Their evening clothes were rumpled, but not torn."

Sir George stayed on the basics. "What about property loss?"

David Johnson, head of security was up. "It was a robbery, but we don't know yet what was taken. The police have called and want some interviews."

"Later. What about PR?" This was the big one, as far as Sir George was concerned.

Peter Davis, the media specialist, was quick to reply, "The Naples Daily News wants to talk to us, as do the four local TV stations."

Sir George was winding this down. "Send all those reporters to me and I'll set up a news conference. Nobody else talks! Tell all your staff to refuse interviews with the press and TV people. Same for the police. I'll set up a room for their contacts, but we'll have them across the street in the administration building."

He certainly did not need uniformed or plain clothed cops wandering among the well heeled guests, those whose wealth was supposed to provide relief from prying law enforcement. Sir George looked at his watch. "Okay, somebody call the hospital. We're going to pick up their tab. When the cops are through with the car, have it brought back here and detailed. Merrick, send Marta to the hospital and have her find out what clothes and toiletries they need. And have her bring back their outfits and get them cleaned and pressed. When they're discharged, we'll provide the limo to the hotel. Persuade the hospital staff to postpone that particular time. Promise a bigger donation! Limo to the side entrance. Move them to the rear elevators and up to the top floor. I don't want a crowd of reporters there or at our gates. Dave, double the valets out front and station two at the entrance. I want all cars screened early, guests only! Are we green on this?" He slid his chair back. Ready or not, they were done.

The last people were still filing out when Sir George reached for the phone to call his "friend" Gerald Kelly, the police chief.

The chief, holding his phone, leaned back in his chair and motioned to Dan to stick around. Dan caught the end of the conversation, the boss promising some bigwig to take it easy on an investigation that had to involve him, or else why the soft seat in the corner? The chief hung up. Dan watched the square jawed Irishman pretend to wipe some sweat from his brow.

"What kind of a job would this be if everyone with money didn't think they could do it better? That was *Sir* George Sherill, of the Hotel Sherill, kindly requesting us to be careful interviewing his employees on site. I guess I can't be offended that he's worried. This is certainly not great publicity for him, even if the crime did take place elsewhere. He's not a bad guy. I've sat next to him at Chamber meetings and he's a great story teller. Been here since before the beginning of the population boom."

Dan did not want to be impressed. This guy's ritzy hotel was so expensive they never bothered to call for a quote for their wedding reception. The Sherill's reputation alone had priced them out. "What did he want, specifically?"

Chief Kelly answered, "He helpfully suggested we interview his staff in the administration building. It's right next to the clubhouses where the guests play golf and tennis. Where are we on the robbery?"

"Right now, I don't know who we're going to want to question. We don't have much - just a little feedback from the restaurant owner and the cleaning guy who found them. And those are the only witnesses. To make matters worse, even they didn't see the crime in progress or the getaway. So from them we got a whole lotta nothin'. As for our victims, the Frothinghams? Here it is: 'It was dark, we were frightened, they wore masks, we were frightened.' Get the drift?"

The chief shook his head. "Snatch and grab. Random or not? What's your call on this one?"

"Hard to tell," Dan shared his mystification. "But it was quite a payday for a random hit. We won't be certain without insurance verification, but Sean Brady added up fifteen hundred in cash, a twenty-five thousand dollar necklace, and a twenty thousand dollar watch, so we are way up there in the grand theft category."

Chief Kelly thought out loud: "Then again, this is Naples. Maybe everyone at the restaurant was swimming in that much liquidity."

"You could be right. Hard to tell if it was the lottery or pre-planned," Dan admitted. "The setting was good for a grab. Not a lot of light, no valets, canal in the back. The first officers on the scene said they had trouble finding the alley. By the time they got there, the kid who let the couple out had calmed them down so what we got from them was clear, the same story. Their report had no helpful facts. It was just a blur for them. The officers said they could smell alcohol in the car but the couple were cold sober by the time we showed up."

Chief Kelly continued to shake his head. This was not looking good in the indictment department. "I don't think we've had any crimes like this lately. Anything similar out there anywhere?"

Dan was positive. "Nothing like this for a long time. The only thing remotely close would be kids grabbing purses."

The chief nodded. "Okay, let's go to the hotel. Sir George has opened the door a crack. He knows the reservation came through his place, but that's the only connection to them, and that's still a stretch. Take Brady and we'll talk to the staff that set it up and anyone else who knew their wealth." Then he added, "Interview them wherever it is Sir George wants you to see them. No reason to anger one of our community's pillars."

Dan was reluctant to bend over for this tycoon, but instead he decided to pull back on his negativity. He acknowledged to himself that his own relative poverty and inability to patronize this resort had put him in a foul mood. And he knew this was all connected to not wanting to disappoint Roni. Dan would cooperate, partly because he, at this point, couldn't see how the hotel was involved in this crime.

Sean was waiting by Dan's cruiser. "Want me to drive?"

Dan thought for a second. "Might as well. I'll go over the file." He shuffled the file's few pages and was not encouraged. It seemed like a lesson in futility, but they had nothing else on the case. "Sean, who do you think we should question first?" Dan needed to hear some new ideas rather than just the noise in his own head.

Sean was ready to jump in. "Well, I guess I'd talk to the person who set up the reservation first, and then anyone else with information on that reservation, or those specific guests."

Dan closed the file. "Good enough for me. Let's go for it," he said with more certainty than he really felt.

As they drove to the hotel on Gulfshore Boulevard, they passed by the new beachfront condos until they reached the older section with smaller complexes. Sean whistled when he saw the top of the hotel, rising eighteen stories from an elevated mound, making it look even larger, and dwarfing anything close to the facility. Dan was also impressed. He didn't drive this road often and wondered what it had been like nearly thirty years ago when this edifice was the only luxury resort on the Naples beach.

They came up to the main entrance and saw a number of liveried staff stopping cars and checking identities. Two television vans were pulled to the side, unable to get by the guards. Dan pointed to the left and Sean crossed the center line to a two-story white building next to the tennis courts. A valet stopped them, but Dan had his badge in his hand, out the window. The valet approached the passenger side.

"How can I help you, sir?"

Dan smiled at the kid. "We're here to see the front end manager," was his deliberately evasive answer.

"Please park in that visitor spot and take the elevator to the second floor. Mr. Merrick's office is number 210."

Dan wasn't used to this level of politeness. "Why, thank you, sir," was the only thing he could think to say.

The valet answered, "It is my particular pleasure!"

As the cops approached the building, two young women walked by in fashionable tennis whites on their way to the red clay courts. Dan had to grab Sean's arm to keep him from doing a 360-degree pirouette toward some very long, very tanned legs.

"Whoa, tiger," he said. "The real prey lies within." He pushed Sean up the tiled walkway. Another staff member had the front door open, directing them toward the elevators. Dan almost flinched when his knee-jerk "Thanks" was followed by the same "particular pleasure" recitation.

The manager was expecting them. "How can I be of service?" was his not unexpected query. Stan Merrick prided himself on having a good hold on all the front end staff, from the servers to the valets and up to the concierges. He knew most things almost before they happened.

Dan first wanted to know how the reservation system operated.

"Guests are free to make their own reservations." Merrick began, "However, our concierges are much more efficient, so most people avail themselves of the opportunity. Our front staff have lists and telephone numbers of all the exclusive restaurants in Naples. Everything is on the computer, so all a concierge has to do is punch in a code and a call is placed to a reservation agent at the restaurant. Our people are on a first name basis with all the agents."

He added, "And those contact people know that it is very important to service the Sherill's guests with VIP treatment. It is basically a symbiotic relationship." Stan was on a roll now. "These restaurants could not survive the season without our patronage and the Sherill would not be as successful without these cooperative referral options."

Dan kicked himself for asking such an obviously open-ended question, resolving to be more specific before opening his mouth again.

Sean's mouth *was* open, as he tried to gather the forensic implications of a run-on sentence that could have been boiled down to "money talks!"

Dan tried again. "How many people have access to the reservation lists?"

Stan smiled at this softball. "All the concierges have the list, as does the valet supervisor who has to arrange the owners' cars, and the limo supervisor for those particular guests who will use that service. And, of course, I get a copy."

"How many is that?" Dan wanted to know.

Mr. Merrick counted in his head. "That would be eight with paper copies, but many more employees would have access to that information at their computer stations."

Dan almost threw up his hands as Sean made a silent but smiling whistle at this news. Dan clarified the obvious. "So, you're saying that a large number of people, or at least all who have computer access, can get the reservations data."

"That is correct, sir" was the manager's reply. "This is company policy. The more staff we have who are aware of guest destinations, the more help they can be in the process. Before guests even sign in, the hotel has their profiles, preferences, food allergies, bedding requirements. Some make restaurant reservation requests before leaving home!"

Dan had heard enough. Privacy at some levels in this place was a sieve. "Can we speak with the concierge that made the reservation for the Frothingham's?"

"It would be my particular pleasure." Mr. Merrick reached for his phone. "Marta, the police are here. Could you come to my office? Do you have coverage?" Marta must have replied in the affirmative because her boss smiled at his compliance success. "She will be here in less than five minutes," was his confident assertion. Then, "Will you excuse me?" and he punched in some numbers on the phone.

"Mr. Sherill? This is Stan Merrick. The police are here and they will be speaking with Marta Shultz next."

Apparently, Sir George had asked to be kept up to date on the interrogations.

Marta was a little surprised at her welcoming committee. The detective was a big man who almost dwarfed his associate who was over six feet himself. "Good afternoon, Mr. Merrick. Gentlemen," was her polite greeting.

"Marta, this is Detective Logan and Sergeant Brady. They're here as part of the robbery investigation."

She sat up straighter and acknowledged quietly, "Yes, I know. It was terrible what happened to the Frothinghams."

Across the street, on the eighteenth floor, Sir George Sherill was consoling two of his favorite (and highest spending) guests.

"I hope you can accept our sincere concern for your awful experience, Myra."

"Thank you, George. It was lovely for you to pay for the hospital. And Albert and I are grateful you protected us from those vulgar news people."

Mr. Sherill was being supportive, but he was tuned in to any change in the conversation that might indicate litigation against the hotel. He did not want to comp their stay, mainly because it was a large chunk of change. Using it as leverage against a lawsuit was only a last resort.

"The best thing I can say," he continued, "is that it is a miracle you were not injured in the attack."

Albert Frothingham, now free from his binding tuxedo, flexed his arms inside his lush Sherill bathrobe. "I guess playing football in college might have paid off for me."

His wife scoffed. "As if you did anything to protect us!"

Albert was quick to fire back, "Hey, it happened so fast, and it was dark. *You* gave them the damn keys to the car!"

Sir George didn't want this domestic fracas to escalate, as the blame game could easily find a more neutral target, namely Sir George, the board, the front end manager, the concierge staff -- an endless list of the potential respondents.

"Come, come, you two. I have some good news. I know you have had a request for dinner in the Saratoga Room. We have freed up an eight o'clock reservation for you for Saturday night. I would be honored if you would be my personal guests at my table."

Myra beamed. "Oh George, that would be wonderful. Albert and I would be happy to accept. We were beginning to think we might miss the chance to eat there this year."

Sir George had no desire to change the subject but he had to be certain the Frothinghams had protected themselves. "Were you both insured against your losses?", he asked.

"George, dear. How thoughtful of you. The police asked us the very same thing. Every year before we come south, Albert renews our theft policy. We travel with so many valuables, our agent *insists* we itemize our entire collection. He keeps saying we may not be covered without photographs and appraisals, so now it has become kind of a habit. The fun part is we get the chance to touch everything and take the jewels from their cases."

Sir George was beginning to feel as if the hotel might have dodged a litigious bullet, and he continued to complete his picture of this event.

"Speaking of the police, have they finished their contacts with you?" Sir George added, "They are across the street right now, talking to some of the concierge staff."

Mr. Frothingham was quick to dismiss the law enforcement. "They're done with us. I'm convinced they'll do nothing. There may be no clues, and Myra and I can't remember details. We may have had a bit too much wine."

Sir George was happy that all seemed to be well and buttoned up, no need for the hotel to get too worried. Now all he had to do was excuse himself, but Myra was holding up a long finger.

"Wait. You say the police are still here? Albert, I think I may have remembered something that I failed to tell the detectives. I just won't feel right if I don't get the opportunity to share it with them."

"What could you have remembered that I didn't? We were walking to the car. I was looking for the keys. You offered me yours and then they jumped us. Case closed."

"Oh, Albert dear. I won't sleep tonight if I don't get the chance to talk to them. George, would you be a sweetie and ask them to come up? It'll only take a moment, I promise. And then they can be on their way."

Sir George looked at Mr. Frothingham who, at this point, was now shrugging his shoulders. He had given up and Mr. Sherill got the idea that failing to comply with this request might set off a more histrionic post-traumatic reaction. So he relented.

"Of course, Myra, I'll go down and bring them up myself."

Mrs. Frothingham was effusive with her gratitude. "Thank you. Thank you so much, George dear."

"It is my particular pleasure," Sir George murmured as he backed through the suite door. In the hall, he punched the number on his phone.

"Merrick, are they still here? Don't let them leave. I'll be right down."

Chapter XIII

Marta was now relaxed. The two policemen were very nice and had gone out of their way to make her feel more comfortable.

"And I wasn't able to get the Saturday night reservation, I'm sorry to say, but Mrs. Frothingham said it was all right for Sunday, as long as it was for eight o'clock."

Dan asked her, "Did anyone else help with the reservations, or were you on your own for the whole process?"

"Richard usually works with the Frothinghams, but he was on his break. And Mrs. Frothingham does *not* like to wait for anything."

Dan was curious. "Richard. Is he another concierge?"

"Yes. Richard Smythe. He's *very* good. Mrs. Frothingham prefers him, but she was in a hurry this time."

Stan Merrick made his only interruption. "She's right. Richard can service more guests at one time than most. He's our Wunderkind." Mr. Merrick secretly had the hots for Marta, and he was hoping his pidgin German would impress her. Then he got the call from Sir George.

"Could you gentleman please wait after you're finished with Marta? Mr. Sherill would like to speak with you."

Dan looked over at Sean. The young sergeant had made sure he had Richard's name in his notebook.

Dan said, "Certainly. We're about finished here anyway. Thanks for your help Ms. Shultz."

Marta got up and stopped short of a curtsy. "I don't think I've been much help. We hope you catch the robbers."

Mr. Merrick opened the door for her and he got a rush from the perfume in her hair.

There was a knock and Stan leapt from his chair to get to the entrance before his chief operating officer had to open a door by himself. Sir George entered as if the obstacle of a portal would vaporize in front of him.

"Gentlemen," Sir George began. "Thank you for waiting. There has been an added development. Mrs. Frothingham has remembered something that she believes could be helpful in the investigation. She wishes to share that with you now. If you would be so kind as to accompany me?"

Dan and Sean got up. Sir George was leaving and they were to follow. This much was obvious.

The three of them entered the elevator and the owner pushed the lowest button. Dan noticed there were two buttons bearing the number one. When they reached the lowest level, he then realized that they had come out into a tunnel. Sir George was not going to take them through the hotel lobby or the Grande Salon. It was four o'clock in the afternoon. At the Hotel Sherill that meant it was time for High Tea. The guests had started to gather. It was the beginning of formal attire. Sean's uniform and Dan's sport coat absolutely did not pass muster. They were going through the employee passage and, although below ground level, they were still above the water line, thanks due to the tons of sand Sir George had brought in to raise the main floor. There were persons of all colors pushing food and laundry carts.

Dan caught up with Mr. Sherill. "Did Mrs. Frothingham mention what it was that was so important?"

Sir George, without looking back, said, "She did not provide any specifics." That was the end of conversation until they entered a side elevator, thus getting an express ride to the eighteenth floor and the Frothingham suite.

Sir George knocked at a wide door and heard a muted voice utter, "Please, do come in."

Mr. Frothingham was still in his bathrobe, pretending to look at a magazine, washing his hands of the whole discussion.

Sir George made the introductions and added, "Well, Myra. Here we are. These two gentlemen are at your disposal."

Mrs. Frothingham was self-effacing. "Thank you so much for coming, officers. I just had to get this off my chest. I thought of something. I don't know if it's important but I remember it now. And it was not there before when we talked to the other police."

Dan was as positive as possible. "We would be grateful for any new information in our search for these crooks. Anything you remember now, or at any time, may have a great impact on how quickly we move forward."

Myra took a deep breath. "It was a smell -- the smell of FISH!" Then she stopped with a smile of accomplishment on her face.

Albert looked up and said loudly, "Fish? You smelled fish?"

Dan and Sean looked at each other. Sir George had turned away in embarrassment. Albert was incensed and saw the chance to gang up on his domineering wife. "What? Myra! You brought these people all the way up here to tell them you smelled *fish*? We were down by the docks, for God's sake!"

Myra looked close to tears. "Didn't *you* smell it? It came from them!"

Dan inched forward on his chair. He repeated what she had just said. "They smelled like fish?"

Myra shot him a grateful look. "The man who grabbed me and tied me up smelled like fish. Even his knife. It smelled the same as he did. I'm telling you the truth, Officers."

Dan and Sean made eye contact again. A break! A break in what, earlier on, had been a case without discernible clues.

Dan was supportive. "Thank you, Mrs. Frothingham. We may be looking for fishermen. We'd appreciate it if you would keep this knowledge to yourself. Please don't share this with the media. If these two do smell fishy, we don't want them cleaning up their acts, so to speak, if you understand what I'm saying."

Myra nodded her head, thankful that someone was taking her seriously. She shot a look at her husband who was rearranging the sofa cushions. "At least *some* people respect my observations," she muttered.

Dan and Sean got up to leave. They were both thinking the same thing: "This guy's in trouble! I don't wanna be Albert tonight!"

They shook hands all around, Myra clasping Dan's wrist and squeezing hard.

Sir George ushered them out and was their shadow on the replication of the circuitous route to the parking lot. "Thank you, and please give Chief Kelly my regards," were his parting words before he strode across the street to the entrance of his Grande Salon and the rest of High Tea.

Dan and Sean took a final look around. The golfers and tennis players appeared to be winding down their athletic pursuits. Sean searched in vain for the tall females he had ogled on their way in. Everything was white, well-groomed and expensive. They saw two limousines turning toward the large golden doors.

"Are we ever coming back out here?" Sean wanted to know if he should be adding to the list in his notebook.

Dan stared at the hotel. "Maybe the Frothinghams are no different than many folks here and in Naples in general. If this is normal, maybe they weren't targeted. What do you make of the 'fish' thing, Sean?"

"I'm with you on the random part. The restaurant is just around the corner from the city docks and the public launch is three blocks east of that."

"They could have escaped by boat," Dan added.

Sean finished the thought. "Pretty quiet on the river, on Sunday nights in particular."

They were really no farther ahead than before the interviews. Dan was happy for Myra's olfactory recall, but his mind fogged over with the realization that Florida had close to a million registered water craft. He was frustrated.

"Okay. So we can check all the pawn shops and fences, but if these guys were from Miami, they're gonna to be tough to catch. I'll tell the chief to make sure Mr. Sherill can get us the insurance information from the Frothinghams. We'll use their pictures and valuations, and send them to the Miami, Sarasota, Orlando and Tampa authorities. And certainly to Palm Beach."

Richard caught Marta on her way back to work. "What was it like? Are they seeing other people?"

"They just asked how I made the reservations for the Frothinghams. I don't think they'll be talking to anyone else because they went with Mr. Sherill. I think they were going to interview Myra and Albert personally in their suite."

Richard wanted to think that the police would guess a hotel connection would be a remote possibility, but he was still apprehensive at the thought of law enforcement at his work site. He was furious at his "partners" for putting his retirement plan in jeopardy. The next meet with his comrades was not until Friday. Richard had intended to create another robbery scenario, thinking he needed one more to fully hook these scumbags into a financial dependency on his clientele and expertise. But the cops had gotten here so fast! He was surprised that they could think there might be an employee who was in any way connected with the crime. Or -- Richard's mind was racing now -- maybe this was just a routine response to ingratiate favor with one of Collier County's most influential citizens. He didn't want anyone doing a background check on him as, at this point, things would be on shaky ground. He was getting paranoid, thinking of all the dynamics that would raise suspicion. Richard's lifestyle up to this point was that of a loner. Even that single fact alone could raise a red flag. Everyone had some kind of family or circle of friends. All he had were the concierges. He'd been careless. The scenario with the police played out in his own mind:

"Tell us about your friend, Richard Smythe."

"How long did you say he has been living here?"

"You don't know?"

"I thought you said you were one of his good friends?"

"What does he like to do for fun?"

"He doesn't talk about things like that?"

"Does he have a girlfriend?"

"You don't know about that, either?"

"What about a boyfriend?"

"I guess you don't know a whole lot about your so-called friend, Richard!"

"He is married to his job?"

"Hmmm!"

"When is his next shift?"

Richard looked up and saw Stan Merrick coming over to his desk looking for Marta. She'd gone on break so it was up to Richard to be as helpful as possible.

"Richard, there's a group of new guests who would like a Spa tour. When you're finished, get their reservation wish lists and you and the others can set the schedules with the Spa manager." With that, Mr. Merrick turned and walked away.

Richard was glad to have something else on his mind beside his imminent arrest. The tour was a mix of youth and age, fitness and sloth. The two young couples were already bonding, the three businessmen were on a conference break, and the two overweight sixty-something men were ready for a nap. Richard thought the older gentlemen would be seriously altering the water levels on the executive Jacuzzis.

The Spa was adjacent to the tennis and golf complexes. It had its own staff, massage schedule, full hair and nail service, saunas, steam rooms, private lap pools, hot and cold tubs, tanning beds, and a meditation area. There was a small café area featuring an array of organic fruits, vegetables, nuts and special waters, teas, and juice drinks. The staff even offered champagne. They had their own laundry, as the facility went through five hundred towels a day.

They formed a conspicuous group with the still fair skinned newcomers, along with the older ones having trouble keeping up. The Spa manager met them at the front door.

"Good afternoon, ladies and gentlemen. My name is Susan. Welcome to the Spa at the Hotel Sherill. What would you all like to see first?"

That set off a disjointed chorus, everyone having a different idea. Susan, gracious as expected, suggested they go to the public sections first, checking out the changing rooms, saunas, steam rooms, hot tubs and showers. She assigned a male attendant for the gentlemen's facilities, and arranged to meet in fifteen minutes at the main desk.

"Then we can go upstairs to the specialty areas. Would that be satisfactory for everyone?" She responded to their professed thankful agreement with, "It will be my particular pleasure!"

Knowing that this 'particular pleasure' of the hotel was the home away from home for the most wealthy, Richard tagged along at the rear, paying strict attention, aware that his skills were not being required until it was time to make the individual appointments. The men in his group were awed at the size of the Jacuzzi. There was a fifteen person limit, but the area looked able to accommodate more. The aromatic vapors rose off the warm bubbling surface and there were cucumber slices on ice to put over eyes as one lolled in the heat. The steam room was occupied by five guests, but it was difficult to discern among the bodies. Some wore bathing suits while others were in the nude, an exhibitionist's wet dream. There were lounge areas with newspapers and free fruit and nuts. An attendant was employed full time just to dispense the iced water, tea, lemonade, and champagne. Guests were to remain hydrated at all costs, and there were red 911 phones just in case. Richard, however, saw no immediate need for defibrillators.

Back at the reception desk Susan remained her effervescent self. She was proud of her facility and of the latest renovations Sir George believed were necessary to compete with the newer area hotels. The Spa had just had its first anniversary and the champagne had flowed. It had been a good year!

She rejoined Richard and the tour while they all squeezed into two elevators to the fourth floor. Here were the massage rooms, she explained. All staff not pressing flesh stood at a modified attention near the open doors of their work areas. Susan asked one of the girls to do a demonstration on another masseuse and a table was rolled out to the center. Linda, the senior staffer, had an assistant lie face down and began to demonstrate the basic techniques, emphasizing that the guests had full control over the degree of hand pressure and nudity they desired.

Susan stepped back to Richard as the demonstration continued and whispered, "How's it going down there? We heard that the police were here today."

He tried to downplay the event, even though his own anxiety was still through the roof. "They were just here to talk to Marta. She was the one who made the reservation at La Rive Gauche. But I think the main reason they came was to talk to Mr. and Mrs. Frothingham. Mr. Sherill shadowed them all the way."

Susan added her own gossip. "People are saying he brought the cops into the hotel through the staff entrance!"

"I think that's true, because we didn't see them come in or leave through the front doors. After all, it was High Tea."

Susan giggled under her breath. "Wouldn't that have been a hoot if the police had walked through the Grande Salon at that moment? Were they in uniform?"

Richard remembered Marta's description. "Marta said the smaller man was in uniform, but the big detective was wearing a sport coat and slacks." He wanted to change the subject. This talk of police was starting to hurt his head.

Richard noticed a new face, a tall girl by the last door, looking a little uncomfortable. "Who's your new beauty?"

Susan punched him lightly in the shoulder. "You *would* notice her, wouldn't you? That's Shannon. She came last month. She's a little green, but she has good basics, and a wonderful body that people would kill for. As long as guests think a Spa visit or membership is all they need to look like Shannon, business will be good! Do you want me to introduce you?"

She pulled Richard to the side, over to Shannon's door. Susan leaned close to the new girl and while holding Richard's shoulder, whispered, "Shannon, I want you to meet Richard. He's one of the concierges in the front hall."

Richard looked into her hopeful green eyes and extended his hand. "Shannon, glad to meet you. Welcome to our family." She had long fingers and a strong grip.

"Pleased to meet you, Richard," Shannon replied haltingly. She liked that he was taller than she was. She wouldn't have to slouch to make him feel better. And his hands were warm and dry. A good sign.

Linda finished her demonstration. She had done a wonderful job extolling the benefits of full-body massage, emphasizing that the longer sessions gave the best relief.

Her 'practice person' Annie was all smiles, and when she announced to all that she had never felt better, everyone laughed at the audacious plug.

Shannon was glad that she hadn't been asked to volunteer her body, remembering with a blush the last time she was the guinea pig victim.

Susan asked if anyone wanted to make a reservation and many hands shot straight up. Richard took their names while they filed out on their way to view the hair and nail salon.

By the time the tour was finished, most of the participants had indicated their desire to use at least one of the services and Susan was beaming. She addressed the group: "Please feel free to wander around the Spa. The Healthy Heart Cafe is still open and your tour tickets entitle you to a free drink." The younger couples had teamed up and left to explore the offerings at the golf and tennis centers. The older ones sat in chairs in the lobby, mesmerized by the two-story waterfall and the meditation music. Richard promised Susan to send his reservation list as soon as he had entered it in the front end computer.

Susan grabbed Richard's arm. She was feeling magnanimous and very happy that the Spa could count on more business, thanks in part to him. Her job depended on close to full occupancy. "A bunch of us are goin' to a favorite place of ours in Tin City after we finish today. Wanna join us? We always have a great time. Great music, great company, and lots of fun."

Usually, Richard took every opportunity to go out with the concierges who shared his shift, but the Spa staff was small, mostly female, and they were, by definition, a livelier group. Richard decided that a broader social life might make him seem more of a normal, single guy. Remembering the police visit today, he said, "Sure. Sounds like a lot of fun! I'd love to. Is Shannon gonna to be there?"

Susan punched him in the shoulder again. "She hasn't come out with us before, but I'll ask her again. Meet us at six? We'll be at Pincher's Crab Shack. They have a great guy named John Friday who sings and plays guitar at happy hour. He's terrific! You'll love him. Everybody does."

Richard determined at that moment to become "Mr. Social." He needed the cover of a large group of friends. When he got back to his desk he looked around at the other staff on his shift. Richard didn't want to be the only male at a bar table. Barry stood two computers over, a newer employee, maybe twenty-six or -seven. He had yet to move beyond their select group.

"Barry, what are you doin' after work tonight?"

"Nothin' much." The younger man was able to type and converse at the same time. As the new kid at the Sherill, he was a little surprised at the question. He was in awe of Richard's speed and status as the consummate multitasker. "Go out with the guys. I don't know. Maybe watch some basketball."

Richard had a better offer. "How'd ya like to meet up with the Spa girls at Pincher's in Tin City?"

"You and me and the Spa ladies?" He couldn't believe what he was hearing.

"Yep." Richard smiled to himself. Barry would be a good distraction for the women, just as long as he didn't fixate on Shannon, Richard's anticipated conquest. He was glad that Barry was short. Too short for Shannon, Richard felt sure.

Chapter XIV

Back at police headquarters, though he had no way of knowing it, Richard was catching a break. Dan and Sean sat at a desk, trying to decide what to do next.

Dan summarized an investigation without apparent leads. "Fishermen, hot jewelry and missing credit cards. Does that tell the tale?"

Sergeant Brady nodded and shook his head at the same time. "I'm thinking of the manpower and the time to check all the possibilities."

"Right. We just have to decide where we're gonna start, and who's gonna do it, and then the slogging through begins."

Then all the phones started to ring at once. A few moments later Chief Kelly emerged from his office, hat in hand.

"Listen up, folks. We need all personnel in Immokalee. The farm workers are organizing a demonstration against Senor Carlos Taco and their packing company. They're walking out of the fields and are going to either slow traffic down or stop it altogether. We could have a thousand people in the streets. There're still school buses on the road and people are beginning to travel home from their jobs."

Dan saw Roni grabbing her gear. Yeah, he thought. They would obviously need her communication skills.

"Dan, you and Roni ride together." Chief Kelly also saw the value of Roni in this situation. He felt the value of the engaged couple staying close together, as well. "Brady, you come with me. I want you to be my liaison at the command center. Let's go, people!"

Dan had the lights and siren going as they weaved through the heavy traffic, dodging dump trucks and other emergency vehicles. Dan thought that they were ahead of Sean and the chief, but he cursed when a TV panel truck ignored his flashing lights and pulled into his lane. He could see another news vehicle trying to stay in the police cruiser's slip stream. Dan hoped one of the following officers would stop any of the ambulance chasers that were trying to stay with the cop convoy. They sure didn't need a pileup on top of the civil unrest.

Chief Kelly called the lead car.

"Set up at the Seminole Casino. There's no way we can reach City Hall. The roads are blocked. So far, they're telling us that the fishermen and their bass boats are backed up all the way to the ramps at Lake Trafford, and the activities bus from the elementary school is stuck in the driveway. They're letting the walkers go, but most of the buses are stopped somewhere out on their routes."

Roni's question was important. "Who are the organizers and where are they?"

The chief said his information was still coming in, but he was able to supply some data. "I don't know their names but they'll be waiting for us at the Casino. Apparently they were surprised at the size of the turnout. They don't want negative publicity, just a larger TV presence. And maybe some national coverage."

Dan was concentrating on his driving. As they got closer to Immokalee, he knew there would only be one lane in each direction. He was able to go faster now, as traffic had ceased to be an issue, everyone socked in somewhere within the town's perimeter. Closer to the meeting point he could see auxiliary police and volunteer fire personnel clearing a path for them to get to the parking area. They could see workers in the street carrying signs, onlookers adding to the confusion. Some of the signs read "Slave Labor" and "Fair Wages for Honest Work." Dan could see Chief Kelly's car in his mirror. Sean could have a second career as a race car driver.

They all walked into the building and were ushered to a meeting room. The gambling continued around them – the faithful undeterred from their life's focus. Together with members of the town council, they sat around the table with maps and hand-held radios to form a game plan. The council's spokesperson brought a middle-aged Hispanic couple over to them. Dan saw that their faces were lined with the effort of just surviving the requirements of seasonal labor. Yet there was a calmness about them that made him feel less apprehensive.

The councilman introduced the organizers. "This is Lorena and Juan Lopez. They have been leaders in the farm workers' union since the beginning."

The chief deferred to Roni. She began by conversing in Spanish, explaining who they were and their chain of command, starting with Chief Kelly. The woman replied in English with only a hint of an accent.

"We will talk in English. It is important that we all understand what is going on here and how we are trying to make things better."

The chief was relieved. "Right now, all we want to do is reopen 846 in both directions. We're not here to arrest anybody. We just need to clear enough roads to get the kids home from school and people home from work."

Some folks with TV cameras were trying to push into the room, shouting questions as news men and women jockeyed for space so they could begin their broadcasts. The chief threw Dan a worried look and the big detective responded.

"Sean, take some men and get those TV crews outside, please, so we can hear ourselves think." Sergeant Brady and several deputies joined arms and pushed the crews back through the double doors. The young sergeant was smiling but firm. "Let's go, folks! There are plenty of good camera angles out here. Look, I see some guys on a flatbed. Maybe they'll wanna make a statement!"

Chief Kelly gave Roni the floor for most of the planning discussion. An auxiliary policeman with a hand-held radio joined in the meeting. Roni wanted to know how many people were out there with radios willing to take direction from the organizers and police.

Lorena responded. "We have sixteen workers spread between here and where Route 29 enters and leaves the town."

Roni asked the volunteer policeman, "Where are the bottlenecks?"

They spread out the town map on the table. The local cop pointed to the north and south.

"Main Street is blocked. That's shut off access to the elementary school on Lake Trafford Road. That's where the fishermen are stranded. Most of 'em are in pickups pulling bass boats."

The chief wanted to know about the side streets.

Juan chimed in. "My people tell me that most of them are open."

Roni pointed again to the map. "If we could get the cars to Second and Third Streets, it looks as if that could get the vehicles out of town."

Dan could see what she was driving at. "If we use the side streets east of Immokalee Road and make them two lanes going in, and we reverse the flow on Second and Third, we can take the pressure off 846"

Everyone was on the same page at that point. Lorena pointed again to the map showing them how the Lake Trafford congestion could be re-routed over Lincoln Boulevard to reach the western outlet.

Roni asked the Lopezes: "Can you get our people to your folks with the radios? They could help us start funneling the cars out."

Juan was quick to cooperate. "We have two ATV's that we can use to go through yards."

They had made the necessary progress. The chief returned to the parking lot to assign staff to the off-road vehicles. The others walked down to the side street intersections to begin the directing process. Dan took the first south street and began moving cars. The other officers stood in the middle of 846 ushering drivers on to the first side street going west, back in the direction of Naples.

It took more than an hour before the Lake Trafford drivers reached their outlet to the main drag. There was a spontaneous cheer from onlookers when the first school bus was able to get through, the harried driver smiling, and the kids waving at the news media coverage. This parade was followed by the fishermen honking their horns, the ice in their fish coolers long melted. Dan and Roni were on opposite sides of Immokalee Road, now able to see each another and wave and smile, as their arms directed the traffic to continue.

In the meantime, Lorena and Juan Lopez were seated at the Casino, surrounded by the four local stations that were now joined by the newspaper reporters. The Lopezes detailed the grievances that had produced this giant traffic jam. The ABC 7 crew announced that the national network had asked for a live feed in time for the late news, insuring the Lopezes' cause would get a larger exposure. On air, the reporters repeated the litany of neglect suffered by the local farm workers.

It was strange that this town was in the same county that, twenty miles to the west, housed many of Florida's wealthiest citizens. Immokalee's demographics were in stark contrast: just four percent were sixty-five or older while seventy percent claimed Hispanic ancestry, and most were at or below the national poverty level. For a brief moment, the organizers could share their hardship with the outside world, and they were going to make the most   of   this   very   precious   opportunity.

Chapter XV

At Pincher's Crab Shack, the ladies from the Spa had commandeered a long table where they could see the water and the bandstand. Richard and Barry had followed each other from the hotel and found parking spaces opposite the marina sales lot. Susan saw them enter and waved the men over. Barry couldn't believe his good fortune. He was to be spending the evening with six gorgeous women, still in their Spa whites, all in great shape and happy to have the weekend off.

Shannon, the relative newcomer, sat at the end of the table. She felt a little out of her element with the older women. She was glad when the familiar man came in. She smiled hello to Richard as he pulled a chair up to her spot in the group.

Susan yelled over, "We better order now. When it gets crowded and John Friday starts singing, you may not be able to find a server." Barry asked for a Corona. Richard called for a Jim Beam on the rocks. Shannon was impressed by his masculine order. She sipped from her White Russian.

Richard was all smiles. "This place is great. How long have you been coming here?"

Shannon perked up at being praised for her good taste. "I just started. Susan likes the musician here, and she felt I'd like him, too."

As if on cue, the guitar player began, starting with a Jimmy Buffet song with a salsa beat. Susan grabbed Barry before any of the other women could move, but the others didn't wait for partners. They jumped up, bumping hips on their way to the dance floor. There were plenty of young men that wouldn't be able to resist approaching these attractive, Swingsing ladies.

Richard held out his hand and raised an eyebrow. Shannon was quick to her feet. He was glad he'd taken those lessons so long ago in California. His dancing skills - along with his accent - were helpful with the circle of rich who wore the expensive jewelry, and also with this lovely young conquest.

Shannon moved easily. The alcohol and this tall man's attention freed her from her shyness.

Richard let her refine her steps before coming in close to hold her and take her sideways, forward and backward. "You're a good dancer." He stated the obvious and saw her blush at his compliment. He let her go again, giving her the freedom to move as she wanted, aware of the looks her beauty generated from those at the bar.

Shannon was impressed and surprised. She thought to herself, "He's not all over me! This must be what real men are like."

Richard let her dance by herself, staying just close enough to hold her hand, or spin her. He didn't want anyone to think she was up for grabs on a Friday night. The first song ended and they all flopped down, warm enough to yell for more drinks.

Barry ordered a strategic pitcher of Bud Light. Five active girls and the heat of John Friday's music were sure to create a giant thirst.

The singer began a slower number and Richard let Shannon take a gulp of her drink before asking her to try it again. This time he held her gently, one hand just above her waist the other cradling her right hand in a noninvasive grip. His slow foxtrot was easy to follow and Shannon seemed happy to move around the outer rim of the dance floor. Richard didn't want to overtly pressure her, but as they moved he felt Shannon come closer, her hips now just brushing his. He concentrated on his steps, on not making his stride too long, although she had no trouble following him.

The song ended and they sat down again. By this time, the weekend hopefuls had come out of the woodwork. When the third number started all the girls had partners. Susan seemed to have fixated on Barry, and Barry seemed satisfied that it wouldn't be necessary for him to have to snow all the Spa women.

Richard and Shannon decided to sit one out so they could work on their second drinks while being better able to listen to this great singer. A young college hopeful approached Shannon, and Richard was gratified when she shook her head before he had to do the rebuffing.

Shannon laughed. She had seen Richard start out of his chair.

Richard smiled too, letting her know that he was willing to look a little stupid over wanting to be the only guy. "Tell me about yourself." Richard wanted to both get acquainted and slow things down.

She was flattered, and embarrassed, mumbling, "Oh, there's not much to say."

He would not be dissuaded. "No, I'm serious! Are you from around here or did you grow up somewhere else?"

"No, I'm a local girl. I grew up in Bonita and went to school there."

He was quick to reward her honesty. "It must be nice to grow up in one place. We moved around a lot."

She wanted more details, but Richard stuck to her life.

"Are your parents still here?", he inquired.

Shannon was not proud of her parents. She knew very little about her father and was ashamed of her mother's marginal existence. "My mom cleans a church and waits on tables. I don't go home much because her boyfriend follows me around. I think he has the hots for me, to be honest." And then she blushed at her own admission.

Richard sided with the man's prurient interest in this beautiful girl, but he was quick to support her family frustrations. "That does sound like an uncomfortable situation. I can understand why you don't go there often. Are there any others in your family?" Richard was pleased when Shannon replied sadly:

"No, just my Mom. All her relatives live back North, and she hasn't seen them for years."

Richard had to know. "And your Dad, does he live around here?"

"He's back north, too. " She was out of tears for him by now. "He left after Mom got pregnant with me. After I was two, she moved down here, and we've been here ever since."

Richard was both sympathetic and glad that Shannon had so few resources. "And you've never even seen him?"

Shannon's sucked back the last of her drink. "Nope!" What a dismal response, she thought. Then she remembered that a tall and very nice gentleman was interested in her, of all people. "Hey, what about you?" she asked. "You're not from here, are you?"

Richard's next step was to let Shannon know how insightful she was. "How'd you figure that out?"

She smiled. "Oh, just the way you talk. And the way you act. You don't seem like a person from around Bonita or Naples."

"You're right." He would toss her a few bones. "I grew up in New Mexico, near Taos. My Dad was a contractor, fixing up old adobe buildings." And before she could ask the next question, Richard filled in the blank: "They are both dead. Car accident when I was nineteen."

Shannon involuntarily put her hand on Richard's arm.

"I am so sorry for your loss," was all she could offer.

Richard used the small interval to order another round, this time with water back. Not knowing how long this night might last, he did not want to match Shannon, drink for drink.

He wanted to dance again before the singer went on break. He heard a country ballad start. They got up and this time Shannon moved in closer and put her head on his shoulder. He could smell the sweet alcohol on her breath. Richard gave up the foxtrot and slowed his pace to a junior prom shuffle. Glancing at the table, he saw that the girls had added more chairs to accommodate their new Lotharios. Near the rear exit, Barry had Susan's undivided attention as they danced slowly. Richard noticed the basket of nachos and Buffalo wings on their table. Would that be enough for dinner and to slow down the intoxication process?

John Friday finished his set and announced that there would be a ten-minute break. Richard decided he was through with large group small talk for the night and he didn't want to get caught in the cacophony of pick-up lines the younger guys were trying on the Spa ladies. He asked Shannon, "Would you like to go somewhere for some other kind of food?"

"Sure!" She was glad for an excuse not to have to converse with coworkers with whom she had barely become acquainted. Their exit garnered little attention.

Barry was trying to get to Susan's mouth by moving from her neck to her ears. She had her eyes closed waiting for his technique to catch up to his ardor.

Richard didn't want Shannon driving, as she was a little unsteady on her feet. She leaned against him for stability. "Is your car around here?"

"It's in the employee parking lot. I rode with Susan." This was making more and more sense. He would have no trouble getting Shannon to that lot. All he had to do was choose a nearby restaurant and the possibilities this time of year were endless. "I know a place near your car," was his encouraging news as he opened the front door of his red Mercedes.

She settled into the soft brown leather, smelling his cologne in the front seat area. He looked different in sports clothes, the tropical shirt and tan pants setting off his darker skin and hair. Richard wore his clothes loose, but the dancing had given her plenty of ideas from which to construct her dreams.

He went west to Gulfshore Boulevard, but turned right before The Sherill, to Crayton Road, then north to Seagate, and on to Shula's at the Hilton. This place gave couples real privacy: booths with high leather backs, behind which to attack football-sized steaks and four-fingered drinks. Richard knew the maitre d', so finding a Friday night table, in season, was not a problem. The restaurant was arranged to impress, with massive oak settees, a shiny bar, and leather covering all seating. Even the menus were in dimpled envelopes that felt like the covers of footballs.

Larry found them a corner booth as far from the bar as possible. The diminished lighting and ambiance relieved the hotel from any responsibility of lovers failing to connect. They sat facing each other, knee to knee. Shannon buried her nose in her pigskin menu as she tried to compose herself. Richard ordered another bourbon and Shannon stayed with her White Russian. He tried again to reduce her shyness.

"How was your week? Any big tips?" Gratuities were always conversation starters at the Hotel Sherill, the largesse or parsimonious behaviors of the guests being important sources of gratitude or disdain. Some of the staff were able to double their salaries. Richard himself received three times his reported income.

"I had both Myra and Albert Frothingham right after their robbery. Mr. Sherill called Susan and told her we were to comp both of them."

Richard was curious. "Who tipped you the most?"

"I got fifty dollars from Mrs. Frothingham, but Albert gave me a hundred dollar bill!"

"Why so much from him?" Richard guessed that Albert had been turned on by this lovely young woman caressing his aging body, but wanted to know all the details.

She blushed her response. "You know we give the males the chance to move from their stomachs to their backs, by leaving the room. We tell them to rearrange the sheet so that they are fully covered."

Richard could see this scene in his head.

She continued: "I waited two or three minutes, and then I knocked. I thought I heard him say it was okay, so I just walked in." Richard was grinning now, and she could see that he was way ahead of her story.

"Well, he had the towel-sheet half on, and there was something he was trying to cover." Richard broke out laughing, letting her know he understood the sometime cluelessness of the paying customers.

"What'd you do?"

Shannon was giving herself some credit now. "I just got another longer sheet from the pile and I covered him, so it was less noticeable, and I started massaging his feet."

"Good job! How long did you stay down there and away from the embarrassment?"

"I have NEVER massaged a pair of feet that long!"

Then they were laughing together, joined by their common understanding.

"What about you?" She wanted to know. "What was your biggest tip?"

Richard had to think. He had no desire to blow her away with the magnitude of his largest gratuity, which was a five hundred dollar bill and five C notes an elderly recluse gave him, just for walking the old man's dog when the billionaire was afraid to travel through the Grande Salon.

"I think one couple gave me two hundred just for signing up their bratty kid to the Sherill Tot's Day Care." Indeed, Richard was used to receiving five hundred dollars in tip envelopes and in fact felt cheated if it was anything less. He didn't want Shannon to be intimidated by the discrepancy in their respective incomes, so he changed the subject again.

"What do you for fun on weekends?", he inquired.

"Oh, not much." Shannon was ashamed of her isolated and dull life style.

"You look in great shape." Richard was helping her again. "Do you jog? Work out? Play tennis?"

"I run on the high school track, and I have some free weights at home. Sometimes I go to the movies with one of my girlfriends."

This required follow up. Richard wanted to know just how social Shannon was. "Do you see these girls much?" He had pegged her as socially awkward and she rewarded his guess.

"I used to see Marcia a lot, but she's engaged now and spends all her time with Charlie and his family."

Then she admitted: "I didn't have a lot of friends in high school. We were poor, so the snobs left me alone."

"I bet the girls at the Spa will make you part of their gang now, especially after tonight!" Assured of her isolated status, Richard turned encouraging again.

Shannon smiled slightly. "I hope so."

It was time to eat. She ordered the smallest sirloin and a side salad, while Richard got the next size up and a baked potato. The arrival of the succulent meat occupied them for a few minutes. Richard got small insights into why this beautiful young woman seemed so insecure. Shannon admitted to poverty and shyness, but what she failed to grasp was that her beauty was the real problem. There were few women with the capacity for generosity when their boyfriends' eyes turned involuntarily in Shannon's direction. Those small inquisitive gestures were enough to terminate any herd instinct the girls might have felt toward Shannon. No one asked Shannon to go shopping because the tall masseuse stopped traffic stepping from the dressing room to ask how she looked. And in terms of guys as friends: as they say in New Jersey, "Fuggedaboudit!" Enter Richard, Mr. Fix-it. They were finishing their meal, and he could see Shannon start again to get nervous. This would have been the time in her routine dates when the male in question would start the inevitable slobber in anticipation of consummating his dream come true. Richard had to take his time, behave like a gentleman.

"Could I come jogging with you tomorrow?"

"Sure. Of course!" was her delighted and surprised reply.

By the end of the meal Richard could see that she had sobered up. The good food and the conversation combined to refocus her eyes. He held her chair as she stood up, then he took her arm and they walked to the parking area. It was a relatively short drive back to the

Sherill's employee area. Richard waited with Shannon until she had unlocked her car. She turned to thank him and he slid his arms around her waist. She raised her face and he kissed her gently and then stepped back. Shannon almost lost her balance at the shortness of the embrace, opening her eyes to see him smiling at her.

"What time do you go running in the morning?"

She couldn't believe it. He was asking her for a kind of a date, one that would not require fighting him off if, in fact, she did want to fight him off, which, right now, she kind of didn't. But there was tomorrow, and who knew what would happen after that?

Traffic cleared in Immokalee by eleven that night. The police reconvened at the Seminole Casino. They were all tired, as it had been a very long day. Roni and Dan sat at a small table. He wanted to reach for her hand, but settled on rubbing knees. Chief Kelly finished talking with the local councilmen and turned to his exhausted officers.

"It looks like we're just about wrapped up here. The organizers have agreed that from now on, they'll rally in a field behind the railroad tracks."

Roni asked about the media vehicles. The chief thanked her for the question.

"We don't have to worry about any extraneous road blocks. We've been assured that there is ample parking, and it looks as if this is now a national story, so those folks will be doing interviews for at least two more days." Then, the good news: "So, we are done! Everyone not on night duty can go home. Thanks for all your help, people. Great job! Have a well deserved good weekend."

Dan cast his sleepy eyes on his beautiful and tired fiancée: "Let's get something to eat. I'm starved."

"Any place where we can sit. My feet are killing me", was her quiet reply.

They drove back to Bonita, seeing few cars in an area that, three hours earlier, had been a giant parking lot. Roni wanted to put her head on Dan's shoulder, but had to settle for holding his hand. They were still in uniform and technically on duty until they logged out. The only place Dan could count on in Bonita was Perkins, and it was close to midnight before they were able to grab a booth. They both said no to coffee. Roni ordered a burger while Dan switched to breakfast -- an egg sandwich. They ate in relative silence, winding down from their extended assignment.

Roni pushed her fries away and sighed as she sipped a glass of skim milk. "I really liked that farm couple." Roni and Lorena Lopez had bonded instantly, recognizing their inherent minority statuses: Hispanic and female.

Dan nodded absentmindedly: "Yeah, they made a great team. All those farm workers and union organizers. I don't know where those two found the time. And they have kids, too."

Roni arched her arms over her head, leaving them resting on her hair. "I know how tired I feel. I don't know which hurts more - my right arm or both my feet."

"Come to my house and I'll give you a foot massage!", he said to her, suddenly quite awake.

She opened sleepy eyes, gave him a lopsided, knowing grin and responded, "Sure you will, Buddy. Anything else you're planning to massage?"

Dan held up both hands: "Seriously, I was just talking about your feet." But then she surprised him.

"Okay. I'll sleep with you, if we literally just sleep. I never *did* understand that expression, anyway. It's twelve-thirty in the morning and I really don't wanna wake up my parents. So, if you promise not to try anything, we can get some rest."

Dan was ready to agree to anything just to have her in his home again. They didn't need to talk on the short drive to his development in old Bonita.

Roni felt a little strange coming up his front walk. It had been weeks since she had been inside. She remembered, with a shiver, the last time they had made love here. Dan was thinking similar thoughts as he turned on the lights. Roni noticed some new curtains and a tropical tablecloth in the kitchen. She was touched that he had been trying to spruce up this place that would be theirs together after their wedding. She then whistled. "Way to go, Martha Stewart! I love what you've done with the place."

Dan grinned at her and grabbed a towel and a pajama top for his woman. "I wondered if you would notice. That tablecloth *is* a Martha Stewart, as a matter of fact. I got it on sale at K-Mart." Dan tried to sound casual: "I'll shower in the guest bathroom. You can use the master."

He was done in five minutes, but decided to get a quick shave while his beard was still soft. He could still hear the water running when he came into the bedroom.

Roni took her time to get all the road smell off. Dan was glad he had upgraded to a fifty gallon, low-energy water heater.

When she came from the bathroom, Dan was on the bed, holding a book - upside down - with the lamp on. Roni struck a pose in the doorway. Her hair was piled on top of her head and Dan's pajama top came to her knees. Roni was, from all angles, adorable and the oh-so-clean soap smell radiated straight to her fiancé's nostrils.

She got into bed very carefully, trying hard not to touch him, or give off any aura that might have been considered sexual in origin. Dan was very glad at that particular moment that he had chosen a king-size bed. He turned away to extinguish his reading lamp but couldn't resist looking at his beautiful bride-to-be, snuggled down in his pajamas. Her head faced the opposite wall. In the half-light Dan could see the lines of her curves. First was her head with the dark tendrils, then those wonderful shoulders, dropping precipitously to her slender waist, before rising again to the hips of a real woman, here again, for a celibate one night stand. He kissed her blanket covered shoulder.

"Good night, Sweetheart...." Roni's mumbled response was an indication that she was almost asleep.

How could she sleep? Dan was wide awake. He tried to control his breathing so he could listen to hers. Very soon, he heard her sounds soften and there was just a hint of a snore to tell him that she was able to block out his nearness in favor of a restorative nap. Dan knew that counting virgins might be a futile gesture, so he tried to get comfortable, adjusting his pillow repeatedly, staring at the digital alarm clock that was radiating one-thirty in the morning. She was on her side of the mattress, but her essence surrounded him, driving him crazy with carnal thoughts that, at long last, finally succumbed to his fatigue.

He was awakened by the sound of a whippoorwill, the first of the early spring. The sun had yet to rise and his room was still holding the pre-dawn darkness. Dan turned toward Roni and looked beneath the covers. Her pajama top had ridden up, exposing some thigh. He snuggled close to her and gently put his arm around her waist. Roni moved to him and brushed against his growing hardness. She moaned slightly and held his arm, so he pulled her closer. Roni's top was higher now, and Dan ran his hand to her left breast, oh so lightly brushing the nipple. He could feel it harden and thought he felt her hips beginning to move against him. He wasn't positive Roni was fully awake and neither was he, really. Her eyes were closed and it was if she was still dreaming -- perhaps something erotic, because her lips parted and there was another hint of a moan. When his manhood pushed between her thighs, there was a sharp intake of breath, and Roni opened her eyes.

They had been moving together for a few moments and it was as if she had been taken over by a woman not in touch with their abstinence pledges. She simply couldn't stop. She raised her hips to take him, moving more quickly now, demanding he keep pace, not wanting to wait any longer. Roni, now wet, backed into him, grinding harder as if daring him to stay in contact. She was getting tighter as she approached her climax. He tried to hold back, but he had been without her so very long. He let go but he kept moving as she came down on him, gyrating faster, until her own explosive cry. They both continued to move, neither wanting this one to end. He stayed hard, moving with her until she finally stopped, kissing his sweaty arm, holding it so he could not move from her. He kissed her neck and her back and held her breasts, pulling her tight against him. She arched her neck and back, letting him look down her front before she wriggled free to face her lover.

Roni put on a false frown: "Well, there goes that plan. What do you have to say for yourself, Danny Boy? You promised you were going to stay away from me."

He held his hands up and started to apologize for this breach of their pre-marital contract. But she grabbed his hands and kissed him, rolling on top. He was surprised by the fierceness of her kiss and her probing tongue. Then she was working her way down his chest, licking his nipples hard, but not stopping there. She slid away, her legs almost coming off the bed as she held his growing manhood, licking the wetness before putting it her mouth, going up and down while she licked the tip. Roni held his testicles in one hand, the other holding the base of his hardness. She was leading and he could follow or get out of the way.

Dan chose to follow, judging his body to be ready and more in control this time, waiting for her tightness and her little yelp to let him know that it was all right to let it all go, coming with her to a place that was real bliss. After that, she was close to sleep again, head on his chest, eyes closed, a little saliva escaping from the corner of her mouth.

He was thinking of breakfast - how he would feed her, bathe her, take care of her, not let her go. Roni slept on him for another forty minutes before sliding off and curling up in a ball, wrapping the covers around herself. Dan watched her for a few minutes. She looked so young now, the worry lines gone. He got out of bed carefully, took a quick shower, and grabbed a T-shirt and some shorts before heading to the kitchen. There were enough eggs and cheese for an omelet plus six pieces of bacon. Dan also had three oranges and a grapefruit, hoping that the juicer would produce two reasonable glasses of fresh Florida liquid. He cooked the bacon in the microwave, and mixed the eggs with half-and-half and a little salsa and grated Romano. There was a half loaf of Italian bread, just starting to get stale, but it was good enough for toast. He punched the button on the coffee machine, grateful that he had filled it before going to work yesterday morning. It was not gourmet, but it would have to do.

The smells from the kitchen roused Roni. She entered the room surrounded by his bathrobe with the sleeves rolled up, the collar high, just the top of her head visible, those sleepy eyes and crooked smile indicating that it just might be time to fully awaken from her sensual trance. But only if the coffee was hot and fresh, which, thank heaven for Dan, it was, and there was plenty of it. She sat curled up in a kitchen chair while he bustled about her, lining up her silverware, finding a clean napkin, snapping it open before taking his sweet time finding a spot in her lap to secure it. Roni brushed his hand away and took a sip of coffee. It was a little too hot, so she tried the juice.

"This is wonderful," she started to say, but he had no time for chit-chat. He brought her a hot plate of eggs with three strips of bacon and buttered toast. Roni couldn't believe how hungry she was. She cleared her plate and then accepted a second cup of coffee while spreading marmalade on an extra slice of toast. "Like I was trying to say a few minutes ago, this is really good. Do you eat like this every day?"

Dan grinned. "Are you kidding? You've been here before. If I ate like this, I'd either be dead in a week or weigh three hundred pounds, whichever came first. I'm a cold cereal kind of guy. Black coffee, juice, a little toast, and it's time for the gym. But for you, Senorita," employing a false Spanish accent, "only the best!"

Dan helped her finish the toast and refilled their coffee cups and stretched out to take a breath and admire his satiated soulmate.

Roni didn't want to go home. "I've got to call my parents and tell them what time you plan to let me go. Then I'm going to call the cops and make a formal kidnapping complaint."

Dan joined the ruse. "I'm beginning to feel guilty for holding you against your will. I've never taken a woman who fought me so hard. They'll probably throw the book at me, and you know what? I deserve it. How can you stand to even look at me? Especially after what I've just put you through!"

She hopped into his lap then and started to lick the marmalade off his mouth. "If you take these handcuffs off, maybe we can think of a plea bargain."

He put his hands inside his bathrobe that she was wearing to discover she was naked underneath. But just then she slipped from the robe and ran to the bedroom and tried to slam the door shut. He pushed through, reaching the bed at the same time to lift her from the floor. Roni put her arms around his neck while he angled her hips and lowered her onto himself. She let him pull her legs around his waist. He felt himself get stronger and it was if Roni weighed no more than a feather. He leaned against the wall to brace himself, moving her faster as he felt himself start to ejaculate, her long hair whipping against his face. When he was done, he opened his eyelids to see her big eyes and open mouth, still coming down from her high. It was only then that he realized that he was still holding her off the ground. He collapsed to the bed with her in a rumpled mess of gratitude. Then they slept.

It was close to two in the afternoon when she awakened to the sound of water running, Dan was using the guest room shower. Roni jumped up and ran to the other bathroom and began her own cleansing process. She found one of her old pair of shorts that she must have left before they started their celibacy experiment (now failed). That was her outfit: the shorts and Dan's smallest t-shirt. It would have to do until they got to her house. They finished the juice and talked about the rest of the day.

"We could go for a bike ride to Barefoot Beach," was Dan's hopeful suggestion.

Roni looked outside at the bright sun trying to penetrate the drawn curtains. She didn't want to be inside any longer on her day off. "That's a great idea. Let's take your bike in the car and then we can ride from my house. I'm closer to the beach!"

Roni's parents had moved to a small house in an old development called Bonita Shores, west of 41, just two miles from Bonita Beach and from the fancier Barefoot Beach area which, at the southernmost end, was closer to Wiggins Pass. Roni called her parents to alert them of her whereabouts. They had just assumed the law-enforcement pair was still on duty in Immokalee.

Ronaldo and Carolina Menendez were always glad to see their future son-in-law, and there were more plates of food ready for them when the lovers pulled up to the front door. Of course, they *had* to eat, even though Roni's stomach was still full from the late morning feast. Dan managed to clean his portion and he encouraged her to do the same, as they were going to be biking at least seven or eight miles and swim if the Gulf was warm enough. They filled backpacks with bathing suits, towels, drinks, snacks and sunscreen and planned to head toward West Avenue and Bonita Beach Road. It had recently turned to Daylight Savings, so they would have plenty of sun for their ride and wave surfing.

Dan took his bike off the car's rack and Roni pulled hers from the garage. It didn't take long for them to doubt the wisdom of their plan.

"Ouch!" That was Roni's response to her bicycle seat after the abuse she had taken earlier in the morning.

Dan looked back as she grimaced again, this time her mouth in a silent "O" to let him know of her pain. He was feeling a little sore, too, so they turned around and went back to her garage, getting off gingerly to store the two-wheeled vehicles in favor of his car and a faster, less painful ride to the sandy shore.

The first two parking lots were full and they could see cars on both sides of the road. Experience had taught them however that this didn't mean the lots were full. It just meant that folks were too lazy to walk the extra two hundred yards from the last parking area to the main facilities building, the one with ice cream and lavatories. There was an onshore breeze chasing some people from the water, so Dan had an idea.

"Why we don't we hike the nature trail inside until we get to Wiggins Pass?"

Roni saw the logic. "We can work up a sweat, and maybe the water won't seem as cold when we get back to the beach."

Dan grabbed her. "I thought we already worked up a sweat."

She broke from him, adjusted her backpack and started to jog the nature trail. He was right behind. They heard the osprey screeching at them before they could see her nest. That section of the trail, between the backwater and the beach, was lightly used, getting downright hot on days when the wind was from the east. Roni pointed to their left, and there she was, with two fledglings and a partly dismembered snook.

Dan remarked, "She sure picked a public spot to make her nest." The tree was adjacent to the path. Once they had passed the angry bird of prey there was no one between them and Wiggins Pass, a narrow opening along the beach where the Cocohatchee River met the Gulf of Mexico. There were small posts along their way highlighting various sub-tropical plants, but now, during the dry season, most of those plants were dormant. Only the cabbage palm, palmetto, and sea grape were showing hints of green along the sandy trail. They ran until the trail ended. Roni was the first one to pass the trees and on to the inlet beach.

Dan followed, and reached down to check the water temperature. "Feels like high seventies, maybe eighty," he said encouragingly.

Roni wrinkled her nose at his optimism. "It's always gonna feel warmer back here in the shallows. We need to go around to the Gulf side and wade there." She led the way past the fallen trees and debris lining the tributary. They could see fishing boats of all sizes taking their time near the sandbars until they could leave the channel and begin the race to the latest hot spot. There were few people at the south end of Barefoot Beach, the majority choosing to be near the amenities at the main building.   A mile below the crowds, they were free to wade without competition.

Roni ventured out to her knees, hesitant about how the saltwater might feel on her particularly sore area. Dan took a running dive near her, getting her wet enough that she relaxed and leaned back into a wave and started to swim after his splashing form. He swam hard to ignore the water temperature, which was warm by Maine standards but still chilly for Florida natives spoiled by summer waters that, in July, could reach ninety degrees.

Dan put his feet down and stood on a sandy shelf that left his neck and head above the surface. He waited until Roni was nearer to him and then grabbed her so she wouldn't have to tread water. They watched the walkers heading north and felt almost invisible.   There were pelicans and terns diving for fish with two dolphins being visible chasing prey along a surf trough, nearer to shore.

Roni wrapped her arms around her man, chasing the goose bumps that were appearing on her arms.

He nuzzled her ears and whispered: "I love you, Veronica."

She kissed his neck. "I want to stay here with you forever, Daniel. "

They remained like that, getting colder but not wanting to move, the sun still high enough in the sky to suggest a day without end. Finally, he started to tremble. "I'll race you to the beach!" He gave her a head start shove and Roni kicked hard, swimming in the direction of the warmer water. Dan took a deep breath and didn't bring his head up for air until he was fifteen feet from shore, looking around to see his beautiful bride-to-be just getting her balance. They held hands, steadying each other, navigating the sharp shells until they were standing on smoother sand. The wind had died down and the air was more than comfortable as they used their towels to get dry before sitting down, arms around their knees. Happiness was leaning against each another.

Chapter XVII

Richard didn't want to answer his ringing phone. The caller ID said it was Jack, as he knew it would be. The concierge felt that the two men wanted to feed again from his list of clientele. It was too early on a Saturday morning to deal with this ongoing catastrophe. But not answering was not an option.

"Yes, Jack. How're you doin'?"

"You know how we're doin', buddy boy." Jack was not in a lighthearted mood. "Louis wants to know what, when, where and who."

Richard squirmed, in spite of himself. These guys seemed driven to undermine his careful approach to a high end haul. All he could do was try and hold them off just a little bit longer. Richard put on his most convincing voice. "I'm glad you called. The next hit we arrange should get you even more cash and contraband."

"We love the cash, podnuh, but I don't know nothin' 'bout that contra-crap part."

"Relax, Jack. Just relax." Richard made himself sound even more reassuring. "I've got the perfect marks, and it could go down as soon as Friday, but we have to get together to work out the details. Let's set up another meet. How's Monday, late afternoon? It'll still be light."

After some inaudible mumbling, Jack came back to his phone. "Okay, Louis says late evening, not late afternoon. Eight o'clock, same place, Monday."

"Right on, Jack. I'll be there," Richard uttered with an enthusiasm that he did not feel. He hung up. He could feel a pulse in his temple throbbing so he took a deep breath and went to the refrigerator for a bottle of spring water. He had to calm down.

"There must be a way out of this", he thought. He unscrewed the top, took a deep swallow and headed for his bedroom. Under a loose board in his synthetic floor, Richard removed a small pistol. He sat on his bed, put the water down and examined the firearm. He removed the clip and checked the firing mechanism. He closed his eyes and thought for a long time. Before his eyes opened again, there was a hint of a smile on his face. Then it was gone, replaced by a straight line grimace. He had the beginnings of a plan that he hoped would bring relief from this nagging problem. Richard mumbled to himself: "Greedy Motherfuckers!" There was a sound of finality to it.

Richard's other important meeting was set for ten in the morning. Shannon was committed to fitness but certainly didn't think rising at dawn was any more beneficial than the later start. The Sea Gate Middle School had a four hundred meter track. Richard got there first and was stretching by his car when Shannon pulled up next to him. She had on white shorts and a pink top. Richard could smell a delightful combination of aromas, coconut being the most predominate.

"Good morning, Shannon," he said cheerfully, trying to force the nagging picture of Jack and Louis from his mind.

"I'm sorry if I'm a little late," she offered. "I'm not really a morning person." She didn't have to worry today. There was nothing she could do to upset her running partner.

"How long do you usually run?", he asked her.

Shannon wrinkled her nose and looked toward the sun, as if to judge how the heat would dictate her answer.

"I like to go for twenty minutes. Or two miles, if I'm counting the laps. Sometimes, if I have my music, I lose track of the time."

She started slowly, jogging the first two hundred meters. Richard could see that her form was good, that she had real lift, her heels coming up high, the suggestion of real speed. At the end of the first lap, Richard picked up the pace. Shannon followed without effort, matching him stride for stride. They kept it going for two more laps, and he was surprised that she was not even breathing hard. Richard did not want to stop first, so he maintained the speed through the first mile.

"Are you okay, so far?", he asked.

Shannon just smirked and went a little faster.

Richard had to work hard just to stay with her now. He grinned to himself and thought, "I guess you *are* in pretty good shape, my dear."

Now he knew that Shannon must keep up a respectable routine and had not exaggerated this part of her fitness. She was smiling, enjoying herself. The challenge now was to try and stay with her as she gradually increased her stride, so that he could hear her hard breathing for the first time.

The second mile was at a much faster pace. When they flew by the finish line, Richard slowed to a jog and let her go. On the turn, Shannon looked over her shoulder and saw him raise his hands in defeat. She laughed and kept going, finishing the loop. And then did it again, just for show. She slowed herself to a jog and let him catch up with her for the warm-down.

"You do this on a regular basis?", he asked breathlessly.

She was happy that he respected her regimen. "I told you I ran three times a week. I just didn't say how hard I pushed."

Richard laughed. "No, you did not! I thought you just went for a little jog, and then straight for the Eddiehnut shop."

"No fast food for me." She replied. "I have to look good at the Spa."

He didn't think a few stops at the take-out would have altered Shannon's spectacular body, but recognized her need to protect a coveted employment. "I see your point. All your co-workers look in pretty good shape, too."

"I had to sign an agreement that said I couldn't gain more than ten pounds." This was news to Richard and wondered at its legality, but the Sherill was a non-union shop, so he guessed anything was possible there. Sir George was the undisputed ruler. He knew that ten dollars an hour was a respectable Naples wage. He also knew that most undereducated workers would be willing to settle for much less. And the tips could be enough to make Shannon a future candidate for middle class status, Florida style.

"Want to grab a healthy breakfast?" Richard wanted to move the date along. "Do you have a favorite place?"

"I don't go out to eat much, but I've heard other spa women talk about the Trail Café in North Naples."

"My treat. I'll follow your car," he answered her. Shannon's smile let him know that she was glad he had extended their workout to include some refreshments, and the chance to get to know him better.

She gave him some instructions to the restaurant, just in case. "It's on the east side of 41, near the light at Imperial Country Club."

He then knew about where it was located. He was thinking it would be just two miles from Jack and Louis, enough information to scuttle the location, but Richard had been thinking of this day with Shannon as if his future had been put on hold.

He was glad for the directions because Shannon was as quick in her Tercel as she had been on the track, running through the yellow arrow, leaving Richard to wait for the light change. He never ran lights and he obeyed traffic laws, checking his lights regularly to make certain he would not be pulled over for any reason.

Shannon was waiting by her car when he entered the parking lot. She had slipped on a green hoodie and explained to him, "Sometimes it's too cold for me if the air conditioner is set high and my head is wet."

Richard thought it more likely that the hoodie was good cover for her physical attributes which might cause some unwanted attention for this shy girl.

There was one booth left. The movement of the help and the piles of plates were an indication of how popular this place was and the size of the crowd that probably had to wait earlier in the day. Richard ordered the signature Belgian Waffle and Shannon kept her promise by choosing the fruit plate. The coffee was hot and dark and the orange juice fresh squeezed. In deference to Shannon's restrictions, he did not order whipped cream, merely the strawberry cover. They ate in relative silence until Richard could see that Shannon was finished with her portion.

"What else happens on your days off?", he asked.

"I just hang around my house. Sometimes I go shopping, but most of the time I watch TV, or clean up. Once in a while, I rent a movie or call my mom." She was embarrassed by the lack of excitement, and asked Richard, "What do you do for fun?"

"Oh, pretty much what you just said. I don't go out much. I probably should clean more, but I do like to read, and watch television sports."

She found it hard to believe that this dark, handsome man did not have a string of women demanding his time. He, in turn, was a little surprised that there were not more men in Shannon's life. He did, however, recognize that her naivety and beauty could be both a draw and a deterrent - enough to keep her out of the social loop.

"I haven't had a lot of luck with guys." She trusted him enough to explain. "They want too much too fast, and get mad if I say no. So I say no first."

Richard was happy to receive that backhanded advice and would plan accordingly. He became upbeat: "What are you doing now? Want some help shopping, cleaning?"

"You want to help me do what?"

"You said those are what you do on your days off, and I just wondered if you would like some company." Then he gave her an out: "I grocery shop on Saturdays, and we could do it together, or not, if you'd rather be by yourself." He gestured for their server, and opened his wallet to get some cash to give Shannon time to get composed around this offer.

She didn't have to think for too long before deciding that Richard meant her no harm. "Okay, you can come with me. Where do you buy your groceries?"

He had no preference. "I'll go where you shop."

"I usually go to Sweetbay, up on the beach road, not far from my house."

Richard could see it would be easy to find out where Shannon lived and reduce her guardedness at the same time. He followed her to the plaza and parked in the next row. He got one cart for them to share and pushed it beside her down the aisles.

"Just like a married couple," was Shannon's obvious thought, but she kept the observation to herself.

Richard followed her lead, buying items similar to her choices. He added to his larder skim milk, fresh vegetables and fruits, organic eggs, and multi-grain bread. She bought some free-range chicken thighs. Most of her choices were without chemicals, more expensive but consistent with Shannon's commitment to healthy living. Richard teased her gently, tossing some sugar cereals into the mix just to get her to throw the boxes back in his direction. He added some organic coffee to his items to show her that he respected the better life. And then they were done.

They got to the parking lot and separated the food bags. Shannon was a little nervous then, not knowing what was going to come next.

Richard relieved the pressure. "That was fun. I guess we have to go before this food gets too warm. What are you doing tomorrow?"

Shannon was relieved and disappointed. He had not hit on her. "I don't have any plans."

He had an idea. "There's an art show tomorrow in Naples, in Cambier Park. Wanna go?"

"Sure. What time do I meet you?" Shannon would have agreed to anything short of a porn exhibition.

He short-circuited that little roadblock. "I can pick you up at eleven o'clock."

"Okay, I'll see you then." She was grateful that he was going to give her time to wake up and get ready.

Richard waited and then filled in the blank. "Can you tell me your address?"

Shannon blushed and then reached into her purse to give him a professional looking card that read: Shannon Scott, Masseuse, 124 North Dakota Road, Bonita Springs, Florida 34135.

"I had these made in case I was going to open a salon in my home, but I never did. My street is off

Dinkins, behind Ace Hardware. You can see the store from here."

Richard looked around the corner to see an almost identical shopping plaza with a huge ice cream cone near the front. He copied her phone number on the card. "Thanks for a great time. Maybe one day I'll be in as good shape as you are."

She blushed again when he leaned over to give her a quick peck on her cheek before turning back to his car and getting in. She was still standing, stunned, by her vehicle when he pulled out waving from his window.

Richard had more shopping to do, but these items would not be groceries. He stopped at St. Anthony's Church and went into their second-hand shop in the rear. There were some things he needed to complete his inventory for Jack and Louis. He saw a jewelry case and an elderly woman behind the counter.

"I'm looking for some inexpensive jewelry for my niece," he told her. "She likes to play dress up and her mother doesn't want her digging through her drawers and losing earrings."

The older lady checked her collection. "I have some pieces with broken clasps and there are some here that are missing pearls or have cracked glass."

Richard chose a few pieces. "Do you have anything that you were going to throw out, something that you don't want?"

"I do have some junk jewelry, and some old things that were too destroyed to even put out for sale." She reached behind her chair and offered a plastic bag bulging with some material pushing through the sides.

"That's perfect. If you don't mind, I'll buy the ones I picked out first and I'll give you five dollars for the broken items here. My niece is three and a half and she won't know the difference."

The sales lady was happy to get rid of the junk and insisted on giving Richard another bag for the intact pieces he had chosen. Richard dumped the jewelry in his trunk and drove to a Goodwill store. There, he checked for small bags in the luggage section and found a black leather valise with a monogram that suggested, at one time, it had been an expensive gift. Then Richard repeated his jewelry quest, getting more castoffs to add to his stash of worthless baubles. Satisfied, he tossed the latest purchases in his car, and headed home before the groceries got too warm.

Inside his bedroom, Richard separated the jewelry, discarding the most outrageous items, putting his purchased pieces on top, and placing them in the leather bag before sliding it under his bed. He went back to the kitchen to finish loading the refrigerator before grabbing a beer and settling into his lounger to catch the end of a basketball game. He gave himself the luxury of a smile. It had been a good day - one with many promises of better times.

The next morning was bright and cool. The humidity that had added to the sweat of yesterday's run was gone. It was still late winter/early spring and dry. Southwest Florida had not yet succumbed to daily rain and ninety-nine percent air conditioner use. There was just a hint of smoke smell this morning, but the absence of wind meant that the volunteers had probably contained this latest brush fire.

Richard put the top down and drove north to Bonita Spsrings. He had no trouble finding 124 North

Dakota Road. She was waiting out front, wearing white shorts and a blue blouse with another sweater under her arm. Her short blond hair was still curly from her hot shower, and she was smiling. Richard got out and opened the passenger door, taking in Shannon's perfume as she gracefully slid in under his arm. He turned to grin at her. "Ready for the big art show?"

"I haven't been to one of these before, even though I've lived here forever, but I'm ready to give it a try."

He reassured her: "You'll have a lot of fun. There's something there for everyone." Then he added, "Have you had breakfast? coffee?"

"No, I got up kinda late." Shannon was embarrassed. It had taken her most of her late morning to get ready. Her shower had been fast, but choosing an outfit had taken too long and then it was time and he was there.

Richard decided to stop at Starbucks. He needed another caffeine hit himself, and there were those scones. Shannon was surprised at how hungry she was. She polished hers off and searched for crumbs in her lap, not wanting to dirty his pretty sports car.

The downtown parking lot was full so they had to look for another spot, lucking out when an early shopper left the curb with a backseat full of arts and crafts. Shannon was amazed at the size of the show. Every inch of the park was covered with vendor tents, and all the side streets had exhibitors. They went down most of the rows. She was surprised by how much she liked the paintings. Many were tropical scenes with palm trees, beaches, sun reflecting from the breaking surf. Shannon recognized some of the landmarks the artists had captured on canvas, pictures of the few cottages that still stood on the alleys near the beach in Naples.

She was especially delighted with the creations of the shell artists. Richard bought her a little clutch of figurines -- a family of owls made from dozens of different sized shells. He got her an extra bag to wrap them so they wouldn't break in her purse. Soon Shannon was hungry again, blushing when Richard heard her stomach growl. They walked back to Fifth Avenue and were lucky to get a sidewalk table at The Mangrove Café, not too far from the festival. She ordered white wine and a grilled chicken salad, and he got the grouper basket and a Corona. Shannon would have been surprised to learn that her date was casing restaurants most conducive to snatch and grab robberies. This one, in the middle of downtown Naples, at the height of the season, was not among the leaders.

"Thank you, Richard!" Shannon was having a good time. "I had no idea that an art show was so much fun."

Richard, despite his worries, was enjoying showing this young woman a new experience. "There's a lot we haven't seen yet. I want you to see the photographers at the end of the park."

She was impressed with all the photographs, the different ways people saw Naples. There must have been way over a dozen pictures of the Naples Pier, from early morning shots to storm tossed photos of waves breaking over the boardwalk. By that time it was getting late. Artists began to break down their tents.

A caricature painter called to them. "I'll do the lady's picture for five dollars!"

Shannon pulled away, but Richard encouraged her. "Come on. Let's do it. This'll be great. I'll pay."

She sat in a chair as the man's hands became a blur of pencil strokes. "You have great posture," he told her. "I'm just going to capture your essence, your lines." He was done in four minutes, and handed them the picture. Shannon didn't want to look, but Richard held it in front of her. In the shot, the man had recreated her wide shoulders, her averted gaze. He also captured Shannon's inherent shyness, with just a hint of her spectacular body. She liked it for the anonymity, not as a Playboy picture, but as one emphasizing her athleticism and strength. Richard gave it to her. Shannon held it to the light, and then handed it back to Richard.

"I want you to have this," she said quietly.

He objected mildly, "I bought this for you."

She was insistent. "Keep it as a memory of today. I know what I look like."

He tucked the cardboard frame under one arm and it seemed natural when Shannon took his other hand.

Chapter XVIII

Louis and Jack had lines in the water south of the Cocohatchee's main channel. They were tied to some mangroves and had not boated anywhere for two hours. The beer was getting warm and their location denied them any cooling wafts of onshore breeze that might have made their situation comfortable. Instead, they were sweating. That, plus being hung over certainly didn't help Louis's temperament any.

"You said your 'amigo' Richard was going to make us rich. We're almost broke again, yo."

Jack was not in the mood for criticism. "You'd have some left if you didn't buy all that new fishing gear. How many snook have you caught today, dude?"

"Fuck you and your gringo bud. He must be saving all the good stuff for himself and giving us the dregs."

Jack had been thinking the same thing, but he didn't want to give his chief critic any legs.

"He'll come through for us. All we have ta do is twist the screws a little more. He's got too much into whatever plan he's cookin' to take a chance with us. You'll see. Ole Rick has his eyes on a trifecta, and when he goes to turn in his ticket, we'll be right there to hold the limo door."

Just then Jack's pole doubled over and he spilled his beer. They saw a sheepshead break water and Louis lunged for the net. Jack was laughing now. "I told you our luck was changin'. And I'm using my old pole."

Louis could only smile while saying, "Fuck you, Jack."

Richard was looking for a restaurant, but not just any eatery. It had to impress Shannon. But more importantly, it must provide access for his partners in crime. Nothing in downtown Naples was going to meet the latter standard, so Richard drove up the Tamiami Trail heading north, toward Bonita. The plazas along the way were too bright, and the smaller joints too close to the well lit road.

Shannon paid no mind. She was having a wonderful time with this kind, handsome man. She had brought a wrap to cover her shorts and was presentable for most places -- Naples having few dining requirements beyond the ability to pay an outrageous bill. Richard tried to concentrate on their conversation, making mental notes of her background, likes and dislikes. They were almost to Bonita when Richard slowed down. He passed a plaza, followed by a flashy restaurant, car dealership, and then an empty construction site. He went to the next light and turned around to case the joint from the other side of the highway. It looked like a good possibility, so Richard did a U-turn at Immokalee, and then right into a driveway and parking lot belonging to The Landmarke Grille.

He turned to Shannon. "Ever eat at this place?"

"Gosh, no! Is it super expensive?"

"I don't think it is any more than most of the Naples restaurants." The exterior front was all glass, giving patrons unobstructed views of the street, but the tint kept outsiders from seeing much inside detail. There were multiple levels allowing some to eat from lofted platforms, looking down on the less favored booths. It was Saturday night, but Richard took a chance and approached the reservation desk.

"Do you have any tables for two?" Richard admitted not having called ahead, but the woman was intrigued by this handsome man and beautiful woman, and they had not been pushy, but appropriately apologetic.

"Let me see if I can squeeze you in," she said, letting Richard see her dark eyes and bending cleavage. She looked at her chart. "I think they are clearing that booth, over there, in the corner, and it's too small for this waiting party of four."

Richard thanked the woman profusely and they followed the server to their booth. Shannon was glad that she had brought a sweater that matched her sarong. The temperature inside seemed almost cold. The air conditioning was more for the hard working employees than the customers, she thought. Shannon shivered and pulled her sweater tight to her neck.

Richard asked their server if something could be done about the chill in the air. She looked around at the other huddled patrons and admitted, "It does seem a little cold in here tonight. You're right. I'll ask the manager if he can raise the thermostat."

Richard slipped her a five as they gave their drink order. Shannon was feeling very pampered and sophisticated, so she asked for a Dirty Martini. Richard stuck to Jim Beam on the rocks. The place was jammed and they each were on their second drink before their server brought their bread tray. Richard was thinking that he might have to ask for Shannon's third Martini when the entrees arrived. Richard had chosen lamb chops, his date opting for grilled snapper, both portions large enough to suggest doggie bags, or relief for third-world countries. Shannon was relaxed now, chattering about her childhood and job. Richard supported her courage, surviving a marginal home, and striving to fit in at the prestigious Hotel Sherill. He told her some fictitious stories from his New Mexico past, dwelling on the beauty of the desert in winter and the summer snow in the high meadows of the Sangre de Cristo Mountain Range. They were both too full for dessert, but instead ordered aperitifs. Shannon had Crème de Menthe, in part to offset her fish dinner, and Richard chose Grand Marnier.

When they left, Richard suggested a short walk before they had to double up again in bucket seats. He held her hand and wandered not-so-aimlessly through the restaurant parking lot toward the adjacent car dealership. He hoped Shannon would think he was quietly remembering their last few days together because, in truth, he needed time to work out a plan.

Richard saw that the two lots had no barriers. The restaurant parking had no choice except to spread out next door after the car lot had closed for the day. Farther north was an empty lot filled with construction vehicles preparing yet another plaza. He was deep in thought: "This just might be the spot. A restaurant set back from the road with nothing north except a dark car storage area, next to a way too small restaurant parking lot. The grocery store to the south is, luckily, too far on the other side of the entrance to mean anything here or to serve as an overflow for this joint. That leaves the car place as our logical spot for a secluded robbery. This is it!" Richard resolved to come back and drive the rear areas to make certain this was as an ideal location as it appeared to be.

He swung Shannon around and they made their way back to his car, which fit in nicely with the other high end vehicles awaiting sale and/or a ride home after a rich meal. It was symbiotic: the glitzy restaurant needed parking space and the car place was happy to have folks take an informal jaunt around their offerings.

Shannon snuggled into her seat, taking off her sweater to enjoy the warm air of a sub-tropical night. She was glad she had ordered a mint drink and had plucked a candy from the reservation desk on her way out. Shannon was thinking about kissing and wanted to be ready.

Richard was multi-tasking, both planning a heist and formulating just how far he would advance this budding romance. He drove carefully in the right lane. As always, he was on the lookout for cops, police out to catch the Saturday night drinker, watching for weavers, speeders, or vehicles going too slowly, clues that the driver's coordination was chemically suspect. He saw the first blinking light as they got closer to the Imperial intersection. Because Richard's car windows were down, they could hear the man attempt to explain why he was having trouble walking in a straight line while his embarrassed wife stared angrily ahead. She was yelling at her husband that she had told him to stop at that last manhattan, but he had *insisted* that he was perfectly capable of driving the eight blocks to their home. This was one less policeman that Richard had to worry about. He found Shannon's place without having to ask for directions and pulled into her driveway and left the car running while he went to her side and opened the door.

Before she could say anything, he offered: "Thanks for coming along. I had a great time."

He walked her to the front door as she murmured, "Me too, and thank you for asking me to come." Shannon was relieved and a little disappointed that Richard was apparently on his way home without even trying to come in and break down her bedroom door.

She lifted her head, giving a clear view of her breasts and long neck. He gave her a gentle kiss while keeping one hand on her waist. She leaned into him so he could feel her upper body against his chest. The kiss was just long enough to let her know that he was interested in further exploration, but was willing to respect some first date traditions.

Richard pulled back. "This was really fun. Would you like to go out again some time? Soon?"

Shannon was ready and willing to make extensive plans, but this offer had contained no specifics, so she would have to wait. "Okay. I'd love to," was her best attempt to let him know she was on board to any and all of his social aspirations.

He drove back the same way and pulled into the restaurant parking lot. It was still jammed. Richard observed patrons walking back into the dealership area to retrieve their cars. He continued to the north end and the start of the construction area. The building spot was sandy. There had been an attempt to separate the two lots, a plastic fence that had fallen, and there were a number of parked backhoes and bulldozers. This arrangement was obviously temporary until the building was completed and there were permanent barricades. It was possible that there would be a driving area connecting all three establishments, but as of tonight that was unclear. What was evident was an absence of lights, and a confusing mixture of waiting vehicles - new, used, and licensed. It might make sense in daylight, but at night, an intoxicated person could all too easily get lost back there among the hodgepodge of commercial interests.

"Martha, where did you say I parked the car?"

"Darling-Dummy, right over there, next to one of those fancy cars."

"Martha, you idiot! They're ALL fancy cars!"

With that scenario playing out in his head, Richard had formulated most of a plan by the time he pulled into his driveway in Naples Park.

Alicia Hernandez was having trouble believing her good luck. She was unloading her laundry cart when she saw the tiny, jeweled evening purse, wrapped in a bed sheet. In a second it was in her pocket, under the apron. It was close to the end of her shift and since she wore her uniform home, there was no one checking her as she clocked out for the day. Workers were encouraged to leave the job quickly after their shifts had been completed. The Hotel did not want employees lingering where they might inadvertently bump into paying guests. Alicia was particularly diligent this day, getting to her car and driving home before checking the contraband in her pocket. She was delighted to find two hundred dollars - the four fifties - rolled tightly. The beautiful diamond earrings were an unexpected bonus. The money would pay for groceries and part of her rent, but the earrings made her uncomfortable. She pushed them to the bottom of her underwear drawer, and changed out of her uniform. Tonight, she thought, they would have steak!

Gloria Esposito was angry. No; she was MAD! She had looked all over for her favorite evening purse. They had reservations tonight in the Saratoga Room, the only chance for this, their first visit to the fancy Hotel Sherill. She was still a little ill at ease here. But Tony had been able to buy out his partners and he was now the sole owner of Esposito Lincoln-Mercury in Toms River, New Jersey. Gloria had been the billing lady, the person who gave the bad news to customers returning to retrieve their repaired vehicles. As such, she often had to visit Mr. Esposito's office to get clarification about this or that egregious overcharge. On those occasions, he had noticed her short skirts and tight sweaters, and the whiffs of exotic perfumes she just happened to add to the package before knocking at his door. It wasn't long before she was lingering longer, the consultations becoming flirtatious, that first exciting grab and kiss laying the groundwork for their future affair. Now the new Mrs. Esposito (the former having retreated to her New England roots), Gloria was also the new head of customer relations. Her sexiness was enough to mollify at least some of the male customers. Their double dipping and a local dealers' conference had financed this visit to Southwest Florida. Tony would write off the whole expensive adventure.

The missing purse matched Gloria's sequined evening gown, and the diamond earrings had been the perfect accompaniment to the ensemble. On top of that, they were an engagement present, Tony's validation of his undying love and respect for his wife-to-be. Now, they all were gone!

She had looked everywhere, even calling the concierge desk to have them quiz the limo driver and search his vehicle. She remembered the couple hundred dollars Tony had said they could take out of the employee party fund. The limo turned up nothing, so it was back to the maids. But the one on duty that day had been an employee there for ten years with an impeccable record. Gloria had almost lost it when someone had suggested that she had left it at the restaurant. Tony, aware of what might follow, had pinched her arm so she would swallow the expletives her family had used routinely in a variety of verbs, nouns, and present participles that were not appropriate for High Tea at the Sherill.

Her husband had told her, without divulging the exact price, that her jewelry had been very expensive, emblematic of his (at the time) passion, and Gloria was going to climb the Hotel Sherill ladder until someone gave her satisfaction. Her first call was to Stan Merrick, the front end manager. Her voice was one level below a scream.

"Do you choose your employees from thieves.com? What kind of security do you people have when a person can't put down her purse before someone steals it?"

The manager was used to guests with better people skills but he did his job. "Yes, Mrs. Esposito. We are very sorry at this reported loss. Did you list this item with the hotel and is it represented among your valuables with your insurance company?"

Gloria knew when she was being stonewalled. After all, these were the same techniques her husband used to get clients to accept an inflated sticker price, or an undercoating contract. Mr. Merrick would have judged the guest's next barrage to be histrionic, but to Gloria this was just how you talked to people who were trying to put the screws to you.

"No! It's a goddamn PURSE! And it HAPPENED to have my diamond earrings and four hundred dollars in it! So it's NOT on any fucking insurance list or whatever you call it. It's just fucking GONE and one of your people STOLE IT!"

Gloria inflated her loss by two hundred dollars, but in situations like this, injured parties routinely rounded things up.

The manager was almost speechless in the face of this violent verbal assault. He repeated his litany of regret. "We are VERY sorry about this. The Hotel's security is rarely breached. Our staff receives very extensive background checks. Perhaps our insurance may be able to help."

Gloria was still unsatisfied. "'Perhaps, maybe, wonderful staff.' Blah, blah, blah. I want to talk to someone who can HELP me! Who is the big boss? I want to talk to HIM!"

Mr. Merrick was flummoxed. He started to stammer. "Why... why... that would be Sir George Sherill, but he is too busy, I mean he has so many issues he is dealing with--"

"I don't care if he's the PRESIDENT of the UNITED STATES. I want to talk to him. NOW! Tell me where he is and I'll go see him, myself!"

Mr. Merrick did not want this woman prowling the hotel for Sir George, screaming obscene threats the whole while. "Please Madam. Let me see if I can contact him and I will call you right back with a solution."

Gloria let him know she would expect something soon. "Make it damn fast, Buster!"

She slammed the phone down and almost missed Mr. Merrick's blurted, "It would be my particular pleasure!"

He could have dumped if off to housekeeping, but Merrick had a feeling that this guest was a true loose cannon and he most definitely had no intention to be one of the staff Mrs. Esposito listed as being unable to meet her expectations. The very last thing he needed was this guest roaming the halls, bouncing off the walls, telling all who would listen (and with that mouth, listening was not discretionary), that Stan Merrick, the Front End Manager, had dropped the ball on her particular pleasure. It seemed to him that chief among her pleasures was ruining his day, and maybe his week, with her obscenity laced calls for satisfaction. And there was always the chance that a rival would be happy to pass along an incident in which he had been unable to provide a resolution. So he called the top floor and asked to speak with Sir George.

After pressing a series of administrative assistants with the emergent nature of his call, Mr. Merrick was patched through.

"What is it, Merrick?" The Boss did not sound happy, and indeed, this robbery had occupied most of his time. He'd been discussing contingencies with a variety of legal types, including his golfing buddy, the corporate attorney. The manager reiterated Gloria Esposito's tale of woe, including her intention to share her frustration among all within earshot, whether they were in a position to help or not.

Sir George started down his list. "Okay, Merrick. Where do we stand on lost valuables?"

The manager could think of no thefts this week. He recited what he did know. "Most of the jewelry reported lost has been returned. There were two watches we thought were on their way to lost and found and they never turned up. One lady told us that she believed there was less cash now in a returned purse. The guests with the missing jewelry items that have not yet been found have been reimbursed through insurance."

Mr. Sherill needed more data. "Would you say we've had less, more, or the same number of complaints this season?"

Merrick knew that Sir George could access a printout on all this data, but wanted to get his feel for the issue. He had to be honest. "I would say, without looking at the sheet, that there are more complaints this season. Little things, like the watches, missing cash, the robbery, and now this."

Sir George was more conciliatory: "I'm with you on this, Stan. Which areas seem to be the most vulnerable?"

"It seems evenly spread out between the pool and the Spa. We really haven't had many incidents concerning the room maids. Some of them have been here the longest of any of our people."

The boss had spent enough time on one guest's concerns. "Okay, call Bob Rosen's office and tell them they have the green light to talk to these people about reimbursement in lieu of litigation. If they have a reservation for one of our restaurants, comp their bill. Send flowers to this lady and tell her that we will be providing an equitable solution to this problem. And do it quickly. Make sure your concierges know who this woman is and have them ready to turn inside out to shut her up. We do NOT need any more bad publicity, comprendé?" Then he hung up.

Mr. Merrick left a message for the Espositos that relief was close at hand. He typed a confidential memo to the front end staff asking for their help in providing exceptional service to a particular couple who had recently lost some valuables. Then he contacted the flower shop and made an order for an executive bouquet to be sent to the room. Merrick checked the reservation list and saw that the couple had an early seating at the Saratoga Room, and wondered how they had found a place at the most exclusive of the Sherill's restaurants. He guessed that Mr. Esposito had greased somebody's palm and had slid in by virtue of a bribe and a cancellation. However it happened, the restaurant was alerted and told to eat the bill. Lastly, he called their attorney, Bob Rosen and left the message as to Sir George's requests and asked for a callback on the restitution issue. There were three concierges on duty, so he had them in for individual sessions, sharing the memo and making certain they knew the Esposito's room number and their rental car description. It was done! For the remainder of their stay, Gloria and Tony Esposito would be treated as VIP guests. Maybe that would be enough to keep her quiet. One could only hope.

It was still twilight when Richard locked his bike to the rack in the Cocohatchee River Park. There were a few boats tied to the sea wall opposite the yacht club. He could see the Manatee Cove tour boat returning from their sunset cruise to the surf line. When Richard walked over the bridge to the meeting place, a line of pelicans flew overhead in a perfect V, dropping close to the channel, beaks into the wind, their wing tips barely skimming the water's surface. Out near the sand bars, he could see two dolphins trying to surf near the stern wake of a Grady White on its way out to look for sharks. It would have been a beautiful, vernal evening, the pinks and whites of the sunset and the balmy air, a wonderful mix of sub-tropical ambience. Instead, Richard had to convince two lowlifes that he was going to enrich them beyond measure.

His partners' boat was nowhere to be seen but he knew it was out there, waiting for the darkness that would provide them all the necessary cover for their clandestine planning. On the other side of the bridge and its narrow strip of water, he could see a sailboat on its side. It was on the bottom, the low tide causing the little ship to tilt, the keel and waterline visible in the twilight. It was either abandoned or a vagabond, waiting for the moon to float it free of the mangrove sands. A little past eight o'clock, Richard saw the red and green bow lights as Louis eased the green craft under the bridge to the canoe launch. Richard put one leg over the side and used Jack's proffered hand to pull himself in and up to a sitting position. The men said nothing as Louis polled backwards, swinging the stern around to take them under the bridge and the protection of the shore growth, south of the yacht club docks.

Richard tried to be jovial. "So how've you boys been? Any new toys, Louis?" He'd seen the shiny fishing pole. "Jack, you feelin' okay? Looks like sunburn. You should wear a hat!"

Jack's sardonic grin was sideways. "We think it's wonderful that you're worried about us, Rick. Try and make us feel better by helping us get rich. That'll show us how much you care. Otherwise, let's quit the bullshit and get to business."

Richard held up his hands in mock dismay. "Sorry y'all got up on the wrong side of the boat. I just thought that because it was such a beautiful night we could enjoy ourselves, but I can see you guys are professionals so we'll get right to it."

Louis said nothing, and Jack just snorted. "I'm still hearin' and smellin' crap, Rick. It's got a bad stink to it."

Richard switched gears. "Okay, business is business. Here's what I have. A place and a time. The place is The Landmarke Grille. D' you know it?"

Louis nodded, but Jack looked confused.

"You know it, Jack," Louis said. "It's that all-glass joint near McDonald's, next to that fancy car lot."

Jack nodded absentmindedly. "Okay, I think I know what you're talkin' about." He was not happy being the last to be aware of anything. "What's so special about that place?"

Richard took his time with these dunderheads. "The parking lot is too small for the clientele, so they have to use the area behind the car dealership. The cars run all the way to the construction site. There's very little light back there. Get it?"

The men were trying to picture the area at the location. It was most probable neither had been in the restaurant or had a salesman try to persuade them to buy a sixty-thousand-dollar automobile. However, it wasn't too far from their apartment or the boat launch. Richard guessed it was probably no more than five miles.

Jack didn't want this to be a congratulatory event. "So, it's next to a car dealership. Who gives a flying fuck? What's so great about that?"

Richard realized he'd have to hold their hands. He knew Jack was teasing, testing his power, glad to have the upper hand. He wasn't going to let them get his goat, so he rationalized that it would be good to go through the heist slowly and by the numbers. There would be less confusion later if he led them through it now. He took a deep breath and started again.

"You'll know better when you drive into the lot, but this is what I think makes this place good for a clean hit and getaway. When you first get to this place, in the daytime, it looks a little crazy. There's a grocery store and little shops, then the restaurant, and beyond that there's the car place, leading to the construction area. At times, all three operations are using some of the same roads. However, at night, all that changes. The dealership closes and the construction crews go home. And now most of the space north of the driveway is dark."

Jack's brow was still furrowed and Louis was picking his teeth. Richard needed something to grab onto and focus their attention.

"Here's the best part," and he waited until they were both looking at him. "After you've got the haul, you can leave from the construction site, in the dark. You don't have to exit the way you came in."

Jack wanted to know more. "How in the hell are we gonna to do that?"

"All you have to do is move a two-by-four sawhorse and you're back on 41 and on your way home. Go to the Beach Road, take two rights and you're near your complex. The construction guys do it all day. There're no cables or tape, just that road barrier."

Now both crooks were leaning forward, elbows on knees, in sync with this, seeing their escape, anticipating more money.

Jack spoke first. "This sounds good. Me and Louis will check it out. When do we pull this off?"

Richard had a time frame, but he would have to see the reservation list before he could be certain of the night. "It'll be one of the three weekend nights. The reason I'm not sure yet is because we don't send guests to this restaurant every day. It's not on our regular list of preferred places. We use it more like a last resort, an overflow option, when the other ones are too full to take any more customers."

Louis was annoyed: "Ya mean there's a chance we'd be just sittin' there, waitin' for nobody?"

"In the summer maybe, but not in season! Downtown Naples is swamped all the way from Friday to Sunday nights. There'll be people goin' all over the place. I just have to choose the right marks." He wanted to stop the negativity, so he said forcefully: "I will know by Thursday night who we're sendin' to the Landmarke Grille, when they're goin', and what car they'll use, just like before." He hoped he would have some choice who they would rob, but didn't want his "pards" to know that it might come down to one patron. He could guarantee a run on downtown Naples but he couldn't count on guests agreeing to go north to a place without the Sherill seal of approval. All Richard knew was that it was too risky to go back anywhere close to La Rive Gauche. The city docks were out.

He was curious as to what these two were going to do with haul number two. "So, when're you guys gonna make your Miami run?"

Jack looked up at this intrusion into their machinations. "Who said anything about Miami?"

Richard shrugged his shoulders. Two could play this control game. "You did. You said you had contacts there who could move the jewels and credit cards."

Louis chimed in. "Don't you remember, Jack? We talked about how we were gonna get rid o' the shit?"

Jack gave Louis a disgusted look. "Awright, I guess we did talk about that. I just don't want him knowin' all our business."

Richard was magnanimous again. "You're right, Jack. It's none of my business what you do with the shit. I'm goin' home. I'll call you by Thursday."

They rode in silence back to the shore. Richard got out and walked to the bridge in time to see the white stern light disappear behind the mangroves. There was no one in the park and no other craft visible on the river - a quiet night for thinking about being somewhere safe, away from the bloodsuckers. A refuge! Richard couldn't remember a time when he wasn't on the run from something... or someone.

Chapter XIX

Gloria Esposito was in fine form. She and her husband were sitting in the fanciest restaurant the Hotel Sherill offered. She was not upset that it was the early seating. When the maitre d' had informed them that no charge would appear on their bill, Gloria had changed her order from chicken to filet mignon.

She regaled her husband on her "negotiations" with the hotel staff. "Then I told that worm Merrick that he wasn't gonna weasel out of his responsibility. You should've heard him stutter."

"I guess you really told that guy. " Her new husband was only beginning to understand the full nature of his second wife's obstinacy. "Was he trying to welsh out?"

"If only you'd heard him go on and on about our insurance! Like it was none of his business that we were ripped off!"

Her husband had seen her hold the line on their office bills, never bending to outraged customers. "I knew when I saw those flowers, you must have rung somebody's chimes. And when that lawyer called to say they'd cover the jewelry, well, that was the icing on the cake. I knew you'd worked it real hard."

Gloria started to work on him. "You said those earrings were two thousand dollars, but we need the receipt."

Now her husband felt some of the heat. "I hope I can find that piece of paper. You know it was a cash deal because I didn't want Maureen to find out. Remember, we weren't divorced yet." He was hoping that this debate would die, and he got back to the compliments: "I guess congratulations are in order. Thanks for the sweet deal!" Tony raised his glass of red wine, the one-hundred-dollar bottle of Oregon Pinot Noir tacked on the meal by his wife after she knew they'd be comped. Gloria touched her glass to his, listening to the chime the fine crystal made. "We should get some of this glassware. It sounds a lot better than our stuff, and it's not as clunky. D'ya know what I mean?"

Tony was just finding out this new wife had expensive tastes, and his costs had just begun.

Richard called Shannon the following Sunday morning.

Her voice was sleepy. "Where are you?"

He chuckled. "I'm at work, the ten to eight shift. Are you still in bed, sleepyhead?"

"Oh gosh, is it after ten already?" She was embarrassed, but in truth, sleeping this late on the weekend was not rare for Shannon, particularly if she had nothing to do but feel sorry for herself. But with this new man in her life, there might be some reasons not to stay in bed. "I didn't know you had to go in so early."

"It bein' the season plus a full house means most of us don't get both weekend days, at least not the concierges. You Spa ladies must have greater pull. If I knew you needed help gettin' started on the day, I could've come over early and helped you get goin'."

Shannon blushed at this suggestion, involuntarily double checking her nightgown to see how much of her body was exposed. The thought of him in her bedroom made her shiver. "My door is locked, Mister. How would you be able to get in?"

Richard continued the flirting. "Oh, I'd ring the doorbell or I could check your door on your lanai."

She was wishing he could have kissed her awake. "The sliders are locked too, so by the time I answered your ring, I'd be awake anyway."

Richard conceded the wordplay. "You're right. I never could've surprised you. What're your plans for the day? Goin' running?"

Shannon had not yet made up her schedule, hoping that he would call with some wonderful possibilities. "I guess I could run, but it would be more fun with you."

"Believe me", he answered. "I would so much rather be with you on that school track than here being yelled at by so many snooty guests."

"Take the day off and meet me and we can have lunch or something later." Shannon was thinking of all the things they could do, and her first choice was back in her bedroom. Suddenly, her covers were too heavy and hot. She kicked them to the floor so she could sit up and concentrate on Richard's call.

"I'm stuck here 'til after six, but I could come over then with some beer and pizza, or I could meet you somewhere else, if you'd prefer."

"Okay. Here would be wonderful, if you want. I can make a salad." She was happily looking forward to later in the day.

Richard was thinking about making sure he shaved before leaving the staff locker room. "I'll call ahead and pick up a pizza from Pontillo's. Do you have a beer preference?"

She was wide awake now. "Any beer is all right, but I'll drink white wine, if you don't mind."

He was starting to get excited himself. "I should be at your place by seven-forty-five at the latest. The phones are all ringing here. See you later." He hung up before she could elongate her good bye.

Shannon didn't know where to start. She knew she had to change the sheets, mop the kitchen floor, and put fresh towels in the bathroom. It was going to be a long day of waiting. She took a deep breath and sat back on her heels, arms crossed in reverie. When would she run? How many showers before the final one? She decided to clean first, staying in her nightgown as she ripped the covers from the bed.

Richard's shift was a blur. They were at close to full occupancy and the calls came in waves. There was an angry guest who, by virtue of a theft, had been elevated to VIP status. Richard had no memory of taking any breaks, and his half hour lunch had lasted less than twenty minutes because Marta called to say that there was a line beyond the concierge desk. It had taken the three of them forty minutes to clear the logjam of requests before returning to a more routine hyperactivity. The dinner hour was the last challenge, but by six-thirty, the Grande Salon was almost quiet.

Barry looked at Richard and Marta and heaved a giant sigh of relief. "Is it over? Can we go home now? If you'd told me it could get like this, I would absolutely not have believed you!"

Marta slumped against her stool. "We forget when we're relaxed in the off season, how hectic it can get here." She poked Richard. "*He* was supposed to warn you. Why didn't you warn Barry, like I told you?"

Richard continued the post shift therapy. "Me? I thought it was you! Anyway, if either of us had told Barry we were gonna be under the gun like this, he would've quit. And *then* it would've been that much worse for us!"

Barry continued the charade. "Thanks a lot guys. I just about ran out of particular pleasures today."

Richard was quick to reward their latest recruit. "You were on fire today, Barry. I would've guessed that you'd been at this for years instead of just starting yesterday. How'd you learn all this in just twenty-four hours?"

Marta continued the praise. "Seriously Barry, you accomplished wonders today. Thanks for the help. Richard and I would have been totally lost without you. You definitely earned your stripes!"

Barry smiled at the accolades. "All I did was try to copy what you all do, only I still can't juggle phones as fast as Richard or speak in three languages like you, Marta."

Richard summed it up. "We were a team today. They tried to beat us down but we rose to the challenge. If I wasn't so tired I'd buy you both a drink at Shula's."

Yawning, Marta held up her hand. "I'm gonna drag my swollen feet home and see if my beautiful daughter is still awake for a bedtime story. Then, I'm goin' for a soak in a hot bathtub until the water freezes over."

Barry headed for the door. "Me, too. I'll take a rain check on that drink at a time I can appreciate it and not fall asleep with my head on the bar. Might embarrass myself a little."

Richard agreed with them. "You all take off. I'll finish up here. I see Charles coming. He and I can cover the last ten minutes. Thank you both so much. We did a great job together today."

"No, thank you. Thank you, blessed savior," Barry was saying as he turned to hustle to the staff changing area.

Marta looked over her shoulder. "I owe you. The next time you have something goin', you can leave first, I promise."

"Get out of here you two, before I change my mind." Richard had work to do.

Charles came in, raising his glasses to look around the almost empty area. "Are you sure you need me tonight? Looks like everyone went home."

Richard slumped in exaggerated exhaustion. "Just take a look at the reservation book for today before you talk about easy times."

Charles lifted the sheets of met demands and whistled. "How many pages *is* this?"

"I don't know, but I can honestly say that in all the time I've been here, we've never had a busier shift."

"I guess that proves why I like the night work the best. This would have destroyed me today. I don't have your speed, and the supervisors know it, so I'm their midnight guy." Just then a couple approached the desk. Charles drew himself to his full five-foot-eight stature and gave them his undivided attention. This gave Richard the chance to review the restaurant reservations.

He flipped to the weekend pages. There was only one reference that piqued interest. He counted six for The Landmarke Grille: two on Friday, three for Saturday and one on Sunday. All but two guests had requested the limousine. The Sunday guests were, coincidentally, the VIP couple, Gloria and Tony Esposito. They would be driving their rented blue Lincoln Continental with the white vinyl roof. Richard was certain that he had not been the one to make the reservation because he would have most definitely remembered running into the oft-described "Bitch from New Jersey".

Richard was in and out of the shower and shaved by seven-fifteen, and had his hot-from-the-oven pizza and cold beer twenty-minutes later. He was only a little beyond his ETA when he rang Shannon's doorbell. She answered in pink capri pants and a white button up blouse with the ends tied, exposing her belly button ring. He could detect a delightful combination of girl smells, soap, shampoo, perfume, and toothpaste. She had primped in the bathroom recently. The house was very neat. The kitchen table had a white cloth and there were two place settings of china plus water glasses. A salad, too big for two, was gracing the center. He handed her the pizza while he took the beer to the refrigerator. Shannon busied herself opening the box and separating the pieces, putting them on a serving platter next to her salad.

Richard was appropriately impressed. "Everything looks great. I love what you've done to the place."

"But you've never been here before!"

"You know what I mean, how nice everything looks."

She could not stop smiling. "Just for you," she said quietly.

He could tell she really meant it.

"Would you open this bottle of wine?", she asked.

He was quick to comply and poured her a glass before opening his Corona. She went back to the refrigerator to find a lime section for his beer. They sat down to a dinner a lot like what working couples accept at the ends of long days. Richard had ordered the pizza with half sausage with the other half vegetarian to give Shannon the chance to eat guilt free. She served him the carnivore portion and filled two bowls with her homemade salad. They ate in silence until Shannon's mouth was empty enough to start the conversation.

"So were you really busy today?"

He then gave her a synopsis of his most energetic shift at The Hotel Sherill. "We have never worked so hard. The worst time was just before dinner. Everyone was either comin' back from excursions, or checkin' dinner reservations."

"Who gave you the biggest headache?" She'd heard Richard refer to problem guests as "headaches", people causing enough trouble to make the concierges go through painful symptoms they couldn't outwardly reveal.

He didn't have to think too hard to come up with an example. "We have a 'full-alert' lady the bosses have warned us about. She's the wife of a car dealer, just elevated from an office employee to spouse and she's getting' used to makin' service people miserable."

Shannon got a good picture in her mind. "Did she do something to you?"

"Not to me, but apparently she was all over Mr. Merrick, accusing him of hiring thieves to do maid service and everything else." Richard was glad that Mrs. Esposito's suspects were not among the front end staff, as he didn't want to be accused of theft until he had left the premises for good.

Shannon offered her own story of guests complaining that they hadn't received the restorative experience that massages were supposed to provide. "I can remember one lady who left her purse in an open locker. She thought it was stolen but had forgotten the right locker number and the attendant later found it where it had been all along. The guest refused to believe that it was her own memory that was the problem."

Richard understood. "That pressure is what makes our free time so valuable, getting away from that potential criticism. Like this great dinner tonight."

Shannon grinned at the exaggeration and pushed the pizza toward him, but he slid it back toward her. "I can't eat anymore. Two slices and a beer filled me up."

Shannon had stopped after one slice and a small serving of her salad. She was waiting for Richard to make his move, any sign that he wanted her. Richard was biding his time. He could sense that Shannon would accept his advances, but was this the right time or would sex between them now cause more potential problems at work? It was nine-thirty. He helped Shannon clear the table and take the few pieces of china to the sink. She rinsed the dishes and loaded the dishwasher. Then she excused herself to go to the bathroom, giving Richard more time to plan his strategy. He rinsed his mouth at the kitchen faucet and opened a packet of gum. When she returned, he had ditched the gum and was still leaning against the sink.

Shannon put the salad away and when she passed Richard, he reached out and took her arm. She turned toward him, so he could put his other arm around her waist. Richard pulled her unresisting body to him and she raised her face to take their first real kiss. He could smell the toothpaste as he caressed her soft mouth, seeing her closed eyes, and feeling her body press against his. There was just the hint of a tongue behind her open lips. He decided that moving ahead wouldn't hurt, so he slid his right hand under her blouse discovering that Shannon was not wearing a bra. Brushing against her nipple, he felt her sharp intake of breath and pushed his tongue between her teeth. She responded hungrily. Still maintaining their kiss, he lifted her in his arms and found the bedroom. Richard placed her gently on the freshly made double bed. Shannon lay there, her body quiet, but her chest rising and falling with accelerated breathing. One leg was bent as she watched and waited to see what he would do next.

"I can go or," he was saying to himself, "I can stay. This doesn't have to happen now." Then he was taking off his shirt. It had simply been too long since he had been with a woman, and this one was beautiful, frozen in time between adolescence and maturity.

Shannon had not taken her eyes away from his as she slowly unbuttoned her blouse, exposing beautiful breasts unhindered by time or gravity. Before he could do more, she was raising her hips, thumbs under her panties, sliding the undergarment and capri pants over her ankles. Now Richard had to catch up, dropping his trousers, kicking out of loafers, and removing his socks. He walked to the edge of the bed and let her look at his absolute readiness. Shannon reached out to touch him, gently caressing him, running her hand down farther, an extra credit massage.

He had to be near her, getting on the bed and touching the inside of her thigh, bending his head to take her right nipple in his mouth. She was moaning now as he turned her toward him, feeling her tight buttocks, running his hand over her bottom and under to her wetness. Shannon was starting to move so he shifted above her, supporting himself on his hands as she guided him to her insides. He stayed there, letting her come to him, feeling her begin a timeless rhythm, her eyes closed, mouth open, hips performing the magic that would stop time and space.

She was in control. He felt her tighten as her moaning became louder, joining her in an involuntary yell as he could hold back no longer, coming faster, moving with her now to their climax. Shannon stayed lifted to him and Richard maintained his pushup, until his strength was gone and he dropped on her glistening body, sliding off to her side. She came closer to him, kissing his neck, reaching down to feel his soft wetness, bringing her lower body back in contact with what had been so hard.

Shannon put her arms around his neck and stretched out against him so he could feel all of her. Richard had no choice but to wrap his arms around her waist and help her mold her body to his. She was into his neck and he could smell the shampoo in her hair. Shannon wanted to slide down his chest and suck him, but he held her fast. He didn't know if he had another erection in his arsenal, but Shannon had her own ideas. He held her tight against him, but there was no one controlling her hips and she began to rotate against his groin. He was surprised at the strength of his response and, as she rolled him on his back while continuing to stimulate him, she sat up on his thighs to get a good look at the power of her intentions. Shannon leaned forward so he could reach her breasts, the nipples becoming hard under his fingers and thumbs. She put him inside her and rode him, leaning away, arching her back, making him reach to touch her as she picked up her pace, eyes closed, mouth breathing rapidly. Just before her climax, Shannon reached back to feel his balls jump as he cried out again. Then she was collapsing on him, quiet now, no energy left for more stimulation. Richard rolled her away and cupped her from behind, holding her gently, feeling her soft wetness. In a few minutes, Shannon was asleep, content to be there in her small bed with the once-clean sheets and the bedspread on the floor. He stayed quiet for five minutes, freed one arm to check his watch, seeing it was then eleven o'clock.

It was difficult for him not to touch her. The misogynist's creed: God gave this woman that beauty for males to enjoy. The line forms on the right.

Shannon had been careful to stay away from places where lines could form easily, avoiding the limelight, such as dance clubs, where she would have been up for grabs. Giving herself to Richard had been a calculated event, requiring only his capitulation to her beauty. She trusted that he liked her and respected her, the key to opening herself to this profound level of intimacy.

Richard couldn't stay overnight, much as he would have wished. The concierge desk required his inspired presence at eight the next morning and he thought Shannon would have a similar schedule. He removed his arms and slid from the bed, pulling the sheets up to cover her cooling body. She shifted and moaned. Richard kneeled back on the bed and kissed Shannon behind her right ear. She turned her head, eyes barely open.

"Are you leaving?" Shannon uttered the sentence that was both a question and an imperative. The man *had* to leave her. He thought about what it would be like to sleep with Shannon, seeing her vulnerability at dawn, taking her before she was awake, a primal beginning of the day. Richard whispered into her ear, "I'll call you tomorrow." Only time and hope would dictate whether that happened. Shannon would wait to be convinced Richard was different.

Chapter XX

The next week was another blur. The front end and the Spa had never experienced more business. All the shifts were expanded to contain the increased activity. Shannon and Richard had time to grab a fifteen minute snack when their lunch breaks overlapped. He was sitting there on Wednesday at one-thirty, thinking that he would dump his tray, when Shannon came in with Susan.

"Hey there, stranger," was Susan's breezy greeting. "I hear you took off early last Friday night."

Shannon blushed and both women sat down with him. He brushed her knee under the table and she let her hand linger for just a second on his thigh, before standing up to get in the buffet line.

Susan was in a good mood. Full occupancy helped her total, and the Spa was always going to have to justify the outlay it took just to keep that facility from going into the red. "What's good today?" was her next question.

He tried to be helpful. "I took the grilled ham and cheese, but they say the prime rib is not too dry." She left to join the others in line trying to decide what was good, versus what was good for them. Shannon came back with her plate, holding only items from the salad bar. She let him know with her eyes that Susan had inserted herself in the lunch plan. Richard liked how she looked in her white uniform. The outfit was designed to be modest, but it did nothing to hide Shannon's spectacular form, the fabric tight at all the right places.

She wanted to know what he was thinking but could only ask, "How're you feeling today?"

He had let her know on Monday that he could hardly walk, and had a difficult time staying awake through his shift. Now, two days later, he was on an even keel. "I'm doing better today, thank you. Slept like a baby last night and hope to be able to last the whole week without calling in sick." They both knew this was an inside joke, as no one could afford to be out of work at this critical time of the year.

"You look great today, by the way," he told her. Indeed, Shannon had a glow on. All that good sex, and being in serious 'like' had given her energy to leap small buildings in a single bound.

"Thank you, sir. I am doing quite well today." And, after a short pause while looking around, added: "Am I going to see you after work tonight?"

Richard tried to slow this down. He had to plan the weekend job and needed to concentrate. "I'm tied up through tomorrow, but Friday and the weekend look good."

Shannon smiled gratefully. Susan returned with her tray. The Spa manager was also anticipating time off.

"Happy Half-Way-Through-The-Week Day" was her toast to them with a glass of skim milk. She looked at Richard. "Are you coming with us to Pincher's again on Friday?"

Richard glanced at Shannon. "Sure, you can count me in. What about Barry?"

Susan was magnanimous. "Barry's a good fit, Richard. He's learning to be a better dancer."

Richard was thinking that Susan had already enjoyed some of Barry's moves, but was willing to hide that budding relationship just as he was hiding his own with Shannon. The threesome gossiped about their overlapping jobs, the guests they served in common, and their idiosyncrasies.

He looked at his watch. "I've got to get back." Then, looking at Shannon he said to both women: "Talk to you later." He saw Susan give Shannon a look, but the younger woman just shrugged her shoulders and looked bewildered, a guise she could pull off.

Richard got back in time to relieve Barry. "If you hurry, you can still catch Susan in the lunchroom."

Barry hustled away. "Thanks, Buddy. That's two I owe you, but who's keeping score?"

Richard, in fact, kept careful track of IOU'S, but waived him off. "Don't mention it. You better get goin'." He double-checked the reservation list for cancellations. The Espositos' name was still the only one for Sunday night at the Landmarke Grille in North Naples. Richard knew that he would not be responsible for sending anyone else there for the last seating.

The rest of the day went quickly and it was six before he knew it. After Richard got home he decided to call early to nail down the weekend hit. He got Jack on the second ring and arranged to meet his partners that night. They had no problem getting on board early, eager for the next payday. Richard got off his bike at seven-thirty and strolled the park waiting for the sunset. The days were getting longer and he had been a little early for this latest rendezvous with his least favorite slimeballs. When he got on their boat, there was a snook flopping in the bottom.

Jack was proud of their catch. "Louis got this on his first cast. Pretty good, huh?"

Richard tried to keep his feet off the fish. "I thought we were gonna talk about the next job, not choose dinner."

"Take it easy Rick. We're all on the same page here," Jack answered snidely.

Richard was still not happy with the dying catch. "Okay, here's the deal. Just keep that thing off me. Your marks are a middle-aged couple. They both have dark hair.

The man has a gut and the woman has a big mouth. They'll be driving a powder blue Lincoln Continental with a white vinyl roof. Are ya with me so far?"

Jack and Louis nodded their heads. Louis kicked the fish to the stern.

"They like to show off, so they could be carrying a wad of cash. No way to know how much." He wanted to know if they still had all the 'tools' they'd used in the previous job.

"You worry too much, Rick. We have two full rolls of duct tape, and don't forget we've got our silencers," he said while brandishing his pistol.

Satisfied at least on their readiness, Richard continued: "They have the last seating, eight-thirty. I expect they'll be in the restaurant at least an hour, maybe more. These two have a reputation for getting their money's worth, so you might have to wait two hours."

Jack played it back. "Couple with dark hair, light blue Continental, nine-thirty at the earliest. Does that cover it, Rick?"

"Not quite. The car is a rental." He gave them the license plate number, just in case another Lincoln with a white top showed up. "Don't forget the rear exit, through the construction site."

"Aw, Rick... d'you think we're stupid? Me and Louis have already driven through there. More than once. You're right about that barricade. I could move it with one hand."

Richard still felt that he had to go over it one more time. "Remember, these two are a little younger. You may have to get rough to get them down and into their car."

Jack was yawning. "Ya think we're weak, Man?"

"This'll be a piece of cake," Louis added.

Richard had done as much as he could on his end. "All right. I won't contact you again unless there's a cancellation. The earliest you will hear from me is next Tuesday. So is this a go?"

Jack nodded. "We'll let you know what we get. For your sake, Rick, this better be a bigger take."

Richard knew of no way to defuse their cockiness, and hoped it wouldn't translate to foolishness. All he could say was, "Take me back. And keep that damn fish away from me."

Richard rode his bicycle slowly back along Vanderbilt Drive. He was in no hurry. There were few cars at eight-thirty, and he had the chance to work on his contingency: what to do when Jack and Louis decided they wanted more than he could deliver.

Shannon was coming out of her shell. Susan's friendship was the catalyst for other women acknowledging her. Some had been put off at first by Shannon's beauty, but her lack of pretense and her shyness convinced them that she was not predatory. By Friday, the after-hours group had bonded and were planning the next party.

Susan had sensed that Shannon and Richard had become an item. And since Barry was in Richard's pocket, Susan saw the benefits of staying close to anyone that could help her romance with Barry. As the Spa manager, Susan still controlled the social schedule on Friday, and she liked the conveniently named John Friday with his laid-back guitar. She'd decided they were going to follow him to whichever bar was lucky enough to have him contracted to perform.

Susan knew he was still playing at Pincher's in Tin City so she arranged for the gang to arrive a little after six. The ladies had taken the time to shower and change in their locker room. Richard and Barry had done the same, parking their cars near the Gordon River Bridge and traversing the boardwalk to the spaces along the water. Susan pulled three tables together, enough for the seven hotel employees and the unknown males the other women hoped to attract.

Barry sat down next to Susan and they kissed in a way that seemed to indicate some fraternization beyond bar hopping. Richard and Shannon were more circumspect, sitting opposite each another, waiting for the music to start. They heard the microphone sputter as the big man adjusted it to his height on the stand.

He said hello to his growing group of followers. "I just want to offer greetings from Pincher's. We want to thank you music lovers for your patronage. So to help y'all concentrate on the guitar and vocals, the owners have agreed not to serve alcohol for the duration of the first set!" His next words were drowned out by the chorus of boos, laughter, and whistles that followed the humorous offerings.

Frowning a little, John Friday looked out at the raucous gathering. "I guess all of you are the kind of aficionados who can drink *and* listen to music, all at the same time!" Then he began with a soft number he knew the locals liked to dance to and the noise subsided. Susan and Barry were first on the floor. Richard held out his hand to Shannon before anyone else got any ideas with whom she was connected. She was grateful for the chance to get close to him again. He pulled her in and she followed effortlessly. Shannon was a natural athlete, light as a feather in his arms.

"Welcome back," he whispered in her ear.

"Glad to be here." Shannon was feeling comfortable with this tall man, the hesitancy gone.

The other Spa girls' envious glances were erased when four young firefighters descended on their table, taking the attractive women to the dance floor before more locals could intervene. Seeing all that activity, John Friday switched to a livelier beat. With that, the ladies took the liberty to pull away from their admirers and show off their toned bodies to the entire bar audience. It was Friday night, and the alcohol had yet to catch up to the natural high of the chase, letting them have time to enjoy being pursued.

Richard and Shannon sat down to give their counterparts more time to parade their respective wares. They had to plan the weekend, the time available for fun and games. He didn't have to get worried until Sunday night, so he was determined not to obsess about his witless companions-in-crime. The rest of the crowd from work seemed to recognize that Susan and Shannon had effectively paired off, leaving the field to the remaining single girls.

It had been done. Richard was now officially a social being, like a normal person, with resolving passions and a life beyond work. If law enforcement expressed curiosity about him, the other employees would attest to his "normal guy" credentials.

Richard was sitting next to Shannon now, so they were able to talk over the music and glass clatter. "Are you running tomorrow?"

She nodded. "Ten o'clock at the school."

He pretended to be cautious, not presuming Shannon's availability. "Want someone to beat?"

"It would be fun to have somebody pace me."

"Is there a place where we can pick up some oxygen?"

She kneed him. "I'll take it easy on you if you can think of a good place for lunch."

He was thinking of a picnic. "What about a boat ride and some snacks?"

Shannon was ready for anything with him, weekends suddenly filled with promise. "Sounds like fun. Will I need a bathing suit?"

"You might, if you don't want to spend the night in jail." The idea of Shannon running naked on a beach exited him, of course.

She wanted to know where they'd be going.

"There's a boat rental place on Bonita Beach Road, near the end of Little Hickory Island. Barry told me it was cheaper there than in Naples, and there's a beach nearby."

Shannon thought of her new bikini, one she had only tried on once. It was white with tiny polka dots. She had been afraid to wear it in public and it languished in her closet. Now, with an admirer/protector, Shannon could parade with pride.

Richard finished his second drink and nudged Shannon's shoulder. "Wanna get outta here? I love this singer, but…….."

She nodded a silent asset, and their departure went relatively unnoticed. Only Susan looked up, giving Shannon a knowing look of approval that seemed to say, "You go, girl!"

The twosome drove north on the Tamiami Trail, until Bonita Beach Road, tuned left, and then into the small parking lot of The Fish House, a popular local eatery on the backwater where they could be more alone. A valet took their car and they got the last table on the outside deck. Shannon wanted to know if this was near their boat rental.

Richard remembered Barry's directions. "I think it's farther north, closer to Lover's Key." They both ordered grouper baskets, asking that the fish be grilled, and choosing cole slaw and chowder over the french fries. He had a Corona, while Shannon (thinking ahead) asked for seltzer with lime. They could see two boats tied to the docks, their owners arriving by water.

"That'll be just like us tomorrow," Richard said, pointing to the pontoon boat.

"Have you driven one of those before?"

He made up another story. "My Uncle used to take me fishing. He lived on a lake." In truth, Richard had worked as a dock hand in a private California marina that catered to those with disposable incomes. This had kept him close to those with jewels crying out for emancipation.

After their dinner, Richard continued north on the beach road, looking for their boat rental place. They found it just before the end of the island, a small establishment just hanging in there until the big offer came from the high end developers. He turned around in their driveway and headed back toward Bonita Springs and Shannon's little apartment.

This time there was little foreplay, Shannon coming to him easily, eager for more intimacy. He left before midnight, promising her barely conscious form that they would have a good time on Saturday. She was convinced that it would be a wonderful weekend.

She still looked sleepy when he showed up at nine forty-five the next morning.

"I couldn't wake up," was her excuse. "You wear me out."

Richard admitted a similar difficulty. "This workout will get us going," he assured her.

After the first lap, Shannon didn't need coffee. The endorphins had kicked in. She lengthened her stride and left him behind, letting him admire her technique, square shoulders and tight butt. Shannon kept it going for another eight hundred meters before joining him for their warm down.

She was wide awake now, grinning and perspiring in the morning heat.

Richard still needed help. "There's a Starbucks out there somewhere with my name on it, and I can't keep it waiting."

They stopped at the one in North Naples, opposite a new development. She had a small coffee with cream, but Richard had to have a Mocha Java Grande. That filled him, and opened his eyes to a whole new life vista.

Back in the car he declared, "Now I'm ready for the high seas, or, for that matter, pirates and tidal waves."

Shannon giggled at his newfound energy. "We've got to shower and change first, before you take on pirates."

He let her use the bathroom first, figuring that his cleansing would be quick. They were ready in thirty minutes. Richard decided to forego breakfast and they went to Sweetbay for picnic supplies, choosing submarine sandwiches, chips, fruit, and lemonade. Shannon had a small cooler and they bought a bag of ice to keep everything fresh. It was one o'clock when they reached Hickory Island Boat Rentals. The dock hand showed them the controls. He gave Richard a cell phone programmed to the facility, just in case they got in trouble. There was a chart on the console showing where they were and the various routes available for the afternoon.

Richard could tell that this rig was not built for speed. The forty-horsepower engine would never be confused with rooster tailing, the owners making sure there would be no racing. The dock hand told them that they could not, under any circumstances, venture beyond the inland waterways, as the open Gulf of Mexico was out of bounds for all rental boats. This was fine with Richard, as this old pontoon platform didn't appear strong enough to withstand any extremes of waves or weather. Shannon helped the hand push them off. Richard backed into the narrow channel and saw that the tide appeared to be ebbing, helping them move north. They were in a no-wake zone, so Richard suggested they dig into the food. Shannon split the first submarine sandwich, a delicious mixture of turkey, sweet peppers, tomatoes, Swiss cheese, lettuce, and honey mustard dressing. He steered with one hand while Shannon stretched out on the bow, removing her sweat shirt to let him feast his eyes on her tiny bikini. She inadvertently dropped some dressing on her thigh. As she reached down to wipe it off, she raised her finger to her mouth, looking back at him before she sucked it dry, then turned back -- letting him think what he wanted.

They saw a variety of roosting birds, herons, egrets, and pelicans. Buzzards circled overhead, and an osprey shrieked at them from her channel marker nest. It was eighty-five degrees and Richard was glad he was under the bimini.

Shannon seemed to revel in the heat, reapplying sunscreen, her hands lingering at her breasts and inner thighs. He steered north until New Pass, going under the automobile bridge that marked the entrance to Lovers Key and the final run to Fort Myers Beach. To starboard was Dog Beach, a place for canine owners to run their pets, letting them swim for tossed frisbees. In front of them was a crescent beach that ran along the main channel to the Gulf of Mexico. A number of pontoon boats were tied to mangroves or anchored just off the shore.

Richard coasted in and instructed Shannon to take the bow anchor and some line and bury it in the sand. In the meantime, he tossed the stern anchor twenty feet behind them to hold the boat perpendicular to the beach. Their rental secure, Richard and Shannon hiked the beach, toward the Gulf. Half way to the surf, they stopped along the channel. The water sloped quickly away from the shore allowing for a shallow dive. Richard took a run and arched through the air into five feet of water, on its way to a depth over his head. When he surfaced he was now twenty feet away from Shannon and being taken by the current toward open water. He swam across the tidal pressure and came back to the beach. Richard lay there, half submerged, and put his head back on the wet, smooth sand. Shannon came up to him and sat down next to his shoulders. The water temperature had gone up, the spring and warmer nights making the Gulf and surrounding waters manatee safe and humans friendly. Richard got back up.

"You have to try this. Dive in, and go for a ride on the current." She was reluctant to take a chance, so he took her hand and backed in until the bottom dropped away and they floated west with the tide. After twenty seconds, he turned on his back and she copied him. Still holding hands they kicked to solid sand.

"See how much fun that was?" Then he took another running dive, came up shaking his hair and motioned for Shannon to try. Not wanting to appear afraid, she stepped off the shelf and stroked in his direction, catching him quickly, as he tread water. By this time they were close to the channel mouth and the Gulf beach. The current was less strong here, and the water more shallow. They were kneeling before they realized, struggling to stand and walk out, this time with the mild surf hitting them from behind. Looking south, they could see the consecutive beaches, starting with the two mile Bonita Beach, followed by the Barefoot and Vanderbilt Beaches, stretching away to the Naples high rises. Somewhere in the haze, the Hotel Sherill rose to dwarf the nearest luxury residences.

They walked back to their boat, holding hands and wading. Shannon's bikini seemed to be smaller, and he could see her nipples though the soft fabric. She leaned against him to maintain some balance and he felt a powerful urge to take her right there in the sand, an act not permitted, at least not during a warm Saturday afternoon with boaters and beachcombers everywhere.

They climbed back onboard and finished the sandwiches and chips under the bimini. The lemonade tasted refreshing, chasing the salt away. The fresh fruit removed the last of the Gulf from their mouths. Shannon sat on his lap and kissed the watermelon juice from his lips. She surreptitiously reached down with her hand and felt inside the band of his bathing suit. Richard was almost hard as she wrapped a towel around them and caressed him in a gentle up and down motion, still kissing him and touching his nipples. He groaned as he started to come. She pressed back on him, not letting him move and he exploded into her hand. Shannon would not stop then until he was spent, feeling his chest and stomach relax, as he sagged back into the captain's chair.

Shannon had a sexy look as she stared into his half-lidded eyes. "Feel better?" she purred, then she used the end of the wet towel to clean him before standing in front of him, legs spread in a gesture of power. "Want me to drive? You look like you could use a nap."

Richard reached for her feebly, but she backed away, still in control.

"I'll get the beach anchor. You can start the motor." Then she added with a little smile: "If you're able!"

He groaned and checked to see if he was still in neutral. He turned the key and advanced the throttle to idle speed. Then he waited for Shannon to climb onboard before he clicked into reverse and reached back to retrieve the stern anchor. They motored back slowly and returned the rental fifteen minutes before their deadline.

There was still plenty of daylight left when they got back to her place in Bonita. Richard carried the cooler into the house and Shannon brought in their clothes and wet towels. He said, "You shower first and I'll dump the ice and put the wet stuff in the washer."

Shannon grabbed her robe and went into the bathroom and dropped her still-damp bikini on the floor. The warm shower felt good on her skin, still a little pink from the bright sun. She was not surprised when she felt him step into the shower stall. He took the soap from her and gently caressed her body. She leaned back against the wall and arched her back as he bent to reach her legs. Shannon's eyes were closed when she felt his hands at her waist. He was on his knees and his face was near her womanhood. She gasped when she felt his tongue flicking her there. Then his tongue was in her and he reached one hand around to lightly finger her bottom.

She put her hands on his head, holding him there, moving into that magic mouth. Shannon had to reach the grab bar to keep from falling. Her knees were weak as she came into his face. Then he was holding her, keeping her from falling, lifting her, wrapping her legs around his waist, lowering her onto his stiffness. Richard pushed her into the shower wall, thrusting hard, oblivious to her cries, this time taking longer to climax, elongating the effort. Now, Shannon was powerless, arms limp around his neck.

He turned off the shower with one hand and carried her into her bedroom and lowered her on the bed. Richard dried her with a fresh towel, put another next to her and rolled her on it to finish the job. Then he covered her with the bedspread and observed his handiwork. "We're even now," he chuckled and went into the kitchen to find a cold beer.

Richard sat there, thinking and drinking. His beautiful woman was in one room while his two hair trigger lowlifes, luckily somewhere else right now, competed for his equanimity. He knew that he would not experience anything close to relief until the bloodsuckers were no longer an issue. Still, despite the cold-heartedness, he had feelings for Shannon. Her vulnerability and beauty were a heady mix, a breathtaking statue he could mold. Richard could see her becoming more assertive, gaining confidence in herself as her trust in him grew. He liked the new Shannon, one willing to try things, and aware of her sexual power. She definitely was unafraid to show affection in physical terms. However, it was time to shift gears and focus on his bête noirs, helping them reach their goals by keeping them from his. Richard wrote Shannon a note: "Thank you for the workout. And the boat ride. And the workout! You were wonderful and a good swimmer. I had a great time. My list of Sunday errands is endless, but I will call you. I promise. Sleep well. Richard. "

He did not use the word "love" as he was still searching for a nice way to say, "I like you."

Chapter XXI

Gloria and Tony Esposito were ready for their night on the town. She wore a flowery party dress and heels. He had on a blue blazer with a white polo shirt and light slacks. Tony had refused to wear a tie. "Fuck the formality," was his salute to the Hotel Sherill's protocols. She had asked for a less snooty, but good restaurant, and Barry, the cute, young concierge had suggested the Landmarke Grille. It had helped that the other traditional referral options had been crowded, and Barry didn't want to juggle a reservation list that resisted last minute tweaking. When they reached the outside doors, their Lincoln was waiting.

As a dealer, Tony had received a cut rate rental on a vehicle much like the one they drove in New Jersey. That one was charged to the company, so the Espositos were used to driving for free. As they exited down the long entrance lined with Royal Palms, he asked his wife, "Should I have tipped that valet?"

Gloria scoffed at the idea: "What the hell... are you kiddin'? For what they're chargin' us for our room, he shoulda been drivin' us! Screw their snotty asses." She was getting tired of the hoity-toity attitudes, getting the feeling that the staff were looking down their noses at them. "Just cuz we don't live on the Upper West Side, doesn't mean our money's no good!"

Tony approved of his wife's temper, particularly when he wasn't the recipient. "Yeah, they think their shit don't stink here!"

The car's GPS directed them past Bentley Village to the Landmarke Grille. The tiny parking lot was full, so Tony kept driving north, along the fancy parked cars next door until he saw an opening in the wall of new and used vehicles.

"Why do we have to park so far away?" Mrs. Esposito was pissed. "They should have a shuttle for us."

Tony tried to be conciliatory: "That Barry guy did say that parking could be a problem here."

Gloria was not mollified. "What if it was raining, huh? And I don't give a flying fuck what that guy said!"

Tony was tired of her constant complaining. He answered her, in none too sweet tones, "You asked for a less fancy place. You got one. They said this isn't on the high end list, just like you asked for!"

"What if I break a heel, huh? These shoes are brand new!" They had to walk by the restaurant parking lot, then along the driveway to the entrance which faced Route 41, at least seventy five yards from their Lincoln. Mrs. Esposito was hot under the collar and her good humor was not enhanced by the line of patrons just inside the front door. She heard the hostess tell a customer that there would be a forty minute wait. When it was their turn at the desk, Gloria made sure the girl knew that their reservation had come from the famed Hotel Sherill.

"Yes Madam. Just the two of you? I'm sure we can accommodate you soon. Gloria looked up to see the second tier of diners looking down at the entrance, bar, and booths.

"We want to eat up there," was her next command.

The hostess, mindful of the referral source, the loudness of this crass customer, and her need to keep this job, called one of the servers over and whispered: "These two are from the Sherill. We don't get a lot from there, and we don't want this one going back and giving us a black eye. Do you think you can find some space up there?"

The waiter waved his hand to one of the second floor servers and held up two fingers. The upstairs worker gestured toward a corner table that was being cleared. The downstairs staffer made a gesture of triumph, locking in the table. The hostess sighed with relief. She picked up two menus, handing them to the waiter.

"Joseph will take you to your table now."

The Espositos hustled off without thanking their harried expediter.

It was nine-fifteen when Louis and Jack entered the parking area from Immokalee Road. They'd gone about ten miles before coming to the plaza near a video store. They continued until coming to the restaurant and the now-closed car dealership. Staying straight, Jack sat in the back seat with a flashlight as they looked for the blue Lincoln. It was easy to spot, the white vinyl top reflecting the light from Jack's vantage point.

Louis was happy with their location. "If they'd parked a little farther, they would've been in the construction."

Jack was in complete agreement. "It's getting darker back here. I had to look hard to see that license plate. Let's check that construction lot."

Louis drove slowly on. They could see the barricade and the sand, firmed by the workers' vehicles. Louis was convinced. "We couldn't get stuck out there even if we spun the tires. It's as hard as rock."

They turned around then and went back to the dealership. Louis found an opening between the foreign cars, three cars down from the Esposito Lincoln. He backed into the spot and Jack looked at his watch. "Nine-thirty. Not long now. Let's check the gear."

They both opened their plastic grocery bags. Louis took out his duct tape, plastic gloves and face mask. Jack looked over. "Where's your knife?"

Louis reached into a rear pocket, shifted the weapon in his hand before snapping the blade open. "You mean thees leetle baby?"

Jack smiled. "That's the one. Keep it open. After we scare 'em, we may need it to cut the duct tape."

Louis had another suggestion. "Start your tape and fold it over. I stretched the mouth on my mask, so I can rip the tape with my teeth."

"Good idea," and he pulled the mask opening to expose a greater area to get at the sticky stuff. He checked his tape and gloves and left the forty-five on the seat. It would stay in his hand as a threat, and, if necessary, a club.

They were whispering now. Jack said, "If we get enough, we can go to Miami this week. I just don't want old Ricky Baby to be in on our schedule."

Louis agreed. "I got no problem with that. I won't talk in front of him. Oh, I almost forgot," and he reached over his head to remove the bulb from the dome light. He took his keys from the ignition and put them in the ashtray. Now there would be no light or noise and they could keep their doors open.

Gloria had enjoyed their setting. The table above the entrance gave them a cliff side view of all the comings and goings. She had particularly liked seeing the frustrations of those waiting to be seated and the harried responses of the host and wait staff. The bar was filled with folks being friendly, people waiting too long for tables, and diners willing to settle for the bar menu in order to get home by eleven o'clock.

Tony loved his spaghetti. He wanted Gloria to know it. "It's so good to get some normal food for a change!"

Gloria had chosen the Prime Rib, even though it had been the 'Saturday Night Special'. It was still the most expensive item on the menu, and she was upset that it had arrived dry (in her opinion). Gloria sent it back twice, but there was not a lot the chef could do to please this patron with tonight's entrée. She finally tore at the meat angrily because her husband was almost finished with his meal and was glancing at the dessert offerings.

"This is the last time I'm coming here," was her emphatic assessment of the facility.

Tony had an entirely opposite opinion of the restaurant and his meal. He'd thoroughly enjoyed himself. He was not going to disagree too loudly, however, knowing full well what would come next. "I really liked *my* dinner. Maybe if you didn't order from the right side of the menu all the time…" Tony had mistaken his own satisfaction as an indication that they would have a tranquil time. Gloria was not happy.

"Well, fuck me, fat boy, if I don't like to eat shoe leather for dinner!" He stayed out of the line of fire by burying his face in the dessert menu.

"What about a hot fudge sundae?", he asked.

She would not be appeased. She made sure the scared server knew that her meal had not been improved upon by sending it back. Finally, the waiter told them he would remove it from the bill and Gloria demonstrated her first smile of the night. She was ready for dessert now ordering, of course, the most expensive one on the menu - a fruit and ice cream pile the waiter set on fire next to their table.

Finally, she clinked aperitif glasses with her husband, announcing: "The dessert was the best part of the meal!" She had liked the dramatic flambé effect and the way it drew the other diners' attention to their table. On the way out, Gloria grabbed a handful of chocolates while Tony took some toothpicks. He started to work the back corners of his mouth as they walked to their car. He was hoping she'd been appeased. He wasn't in the mood for any more of her grousing.

It was much darker now. Gloria took her husband's arm as she tried to maintain her balance and peer into the sea of cars behind the car dealership. Tony tried to juggle his keys, the toothpick, and keep his wife vertical.

They had been walking a few minutes when Gloria offered a suggestion. "We must be getting close by now. Hit the unlock button so we can find our way." Tony pushed the remote and they saw a light flash thirty feet ahead. She held his arm tightly while her husband left the toothpick protruding from his mouth and arranged his ring, key facing forward.

Jack and Louis waited until their prey were seated and Tony had his key in the ignition.

At that moment, the two whispered dead serious instructions to the victims. "Shut up and don't move or we'll kill you both."

Tony foolishly pressed his alarm button and Jack hit him over the head with the forty-five and rolled the man out so Jack could grab the key and shut it off. Tony was bleeding and trying to crawl away but Jack came down on his back and pushed him flat on the ground, taping the man's mouth and forcing his hands together behind his back.

"You stupid motherfucker," Jack cursed. "I told you to stay still!"

Louis was having some trouble with Mrs. Esposito who seemed unafraid of his knife, kicking him repeatedly in the leg. Finally, he slapped her sideways, pinning her to the side of the car long enough to wrap tape to immobilize her arms. She was just starting to scream when he got some tape over her mouth, silencing Gloria for the first time that evening. They could then complete the trussing, taking extra precautions.

Once the victims were secured and quieted, Jack looked around to see if the commotion had alerted anyone. Their location appeared to have given them enough privacy so Jack got Louis to help him load Tony face down in the back seat of his rental. Louis took the man's wallet, pinky ring and watch, searching the front pockets for extra cash. Then they bent Tony's legs and taped his ankles to his wrists. Louis was beginning to feel bruises forming on his shins. He was not gentle when he and Jack lifted Gloria and pushed her down almost on top of her husband. They repeated the tape procedure, adding extra to tie the couple together in such a way that helping each other was impossible, as was access to the front seat and the horn. Louis checked the woman for jewelry, and was disgusted to find only a watch and a ring, hoping the two were more valuable than a clutch of pearls. They were sweating and breathing hard, Louis being in pain.

"Have a nice night, bitch!" was Louis's goodnight to Gloria Esposito. Jack had the one cell phone. There was nothing in the glove compartment or trunk. He threw the keys three rows deep, amidst the collection of cars. Using the flashlight he emptied Tony's wallet of all credit cards and money, surprised to find only two twenties and a ten. Jack then heaved the wallet in the direction of the keys. He handed the flashlight to Louis to go through the purse. Apparently, Gloria had left her wallet back in the room, as there was nothing there in her name that could be sold. She was dependent enough on her husband to not have any money of her own. Convinced that there was nothing further of value, Louis sent the purse winging between the other cars. He wanted to cut the woman up, reluctant to put his knife away.

Jack grabbed his friend's arm. "Come on! We got what we wanted. Let's go. We don't wanna increase the heat, understand?"

Unhappily, feeling he'd wanted to do more to her, Louis walked back to their car. He took the keys from the ashtray while Jack returned the bulb to the dome light. They drove with their lights off until they reached the construction lot barricade. Jack got out and rotated the two-by-fours until Louis had passed the improvised entrance. Returning the boards to their original position, he got back in the car. Louis turned on his lights and moved into the right lane, heading north, to Bonita and back to Old 41 and their apartment. They would not take a shorter circuitous route this time, wanting to be back, parked, and in their place, shades drawn, before the first possible alarm. The robbery itself had taken seven minutes.

Richard was in his living room, lights dimmed. He wondered how the grab had gone down. "Anything could have happened," he was thinking. "With those idiots, they could botch taking trash from a garbage can." Richard was worried and glad nothing had revealed his identity, so far at least. And he wanted it to stay that way. But he realized that it had only been luck and greed that had kept these two from giving him up. It would merely take a good interview and a plea bargain to be named as the mastermind of these heists.

He picked up the black briefcase. Richard had oiled the leather and it gleamed, setting off the bronze fastenings. Inside this little beauty was the cache of junk jewelry he had bought from the Goodwill and Salvation Army stores.   It looked as if the baubles had been lifted from a high end store - like Tiffany's, for example - someone's lifetime of collecting. He picked up the pistol, checking the firing mechanism before inserting the full clip. Richard put the gun inside his pants, reaching back to practice finding it and bringing it forward, holding it with two hands, sighting over the end of the barrel. The call could come at any time. They had agreed on Tuesday for the first possible meeting, but with these two, they were just crazy and stupid enough to break all the rules.

The phone rang at midnight. Richard was awake but he still jumped at the noise of the ring in his quiet house. There was no mistaking Jack's anger.

"Hey, high roller. We're still waiting for the big score!"

Richard kept it light, pretending to be clueless. "Didn't that couple show up?" Richard could hear the sarcasm.

Jack was having trouble controlling his hostility. "Oh, they showed, Ricky Boy, but they left their cash at home." Then more loudly, "Fifty fuckin' bucks, Rick! FIFTY FUCKIN' BUCKS! And maybe a K-Mart watch. With these two, I'm surprised the watch didn't have two ears and a tail!"

Richard tried to keep his voice low and rational. "Anything else besides the cash and the watch?"

"We don't know about her jewelry, a watch and a ring, but beyond that, her purse was empty. EMPTY!" His voice rose again, overwhelmed by his disappointment. "And that bitch kicked the shit outta Louis. He's had ice on his shins since we got home. We should've killed those cheap motherfuckers. Where did you FIND these people, Rick? Was it two-for-one night at the Cheap-Is-Us motel?"

Richard didn't foresee the conversation improving, but he also knew he didn't want to hang up on Jack, fearing some reckless, hate-motivated revenge. "Steady, Jack," he cautioned. "I can see why you're upset. I would be too, if I'd gone through all the work you guys did." He was grinding his teeth. The lazy bastards had sat back and waited to be fed, just like babies in high chairs. "Look, I've been afraid we might run into some pikers, and I've got some valuables to compensate for the bust tonight."

"See, Louis? It's just like I told ya. Rick's been holdin' out on us. What're ya talkin' about, Rick?"

Richard made his voice sound apologetic. "To tell you the truth, I've been hoarding jewelry since I started at the hotel, almost three years ago. I've been able to stockpile lost and found items since the beginning."

Jack was still suspicious. "How've you been able to keep this stuff without gettin' caught?"

Richard put on the full act, as if he was reluctant to reveal his strategy, but was giving in under the onslaught of his conspirators' apoplectic indignations. "Well, Jack, it works like this. Every week someone at the hotel loses something. They report it. Sometimes we find it, sometimes we don't. These guests have insured all their valuables. In a couple of weeks, if the items don't show up, we notify them, they call their insurance people, and everybody goes away happy."

"How does the stuff end up with you?", Jack wanted to know.

"I can't tell you who, but a couple of us have access to the lost and found safe. Someone brings in an item, we thank them, pretend to log it in, and somehow the bauble doesn't get to the vault. If the guest won't let it drop, or refuses to use the insurance option, the item reappears, like magic, and the guest is convinced we are the most honest people in the world."

Jack was beginning to sound intrigued. "And how long have you been doin' this, again?"

"Like I said Jack, about three years."

"How much do ya think all this shit is worth now?" Jack couldn't let *this* one go.

Richard was very slow in responding. "You know how hard it is to tell, without actually gettin' it to the fence."

Jack was sarcastic again. "Ball park Rick, ball park. Give us a guesstimate."

"Well, if you want ball park, I'd say my share might, and this is just a guess now, it could be one and a half million, more or less, give or take the market." He heard Jack whistle, then cover the phone to whisper to his buddy that their luck just might have suddenly improved.

Then he was back on the line. "Me and Louis want our piece." There was no mistake in his voice. There would be consequences if Richard did not cooperate.

"Like I said before, Jack. I was afraid we might run into a roadblock with one of the restaurant jobs. I was hoping we could hit the mother lode, but I guess I was wrong this time."

"You were dead wrong, old Buddy. All we got tonight was aggravation and Louis got a bloody leg! I'm askin' again, Rick. When do we get ours?"

Richard continued to sound forced to giving up a significant chunk of treasure. "I can get a bag together by Tuesday. How does Tuesday sound?"

He heard Jack whisper to Louis again. Then, aloud, he asked, "How's Tuesday sound, Louis? Do we have any plans that night?"

Richard heard Louis respond. "Sounds like a good night to go fishing."

Jack became more assertive. "We'll meet at the usual time, same place, Rick, and no funny stuff. We know where you work and live. You wouldn't want us showing up all dirty, asking for our old buddy."

"I'll see you Tuesday night. Something tells me you both'll be happy to plan that trip to Miami." Richard left them with those 'visions of sugar plums' and hung up.

Chapter XXII

Officer Ted Simmons made his regular late night run behind all the businesses on 41. The ever-increasing number of plazas took hours. By the time he reached the Landmarke Grille it was just after two AM. His cruiser circled the rear areas first, and went on to the restaurant, going through their almost empty lot to the storage area for the car dealership. He slowed near the end of the line of cars. A blue Lincoln stood out among the regularity of the foreign vehicles. The policeman shined his spot through the back window. He saw some bundles that began to move, pulsating under the glare. Looking around, he opened his door carefully while loosening his service revolver, and called in.

"Officer Simmons here. Investigating parked car with movement inside. Possible carjacking. Behind Landmarke Grille on 41."

Moving in closer now, the cop could make out what seemed to be two bodies that had been restrained with tape. There were muffled sounds coming from the back seat. The doors of the car were locked. The policeman informed dispatch that he was going to break a car window to access two citizens in extreme distress. After he freed the hands of the person closest to him, he removed the tape. The man had blood on his face from a head contusion.

Tony's first words to the cop were: "We were robbed! Please help my wife!"

Officer Simmons went to the other side of the Lincoln and performed the same intervention on the woman. He could see a large bruise on the left side of her face. "Are you all right, ma'am? I'm calling in for an ambulance."

Gloria's response was definitely more blue: "Those fucking bastards hit me and stole my purse! Of course I'm not all right, you stupid idiot!"

At that point, Officer Simmons decided that the woman would certainly survive until she got to the emergency room and he would get better data from the man. He returned to the husband who introduced himself as Tony Esposito. The officer was hoping to get more specifics from him without the coarse language of the wife. A cursory glance at his head injury revealed what appeared to be a surface wound. Trying to ignore Mrs. Esposito's expletive-laced interruptions, the cop called for backup and an ambulance and then got the following description: The couple were from New Jersey and were staying at the Hotel Sherill. The concierge desk had arranged for an eight-thirty reservation at the adjacent Landmarke Grille. At or around nine-forty-five PM, Mr. and Mrs. Esposito were returning to their parked car.

It was at this point when Mrs. Esposito added, and none too quietly, "This is what happens when a goddamned restaurant is too fucking cheap to build a big enough parking lot. We were parked way the hell back here in East Jesus! It's a wonder we weren't killed. We're gonna sue every motherfucker responsible for this fucking mess. And did you *have* to break our window?"

Officer Simmons was still hunkered down with Mr. Esposito when the first of two ambulances and a fire truck arrived. Gloria resisted being put on a gurney for the ride to the hospital, but the attendants were worried about that bruise and any possible neck injury. Immobilizing her neck and head produced more anger along with a higher level of hysteria, so the ambulance people were forced to administer a sedative in the IV after which the stream of vulgarities finally stopped. Tony got the chance to ride sitting up, in the second ambulance, without her, for which he was extremely grateful.

The crime scene was taped and searched. They found the empty purse and wallet, the keys winding up on the hood of a green sports car. By this time, it was dawn and the first construction vehicles started to arrive next door, eliminating any chance of checking for suspicious tire prints in the adjoining sandy lot. The items that were allegedly stolen were two watches, two rings, earrings, and one credit card. In addition, the Espositos reported losing five hundred dollars in non-specific bills. Tony had been ashamed to admit that he had only been carrying fifty dollars.

Richard didn't get much sleep and felt unprepared to deal with the drama unfolding at the Hotel Sherill. The place was buzzing with the news of their latest crime wave. Reportedly, two people had been robbed and beaten behind the Landmarke Grille. The gossip did little to delineate between fact and fiction. Some accounts alluded to broken bones and thousands of dollars lost. Mr. Merrick had already met with the hotel's crisis team which is, of course, led by Sir George himself. They had followed the same regimen prepared for the previous robbery. This time the session had lasted just ten minutes. As before, the hotel would pay for the hospital visit keeping all news media away from the main facility only allowing interviews across the street in the administration building. Marta was already on her way to the hospital to retrieve clothes that were to be cleaned or replaced. The hotel's flower shop was preparing a gaudy arrangement and a card to be transported to the Esposito's private room in Naples Community Hospital.

Mr. Merrick met with the other remaining concierges. "Barry, you made the restaurant reservation. Anything special about the transaction?" Richard said nothing, but he was seething. If the guests were hurt, it was because these morons had probably gotten too cocky, high on their perceived "toughness."

Barry responded to the loose question. "I made the reservation because they asked for a dinner place, away from downtown, and not on the preferred list. They wanted to drive their own car just in case there was another club they might want to visit after dinner." Everyone was aware that the Esposito's VIP status was not based on olde money, but was a result of Gloria's lost evening purse and diamond earrings. And she was a loose cannon, capable of gathering a large audience to proclaim her injuries, real and imagined. Sir George had managed to get the couple moved to a quarantine suite, away from the general population. The hospital administrator had agreed to try and keep the news media from finding the location of these latest crime victims.

Richard tried to just focus on doing his job, appearing to very interested in a couple's need for a nanny for little Suzette, while he sorted out the confusion of trying to shoehorn twelve people in a single sightseeing limo. In the back of his mind was the Tuesday night meet -- that shadow obliterating any sun left in a spring sky. Shannon rang him on his cell phone. She was missing him and wanted to know if they could steal a snack together. He realized that Shannon might be just the tonic to help him get through the rest of this miserable day.

Back at Police Headquarters, Dan and Roni were touching toes while they waited for The chief to call them in. They'd heard of the snatch and grab behind the car dealership and restaurant. Roni asked Dan: "Do you think this robbery is connected to the other one?"

Dan nodded his head. "From what we've heard so far, it's the same M.O. They used duct tape, just like in the other job. Two men, dark parking lot. Too many coincidences." He had expected to be helping interview the victims at the hospital but The chief had asked them to wait a bit. "Why do you think he wants us?"

Roni shook her head while rubbing her foot on the inside of Dan's leg. "Could it be he wants us to split between the husband and the wife?"

Just then, the boss looked out his door and motioned them in. The chief was pacing but he wanted them seated, so they took the two chairs closest to the desk. "I got another call from Sir George Sherill this morning. He's worried about the connection between the hotel and his guests getting robbed. Hoping it's not an inside job but aware it might be."

Dan started to say something, but Chief Kelly held up one hand. "Let me finish this thought, then you can both jump in. There's more for him to be concerned about than just these two events. Apparently, there've been more reports of stolen articles this season than in any year he can remember. The hotel has avoided publicity by handling these things internally, most of the losses covered by either the hotel or the guests' insurance policies."

Roni spoke first. "So he's concerned there's a connection to the robberies off site and the hotel thefts?"

The chief shook his head. "That's the confusing part. I don't want to say it's panic. This guy doesn't scare easily."

Dan put his oar in. "We started an initial investigation, I know you remember. Then we had the labor demonstration in Immokalee and, for lack of leads, we sort of let it go."

Roni continued the brainstorming: "This Sherill guy wasn't on the bandwagon before. Is he thinking conspiracy now?"

Chief Kelly nodded. "You're right. That's the major difference at this point. He *is* thinking something may be going on. And trust me on this one. Sir George is in a position to measure his vulnerability right now."

Dan wondered, "So where do we come in?" Then trying to make a joke, he smiled and added: "Roni and I could come in undercover and try out the honeymoon suite!"

She kicked him in the leg. The chief laughed, and then got serious again. "Good guess, Dan. He is talking about having some kind of undercover personnel on site there."

"Well, it can't be me," Dan said. "I've already blown my cover, going in there interviewing staff and guests."

But The chief wasn't looking at him. He was looking at Roni and she shifted uncomfortably in her seat.

"Me? You want me in there? I don't know the first thing about running a hotel!"

The chief coughed. "Actually, we were thinking of starting you a little farther down the hospitality pecking order."

Roni didn't like the sound of that. "Just how far down this 'pecking order' do you and Mr. Sherill have in mind?"

He looked at Dan and half shrugged apologetically. "Sir George thought a female officer could hide best if she started as a laundry maid." Dan tried to make another joke, but she froze him instantly with a look.

Roni was hot. "And since you just happened to have a female Hispanic cop, you and Sir George figured why not add another wetback to the hotel roster?"

Chief Kelly had both hands up now and moved back behind his desk for extra protection. "Roni, it's a perfect fit. With your Spanish language ability, you can hide down there. Be a fly on the wall of the whole operation."

"Yeah, the 'step and fetchit' operation. That's what you mean. Why not call it what it is?" She was not a happy woman.

Dan couldn't resist. "You'll be literally under the covers!"

Roni kicked him again, but this time she started to grin. She was a cop, after all, and had never done undercover work. It was a chance to shine. But she knew that Dan's was just the first joke of many to come. Before long, she knew she would be finding pillow cases stuffed with dirty clothes under her desk, and notes requesting "starch only" for uniform collars.

The chief appeared relieved. "So I can call Sir George and get the ball rolling on this?"

Roni nodded her head. She was miles ahead of them, her minority status giving her an acute awareness of the 'starting places' for first generation Hispanics. At the same time, she was excited by this new tongue-in-cheek "opportunity" she'd been given. Roni could see herself mixing with workers who had marginal English skills, eavesdropping on guests and personnel who were convinced she was clueless as to what they were saying. Then there was the inherent prejudice of people who considered non-whites as sub-human, sometimes not seeing them at all.

She said out loud: "You know, it could be the next best thing to being invisible. I'm on board."

Chief Kelly let out a sigh of relief, coming around from the safety of his desk to clap her on the cooperative shoulder. "Thanks, Roni. I don't know if we do have a conspiracy at this place, but with you on the inside, and your crackerjack fiancé helping with the grunt work on the street, at least we can try to find out." Then turning to Dan, he added, "In the meantime, you and Sean can start with the victims. Get the notes from the first squad on the scene and coordinate that information with another visit to the hotel. I don't want Roni in uniform again until this is done. And Roni, no more driving the cruiser. Sign out a junker from the auction lot and that will be what you drive to work. You and Dan will have to see each other on the sly, and try not to have any conspicuous dates."

Now it was Dan's time to be indignant. "Hey, nobody said anything about us not being together!"

She had to tweak him, and whispered in his ear: "And no 'under-the-covers' for you, buster!"

It was his turn to kick her, but he was thinking that Roni's assignment was a good way for her to maintain her situational virginity until their marriage. Their recent lapse, although delightful, had not led to further dalliances. He would still see her, he thought, but their dates would have to be at secluded spots or at her house.

"I'll call Sir George and get their contact person and the schedule for Roni." The chief looked again at his favorite female employee. "You sure you're okay with this? I never meant to insult you. It just looked to me like it might work. A perfect fit."

She gave him a friendly hug. "Its fine, Chief. I'm good to go."

He clapped her on the back again. "Good, good. Make sure you change into your civilian clothes and get that car before you leave. We'll meet off site after you're settled at the hotel. And Roni, thanks again. This will look good in your dossier."

Dan felt a twinge of professional jealousy. He walked with Roni to the locker room. He put on his best forlorn puppy face and said plaintively, "When will I see you again?"

She laughed, looked around and gave him a big kiss, with just the hint of tongue.

"Come for dinner. Mama's making Paella." Then she patted his fanny. "We can play scrabble."

He reached for her, but she ducked into the women's bathroom.

Chapter XXIII

Richard barely got through the day. The post-crime activity just added to his fatigue. He was now resolute. "This kind of shit has to stop," he said to himself on the drive home.

He locked in on his immediate task. Stan Merrick was surprised when Richard had asked for Tuesday off. Richard said he felt he was coming down with something and a day off might kick it away. The boss was used to juggling schedules, but not with his fastest concierge. Richard was usually so unwilling to lose any time when the tips were at their most frequent and outlandish, no matter how ill he felt. But the boss relented and said yes, of course. Richard promised to be back on duty bright and early Wednesday morning, feeling much better.

He went to sleep early and was up by eight. To shake the cobwebs from his brain, he went for a run at Veterans' Park off Immokalee Road. There were adjacent soccer and baseball diamonds, natural turf with a combined half mile perimeter. Richard stretched a little and then jogged on the soft grass for fifteen minutes, not minding the dew soaking his running shoes. He went to some bleachers and stretched seriously now, first hamstrings, then back, quads, and finished with his Achilles tendons. Loose now, Richard started doing intervals, building speed until he was almost sprinting, going one hundred yards, jogging fifty, and repeating the hard striding. He kept this going for a half hour, until his chest hurt and he was having trouble getting his breath.

After that, he settled into a twenty minute warm down, losing himself in the synergy of his fitness, able to dissociate mind and body, focusing not on the leg repetition, but on what his evening had in store. When he was done, Richard was clear-eyed and ready. There would be no equivocation.

He ate sporadically during the day, a little cereal and later snacks of fruit and nuts. At six, he emptied the leather bag on his bed and sorted through the jewelry. The prettiest pieces he isolated and wrapped in bright cloth. Other larger stones and necklaces he put in jewelry bags that tied at their tops. Richard's goal was for Jack and Louis to be occupied like a child on Christmas morning, with the sequential opening of a wonderful array of expensive looking baubles. The wrapping finished, he repacked the leather bag, picturing the two men fighting to get through the narrow opening to the larger pile below. He opened a box of surgical gloves and stuffed three pair in his back pockets. Richard chose cargo pants and already had his ideas what would go in which compartment. He put a sweater and hat in the backpack, added the jewel bag, and checked his pistol. He owned a flat holster. He fit that between his underwear and the back of his pants. The belt held the holster firmly. He practiced one more time, reaching back, grabbing the weapon, and aiming it. His sailor shirt covered the mound of the gun, and he was counting on the sweater later on to add to the camouflage.

Everything ready, Richard lay down on his bed and took a quick nap. Thirty minutes later he put on the backpack, locked the front door and began pedaling west to Delnor-Wiggins State Park. There he locked his bike to a rack and started walking east on his access road, back to the Cocohatchee meeting place. The hike was a mile and a half, and it was close to eight when he reached the canoe launch area. The sun had not been down twenty minutes and there was still enough light left to see the roosting birds. The water reflected the last of the purples, oranges, and pinks.

Then it was almost dark. Richard had to stare intently to see their boat lights. He almost missed them before they vanished beneath the bridge. Louis was hunching over as he polled the last few yards to the muddy bank. Richard realized that the two men were giddy with anticipation, their quiet laughter echoing over the water. Securing his backpack with his left hand, Richard made sure that Jack was occupied trying to help him into the old boat. Richard moved to the bow and removed his pack and took out the leather bag, letting them see its shine in the twilight. Louis polled backwards, but his familiarity with the river enabled him not to take his eyes off their prize. Jack leaned forward and rubbed his hands together.

Richard tried to be helpful. "Let's pick a place where no one can see the jewelry. We don't need prying eyes."

Louis found an opening between the mangroves. The rising tide assured them that they would not be stranded there. When the boat was tied off, Richard handed a flashlight to Jack and then passed the leather valise. The two of them were about to rip into it when Richard whispered loudly, "Wait!" The startled men looked up suspiciously. "I just want you to know that each item is wrapped individually or in a jewelry bag. The challenge for you is to guess which stone or necklace is worth more."

They bent over the bag again and Richard said, "Remember, in this case, bigger may not be better."

"Fuck the games, Rick," Jack snarled and the two began to paw through the waiting treasure.

Richard reached back slowly behind him and pulled the surgical gloves free, putting them on quietly, and just as silently grabbed hold of the pistol. He settled his seat and braced his feet on the side supports. He shot Louis first, then put two in Jack's chest before hitting Louis again. Both men were dead or dying, making wheezing sounds as they drowned in their own blood. Richard listened. The night was still quiet. There were no new lights, no shouts for help. He could hear a steady stream of traffic going over the Cocohatchee River Bridge. There were no boat sounds, no one coming to investigate the backfiring of a bad motor.

He reached forward and grabbed the leather satchel and returned it to his backpack. Then he went through Jack's pockets, taking his gun, wallet and the watch Richard had provided. He did the same to Louis, removing the wallet and key ring. Richard focused the flashlight on the keys. There were three: one for the car, another for the apartment, and the third for the motor lock. All of that joined the valise in the pack. Moving carefully, he pulled the bodies away from the stern, getting them to the middle of the boat, and threw a small tarp over the dead men. Next he untied the line from the mangrove and put the engine in neutral, squeezed the gasoline bulb, and tried to start the engine without the choke. He had been on boats with warm engines that were rendered inoperable after someone tried to choke them when it was unnecessary. The old two-stroke fired on the second pull. He idled down and shifted to forward and headed the boat toward the main channel.

Richard was watching for Coast Guard vessels, their big lights a sign that they were on patrol. He had decided he would stay in the backwater if he saw any suspicious boats, but the channel was empty when Richard finished passing the Yacht Club docks. It was unseasonably cold this evening, frigid for February or March in the subtropics, but nothing like what folks were probably enduring in Buffalo. Luckily for Richard, the cold had been enough to keep boaters home on a cloudy night. He headed west, leaving little wake, the old engine fairly quiet. Richard could barely see the roosting birds and the channel markers weaving their way through the sand bars. The tide was helping as he made the last corner and saw the "Resume Reasonable Speed" sign. For larger boats, the notice was the chance to bury the stern and swamp some poor fool in a canoe or kayak who'd been too naive to leave the open waters for the big boys. Richard headed straight west, fast enough for a modest plane. He was glad Louis had maintained the lights, not wanting to be pulled over for that infraction at this particular time.

Richard got out to a distance from shore that made distinguishing beach structures difficult. He guessed that they (he and the two former crooks) were at least a mile and a half from land. He used the anchor line to tie the two bodies together, using all of it up to the chain and the anchor itself. Richard rolled Jack over the side and then Louis. They floated against the side of the boat. Richard took the end of the tarp and covered the barrel of his pistol and shot both men in the back of their heads. Then he tossed the remaining chain and anchor over the side and watched the bodies disappear from view. Next, Richard threw in the pistol and Jack's forty-five. He reversed from where the bodies had been and turned in the direction of the Vanderbilt Towers. Richard beached the boat at the halfway mark between the Cocohatchee channel and the Delnor-Wiggins Park entrance. The engine still running in neutral, Richard slipped over the side, ripping the light wires from the battery, and swung the bow heading southwest, in the general direction of the Yucatan. Then he pulled the drain plug and put the motor in forward and pushed it away from the beach. The locked tiller was maintaining a straight line toward the horizon. Richard didn't know if the old boat had any internal flotation, but he could see the stern slowly settling to the waterline. As long as he watched, Richard could still hear the small engine driving the craft, he hoped, toward a deep water reunion with Davey Jones Locker. It was close to ten PM.

His wet feet were feeling the cold. He put on the backpack and trudged the beach back to the park and his waiting bike. Richard rode back up to the Cocohatchee ramp. There were only two vehicles and boat trailers left in the parking lot, one with a boat belonging to a dealer waiting to be first off tomorrow and Louis' green Caravan. Richard looked around and unlocked the car, then loaded his bike in the back compartment. Richard took his time driving to Louis and Jack's home, staying right, taking the green arrow to Old 41. He could see the lights of their apartment complex four hundred yards north. It was eleven o'clock when he entered the driveway. It was too cold for grilling, and all the doors and windows were closed. Richard backed the car and trailer into a spot near the rear of the facility and walked to the front door. He saw the name Louis Gonzalez, 402, and let himself in the lobby, taking the stairs to the fourth and top floor. The key stuck for minute, and Richard had a moment of panic before the lock gave and he was inside, closing the door quietly.

He stayed in the dark until his eyes were more accustomed to the reduced visibility, then he walked to the windows and closed the blinds before putting on the first light. Gloves still on, Richard went from room to room, looking for any evidence that might prove a connection with him. In what he figured was Jack's room he found material from both robberies: some rings and womens' watches. The credit cards of both male victims were atop the bureau.

"Greedy bastards didn't consolidate," Richard muttered, knowing that he would also have to find Louis's stash of contraband from the heists. He began his search under Jack's bed, then in the closet, and finally went through his drawers, finding extra ammunition for Jack's forty-five. All of this went into the leather case. In the next bedroom there were few surprises. This time the bulk of the stolen items were in the bureau's top drawer: cash, cards and jewelry in a pile, awaiting the trip to Miami. There was one picture, face down, of Louis, an older woman, and three younger children, in what Richard guessed was some kind of a family portrait. In it, Louis was pulled to the side, a reluctant participant in the construct.

Richard had, he hoped, all the material that could possibly link these two to the hotel and its quickest concierge. He checked the bag, two cell phones, credit cards, jewelry, and cash. It was time to go. Richard opened the apartment door and looked down the hall: empty. He walked to the exit sign and took the stairs, looking through the glass to make sure the lobby entrance was clear, slid through the front door, and around the corner to the rear of the building, and back to the hedge where he had stashed his bike.   Richard put up his hood and rode on the right, back to 41, then south to Naples Park and to his small, rented house.   He checked his watch. Operation Return-To-Sanity was completed by one-thirty Wednesday morning.   He would have barely six hours for much needed sleep before returning to the Hotel Sherill's busiest workstation.

Chapter XXIV

Dan and Sean met the crime scene investigators at the hospital. They all sat together in a staff room near the family waiting area. Officer Ted Simmons desperately wanted to go home. He'd experienced enough of the Espositos, particularly Mrs. New-Jersey-Foul-Mouth. "I've never heard the word 'fuck' used to describe a crime scene that much, ever before."

Dan was sympathetic. "It's tough when they take it out on you, Ted. After you've been on the job a little longer, you'll learn to tune that stuff out and hear only the important facts."

Officer Simmons was encouraged by that and by the impending end of his elongated shift. "I'm sure gonna be glad when *that* happens, Detective. That woman's attitude needs a serious upgrade."

Dan shifted from sympathy to information. "Give us your take, including anything the crime scene people found." Sean had his notebook open, pen in hand. The investigating officer didn't have much to encourage the next team.

"These folks got jumped and tried to fight back. The husband hit his alarm key, and the woman kicked her assailant in his, she thinks, his left leg. Both victims were assaulted, the husband in the head with a gun barrel while the woman got a bruise to the side of her face. The perps were wearing ski masks and used duct tape. Just the same as the job near the docks. The victims remembered the bad guys using gloves, so no fingerprints."

Sean asked the crime scene guys if there were any tire tracks. Any *anything.*

"Not anything useful. Trucks coming in and out of the construction site destroyed any tread evidence there, and the pavement was clean. We think they may have driven through the building area, and moved the barrier to get back on 41. They're gonna check for prints."

Dan had heard enough. "Thanks, Ted. Good job. Let us have your notes and we'll take a stab at the couple. Go home and please try to get some rest."

"It can't come too soon for me. Thank you. " And he was on his way back to Bonita and seven hours behind double shades while his wife tried to clean and keep the kids quiet.

On their way up to the isolated room, the detective and sergeant tried to decide who was going to interview whom. Dan leaned into the younger officer. "Sean, maybe you should be the one to talk to her. You're younger. Who knows -- maybe she'll get the hots for you."

Sean wasn't so sure about that. "I don't know. Ted Simmons is younger than I am and look at the beating he took. You, however, are bigger and you could intimidate her better. Give me the husband. I could remind him of his son."

Dan could see some logic in the younger man's thinking, once he got beyond the chickening out part. "All right, all right. I'll question Mrs. Esposito. If the room is big enough and if the beds far enough apart, or one of them can walk, we could do them at the same time, break, and then compare notes before we finish. How's that sound? Okay with you?"

"Anything you say, boss," was Sean's relieved answer.

The Naples Community Hospital wing was new - so new, in fact, their VIP guests inhabited the only room. In this way, the administration had accommodated Sir George's request that the patients be kept safe from the prying press.

His yearly gifts were, again, being utilized as an important part of this institution's acquiescence. Gloria was sitting up in her bed while a young Spa employee from the Sherill did her toes. Fleeing from the lacquer smell, her husband sat in a chair by the window watching sports on ESPN.

"Well, well," the young matron exclaimed, "more of Naples' finest, here to tell us why we'll damn well never see our money again!" Apparently, Officer Simmons had not been very encouraging to them.

Dan tried to keep it positive. "Good morning, Mr. and Mrs. Esposito. Are you feeling any better? Have you had breakfast yet?"

"You call that shit 'breakfast'?, she yelled. "Our dogs at home eat better than that!"

He kept the apologies coming. "We're very sorry about the robbery. Anything that you can remember, beyond what you've already reported, could be helpful catching these guys."

Sean was trying to sequester Mr. Esposito, giving the man a specific forum to tell the story his way. It was clear that his wife believed her version should be the one to receive the most attention.

"Oh, Tony got hit on the head. I don't know what he remembers, except that he liked the spaghetti." Her husband seemed to be immersed in the sports programming and ignored his wife's assessment of his acuity.

Dan shook his head at Sean, giving him permission to halt the double questioning. Mrs. Esposito was not going to be denied her front and center status. "Would you mind going over it one more time?" he asked.

Gloria waved her hand and the Spa girl gratefully left the room. "We had a lousy night even before this shit happened." Mrs. Esposito was going to share all her dissatisfactions. "That parking situation *has* to be changed. We walked literally to hell and gone to get to our car. The only thing missing was a fuckin' neon "ROB US NOW" sign. We were sitting ducks out there! No lights, no security, accidents waiting to happen."

Dan tried to move to the robbery itself. "Do you remember anything about the men?"

Tony started to speak but Gloria shot him a look, and she continued without interruption. "They had on masks. My guy hit me, but I gave 'im something to think about. I think I kicked 'im at least seven or eight times. I tried for his balls, but got his leg instead, I think. He had a knife and I thought he was gonna cut me. He said he would."

Dan decided to push a little more. "Do you remember what they smelled like?"

"Smell, what do you mean, smell? They weren't wearing cologne, if that's what you're after. They were dirty scumbags. They smelled like fuckin' lowlifes. What do ya think they smelled like?"

Tony finally spoke. "They smelled like fish, a fishy smell. At least, that's what my guy smelled like."

Gloria was quick to denigrate her husband's olfactory recollections. "So they ate MacFish-take-out. Who gives a flying fuck what they had for dinner?"

Dan looked at Sean. They had their connection to the other robbery, icing on the cake of the other similarities. Dan saw no need for much more. "And the stolen items?"

Tony jumped in then to make certain he repeated the same story, afraid his wife might embellish their losses. "I lost a ruby ring, watch, and five hundred in cash, plus my credit card. I don't remember the specific bills."

It was Gloria's turn. "And I had a diamond ring, earrings, and a watch *taken off* of me!"

Dan asked his last question: "And how did you choose this restaurant?"

Gloria was quick to assign blame. "Tony asked the hotel to make a reservation there. *He* said he was tired of the fancy places."

Sean could see that Tony had started to protest and decided against it.

Dan thought of just one more question. "Do you remember which staff member made the reservation?"

Mrs. Esposito had no problem with that one. "The cute concierge. I think his name was Barry."

It was time for them to go. "Mr. and Mrs. Esposito, thank you for your patience this morning. We will do everything we can to catch these two and return your valuables."

"But what about our damn money? Won't they just spend it as fast as they can?", Gloria all but screamed to them.

Dan had no answer to her question. "We're sorry about the loss, and we'll do our best to apprehend the criminals."

Sean already had the door opened so the two police could duck out quickly. Gloria was still asking questions about the lost five hundred bucks.

The two cops went back to the waiting area and sat down with their notepads and the folder. Sean spoke first. "Same guys, same M.O., and they fish. A lot."

Dan added his take. "And same hotel, same referral technique, and vulnerabilities. Are you thinking what I'm thinking?"

Sean nodded his head. "How'd these two just happen to be there when the victims chose very out of the way parking? Were they just hangin' out in restaurant lots that gave 'em hiding spots, or were they tipped off?"

"If we had five robberies, and they were all from the Hotel Sherill, we could be pretty sure. But just two crimes?" Dan wasn't absolutely positive about anything just yet.

He was feeling better about the value of Roni's assignment. "The chief is putting Roni in the hotel as an undercover officer," he told his partner.

Sean was impressed. "She's so lucky. All those rich babes. Under one roof."

"Sean, Roni, as you may have noticed is a girl, a woman. Now we know why he didn't choose YOU to go in there."

Sean was thinking of the ladies in tennis whites he had seen strolling near the hotel. He could just see himself: lounging by the courts, tennis sweater over one shoulder, sipping from an exotic drink, no one the wiser to his clandestine role.

Dan decided not to elaborate on Roni's less than romantic new job description.

Richard started his shift at the front desk the next morning bone tired. However, he also felt a long-awaited sense of relief, despite the rampant staff gossip about the Hotel Sherill's latest off site robbery. He was free! Free from Jack and Louis and free from that unwanted link to his California past. Anything that happened now would be of Richard's own choosing, come from his own actions. The Florida spring seemed brighter and greener today. The clouds of Tuesday had given way to perfect sunshine. That, coupled with the absence of the nagging humidity that sometimes follows spring rains, had invigorated him. He noticed the flowers lining the access lanes to the hotel's front entrance and marveled at their beauty. It was as if the colors had reappeared from a hiatus of monochrome hibernation. He felt no guilt. He had done what needed to be done. They had left him no choice. There was no room for three where, previously, only one had stood on the threshold of riches. Richard was alone again in his resolve.

His rumination was soon shattered against a growing panic setting in at the Hotel Sherill. The police were to be again on the scene questioning staff and Mr. Merrick called a meeting with the concierges to explain the damage control strategy.

"Thank you for your attention on this latest problem," Stan Merrick began. "As you may have heard, we sent Spa staff and Marta to attend to Mr. and Mrs. Esposito at the hospital. These guests will retain their VIP status until they check out. We're going to comp them on their room, their breakfasts and lunches. The valets out front will again direct the media to the administration building. Law enforcement will also conduct their interviews there. If you see people you suspect are police, please usher them to staff elevators and a tunnel exit to the buildings across the street."

Richard raised his hand. "Have the cops indicated which staff they wish to interview?"

Merrick shook his head. "We assume they'll want to talk to Barry, or anyone who helped make the reservations at the Landmarke Grille. Other than that probability, we're in the dark as to what direction the investigation will follow."

Richard grew hopeful. He thought it likely the current process would parallel what happened at the previous robbery. At this point, he felt relatively secure that he had thoroughly removed every single one of the clues that would connect the thieves with him and lead to his back door.

Back at the police station, another kind of interview was taking place. Sitting in Chief Kelly's office were Sir George Sherill, the hotel's Director of Human Resources, and Corporal Veronica Menendez.

The chief set the parameters of this operation. "I would like to thank Corporal Menendez for volunteering to go undercover at the Hotel Sherill. We hope her Spanish language skills and ability to assimilate will help discover if there's a theft conspiracy among staff there." He raised a hand to give Sir George his opportunity.

Sir George didn't waste any time. He looked at Roni and said, "This will be the last time you'll see me until we hear your report. But I would like to share my gratitude for your service." He gestured to the attractive, middle-aged blonde woman beside him. "This is Sandra Barton, our director of personnel. She has been briefed on your job title, Ms. Menendez. She will take care of your orientation. You will contact me through Sandy, please."

At this time, Mrs. Barton straightened in her chair and became alive for her presentation in front of the big boss. Looking toward Roni, she said, "I would also like to thank you for volunteering for this assignment. As you may have been told, it's been decided to start you among our laundry staff. That group is the most English language challenged and most require some help translating Spanish to English. Your supervisor will be Juan . He doesn't know you're a police employee and we're not going to tell him. He should respond to you as someone needing help communicating in English."

Roni nodded and folder her arms across her chest.

Sandra Barton continued. "We'll add you to his group of new employees and he'll give you the same tour all recent hires receive as part of their training. From what I have been given to understand, no one outside this room will know your true identity. You'll work a regular shift until you believe that you have all the information required for a full report. We did suggest to Juan that his new employee could best be utilized servicing the VIP suites, but that's been our only intrusion." Mrs. Barton looked to Sir George, who nodded his approval of her summary.

Roni figured the gaps in her understanding of the setting would be answered on the job itself and she asked only one question: "When do I start?"

The chief replied with, "When they're ready for you."

Sandra Barton indicated, "We can begin at any time."

Sir George did not equivocate, saying firmly: "TOMORROW!"

By the end of the day Roni was tired, her fatigue enhanced by the upcoming change in her routine. She was glad that Dan was coming over for dinner. It would give her the chance to share her apprehensions and get some feedback on the crime investigation. And she needed to kiss him. A lot!

It was still light when Dan turned into his fiancee's neighborhood of Bonita Shores. He noted the "new" old Corolla in the driveway, the beat up vehicle evidence of Roni's marginal income at the bottom of the Sherill's work totem pole. She met him at the door and jumped into his arms before he could reach the top step.

"I hope you're hungry," she admonished. "Mama has enough Paella for the whole Cuban Navy!" Dan wasn't going to talk until he had his fill of her mouth, taking a peek over her shoulder to make sure that Roni's parents were not observing their passion. Temporarily satisfied, he sat down on the steps and held Roni on his lap.

"I like your new ride," he kidded. "How many different colors is it?"

She nuzzled his ear and whispered: "As many colors as the number of accidents it's had. My best guess is eight."

Dan was amazed how sexy Roni got when she talked about cars, and was thinking how to get his hand under her blouse when Carolina Menendez came to the door to announce that the food was ready. Dan lifted Roni from his lap and stood up. Carolina gave her future son-in-law a big hug, and her husband Ronaldo showed Dan a firm handshake and its companion, a strong clap on the shoulder. They both wanted to know about the big news of another shakedown of high end guests of the Hotel Sherill.

Dan winked at Roni and gave a cursory description of nothing more than had already been revealed on the six o'clock news. Her parents had to know of Roni's assignment, but Dan didn't want inside case information leaked to anyone until they were finished. Carolina and Ronaldo had been sworn to secrecy. Their neighbors would only see Roni leave for work in civilian clothes, not in the maid's uniform she would change into later, at the hotel.

Over dinner it became clear that Roni's father was not happy with his daughter's assignment. "I worked to send you to college so you would not have to sweat in a hot laundry! And now, this is where they place you? There was no room on the bathroom patrol?"

Carolina patted her husband's arm. "I am sure there was a good reason to put her in that job, but for now we can't know what that is."

All Dan could do was shrug his shoulders and, with his eyes, beseech his fiancée to bail out the department.

Roni was enjoying the whole thing. Let Dan take some heat for the brass brain trust that had come up with this scenario. But soon she let them all off the hook.

"This job puts me in the most invisible spot in the hotel. I'm getting' the idea that even most of the other hotel staff don't recognize these workers. I can listen to gossip in two languages, spy on guest behavior, and maybe catch someone breaking the rules, without anyone being the wiser." Then, she smiled.

Dan added, "And if there *is* a hotel conspiracy, she gets the chance to break the whole case!"

Roni just had to get in one more dig at her Anglo boyfriend who, by ethnic experience, was clueless. "And I owe all my surveillance advantage to the real and latent prejudice we Latin-Americans enjoy here in sunny Southwest Florida. Thank you Naples and Bonita for this unique opportunity to shine in my chosen career!" Roni jumped up then and ran around the back of Dan's chair and hugged him. "And thank YOU, big guy, for being in my corner. I need you and I love you so!" All he could do was sit there, smile, and blush.

After dinner the two went for a walk. Dan was setting their next time to be alone. "Call me after you finish at the hotel, even if you're bushed. We can still go to dinner."

"Where can we go where we have privacy?" Roni asked. "I don't want to mess up this detail." Then she slapped her head. "No one will recognize me out of the maid's outfit. They won't be looking at me, anyway. I'll be invisible in the uniform."

Still, Dan wanted to be careful. "I have a 2-for-1 coupon for the Greenhouse Restaurant. Sorry to say, I have never seen a non-white person in that place."

Chapter XXV

Richard drove to Shannon's home because she said she wanted to feed him, for a change. He was glad to see her.

"Hey, want a drink, or a beer?" Shannon had changed into shorts and a sleeveless blouse and was bustling about the kitchen. He could smell onions frying.

Richard didn't want anything until right then, realizing how good a beer might taste. "Sure. Can I get one for you?"

She pointed to an open Corona on the counter. "I'm set. There are lime slices on the cutting board."

He popped the cap and sat back down to watch her work. Shannon from behind was as good as the front version. Richard felt a wave of fatigue and relief and closed his eyes for just a moment as the beer swirled in his mouth. She smelled wonderful. He guessed she had taken a quick shower before tackling the kitchen duties.

As far as he was concerned, Shannon need not hurry on his account. What he needed was some time to decompress. Last night's viciousness followed by the search for clues, plus the hotel confusion, had wiped him out. He closed his eyes again.

"Tired, honey?" Shannon was the exact opposite, full of energy and excited to be able to cook for him. She had water on her blouse from rinsing the lettuce and he could see one nipple against the dark wetness. Shannon came close to him and offered part of a carrot she had been peeling. She sat on his lap just long enough for him to get the essence of her athletic perfection, and then she was back to the stove and sink. As much as Shannon was a tryst waiting to happen, Richard absolutely did not need more excitement. A beer and a meal was just the tonic. Any sort of dessert would be an unnecessary extra.

She spun around. "Italian okay?" She was holding her only bottled dressing, and the hamburgers simmering with the onions was just about the girl's culinary zenith. Richard would have been satisfied with Alpo Alfredo, just so long as he wasn't responsible for the preparation. He also was happy not to have to say that it was his 'particular pleasure' that any wish be granted.

It turned out the dinner was wonderful. Hamburgers done to perfection served on buns with sautéed onions, lots of ketchup and a green salad. Richard was stuffed. Between the beer and the buns, he had to refuse Shannon's offer to try thirds. He was ready to crash, and was even reluctant to get behind the wheel of his car. When Shannon suggested a walk, it was the only reasonable choice.

They went down Pennsylvania Avenue.. There was a sidewalk that led all the way to the old part of Bonita Springs. It wound around, over the trickle beginnings of the Imperial River, this far up called Oak Creek, ending at a community park. It was a peaceful place, shaded by a combination of slash pines, cabbage palms and live oaks. There were families there, children running while fathers grilled and women talked. Shannon took his hand and they skirted the people to wander near an old railroad station. He was content with this level of closeness, no immediate demands, and no long term planning. Shannon was falling in love, but she was too much in awe of this older man to ask for anything that might provoke rejection. So she kept those special words to herself.

The walk had erased a good part of Richard's post-trauma fatigue, leaving him with just his loss of sleep tiredness. They talked of their job experiences and the drama of the Sherill's latest notoriety.

"Karen had to go to the hospital to do a manicure and pedicure for Mrs. Esposito, and she didn't even get a tip. Mrs. Esposito said that they had lost all their money, five hundred dollars! And all she did was swear the whole time, even in front of the police officers."

Richard's ears pricked with this new information. "Did Karen have any more stories about the police, what kind of questions, anything like that?"

"Well, she did say that the couple was hurt, a cut and a bruise, I think."

"Anything else?" Richard was letting his curiosity show.

"Karen said that it was dark and they wore masks." Then she remembered: "After the police left, the Espositos had a big fight, something about the men smelling like fish. And Mrs. Esposito thought her husband had made that up just to get some attention. Something like that."

Richard added a couple of comments about the VIP status and comping meals, but he was thinking that he was going to wash all the clothes that made contact with the boat, in hot water, twice. He also resolved to throw out the shoes he wore that night, grateful for Shannon's sharing. On second thought, he would throw out all the material that might receive forensic consideration.

After that, they walked in silence, holding hands and touching shoulders, each with different thoughts.

Richard's ruminations were of the staff, a balance of professionalism and companionship, a young man on his way up, but still capable of enjoying himself along the way.

Shannon was thinking how lucky she was to be with Richard, and wondering if he would want to make love tonight. She was too insecure to plan beyond what some people might erroneously think was immediate gratification.

He did not re-enter Shannon's house, standing beside her as he unlocked his car.

"Shannon, thanks for the great dinner!"

She wanted more. "Did you really like it? It was just burgers."

"Are you kidding?" he assured her. "I would have ordered it at a restaurant tonight, only yours were better than any commercial place."

She hugged him spontaneously. Richard took her face and gave her a long kiss, feeling her sag against him while knowing that she was putty in his hands which would have to wait to be formed.

"Let's see if we can go on break together tomorrow morning," was the best he could offer her now. Shannon's pretty pout let him know what he was missing, but he had been there and knew that there would be other times to wander her exquisite body.

Roni was up early, too nervous to sleep. She was not expected until eight-thirty, the time when she and the other newcomers would find their way to the personnel office and complete paperwork.

She parked her car in the employee parking area behind the administration building. There was a high hedge shielding those cars from the view of guests. Many of these vehicles, like Roni's beater, had long passed the one hundred thousand mile mark and their dark rear bumpers showed the need for long postponed valve jobs. There was another lot, closer to the front entrance where the guest cars were parked, waiting for fleet valets to fetch them. Any similarity between the luxury motorcars of the hotel's patrons and the staffs' modes of transportation, ended at the tires.

Roni locked her car and followed the signs to the rear of the administration building. She was directed to Human Resources. Outside those offices the latest hires awaited. There were five new employees: three Hispanic and two

Haitians. The Haitians had no trouble speaking English but whispered Patois between themselves. The Spanish speaking girls were able to get by, it seemed. So Roni decided to have the most trouble herself, figuring that would create a dependent relationship with someone sympathetic, perhaps close to her age. That someone turned out to be Katina Rodriguez, a twenty-five year old single mother. Roni directed all her questions to Katina who seemed to enjoy being better prepared than at least one hotel person.

Sandra Barton and Juan Delgado ushered the women into the personnel office. They would have a short orientation letting them know the strict narrow lines of their duties and the infrequency of their interaction with guests. They would not be 'particularly pleasuring' anyone directly. Their jobs would simply be collecting, washing, folding, and delivering sheets, towels and pillow cases.   The Human Services Director welcomed them into the "Hotel Sherill Family," the finest hotel in Florida, if not the world. Mr. Delgado repeated the sentences in Spanish.

Roni noticed that neither supervisor looked directly at them, and she, too, made no attempt at eye contact. She found herself leaning into her new "friend" for clarification on half the presentation. They would operate in two person teams as the laundry carts were heavy, particularly when loaded with wet towels. It would take two of them, one pulling and navigating while the other provided the push power required to get from the hotel to the washing machines across the street. Roni saw Sandra Barton whispering and gesturing to the supervisor and would find out that she had instructed him to pair Roni with Katina Rodriguez. Then she saw him shaking his head, only to be overruled, this time his supervisor telling Mr. Delgado to assign Ms. Rodriguez and Ms. Menendez to the VIP floors. That was the last time Roni saw Sandra Barton.

Juan Delgado did not like being told how to do his job. He wondered how these new maids could function with the

VIP's. Juan decided to form an instant dislike for Roni, his pretty newcomer. At the same time, there was a glimmer of lust. He was turned on by Roni's beauty and vulnerability. "There will come a time," he thought, "when this new one will need me, and those soft piles of towels, in the dark, could seal the deal."

In the meantime he gestured at them, as if they were illiterate even in their native language, until Katina said straight out in English: "Just tell us what you want. I will translate for this one," taking on the responsibility with the idea that she, Katina, would be team leader, leaving the hardest work for this simple wetback.

Juan was already tired of these two and decided for now to delegate their on-the-job training. He called over an older woman and told her to take them and their wagon to the VIP floors and assist in the completion of the bedding changes there. The experienced maid told them to push a loaded cart to the staff elevators and they went all the way to the eighteenth floor. The VIP suites had multiple bedrooms and the executive maids spent most of their time making sure the amenities were up to date. Outside each door was a table on wheels capable of holding all the clean linens required to complete each group of rooms. The older woman, Mrs. Marin, instructed the new laundry workers to put all the towels, sheets, wash cloths and pillow cases on the rolling tables. When the entire hall was finished, the laundry cart would be empty.

Roni was breathing hard, glad that this first hall was done. She was wrong. Mrs. Marin then had them enter each suite and remove all the bed linens and retrieve the dirty towels from the bathrooms. They took the used linens and began filling the now empty laundry cart in the hall. Roni began to see the division of labor. The laundry maids folded and delivered clean linens to the rooms, leaving them all for the executive maids who were in charge only of making the beds, not stripping them. Handling the dirty laundry fell only to the laundry maids, like Roni and Katina. When all the rooms were empty of detritus, Mrs. Marin instructed them to return the cart to the service elevator for the ride to the basement and the trip to the laundry proper.

Roni was told by Katina to push, while her new compatriot directed their route by holding the front and exerting some lift. However, it fell to Roni to provide most of the horsepower required to keep the full cart moving toward its final destination. Roni was not happy. Despite the air conditioning, she was sweating through her uniform. She started to wonder to herself, "How am I gonna uncover anything, buried under a mountain of moldy towels? This better improve, or I'm outta here!"

It took ten minutes to complete their journey, through the staff tunnel to the laundry building at the rear, near the employee parking lot. There, the young women unloaded their wagon on a conveyor belt taking the soiled material to the washers, where trained staff fed the huge rotating machines, twenty-four hours a day. Mrs. Marin then took them to a room where they were overwhelmed by the piles of now clean materials. The supervisor had a list, and instructed Roni and Katina how many sheets, etc., each floor required, and the maids began loading the cart for their next run.

They were told that they were entitled to two breaks a day of fifteen minutes each, and a half-hour lunch in the staff cafeteria. The Hotel Sherill did not have unions, and each maid was to be paid minimum wage, plus an additional fifty cents, to give them a sense of superiority over fast food employees. The benefits package was competitive. Still, the 'honor' of working at the Hotel Sherill guaranteed their continued poverty and the good chance that if they got the opportunity to steal something, they would.

At ten AM they took their first break. Mrs. Marin showed them how to get to the cafeteria and Roni welcomed the chance to sit and grab a cup of coffee. She let Katina control the conversation, talking about her six-year-old daughter and her boyfriend who had been deported when the INS raided a development's landscaping unit and found that ten of the fifteen man department were illegal aliens. Roni was happy that her new "pal" did not seem the least bit interested in her life, probably believing that Roni, although attractive, must lead a dull existence commensurate with her inability to learn English, guaranteeing a second class (i.e: victim) status.

While Katina yammered on, Roni was able to look around. The tables seemed segregated by ethnicity and job title, the different uniforms telling who did what, where, and how high up. The Hispanics seemed to cluster together, as did the Haitians. The Blacks appeared to have cornered the beachfront jobs as they were the only workers wearing shorts. The valets wore white, as did the doormen. She saw a small group at a table dressed in tuxedoes. She asked Mrs. Marin who they were and what they did.

The older woman answered in Spanish. "Those white people? They are the concierges. They get the big tips, and they think that their shit don't stink!"

"And what about those people in white?", Roni inquired.

The supervisor dismissed them as well. "Those stuck up girls work at the Spa. They just sit around all day and spray each other with perfume and do each other's nails!"

It was clear to Roni that there was a hierarchy here and she was last in line. "Now, which one of you is stealing?" she thought. "And if all of this is just coincidence, and the hotel is just going through a bad time, I could be breaking my back for nothing." The fifteen minutes were over too soon, and getting up was not easy. "Back to the salt mines," Roni thought in English. Maybe lunch would be better.

In another part of the hotel, Dan and Sean were talking to Barry. He gave them little that they didn't already know. He was part of three person shift, usually shared with Marta Shultz and Richard Smythe. This group primarily worked days. There were four rotating night staff and all had good reputations, the position requiring the highest level of competence and responsibility. Their supervisor, Stan Merrick, had given them all good marks. They all made his job easier, he said, requiring only minor tweaking to keep them on task.

As in their first investigation, the number of people who had access to the reservation lists was almost too many to count. Anyone with computer knowledge could have found out that the Espositos had eight-thirty reservations at The Landmarke Grille on Sunday night. All of the concierge alibis had been verified. They were digging for water in a dry hole. They had a list of the items that had been reported lost. The Sherill did not itemize these as stolen. They had been 'misplaced' or 'not yet found'. Depending on the time limited recall of the victims, the lost valuables could have been taken by valets from cars, servers from restaurants, room service staff from guest suites, maids from the same places, and limo drivers from back seats. This was probably not the total list, but the concierges seemed least liable for on-site theft, unless they personally handled the lost and found which happened to be part of the Security Department job.

Dan found it interesting that the event that had pushed Sir George into action was an attack on the voluble and common Gloria Esposito. She was everything he detested -- with the exception of the fact that her money was good. As Sir George well knew, in the lean times, it was the Espositos of the world that helped put the hotel over the top. Most of the old money guests wouldn't have even reported a lost purse, except as precursor to an insurance claim. Not so with the young matron from New Jersey, and Sir George was as afraid of her first TV interview as he was of the arrival of real hotel competition. He knew the Ritz, the Parma, and the other resort hotels would start to trumpet their electronic surveillance and, without mentioning the Sherill, try to intimate that Sir George had lost his edge. And now their establishments, besides being younger, were somehow safer, more secure places to flaunt expensive jewelry.

Roni was not feeling exceptionally police-like as she trudged behind the loaded carts. She could hear a lot but otherwise the view from the rear of these wagons revealed few insights into hypothetical hotel criminality. Lunch couldn't come fast enough. She stayed with the Mexican food, sitting with Katina and Mrs. Marin. She let them chatter and continued to check out the other staff. There were two attractive young ladies in white sitting with two men in tuxedoes. "So you all are the top of the ladder," she was thinking. "Does that give you access and opportunity?"

Roni took the tray to the return area and took her time scraping the food into the garbage and putting her silverware in the tub. She tried to eavesdrop on the conversation among the attractive foursome sitting close by. One of the two women was lining up the end-of-week festivities, wanting to make certain her man didn't neglect her.

Roni listened as well as she could. The names of these four soon became known to her.

"You all *have* to come to Pincher's. It's John Friday's birthday. I think he's going to be forty and we should get him a cake or something. We have to let him know we are his biggest fans," Susan said.

Barry was on board. He liked to be seen with the Spa girls -- Mr. Lucky.

Richard needed to be a part of this. If anyone asked about his social life, as he had already thought this through, there would be witnesses to his active participation. "I'm in," he said, looking at Shannon, "Feel like dancin' to Friday on Friday?"

She was eager to be close to him again. "Sure, I'd love to go. And I really like his music." Susan had her nucleus now. "I'll talk to the other girls. I think we'll have enough to have our own table again."

So this group played together, Roni thought. Maybe their jobs overlapped too, as the employees seemed to gather by function, as well as race. What she was also finding out was that nobody hung out with the laundry maids except the other laundry maids. They had the least direct guest contacts and their tips came from a kitty, the leftovers from the executive maids. Tips or no tips, the laundry maids did visit all the rooms. Roni wondered at the chances all the staff had at other people's valuables. She thought of her sister maids. If one was a thief, it would be difficult for the other team member not to know. "Still," she mused, "if they were both in on it, the possibilities seem endless." Roni looked forward to talking with Dan to find out what the interviews had turned up.

After all the VIP rooms had been serviced, Roni and Katina spent the remainder of their shift folding sheets and towels for tomorrow. This activity involved a number of employees and Roni got the chance to listen to some gossip. Much of the talk involved the recent robbery and the chance that the media would be visiting to take some pictures. All the staff had received a memo to refrain from public comment. Those caught divulging their insider status to reporters faced possible termination. The consensus among the maids was that the off-site robberies were random and that the perpetrators were targeting restaurants with dark parking areas. The fact that the victims of both events were guests of the Hotel Sherill they saw as mere coincidence. Without significantly more evidence, Roni could see their investigation would be forced to come to the same conclusion.

The day seemed endless. At 5:30, Roni dragged her aching body to the parking lot, looking for police vehicles. She saw Dan's cruiser, but no one was in the car or approaching it. There could be no meeting here so Roni headed to Bonita, taking the back way to Vanderbilt Drive, driving slowly as she sorted out her day. She could see thunderheads developing to the northwest, and the winds had increased. The radio was predicting rainstorms more consistent with the summer months, but any precipitation during the dry season was almost universally welcomed. They had been under water restrictions for six weeks, and the threat of brush fires was a daily event. When Roni pulled into her parents' driveway, she could see her father reinforcing some new plantings in anticipation of the predicted blow. She greeted him with a hug and a kiss, as he held his arms back so as not to cover her with dirt.

"*Como estuvo su dia los sirvientes espanoles?*" She knew he was asking how her day had been among the Spanish servants. Roni could see that he was still upset at the choice of her undercover positioning.

"Papa, you wouldn't believe how hard these women work. I have to help push this huge laundry cart. I swear it weighs three hundred pounds!"

He was shaking his head as he cleaned his tools in a bucket of water. "*Que puede encostrar usted toallas que lavan y las hojas?*"

As Ronaldo asked her what she hoped to find out by washing sheets and towels, Roni had to admit she didn't have a clue - as yet, anyway. "So far, not much, Papa. The women don't believe anyone in the hotel had a hand in the restaurant robberies."

Just then Dan pulled into their driveway and Roni ran to his car. "Want to join us for lemonade?" She leaned against his door and all he could do was bend over and kiss her elbow.

"Step away from the car, Lady, or I will have to make an arrest for defacing a police vehicle."

Roni jumped back so he could get out and hug her properly. They held hands as they went into the house. Carolina had a pitcher of juice all ready out on the lanai so her daughter and her future son-in-law could enjoy a private conversation.

"Thanks, Mama. Papa looks thirsty, too."

"Don't worry about your father. I'm bringing some to him outside. He's not coming into my house until he gets all that dirt off himself."

Roni slumped in her chair, too tired to lift her glass.

"You look really beat," was Dan's timely observation. "What'd they do to you today?"

"Worked us like dogs, that's what they did to us. I know it's only been one day, but I don't think there are people there that work harder than these laundry maids. We didn't see any guests but we got into a lot of rooms. We could see some valuables lying around, people's clothes on the floor, open purses on bureau tops, money here and there."

Dan had to agree on the suspect list. "We figured that almost all the staff have the chance to steal, some more than others. And the reservation lists are available to anyone with computer knowledge."

"So what do you do next?", she asked her love.

He shook his head. "We interviewed the concierge, Barry, who made the reservation. And we got an alibi list for all the front end staff. They all checked out, at least initially. Besides interviewing them, the next step would be to review personnel files, although they tell us that the hotel does strict background checks, and they don't hire anyone that fails the drug screen."

He wanted to know what Roni had found out. She felt inadequate. "This may not be the best position to find our perps. But I did see how the employees group themselves. People don't seem to notice the maids. I overheard some Spa women making weekend plans with two concierges. I was right behind them, and they acted as if I wasn't there. It sounded like they were going to Pincher's on Friday night to hear some guy named Friday, believe it or not, play guitar and sing."

This didn't excited Dan. "So two groups hang out together. And there may be some relationships going between the two departments? If there is collusion between the Spa and the front end, dating doesn't prove anything."

Roni nodded her head. "This was just the first piece of information I was able to overhear. The maids don't think there's any connection between the hotel and the heists."

"Based on what? What do they know?", he wondered.

Roni put a hand on his arm. "Nothing. They don't know anything. They're guessing that the bad guys hang out in dark areas and jump restaurant goers, and these are isolated, random events."

"All we can do is just shake a big tree and hope something falls out," he stage whispered.

He sounded discouraged and she didn't feel a whole lot better. She was facing another day in the salt mines tomorrow, without any clues. "I'm gonna call in sick tomorrow and then go on vacation. You can reach me at my villa in Boca Grande!"

He groaned with her: "Take me with you. We can start our honeymoon early."

She poked him. "Who said anything about you? And by the way, have you seen any strange looking objects around my desk, yet?"

He grinned innocently. "What are you talking about? I did   notice a pillowcase, stuffed with something. Did you leave   anything there?"

She was frowning now. "Anything I get that is laundry related is going to end up in the back seat of your car, flies or no flies, so please try and slow down the practical jokes, *comprende*?"

Carolina joined them. "If you want, I can bring your plates out here. It's just chicken salad. If that storm comes, you'll have to come in and eat with your father and me."

Roni looked through the screen at the darkening sky, watching the tops of the palms waving in the building wind. She decided not to chance getting wet out there.

"We'll come in now." She pushed the wall button and the shutters were almost down when it hit. A wall of water came across the lawn, the thunder and lightning close behind. They heard a crash and saw a neighbor's pine tree fall on their carport, crumpling the roof and metal supports. They rushed to finish closing all the windows and watched as the wind bent trees. The lights flickered but stayed on as the storm continued, less violent now, but still blowing the water in horizontal sheets. Ronaldo and Carolina looked out the window. They could remember surviving a big storm on their run from Cuba almost thirty years ago.

Roni checked their flag. "It's coming off the Gulf. It looks like it's from the west-northwest." They sat and listened to the storm, eating quietly, warm and dry in a house that had withstood two hurricanes, most likely with more to come - this summer or the next.

Chapter XXVI

On his next shift Richard gave Barry his own style of interrogation. "What'd the police wanna know?"

"Pretty much what they asked Marta last time -- when I made the reservation, how long it had been on the computer, that kinda stuff."

"D'ya think they have a clue what's goin' on?"

Barry shook his head. "It seemed as if they knew the answers already. There was no sense that they were on to something."

Richard was temporarily relieved. He knew that the investigation was ongoing, but hoped the cops would get frustrated at the lack of real leads and leave them alone. He decided to bury himself in the job, volunteering to fill in for people reporting sick, and doing all the multi-tasking for which he'd received past accolades.

The Espositos had returned from the hospital. Gloria was basking in her VIP status, taking compliments for her bravery and ability to bounce back from her terrible ordeal. Once told of their comp level for breakfasts and lunches, she and her husband made certain they ordered only the most expensive entrées. And they availed themselves of all the Spa services, massages, pedicures, and mineral baths. Shannon told Richard that she was seeing Gloria every day for benefits that, if a la carte, would have doubled their hotel bill -- which, for the couple from New Jersey, would now no longer be a problem.

Dan and Sean were back at the hotel the next day. They agreed to split the assignment. Dan would interview the front end staff while Sean tackled the Spa workers.

Delighted with this arrangement, Sean set up in Susan's office. He listened to the manager's description of their set-up. Susan's answers sounded memorized to Sean.

"There are different layers of staff and expertise represented among the thirty employees in the Spa. There are locker room staff who dispense keys, towels, and directions to the pools, sauna and steam room. The health food restaurant has three workers who sell juice drinks and veggie wraps. Our specialized staff provides the manicures, pedicures, and massages. The beauty salon employees do cuts, colors, and styles. Their staff of six are particularly busy on the weekends, preparing guests for their respective evenings on the town."

After that overview, Sean was not sure where to go next. He was guessing any losses in the locker rooms would be reported immediately. Still, he asked Susan how the Spa responded to these requests for assistance.

"We get very little complaints for lost property," she explained patiently. "In most cases, people lose items in the lockers, and then find them, when a locker attendant helps them search the space." She went on: "Sometimes guests think they have lost something, report it, and call back later to say that the object had been in their hotel room all the time."

Sean was getting the idea. "So guests don't bring a lot of belongings here."

Susan was glad the officer seemed to be catching on. Sounding a bit more relaxed, she answered, "That's right. They'll be wearing very little in here, so they don't want to have to store valuables, which might get lost or fall behind a bench."

The young sergeant needed to begin somewhere, so he asked, "Who are your most recent hires?"

Susan had an idea, but nonetheless checked her the computer database to be sure.

"Shannon Scott is our last hire. She is one of our masseuses, and has been here about a month.".

"Do you get the restaurant reservation list on your screen?"

Susan nodded. "Of course. All the guest activities are available to us. Sometimes we have to work quickly to accommodate a dinner reservation. Guests forget how long it takes for us to complete a service, and for them to shower and change. We might need to remind them and alter our speed. It's our responsibility to overcome any mistakes they may have made in their planning."

Sean whistled to himself. Dan wouldn't be happy to know of yet another group who could have helped plan the robberies.

"Would Shannon Scott be available now?"

The manager checked the appointment sheet. "She doesn't have a client until eleven. I'll get her." And by way of caution added, "She's a little shy."

Sean was taken aback when Shannon paused in the doorway. He couldn't remember seeing a more beautiful girl, tall, blonde, with wide shoulders and more than filling her white uniform.

"You wanted to see me?" Sean tried to compose himself, shuffling some papers, opening his notebook. There was a chance he could get lost in her blue eyes.

"Yes, Miss, I, uh, we need just to ask a few questions, if you wouldn't mind." He slid out a chair so that Shannon would be opposite him, across the table. "My name is Sergeant Sean Brady," he started. "My partner, Dan Logan, is talking to front end employees right now." He tried not to stare, but her looks were impossible to ignore. Sean was impressed that Shannon didn't seem aware of her effect on males, or the young officer would have been in trouble. "I was talking to your supervisor, Susan. She said that you were her most recent employee. How do you like it here?" This was a safe topic, a way to reduce any anxiety and distrust the young lady might have been feeling.

"Oh, I love it. It's the best job I've ever had."

Sean suddenly wanted to work there himself, ready to leave his previously chosen career as a law enforcement professional. He had no training in massage, of course, but would have been an eager student if Shannon was giving private lessons. He shook his head to chase the fantasy, and continued on the positives. "What do you like about it?"

She was happy to give him details. "The people here are friendly, and everyone gets along. We even go out together on Friday nights."

"Is it just the ladies, or do you go out with the male staff?"

Shannon dismissed the Spa boys. "We don't socialize with the locker room staff.. Our group goes with some of the concierges, from the hotel's front desk."

At this, he noticed a slight blush and was instantly jealous. "What am I doing?" he thought. "I just meet this girl and I want to kill anyone who might hurt her!" He had to know: "Do you have a boyfriend, one of the concierges?" This was not any of his business, and there was no real need to dissect this beauty's social life, but she hadn't reacted against the questions, so he pressed on. She was blushing, hesitant, but he couldn't stop, asking again, "One of the front end staff?"

"Uh, I guess you could say that Richard and I are going out?", making it sound like a question at the end.

Sean could see that she was naïve, but willing to trust that a police officer would have a reason to want to know about her private life. Sean knew that he could only go so far with this line of questioning. He was already over the line.

"And Richard's last name?"

"Smythe. It's spelled S-M-Y-T-H-E, but you say Smith." All the while she was speaking, she was turning pink because of this level of sharing.

He switched subjects to her tenure. "And you have been working here how long?"

"A little over a month, almost five weeks." This was said with real pride, the girl's head raised, jaw out, happy and surprised to have found her niche. Sean found himself happy for her too, and got a sense that Shannon had not been successful before this placement.

"And how long has Mr. Smythe been at the hotel?"

"He's been here almost three years," she said. "Richard is the fastest concierge."

Sean was a little confused and also hoped that the speed attributed to this guy was not an indication how quickly he was getting into this gorgeous girl's pants! "Fast? Does he have to run in his job?"

Shannon laughed. She was starting to relax in front of this policeman. He seemed nice and he was good looking, too. "I didn't mean running fast. I meant that he can solve problems quickly and do two or three things at the same time. I guess I should have said 'quick'".

Sean was resigned to his jealousy. It looked as if this Richard character was not going away any time soon, and had made an impression on this beautiful woman. He changed the subject. "Can you tell me something about your job here?"

Shannon was happy to oblige. "There are six of us. We do full body massages for women and men. We use soft music, mostly classical, and the rooms are scented."

He pretended to be more curious. "Do the guests wear clothes, special garments?"

She could see that he had never had a massage at the Spa. "Most guests are naked, but there is a blanket that covers them. We do both top and bottom massage, so when it is time for the men to turn over, we leave the room until they are covered up again."

Sean was looking at her long fingers, wondering what it would be like to be under a blanket in one of the rooms, thinking, "Why didn't they put me undercover in *here*?" He was certain he'd be able to find out a wealth of valuable information. And then he could get to know this incredible beauty right across the table from him.

She continued, "We give the guests their choice as to how firm the massage will be. You'd be surprised what a massage does. Sometimes people have trouble walking afterwards. We try to encourage them to drink water and maybe take a nap later."

Her eyes were glowing, and Sean could see that she loved doing this kind of work. "Well, Miss, you certainly have convinced me. I would guess that this place is lucky to have someone who is as dedicated as you. And you look very healthy, so I'm guessing that you are a good advertisement for the services here."

Shannon blushed at the compliment, but was pleased that she had been able to describe the facilities in a way this gentleman seemed to understand.

Sean was kicking himself. How stupid had he just sounded? She had bewitched him. He had to terminate the interview before he made a complete fool of himself. He stood up, and Shannon rose to take his outstretched hand. "Thank you, Miss Scott. Do you mind if I call you Shannon?"

She was not in a position to question his technique, or his motives. "Sure, of course you can call me Shannon."

Sean was impressed by the strength of her grip, guessing the work must really firm her wrists and fingers. "The department appreciates your cooperation, Shannon. If we can think of some other things that may help our investigation, would you mind if we talked again?"

Shannon found herself impressed with this officer's politeness, and with his interest in her career. "If you think I could be helpful, I guess it would be okay? Would you be the person I would be talking to?"

"Yes, Miss, if it wouldn't be too much of a bother."

She smiled at him and he could feel just the beginnings of his own blush. Shannon stood to her full height, shoulders back, as she said with more confidence now, "I would be happy to help, if you need me, Sergeant."

He held the door for her, and almost swooned at the combination of scents emanating from her skin and clothing. He sat down but he was having trouble concentrating. He needed a change of scene, and called Dan.

"How're you doin' down there?"

"I've talked to a couple of the front end staff. How 'bout you?"

"Just one so far here." Sean wanted to clear his head. "Can we get away for a cup of coffee and a conference?"

"Can't it wait for lunch, or do you have some info we need to do something about right now?"

Sean really needed a break. "I just feel if we could talk a little about what we have, it might help me focus the next group of interviews."

Dan didn't think taking a break would slow them down any more than not. "Okay, sure." he said. "Meet me out front. We can go to Dunkin' Donuts and sit outside. It's just five minutes away."

Sean left the room and knocked on Susan's door. She opened it and he told her that he had a meeting but would be back later.

"How was your interview with Shannon?", she asked.

He told her that Shannon had been very cooperative. "She seems to like working here."

"Thank you Sergeant. That's good to hear. She is new but wants to learn and be the best she can possibly be."

Sean was more than ready to go. All the women here seemed to have access to some intoxicating fragrances!

Dan was waiting by the car. They rode in silence until arriving at the coffee shop and making their purchases - the big detective choosing black coffee, his partner opting for café mocha, the biggest cup available.   Sean needed a boost. The Spa's ambience had suffused him with the desire to relax, preferably under the hands of one beautiful masseuse in particular. Dan looked for any hunch that could get them going. He was willing to settle for the smallest crumb.

"What do you have for me, Sergeant?" Dan pretended to be strict, frowning over his coffee cup.

Surprised at the tone, Sean looked up quickly, eyes big, as if caught in a trap. The line of whipped cream on his upper lip and the added look of utter cluelessness broke Dan up. He started to laugh, took a sip, and then began coughing, finally having to stand up to clear his throat.

Sean was glad to have his friend back. "What was that all about?"

Dan was still trying to stop coughing. "If you could have seen the look on your face. And with the white mustache, you were Inspector Clouseau!"

The sergeant was relieved that the big detective had not guessed at his partner's infatuation, and seemed ready to do some brainstorming, even if there was not much to discuss.

"Okay, it's not much," Sean began. "The guests that go to the Spa don't bring many valuables because most of the time they're in bathing suits or naked. There are about thirty employees, some with the chance to steal what little there is around, the restaurant staff with the least access. But get this: they have computers and they look at the reservation lists to find out how much time they have to finish their massages, pedicures, and hair appointments."

Dan was not happy about this bit of news. He'd hoped they could rule out blocks of workers, but even in this other building, they all shared the same database. "That's just great, Sean! Any other bad news breakthroughs?"

"Well, this may not be worth much, but some of the Spa girls hang socially with the concierges. The one I talked to is going out with one named" and he checked his notebook to be sure, "Richard Smythe. That's a fancy way to spell Smith. Almost sounds phony."

Dan was mildly interested: "Okay, if you were looking for a conspiracy, the Spa and the front desk would have all the information to alert robbers that dinner was on its way. What about the one you talked to? Did she seem like the type to be in on a scam?"

Sean was quick to defend his new lady love. "Not Shannon, I mean Miss Scott. She's been there the least amount of time, and is really into her job. "

"We can't afford to write anyone off just yet, not until we have a chance to review the personnel files." But he gave his partner some credit. "You're probably right about this, and I agree we should look for some strangeness in one of these workers before we really start digging. If someone hits us funny, or the file is short, we can check them out against our data bases."

Sean wanted more direction. "What do we do now?"

"Go back and interview a few more. When you have about five, we can meet with the personnel director and go over their files. Something may show up that way. Let's pick four o'clock. If you have the five or not, meet me in Human Resources."

"I'm with you, boss." Sean was glad to have a time and numbers limit, so they could switch to something that might give them more information. "So we do that. Then what?"

"We'll meet with Roni after her shift. She'll have two days in and we can pool what we all have. We'll see if there're any facts that we can call leads. We can only hope."

Chapter XXVII

Richard was busting his butt, being all things to all people, when he was interrupted by Stan Merrick.

"When you're finished with what you're doing, take a break. It's your turn with the police officers. Let Marta or Barry cover anything that needs an immediate response."

Richard had seen the other people leave and return and had quizzed his mates. No one had been upset, but then again *they* didn't have anything to hide. He went to the bathroom, washed his face with cold water, took a deep breath, and headed for the administration building.

Dan was just back from his break when Richard was ushered in. He saw a young man, looking about thirty, with black hair and an air of quiet intelligence. Maybe a little over six feet. Richard shook hands with the big detective, his grip strong, making just enough eye contact before sitting in the proffered chair. Dan started the conversation casually.

"Good afternoon, Mr. Smythe. Is it pronounced Smith or Smithie?"

Richard smiled back. "It's pronounced just regular old Smith. I changed the spelling to make it seem higher class for the clientele here."

Dan reflected the conspiratorial smile, understanding the upper class need to separate from those below. "How long have you been with the hotel?"

Richard responded with just the right amount of pride. "I've been at the Sherill for almost three years."

"And how long have you been at the concierge desk?"

Richard continued his charade of prideful gratitude. "I was appointed concierge sixteen months ago," letting Dan know he was appreciative of the change of status and had marked the transition date.

"What do you like about the job?"

Richard appeared to relax, sitting back in his chair, happy to get the chance to share the complexities of his appointment. "I like the excitement. No two days are alike. And *we* are the problem solvers, helping the guests get the most out of their stays with us." He was letting Dan know that he had identified fully with the hotel's goal to provide the best possible guest services.

Dan switched gears quickly, to see if this employee could be put on the defensive. "Were you on duty the night of the robbery?"

Richard paused what he thought was the right amount of time to reflect careful consideration of the question, not rushing a response, or taking too much time to make up an answer. "I had that weekend off, Saturday and Sunday."

"Did you make the reservation at the restaurant?" This was a trick query, to provoke anxiety. Dan knew that everyone was aware who had made the call to the Landmarke Grille, but he wanted to see if the question of a conspiracy or the possibility of malfeasance would evoke some fear.

Richard refused to get sucked into the ruse, answering as if the police officer had forgotten, or needed confirmation of a known fact. "Barry made the reservation. I think it was early in the week." He was also letting Dan know that the concierges shared their jobs and assignments, the work responsibilities being an open book.

Dan was not getting anywhere. Either this guy was Mr. Service, or a slick operator. Nothing defensive in his demeanor or answers. Dan had noticed a similarity of response, most of the employees having bought into the hotel's mantra of being the best. That status had somehow transferred to the staff, especially the ones with the most guest contacts.

"Where did you work before starting here?"

Richard took a moment, and then recited the restaurant jobs that had preceded his first laundry position at the Sherill. Dan could see the pattern. Everything pointed in the direction of customer service in a resort community.

"Have you always lived around here?" He was running out of ideas, deciding to move to broader questions.

"I grew up in New Mexico, then my family moved to California."

"Do you still have family out there?"

Richard paused, and his face saddened. "I was an only child, and my parents died in a car accident when I was twelve."

That closed that direction of inquiry. Dan was thinking, "Pretty convenient, if that's true," but he said: "Sorry to hear about your parents. What made you decide to come to Naples?"

Richard appeared to relax again, as if this was his favorite topic of discussion. He knew he could answer that one easily. "I was looking for a high end tourist place, like the Palm Springs area of California, and it had to be warm. So Naples, Palm Beach, or Miami was why I came to Florida."

"Very neat," Dan thought, "all tied up in a little ball, but if you wanted to steal, you would have chosen this spot." He resolved to make sure they reviewed this gentleman's file among the others they chose in the Human Resources Office. "I think that's about it, Mr. Smythe. Thank you for your time." And as Richard was getting up, Dan added, "If we think of anything else, we may call you again."

Richard was Mr. Compliance: "Certainly, officer. I would be happy to help. It would be my particular pleasure!"

Richard walked slowly back, making sure he seemed unhurried, not looking over his shoulder at the administration building.

Barry asked how the session went.

"Oh, that," Richard conveying his studied disinterest. "It was just like you said, a fishing expedition. He seemed to already know the answers to his own questions."

Barry liked the confirmation. "Yeah, I told you that they were just goin' through the motions. How could they think that any of us were involved in these crimes?"

Richard changed the subject as if they had spent too much time on something soon to become irrelevant. "Do you want a ride to Tin City on Friday, or are you going to take your own car?"

Barry was only too happy to start to think about the weekend. "I'll drive. I'm gonna take Susan. She wants to steal me away to a friend's cottage on Keewaydin Island!"

Richard pretended to be jealous. "You have all the luck. I've never been over there. It's mostly private, isn't it?"

Barry was glad to have one over his older, more accomplished workmate. "Those cottages are handed down from generation to generation. They don't allow any more building there."

Richard gave Barry his due. "I hear that it's like a trip back to olde Florida. Very quiet and noncommercial."

Barry decided that he'd gloated enough. "I'm not feelin' sorry for you, buddy. I think Shannon'll keep you plenty busy."

Richard smiled, his eyes getting big. "Whatever are you talking about?"

Barry grinned back. "Don't give me that innocent look! I can see the way she's all over you. And what a body!"

Richard continued the guy talk. "You didn't mention anything about her mind."

Barry pushed him. "Okay, I guess that *would've* been the first thing you noticed about her."

Roni was getting in shape. She developed a rhythm, using her legs and back, pushing from a lower point on the laundry cart to maximize her leverage. It was getting easier, all of it, the routine mindless enough for her to be able to focus on what was happening around her, the sights and sounds of poor people waiting on rich people. Sometimes they had to wait for guests to clear a room before stripping the beds. The executive maids made certain Roni and Katina knew who were in charge, nodding regally to grant final permission for the dirty work to continue. It was then up to Katina to reinforce her meager status by having Roni do most of the bending, leaving her the bathrooms where the towels were most likely on the floor, sometimes still in the tubs and shower stalls. There were no dogs for Roni to kick, so the hierarchical work structure ended with her.

They sat with the other laundry maids on break and at lunch. Roni let Katina chatter on again as she tried to establish herself, the cop staying mostly quiet herself, responding in Spanish-only, one word sentences, not even trying the English slang her peers practiced. It was on lunch that Roni learned that there were lists of maids that were going to be called for questioning. There was general anxiety that any pilfering would receive the harshest punishments, including termination.

Alicia Hernandez thought about the purse with the diamond earrings hiding in the bottom of her underwear drawer. The money had long since been spent. She'd been surprised when Mrs. Esposito had caused that commotion following her loss. Most of the guests didn't do much more than report missing valuables, but this one had made her lost cash and jewelry everybody's business. Alicia had never taken anything before. The executive maids did a consistent inventory of items that were left out, before and after the laundry pick-ups. Finding that purse wrapped in a sheet had been a lucky surprise, but she still worried about the diamond earrings she could never wear. She didn't know how to get rid of them. And now the police were beginning to talk to the maids.

Mrs. Marin was quick to stifle any hysteria surrounding the police investigation.   She scoffed, "They won't want to talk with US! We don't count here. We just wash their laundry. The police are only interested in the bigwigs, mostly the white people who talk to these guests every day."

Alicia relaxed. For once, she was glad to have one of the least respected positions. She was thinking, "Maybe I'll just put the purse and earrings in the Goodwill bin." Then she got frightened again, worried about fingerprints. "No," she thought, "I'll throw it in the river on my way to work." Alicia relaxed then, the situation resolved, and joined in the gossip concerning a certain maid and their supervisor, Mr. .

Roni learned that the laundry staff assumed there was wanton pilferage among the higher status employees. There were rumors of missing jewelry, thousands of dollars of lost cash, intimations that the VIP staff made hundreds extra, thefts being a part of their regular incomes, in addition to the larger tips denied the towel washers. The hopeful consensus was that the snooty white workers were going to finally get their just desserts and the idea of someone in a tuxedo being hauled out in handcuffs was too delicious an image. Roni was ready to release the idea of her workmates as suspects, particularly those assigned the VIP floors, as they received daily scrutiny by their supervisors and the executive maids.

After work, Sean and Dan met at Dan's house. The two men were sitting on the lanai enjoying drinks when they heard Roni's clunker rattling up the driveway. She exaggerated her fatigue, dragging her feet up to the screened area, leaning against the door jamb, as if too tired to even reach the handle.

The cops joined in the game, jumping to their feet, Sean grandly opening the door, Dan leading the exhausted worker to a lounge chair. She ran a sleeve across her brow, languidly wiping the imaginary sweat, before beating Dan to his glass of seltzer and sucking from it as if she had just crossed the Sahara.

"Hey, I would have gotten you one!", he yelped.

She took another swig, as if suffering from an unquenchable thirst. "Old friend, by that time I would have been sooo dead." Roni shoved the glass back to him, and he looked in mock incredulity at the small amount left at the bottom.

"May I get you one of your own now, Senorita?"

She smiled in feigned civility and answered, "Why yes, my good man, and please don't forget the slice of lime, if you would be so KIHND," accentuating the broad vowel sound.

Sean picked up on it. "Now you're starting to sound like *them!*"

Roni held up her fingers, peering at him, as if supporting a monocle on a stick. "What evah do you mean, young sir?"

They were all laughing now, glad to be away from all that wealth and work. The drinks replenished, Dan looked at them both and raised an eyebrow. "I guess this means that we still have a lot to do to solve this case."

Roni, still aching, chimed in, "If we even have a case."

Sean agreed. "Yeah. Just what is our situation here?"

Dan pretended to be the father, explaining to the kids why they couldn't, just yet, go out for ice cream. "I realize it doesn't look promising at this point. There're two unsolved robberies, one with bodily injuries, and as yet unspecified number of hotel thefts, most of which have not been reported. I'm hoping that someone will talk, or something will happen that will give us a better shot at this thing. Maybe the perp will confess to Roni, and we'll be done."

Sean was not discouraged. He'd met the love of his life. Shannon had not yet been notified of the change in her future plans, but Sean had promised her another interview and, as the hopeless romantic of the police force, he had begun his latest fantasy trip. "I should be finished with my first group of workers tomorrow. Then we can start checking the personnel files."

Dan was surprised at this new enthusiasm, as he was expecting his partner to request a transfer to another crime scene.

"Wait a minute! Yesterday, you said this was all a huge waste of time." Then, more suspiciously, "So what happened? Come on. Out with it."

Sean was not about to give up his incentive, not until she gave him a nod, so he pretended to be the consummate cop. "I'm just hoping some of the grunt work pays off. Maybe a second interview, or one of those folders will give us a break."

Roni was less positive. "All I know is that I'm exhausted. And some of those women are over forty!"

Dan tried to be sympathetic. "We know this is hardest on you. If somehow we could change places we would, but Sean and I have been compromised by the other investigation in the hotel."

Sean was less magnanimous. "Not me! Could you see me in a maid's uniform?"

"Why yes, Sean," Roni needed more relief. "If we got you a wig, and let out some seams, you could pass. A blonde, Irish immigrant among all us Hispanics. This time, though, *you* get to push the cart from behind!"

Just the idea made Sean shiver with disgust. "Don't even joke about something that terrible!"

Roni laughed. "Nothing scares guys more than sexual vulnerability and manual labor."

They all laughed and relaxed a bit more.

Chapter XXVIII

The rest of the week flew by for the concierge, the hotel full, people paying a thousand dollars a day and determined to get their money's worth. On Friday, Richard allowed himself a little moment of worry. He saw other staff going and returning from questioning. When that activity stopped he wondered out loud to Barry if the cops were finished. Stan Merrick overheard the conversation and jumped in, eager to show them that he was privy to a greater amount of information.

"Sir George told us that they were gonna start reviewing personnel files, starting next week. It may have already begun."

Richard felt a cold sweat starting. Shannon had told him that she had been interviewed, but it had gone well. She was not as anxious because the policeman had been very polite and considerate. Richard was not impressed. "Yeah," he thought, "I bet he was *very* polite, but only after he had retrieved his teeth from the floor after seeing you, Shannon, for the first time! Who wouldn't be mesmerized?"

He was happy it was the weekend. Richard needed time to plan and unwind. The police presence could mandate he ratchet his plan and exit time frame. If there was a tightening noose, Richard needed to feel more pressure before he made the next move. In the meantime, they were going to gather at Pincher's Crab Shack in Tin City. Barry and Susan were packed for the weekend. Richard saw them combining luggage in Barry's car, stealing a quick kiss before everyone

245

came out of the Spa. Shannon came to his vehicle. She was going to leave hers, returning with Richard only at a time when she was capable of driving safely.

Susan and Barry got there first. She had given the bartender John Friday's birthday cake, planning to surprise him at the end of his first set with a cacophony of serenading from the table of Hotel Sherill employees and their hangers-on.

The big man with the guitar was a little surprised at the size of the early bird crowd. He looked out at the gathering as he adjusted the microphone, saying, "I'd like to think all you folks are here to listen to me play and sing. It might be a tribute to the musical sophistication of this fancy town. But it's hard for me to be certain. I saw a sign out front that said it was 'two for one night' between five and seven, and there was something about pitchers of Bud Light for three dollars? And there's a big picture of a giant frozen Margarita that's the featured drink here tonight. If a troubadour was paranoid, or had low self-esteem, he might assume you all were here, after a hard week, to get loaded on the cheap! But I have a higher opinion of your appreciation for good guitar work, so here goes," and he began his first selection among a chorus of good-natured laughter and the clinking of glasses.

They ate nachos and chicken wings and drank beer, Richard preferring Heineken over Bud Light, most of the others chugging from the inexpensive pitchers. The girls started dancing almost immediately, weaving to the music, showing off their Spa bodies, laughing at nothing except the inevitability of attracting the bravest of the salivating males at the bar. Soon their table was overflowing with the new lust-interests, and Richard started to feel cramped. It was hard to hear, people shouting over the music, not helpful to the performer who was thinking that he just might as well end the first set and let the crowd settle down a little.

As he turned on his stool to reach for a waiting beer, Susan emerged from the bar with a birthday cake. She handed the surprised singer his goody and took the microphone and announced, "Today is John Friday's birthday! We just wanted him to know that we love him and his music." There was loud applause and yelling. Susan held up her hand for relative quiet. "We want you to know that the people at the Hotel Sherill are your biggest fans! I can't tell you how old John is, but if you could add twenty and twenty together, you'd be close." Susan then gave him a big wet kiss.

The singer put the cake down on the top of one of the speakers and, looking around the room, picked up his guitar. "Wow! I guess we have time for one more song before the break. I want to thank you all for the cake, which my kids will love destroying. And I want to show my appreciation to the Hotel Sherill for their support. You know, I've never had the pleasure to sleep there because I don't make enough money *here* to even park my *car* there! But, this would be a good time to draw your attention to the tip glass over yonder on that other speaker. If that receptacle ever gets full, maybe I *could* afford to spend a night at that special place on Gulfshore Boulevard!" Then he led them all in a rousing chorus of Happy-Birthday-To-Me, and took his first time out.

By that time, Richard was ready to go. Shannon? Not so much. She liked the attention she received when Richard let her go out on the dance floor alone. And there was that safety net, a big boyfriend to protect her if someone got the wrong idea. Without Richard, Shannon wouldn't have paraded her wonderful body in front of anybody. As it was, she couldn't walk alone by a construction area without having to withstand the most primitive of overtures, promising her endless nights of sexual bliss under somebody's dirty coveralls. Richard didn't mind Shannon dancing with others and the lift she obviously got from all the males. He knew, however, that the drunker they got, the uglier this could become. Drunk guys were more likely to think that, with a well-placed punch, somehow Shannon would be theirs for the drive home, wherever that might be. He whispered in her ear that he thought it was time to go.

When he gave her the option of staying without him if she wanted, Shannon grabbed her sweater and jumped to her feet. There was a loud groan from the single men. "Shannon, don't goooo!" She turned to look back over a pretty shoulder and waved at them. Shannon was just a little drunk, high enough to flirt, with her boyfriend close enough to bail her out of any jam she had inadvertently created.

They rode in silence. He was thinking about his eventual departure, and how to make that happen in its most productive form. She listened to the radio, letting the warm wind blow her short hair, and deeply wanting to make love to her dark and silent friend.

Shannon put her hand on the inside of his right leg. He looked over at her beautiful face, eyes closed, lips parted, just the hint of a smile. She came to at the sound of her driveway gravel under his sports car's wheels. He was quiet as she searched her purse for the front door keys. There was no talk. Shannon let him lead her to the bedroom. She lay down on the bed and he began to remove her clothes, starting with her skirt and panties. Shannon lifted up on her elbows, removing her blouse and bra, before flopping back on the coverlet. He watched her until her eyes opened. She saw him take off his shirt and pants and pull back the bedspread. She hiked up farther on the bed to give him room to come to her. Shannon put her hands behind her head, giving him permission to do what he wanted. He started with her eyes and neck, moving down to her nipples, and continuing until she was grabbing at his shoulders, begging for him to come back and be inside her, so she could please finish.

When Shannon awoke it was dark. The clock radio said one AM. Her mouth felt fuzzy from the margaritas and beer, and there was that headache. A shower, toothpaste, and two aspirins and she fell asleep again, not to reawaken until the morning light shone through at seven.

Before her shift, Alicia Hernandez had time to go to the post office. She had a small envelope addressed to her sister in Mexico City. When the clerk asked her if she wanted to insure the package, she responded: "No, thank you. It's not worth nothin'." Then, he drove back to the Cocohatchee River bridge. Going over the water, Alicia had the purse in one hand, planning a long throw, but there was a bicycle coming toward her, and she tossed the object awkwardly, seeing the purse hit the guardrail, and thankfully fall over the other side. She was just able to avoid the bike rider and a car in the other lane. Unable to look back, the maid would have been very surprised to see the Manatee Cove tour boat emerge from under the bridge on its first run to the Gulf. The captain had seen the purse bounce off his steering station. He pointed to one of the mates to pick it up. "Give me that, Jorge. I can't reach it and steer." The mate handed the purse over and the captain put it on a tray by his hand-held radio. "What d'ya think, Jorge?"
The young crew member had a quick response. "Stolen property, boss. Anything in it?" The captain pressed his belly into the wheel and opened the purse. "Nothing but a parking slip." Looking more closely he could read that it was a valet chit from the Hotel Sherill.

Chapter XXIX

Shannon waited all day Saturday for Richard to call. She'd heard nothing since their date last night and she had a strange feeling in her gut, a not very good feeling. When there were no contacts by six o'clock, the self-recriminations began. "He doesn't really like me. I'm not smart enough for him." By seven, she was beginning to drown her anxieties with vodka and orange juice. "I was too easy. He thinks I'm a slut!" Then the paranoid thoughts started: "He's found another girl, and he's out with her!" Shannon resolved to catch Richard in the act. She was crying as she dressed for a big night on the town. The decreasing level of vodka in the bottle accounted for the trouble Shannon was having connecting the straps on her high heels.

"Where would he take her?", she was wondering. She headed for downtown Naples and Fifth Avenue. There were all those Irish bars, and Virginia's. She would try Yeti's first. Sooner or later all the hot dates ended up there.

There was no one she recognized on the outside bar, so Shannon went inside and took an elevated table. The waitress came by. "Dirty Martini." Shannon said, before the server opened her mouth to inquire. That one was gone in a gatorade moment and she ordered another. Shannon tried not to cry. She was thinking about moving to another night spot, when a man sat down in the adjoining seat. "Hey, Beautiful. What's a hot girl like you doin' in a dead spot like this?"

Shannon wanted to say, "Looking for my boyfriend," but that would have required a lengthy explanation and, all of a sudden, she was very tired. The man's next question was more easily answered.

"What are you drinkin'?"

She looked at her almost empty glass: "Dirty Martini."

Dale ordered one for this gorgeous young woman and a Corona for himself. He couldn't believe his luck. "How is this one is unattached?", his mind was asking. She seemed oblivious to the way he was looking at her, staring into her drink. He couldn't tell if she was bored with him or possibly drunk, but those slurred words seemed to indicate the latter. Dale wanted to energize her, get her to notice him.

"What's your name, Hot Stuff?"

Shannon looked at him for the first time. He wasn't ugly, and he seemed clean. Trying to articulate she said, "My name is Shannon, Shannon Scott."

She looked away from him, just as he came back with,

"Dale Aduino. I own a garage in Estero." Shannon checked his nails. Dale had been successful in removing most of the grease associated with his employment. "This place is dead. How would you like to go to Swings?"

Swings was the local dance club of the moment, the only real night club in town, catering to young people, most of the country club set staying away from the place. Shannon had heard the buzz, all about the dramatic lighting and state-of-the-art sound system. There were reports of waiting lines, beefy attendants deciding that only the very attractive could bypass a long wait.

"Maybe I would feel better", she thought, "if I could just get the chance to dance?" And then, "What if Richard and *that* girl are there?" With that scenario in her mind, Shannon said yes to Dale Aduino.

On the five minute ride, Dale tried to carry on a conversation. "Do you live around here? I've never seen you before. Are you new to Naples?" Then he decided to change gears. "This old Chevy is a collector's item. I've seen some of these babies auctioned off for over fifty thousand dollars!"

Shannon had noted the venerable nature of Dale's car, thinking it just beat up, but had been impressed by its acceleration. Nonetheless, she didn't respond because she was busy imagining Richard dancing with someone else at this night club.

Dale opened her door grandly, proud of his smooth chivalry, even if this beautiful girl had a talking problem or rather, a problem of not talking. He had a gift certificate to pay for the twenty dollar cover, not the classiest of moves, but expensive situations called for cheap responses. The dance floor was alive with people, the lights in continuous motion, highlighting couples, moving on to leave them in relative darkness. Shannon swayed to the music on the dance floor. Dale's choice was to join her or leave her alone. No contest. He'd lose her for sure out here at this joint.

She seemed to be in her own world, looking over the crowd for a tall, dark, handsome man to be her knight in shining armor. Dale tried to keep pace. He wasn't a great dancer, but realized that if he didn't stay close to this beauty and create the illusion of being a couple, it would be open season on this pick up date that had now cost him close to thirty (and counting) dollars.

After the music stopped, Dale found them a small table. The servers were on them immediately demanding that they choose a libation. Shannon changed to an expensive Long Island Iced Tea, and Dale got another beer.

With her head on a slow swivel, Shannon was sweeping the dancers for the chance to see her absentee lover. The whole process was making her dizzy. The next time she tried to dance, Shannon tripped and almost fell with Dale catching her before she hit the floor.

"Whoa, girl. Looks like somebody may have had tee many martoonies!" He led her back to a chair. "Maybe we need to get outta here and get some fresh air." That was his way of moving his flirtation toward a real payoff. Shannon let him help her out the front door, past the still waiting, plain ordinary folk. Earlier, they had parted the velvet rope for Shannon - almost stopping Dale - but he had been holding on to her arm so tightly, the bouncers had been unable to separate the unlikely pair.

They headed toward Collier Boulevard. It was then that she saw the signs for Marco Island and wondered if he had a house or a condo there. Shannon put her head back on the seat and closed her eyes. "Maybe Richard went to Marco Island," she thought. "but it's so far. Why would he come all the way out here?"

She felt the change in terrain, the wheels bouncing on the rough limestone road to Rookery Bay. "Where are we going?"

Dale was feeling it. He said to her, "Come closer, darlin'." He breathed a little too heavily. He was getting desperate. "My roommate is shacked up at our place, so we can't go there."

Shannon sat up a little in her seat, as the common nature of the assignation began to hit home. But if Richard was out with some floozy, two could play that game! Car stopped, parking lights on, she let him start to kiss her.

"Maybe" she thought, "he's a good kisser." Dale may have been a lot of things, among them one of the faster employees at Bonita Grease and Tire, but a good kisser he was not! She tasted so good and those smells from her hair! Dale was in heaven, or close enough to put his hand on Shannon's crotch.

That was her wake up call, the alarm button that required serious attention. "Oh my gosh. I've got to get home!"

"Whoa, wait! We just got here." Dale's entire plan was beginning to go up in smoke. She was sitting up straight now, moving to the passenger door. He almost fell over into the warm space she had so wonderfully occupied. "Wait, wait, I'm sorry. Can we start over?"

Now Shannon had become the diligent, responsible one, and still capable of sounding adult. "I forgot. I have the first shift at the hotel tomorrow morning.." Now more loudly:

"I have to get enough sleep. If I'm not alert, they will *fire* me! Take me home *now!* Please!"

He was beaten. The ephemeral fantasy was evaporating like the mist from the dark waters. There was nothing to do but to tear-ass out of there, horsing the big V-8, feeling the rear end break free from the road, hearing the limestone spatter the water behind them. The big car's turning radius was too narrow to accommodate the violent circle, so Dale had to stop or risk going over the bank. Then, the headlights illuminated the floating bodies.

"Oh shit!" was Dale's initial reaction to a situation that required immediate action. "Let's get the flying fuck outta here!"

But Shannon had already punched 911 into her cell phone, not knowing at that point that her evening would be elongated by another three hours of questioning in the damp night air.

Richard had indeed been busy, but not with another woman. The thought of the record searches in personnel had alarmed him. He'd been on the phone all day to Mexico. Unable to get through to his contact, Richard left a series of messages and went out for a quick meal. He'd been gone barely an hour, but his phone was flashing a message. Antonio had promised to get back to him in the next three hours. Richard sat there, the TV on mute, waiting for the call. He'd been afraid to call Shannon back for fear of missing his friend. Finally, at eight, the cell phone rang.

"Antonio, old friend, how are things in San Miguel?"

"Ricardo, everything goes well here. We are looking forward to your visit. When should we expect you?"

Richard leaned back on his couch. "I may be seeing you sooner than we planned. Some developments have taken place that could force me to accelerate my departure from this place." They talked of the police and the investigation at the hotel.

"Should you leave now? What if you are already a suspect?", Antonio wondered.

Richard used his calm voice. "I do not believe there is any hard evidence connecting me to the robberies." He didn't mention the homicides, not wanting to alarm his Hispanic friend. "I wanted you to know that I may have to get rid of my cell phone soon. After that I will be using disposables and you will have to wait for my calls. This could happen at a moment's notice."

"There is much at stake here for you to be captured now," Antonio answered.

Richard tried to sound confident: "Not to worry, my friend. I have avenues of escape that are still free and clear."

They hung up and Richard called Shannon. He let the phone ring and left a message. "Shannon, I'm sorry I didn't call sooner. I was tied up all day with errands and calls. Maybe we can get together tomorrow?"

It was in all the news media on Sunday. The chief pulled everyone out of the hotel until they had progress on the murders. Sir George had understood. The Director of Human Resources told Mr. that his latest laundry maid had an emergency involving a sick mother in Mexico, requiring an indefinite leave of absence. The hotel, he was informed, without setting a precedent, would try and accommodate this employee. It might help with the morale of the Hispanic staff.

Mr. was not impressed. "Who'd she think she was? A white concierge?", he asked himself.

Shannon had fallen into bed at three AM without noticing that she had a message. It was ten before she was able to rouse herself and notice the flashing machine. She almost levitated at the first one, Richard apologetically explaining yesterday's failure to call. "He does care," she thought. "He wasn't out with another girl." She said out loud, "How could I have been so stupid?"

The other calls were from friends that had seen the television reports or had read her name in the Sunday paper. There were two messages from the media, one from Channel Two, and another from the Naples Daily News. Suddenly, Shannon felt claustrophobic. She called Richard. "Did you see the news?", she asked him.

He'd read the brief article and had the TV on for the latest developments. "Yes, I read it. I didn't call because I thought you probably needed your sleep. Who is this Dale character, anyway?"

Shannon started to cry. "Can you come and pick me up? I'll tell you everything then. I think there's a reporter in a car across the street."

Richard was thinking quickly. He'd been surprised at the location of the bodies. The paper had speculated that the recent storm may have moved the deceased from their original placement. "You've got that right!", Richard had mumbled when he reached that part of the article.

He gave Shannon some instructions. "Sneak out the back and walk through the yards until you get to the Sunshine Plaza. I'll pick you up at the ice cream place behind the bank."

Shannon finished getting dressed, packed a small bag with a bathing suit, towel, and a bottle of water. She opened the bedroom window, and pushed up the screen. Tossing her bag, she slid on her tummy, backward to the rear of her property, cut through a quiet side yard and to a back street to the nearest shopping area.

Richard was there when Shannon approached the ice cream stand. He motioned her to stay away and walked to the counter and ordered two cones. Then he went over to her and his car, which he had parked half way between the bank and the hardware store, the biggest store in the plaza. She got in, licking her strawberry ice cream. Richard leaned over and kissed some of the sweet stuff from her lips.

"Stay down," he cautioned. "Wait until we're out on the beach road, heading away from Bonita." Shannon did as she was told, the top of her head barely visible as they drove toward Fort Myers Beach. Richard stopped at Lovers Key State Park and paid the entrance fee. He decided not to take the beach shuttle but to stick to the walking trails so they could have their private conversation. She finally got the chance to hug him then, and they held hands as they went between the mangroves on the shell path.

"Were you scared?", he asked her.

Shannon shook her head. "I was more afraid of the cracker," she confessed. "And I was cold. I'm sorry I doubted you. I was really looking for you, and this guy was gonna help me, but actually, I don't think that was his idea. He just wanted to get in my pants, and in that old car, on a back road." She shivered at the thought of how she had put herself in danger, saying quietly, "And I was a little drunk."

Richard guessed more than a little, but no harm done. "What'd the police say?"

"They just questioned us. Why we were there? How long had we been there? Where did we work?"

"What'd you tell 'em?"

"I said I worked at the Hotel Sherill, in the Spa. There was a big cop. I think he was one of the police that came to the hotel after the robberies. The officer that came to the Spa was not there last night."

Richard was certain that Shannon was right. The question for the concierge was whether there was anything or anyone that could connect the different crimes. He was hoping that the evidence he'd collected from the apartment was all that was required to cleanse the scene of motive and relationship.

"Maybe you need a lawyer," he suggested.

Shannon was shocked. "A lawyer? Me? What for? I didn't do anything."

He tried to be patient and spell it out, as the thoughts came to him. "All the media are gonna try and make a circus outta this. Robberies and now murders. There's no connection, but you're a beautiful young woman who just happens to work at the very same place where the robbery victims are guests. If I was a reporter, I'd wanna interview you and have your picture, just to keep the story going. It's money in their pockets, and they don't care if they have to violate your privacy to do it."

She asked, "What would a lawyer do?"

He wanted to do damage control. "Lawyers protect you. They can dictate when reporters can talk to you and where that talk takes place. Otherwise, it's open season on you. At any time, those guys can crawl through your window, notebook and recorder in hand to ask you questions."

Now, Shannon was frightened. "What can I do?"

Richard had a few ideas. "I think you should move until this blows over. Do you have any friends that would keep you out of sight?"

Shannon shook her head. "No."

"Maybe you could stay with Susan. I could call her if you want."

Shannon nodded and quietly answered, "Okay."

"We could shield you as you get to and leave work, a disguise, a hood, a different car. Once inside the Spa, our security can keep the media away. There are ways to help you, and it's in the hotel's best interests to keep you out of the spotlight, because that keeps them safer from criticism."

Richard could see this as a project or a game for the close knit staffs from the Spa and the Hotel's front end. But it would get old quickly, and all it would take was one publicity driven employee to anonymously spill the beans to a hungry scribe or tabloid, and his identity would be toast. At best, he might be able to buy a few more days, and he needed forensic confusion and police ineptitude to help.

They stopped and sat on a park bench. Shannon could see egrets dipping for minnows in the ebbing tide from the saltwater ponds. Osprey and buzzards wheeled high above and the pelicans skimmed the surface of the placid waters. It could have been the most beautiful of sub-tropical afternoons. But they were under the gun. Shannon couldn't believe how helpful Richard had decided to be.

"Maybe I'll be able to get through this without a nervous breakdown?", she wondered.

Her lover, she didn't guess, was just trying to cover his own ass. Shannon had become his inadvertent Achilles heel. She was supposed to be a buffer against suspicion, and now their relationship could link him to all the crimes. He had to keep her out of the public eye at all costs.

He called Susan on her cell, apologized for the intrusion on her weekend with Barry, and explained the plan. "We'll all share in the responsibility of keeping Shannon safe. You'll get some good stuff out of this, too, because I'll make sure the powers that be know what you're doing and how you're helping. It won't hurt Barry, either, by the way."

Richard pointed out the benefits to the hotel, and indirectly to her career as a service professional in the most prestigious hotel in Southwest Florida. He reiterated that he would make sure there were accolades placed in her personnel file, and that everyone would be eternally in her debt. That was enough to convince Susan.

Then he called Stan Merrick, intimating that Susan had helped formulate a solution to the bad publicity the murders could generate. Richard said, "The gratitude you'll get from Sir George and the rest of the bigwigs won't look too bad in your file, either."

By the end of that conversation, Stan was in total agreement - with dreams of rapid promotions and an office on the fifteenth floor. The "plan" would become Mr. Merrick's *own* next big idea.

Richard went to a department store in Bonita. Shannon had written down her size and minimum clothing needs, enough for three days, plus toiletries. He took the list and was out in thirty minutes with the gear Shannon required so she wouldn't have to go home. The Spa supplied her uniforms, so the young girl's wardrobe was minimal.

Susan greeted them with hugs all around. She and Barry had just returned from Keewaydin Island, their suitcases still in the trunk.

Richard let the women commiserate and took Barry aside. "The hotel is in a pile of shit here, and there may not be enough shovels."

Barry was eager to be a team player on this. "Susan and I already talked about this mess. What d'ya think we have to do?"

"I've called Merrick, and he wants to help. He thinks anything we can do to keep the media from body slamming the hotel will be appreciated by the big boys upstairs."

Barry's eyes grew big with the wonder of all the publicity. "Will we actually be able to keep them away from Shannon? She doesn't exactly fade into the woodwork very well."

"I know, but I think it's possible. Maybe for a few days, anyway. We really have to be careful who knows what, but the rest of the Spa women will have to be in on it, or any one of them could spill the beans. And we'll have to tell the other concierges, emphasizing the costs to the hotel and our reputations." Richard was thinking that one way to halt the carnage was to turn himself in or run, both of which would stop the bleeding for Shannon and the Sherill. He was *not*, however, of the suicidal persuasion, so he'd have to choose from other alternatives.

Barry was still wonderstruck. "What were the chances that Shannon would be the one to discover these bodies? What was she doing out there in the middle of the night?"

Richard wanted to stick to the remediation, not the disease. "She was looking for me. I didn't call her, and she panicked. It's partially my fault, and I can't let her be fed to the wolves. It could have been any one of us. We may not be as beautiful as she is, but our hotel connections would still have provoked a lot of curiosity. And everyone would love to knock off a snooty hotel for the very rich."

They went back to the ladies, who had both been crying. Susan hugged Richard and quietly said, "Thanks for looking out for her. I'll do all I can to help."

Richard wanted to focus that generosity. "What you can do, besides hiding Shannon, is make sure your girls at work are all on the same page. They have to know that this is priority number one for the hotel, and that failure to protect the Spa could jeopardize their jobs. So this is a God and Country thing, us against the bad media hounds out to get the Hotel Sherill and bring it tumbling down."

Susan got the drift. "I'll call them all tonight and tell them there will be a meeting fifteen minutes before the start of the shift tomorrow morning."

Richard added, "And please tell them not to respond to reporters' calls before they hear your presentation."

Barry wanted to know, "What about us?"

Richard had already delegated this department. "Mr. Merrick will meet with the concierges and review the need to keep our mouths shut. He knows that if he can help hold this together, there may be some larger bonuses in his future. Is there a back door in the Spa building?"

Susan responded quickly to Richard's question. "We take deliveries for large equipment through a rear entrance. It's at the end of a small driveway off the employee parking lot." She could see where he was going with this. "We could have Shannon 'delivered' in a mini-van or panel truck. She could come in wrapped on a settee, or in a packing box."

Richard liked that Susan was warming to the task. "See if you can set that up tomorrow. In the meantime, dress her as a building maintenance worker until she gets inside that back door. She can take the elevator straight to her massage station. She's tall and can get away with a few extra layers of clothes."

He grabbed Shannon, working the angle that this was a giant game of tag, fun for the whole family. "D'ya think you could pass as the massage table mechanic?"

She managed a feeble grin, her mind spinning at the rapid fire machinations her friends were in the process of creating to protect her. "I don't know. I hope so. Susan, you are wonderful to help me hide. We hope it's just for a few days, right Richard?"

"Yeah, right. Just a few days until something else stupid happens, like another labor strike in Immokalee, or a hundred car pile-up on Alligator Alley! Then we can all get back to normal at the plain old boring Hotel Sherill!"

It was getting late. Shannon didn't want Richard to go. How could he love her after all she was putting him through? She excused herself, took a shower and put on her new nightie. Richard was still talking to Susan and Barry near the front door.

"Do you have to go?" she pleaded.

Susan grinned. "We could have a slumber party. We have enough room!"

Richard was the voice of reason. "You kids have a good time, but I am BEAT! Somebody has to be alert tomorrow morning, and something tells me that Shannon would keep me awake. For a very long time."

Shannon still protested, "Nooooo, I'd let you sleep! Stay. Please, stay."

He held her and kissed the top of her head. "It's me, Shannon. I wouldn't let me sleep. Besides, you had a rough time last night and need more rest than I do."

He looked over her to Barry and Susan. "9-1-1 tomorrow, friends. Let's all be the best we can be. And if you think Shannon could use help sleeping, do you have anything for that, Susan?"

Nodding her head, Susan showed Richard the door.

Richard had taken over. His defense would be the same as the hotel's. They would all help to keep the authorities at bay. He drove home very carefully. There would be no traffic violations this night.

Chapter XXX

"When are you going to visit Mrs. Gonzales?" Dan wanted to know.

Roni pretended not to hear. He hadn't been grateful enough. In a pseudo Spanish dialect she answered: "What Sen~or , ees eet you whant me to do?"

"Are you going to do the visit today, or not?"

Roni was straight now. Neither one of them was in any mood to be teasing. "I'm going this afternoon. When are you going to toss the residence?"

Dan was serious, too. "We'll do it today. If we finish by four, do you think we can meet and combine the visits?"

Roni rechecked her timetable. "That's okay with me. Back at the office by four-thirty?"

Dan gave her a big kiss. "See you then, beautiful!" Roni staggered backward as if overwhelmed by the caress.

"Only if I get out of the hospital by then, big guy!"

The cops drove slowly down Old 41, looking for the apartment complex. "It's the first one past the storage units." Sean gave the directions while Dan drove. They pulled in and did a perimeter of the facility before parking near the "office" sign. Dan had the warrant.

The superintendent was not surprised, but still curious. "What's this all about, officers?"

Dan gave him the minimum. "This is part of an ongoing investigation. We're looking for Louis Gonzales and someone named Jack Burdine. Do they live here?"

The apartment manager didn't have to look at his book. "Louis Gonzales rents 402. We think his roommate's name is Jack, but his name isn't on the lease."

"When was the last time you saw these gentlemen?", Sean asked, letting the man know that he was also going to be involved in the questioning..

"Nobody's seen them since Monday, last week. And the rent is back due." And he had more information. "Their car and boat trailer are here, but nobody's seen the car be moved."

Dan decided to start there. "Show us."

They walked to the rear of the property. There were a number of trailers, boats, and other recreational vehicles. The man pointed and said, "That's their car and trailer."

Dan took a chance: "Do you have a key for the vehicle?"

"Only the owner has his key, but if they don't pay, we have their stuff towed to a commercial lot, and they charge daily."

Sean asked, "When would you tow this car and trailer?"

The manager was firm. "Two months and we tow, plus we take the deposit. Then we clean and lease again."

Dan didn't want to lose the superintendent. "We'll need to get into 402."

The man merely shrugged, letting the police know how little he cared. "I'll open it now. Lemme know when you're done."

Sean and Dan checked the car and boat trailer. They looked through the windows. There was nothing visible inside the locked car. Everything smelled liked fish.

"Pheew, what a stink." Sean was checking the trailer. "If this smells bad, can you imagine what the boat is like?"

Dan had no trouble with the connection. "A convicted Californian snatch-and-grabber and a habitual juvenile offender, smelling like fish. Is this some kind of a weird coincidence? Somehow, I doubt it."

Sean nodded his head. "Yeah, but you know it's circumstantial. We still need some hard evidence."

Dan was done with the parking lot inspection. "Maybe we'll find something up on the second floor. Then we can get a release to break into their car."

Upstairs, the rooms were a mess. Sean acknowledged the confusion. "Either these guys were slobs, or somebody else has been through this place." The closet doors were open, as were the bureau drawers. Even the bathroom cabinets had been emptied.

Dan wanted fingerprints, but was not optimistic. "We'll print everything, but I'm guessing the perp wore gloves like ours." They went from room to room, duplicating Richard's route. "Let's hope he was in a hurry and missed something."

They opened all the drapes and the windows, flooding the interior with light rarely seen there. It was difficult to discern which room belonged to whom. They saw that both beds had been checked, the mattresses not squared to the frames. Dan flipped Louis' bed and they examined the underside. In one corner there was a tear secured with tape, a clear sticky adhesive that would have been hard to see in the dark.

Dan pulled the opening wider and reached in. "I think our boy might have missed something," he said as he lifted an expensive looking watch. They checked the object closely. Neither man had seen one like it before. "Patek Phillipe. Does that name ring a bell?"

Sean whistled, as Dan held it to the light. What they were seeing was a twenty-four caret time piece with diamond hour markers and a hidden clasp, worth between thirty-five to forty-thousand dollars. There was an inscription on the back identifying the owner and the significance of the gift.

"This has to be on the loss inventory from the hotel robberies." Dan was getting excited. "Let's call the crime scene techs and they can dust this watch too, as well as the car and trailer." He wanted to share the find with Roni, and bring Chief Kelly up to speed. It was a good beginning, at long last.

Corporal Menendez was driving slowly down Dean Street, looking for the correct street. She liked this section, highlighted by a pretty elementary school covered in Mexican tile. There were live oaks with Spanish moss hanging delicately down as well as cabbage palms and purple bougainvillea shading the playground. The houses were small but the yards showed community pride.

"I know it's not far from the school," Roni remembered before slowing in front of a cement block ranch house with bright yellow paint. She parked the police car and walked the red pavers to the front door.

The door bell hung by a wire, so Roni knocked. She could hear children laughing from the back yard. A small woman answered the door. Her hair was tied back and she was holding a broom. "Yes, can I help you?"

"My name is Corporal Menendez. I'm with the police department. We met before, some time ago. I have some bad news concerning your son, Louis."

The woman, put her hands to her mouth and took a step back. Roni thought that she might fall. "Is he hurt?"

That question was uttered as a desperate hope that the information would not be worse, but the officer was guessing this mother had long expected such a visit. "May I come in, please?"

"Oh, yes. I'm sorry. Come in." The mother was still covering her mouth and backing away, as if her retreat could somehow postpone the inevitable. "What about Louis, Miss?"

Roni gestured to a couch. "Please sit down and I will explain."

The older woman reached back for the cushion, never taking her eyes from the policewoman's face.

"I am sorry to be the person to tell you, but I am afraid that your son is dead."

The older woman still sought a way out: "How... are you sure? Please, could there be some mistake?" Anything, anything to repudiate the claim.

"It is unfortunate, but there is no mistake. We verified his identity through fingerprints and dental records. He was the victim of a homicide." The corporal was speaking quietly.

"What happened? Was it a drive-by?", Mrs. Gonzales asked.

"No, it was not a drive-by. We still don't know what happened. He was shot along with another man who also died. His name was Jack Burdine. Did Louis ever speak of him?"

The mother was crying silently now, shaking her head. Roni wasn't sure if she was saying no to the question, rejecting the bad news, or acknowledging the fruition of all her fears. After a few moments of gathering herself, Mrs. Gonzales began a litany she had rehearsed and shared with others.

"I have not seen Louis since before last summer. He stayed away from us. I know he had a place on Old 41, and there was another man, but I never met him. One time, Louis told me his friend was from California, but that is all I know. My son was always running from something. He was in jail many times. Sometimes, after jail, he would come home, but only for a short time, then he would go, and we would hear that he was back in jail. The only time Louis was happy was when he went fishing." She smiled now, remembering the few good times her son experienced. "He had a little boat and he would fish for hours. It did not matter if it rained. He would still go."

Roni thought of the robberies and wondered what Sean and her fiancé had discovered. "Would you like to see the body? I could take you to him."

The mother's shoulders drooped again, as she was brought back to reality. "Yes. I would like to see my son one more time, please."

"I must tell you that he was shot a number of times, Mrs. Gonzales. And you should know that he had been in salt water for quite a while."

"Thank you for telling me, but it is important that I say goodbye. And that I am able to tell his brothers and sister what happened. Maybe this story will keep them from trouble. Do you have any idea who did this to him?"

"We hope that someone will talk to us, but right now we don't know who did this, or why. Is there a time soon when I could take you to the morgue?"

"Tomorrow the children will be in school. Could we go at ten?"

"That would be fine. I will pick you up and we can go have coffee. Is there anything else I can do for you now?"

The mother reached out and touched Roni's arm. "Thank you for your kindness today. I am going to call my sister. She will come over."

There was nothing the officer could do except pat the woman on the shoulder and let herself out to the bright sunshine. The rest of the neighborhood was proceeding as if there were no clouds over 142 Dorau Street.

The Manatee Cove tour boat driver walked up to the concierge desk. He was not as presentable as the other patrons, but Marta greeted him as a guest.

"May I be of service, Sir?", she inquired.

The captain responded. "I hope so. I think someone from here may have lost this. I run the Manatee Cove tour service. This morning it was tossed over the bridge guardrail and landed on my boat." He held up the jeweled evening purse for Marta to see. "I found one of your hotel's valet receipts in it, stuck in the bottom. It looked like a part of the purse."

Marta was excited. "That could belong to Mrs. Esposito, one of our guests. She reported a purse lost or stolen two weeks ago. Thank you for returning it. Could I have your name and number? There might be a reward."

"Naw, I don't need no reward. Just glad to get it back to the rightful owner," the boatman answered.

Marta insisted. "If this was stolen, the police may need to talk with you."

The older man was backing away now. "Like I said, not necessary. Just happy to help." He was sorry now that he hadn't just flipped it in the garbage.

Marta tried again to get him to stop. "Please, wait, Sir. Mr. Merrick might like to speak with you. Could you wait for a very few minutes?"

"Lady, I gotta GO! My next trip is in twenny minutes, and I gotta gas up first."

He turned on his heel and walked out more quickly than he had entered. Marta looked around. Richard was on break, and Barry was showing someone how to get to the Spa. She dialed her boss.

"Mr. Merrick, this is Marta. A man was just here returning a lost purse. I tried to get him to stay and talk with you but he just ran out, saying he was late for his job. I think it belongs to Mrs. Esposito, the one she said was stolen."

Stan Merrick was glad to come out, if only to smell Marta's hair. This might be connected to the robberies, a chance to shine in front of the bosses. She showed him the purse and he examined it against the written description on the loss sheet.

"Marta, you're absolutely right. This *is* the missing item. Where'd you say the man found it?"

"He's a tour boat captain for Manatee Cove. He said someone threw it over the bridge guard rail and it landed on his boat as they were coming through on the Cocohatchee River.

"Did he leave his name?" the manager wanted to know.

Marta was apologetic. "He wouldn't say. And, he didn't want any reward. Don't worry, though. He should be easy to find."

Mr. Merrick rubbed his hands together. "Good work, Marta. Sir George will be happy to hear this bit of news. We'll leave it to him if he wants the police called." Stan went back to his office and called the executive suite, waiting for the assistant to patch him through to Sir George.

"Yes, Merrick? What is this about some of our stolen property?", the master asked.

Merrick repeated Marta's story and said the purse matched the description on their stolen goods sheet.

"Good work, Merrick. Bring the purse to me. I'll return it to Mrs. Esposito and try to continue the damage control. You can detail the other concierges, but tell them to keep that info to themselves. And I'll take care of calling the police."

Soon the three cops were sitting in the conference room. Sean had his tired feet on a chair. They were all drinking seltzers from the machine.

Dan handed the watch to Roni and asked, "Ever see something like that? We found it in a hiding place under one of their mattresses."

She held it up to the light coming through the window, admiring the sparkle from the tiny diamonds. "Nope. I've never seen a watch this expensive." Roni then frowned in mock thought. "I think this *could* be worth even more than my engagement ring! And I thought I would *never* see anything that was worth *that* much!"

He ripped it back from her. "Gimme that ring!" She covered her hand and turned away from him.

"No, it's mine, buddy. You can't have it!" Dan was wrestling with her when the chief knocked on the door and entered the room. That brought them all back to attention.

"What do you have there? Is it part of the stolen goods from the hotel?", Chief Kelly asked.

This surprised Dan. "How'd you guess that?"

The chief chuckled. "Not so hard. You *are* working on the robberies and the homicides. Any connection?"

Then Dan filled him in on what they'd discovered. "We found the car and trailer, but no boat. There was a fish stink on everything in the apartment."

The chief sorted through their report. "You say someone got there first, looking for something?"

Dan nodded. "Yeah. Whoever it was, tossed it good. Went through all the drawers and closets. But he missed that one corner of the mattress. That light tape happened to match the fabric color. Pretty hard to see it in the dark."

The boss took a little time to collect his thoughts before adding his new information. "Okay, here's another piece. Sir George just called me. Somebody threw one of the missing purses over the Cocohatchee Bridge and it landed on a tour boat. The captain brought it back to the Hotel Sherill because of a valet chit and they identified it as belonging to one of the robbery victims."

Dan started to interrupt, but the chief wanted to finish. "But get this. The lady reported the purse stolen from her room, *not* during the heist."

Now they were all talking at once. Chief Kelly held up his hand. "One at a time, please! Dan, you were first."

"This happened today?", he asked.

The boss nodded. "The guy came in around eleven-thirty."

"Can we find him?"

"We know where he works. He may be the only Manatee Cove tour captain. If not, we can still find him."

Roni wanted to know, "How'd he know it was from the Sherill?"

"There was a valet slip, folded over and pressed into the bottom seam. I guess it looked like it was part of the purse. Hard to see." The chief was keeping nothing from these three.

Sean had his two cents. "We have two articles. One's a confirmed loss and the other's a probable. What now?"

The chief was encouraged. "This could be our break! Do you see it?"

Dan, too, was feeling better. "The fish smell, a stolen watch, a tossed residence, two dead men, and now a returned purse. Motive, anyone?"

Roni started. "My guy from Bonita? Small potatoes until now."

Dan continued. "My perp from California, a career snatch-and-grabber. Was he out of his league?"

Sean needed to say something brilliant, he thought. "We're missing a ring leader, the mastermind, if this was really a conspiracy starting at the hotel."

The chief liked what he was hearing. "We thought the killings were unrelated, that we'd have to abandon the robberies and concentrate on the homicides. We have to be careful. This guy could bolt. Dan, have you called that cop from California?"

"I'll do it this afternoon." Dan was thinking of a certain concierge who said he used to work on the west coast. "We need to go over some personnel files, tighten the noose that way. Roni, anything from Mrs. Gonzales?"

She shook her head. "Nothing really substantial. She confirmed the fishing hobby and that he had a roommate named Jack. And lived off Old 41, so those facts fit what we now know."

Chief Kelly was serious. "We're closer than we were. I'll call Sir George and tell him Roni's coming back from her emergency leave. He'll clear the way for that to happen."

Roni jumped in. "I promised Mrs. Gonzales that I'd take her to the morgue to view the body for the last time."

"All right. Go back to the hotel the next day. Dan and Sean, you continue to review records and talk to anyone you think may be able to give us more than in your first interviews. Let's wait to return that watch. If the ring leader is a hotel employee, we don't want him to know that he left a loose end. You two will tell me what the crime scene team comes up with from the apartment, car, and that watch, too. That's all for me. Let's all meet again at the end of the day tomorrow, six o'clock here."

"Sergeant Avila, this is Detective Dan Logan from Naples, Florida, calling you back on our deceased, Jack Burdine. What's it like out there?"

The officer sounded tired. "Cold winds off the Pacific. We don't think it will ever warm up around here. How 'bout you?"

Dan was apologetic. "You don't wanna know. Eighty-seven yesterday, eighty-nine today. The hot spot in the nation."

"You're right. I don't wanna know. Sometimes, sunny California is cloudy and cold California, not much to dreamin' about. How're you doin' on your investigation?"

Dan didn't want to give away too much information. "We haven't found much so far. Someone tossed their residence and took most of the clues. What could you tell us about our victim?"

The California cop snorted, "That's the first and last chance anybody will ever call Jack a victim. Most of the time he was victimizing other folks, taking their valuables, scaring them to hell and back, plus, just to make him a sweeter guy, he hurt a few that tried to fight back. We had some missing pieces, questions to ask, and then he left town."

"Like what, Sergeant?", Dan quietly inquired.

The man sounded embarrassed. "Well, there was this little problem with a missing service revolver, a forty-five that was taken from a policeman's car. We think light fingered Jack may have run off with it. So far, we don't have any reports the gun was used in any crimes out here, but if you get any there with that caliber weapon, that would worry us."

"These guys were taken out with a thirty-eight, if that makes you feel better."

"A little, but my partner was on desk duty for nine months and I had to break in a rookie."

Dan was sympathetic. "Old Jack is done scaring people and that pistol could be at the bottom of the Gulf of Mexico, a new hiding place for small fish. Anything else we can do for you?"

The officer switched gears. "We had some jewel robberies that Jack helped us on. He had a friend, acquaintance, buddy, hard to say what they had together, because old Jack, the sweetheart, saved himself some jail time by ratting this guy out. We were able to recover some stolen property and we expected Jack to continue helping us, but he skipped town, along with his probation agreement."

Dan's interest was growing: "Did you catch this other guy? Know anything about him?"

"Nope. He slipped through our fingers. We never knew if Jack tipped him off or what because then Jack was gone, too."

"Do you have a name or a description?" Dan was getting one of those feelings.

"We think the name was a phony, Dick Smathers, something that sounded like that old comedian, and we never got a picture. It was all coming together, and then it fell apart just as quickly. Jack was the key. He gave us a little, but we guessed that he knew more and would have told us, if we'd been able to back him into a corner. All we knew about the jewel thief was that he was young, smart, and had some priors. We needed fingerprints, and a lineup, and we thought we had this guy, but his place was clean. It was as if he knew we were coming."

Dan's mind was whirling. Was this perp here, at the hotel? And if so, which one was he? "Well, Sergeant," he said, "thanks for the information. If we turn up anything on that forty-five, or your jewel thief, I'll give you a courtesy call. And if we strike out, I'll tell you that too."

"I appreciate your time and trouble, Detective. Have fun in your sun."

Roni called Old Doc Weeks and described the situation. "Can we give this poor woman some privacy tomorrow? She hasn't seen her son in over a year, and now he's on a slab."

The Medical Examiner liked Roni. He regularly kicked himself every time he saw her for not being forty years younger, but he was happy for Dan. "I'll make sure we don't have any stiffs out at ten-thirty, and you'll have the room to yourselves. I'll try to clean him up as best as I can."

"Thanks Doc. I owe you."

"Just save me some wedding cake and a kiss."

"You can eat all you want at the reception, but you get the kiss tomorrow," she promised.

Sir George knocked on the VIP suite door. Gloria called out: "Who's there?"

"It's Sir George Sherill, Mrs. Esposito."

She pulled the lush complimentary robe around her newly massaged body and ushered the CEO into their living area.

"Good afternoon, Madam," Sir George said in his best British accent. "It seems that we may have found your lost evening purse," and he presented the object at arm's length, for her perusal. Sir George heard the toilet flush and Mr. Esposito was soon interrupting the ceremony. He, too, was wearing his monogrammed robe and was smoking a very expensive cigar.

"What's going on here?", Tony asked.

Gloria went into her act. "Sir George has found my evening purse." She made an elaborate display of opening the purse and staring into its empty space. And with a rising voice declared, "And there's NOTHING IN IT! Where are the diamond earrings? They were a VERY EXPENSIVE ENGAGEMENT PRESENT FROM MY HUBAND!"

Sir George was questioning the wisdom of returning the item. He had hoped to keep this guest's injured innocence out of the hotel's daily contingency plans.

"Tony, tell the man. How much did you pay for the earrings?", she continued to harangue.

Mr. Esposito was squirming, not wanting his fairly new bride to know how much of a deal the "fell off the truck" jewelry really was. But unrecovered losses could be inflated, he knew. So, he responded grandly, "I don't have the receipts, but my best recollection is that I paid ten, uh, two thousand dollars for them."

Gloria stood up, hands on hips. She was good at catching people by the short hairs and the faint idea that she was quite possibly persona-non-grata among these fancy types just made her even more obnoxious. "Well, Sir George, what do you have to say for yourself?"

He was flabbergasted and flummoxed. Few people had been able to bring him to his knees, but this one knew no fear. "I am certain we can reach an acceptable solution. Our attorneys are coming up with a settlement proposal we will share very soon. Now, if you will excuse me, I must attend a meeting."

As he was backing out the door, the last thing Sir George heard was a now brave husband yell, "And don't forget my five hundred dollars cash!"

Sir George immediately called his "friend", the police chief, Jerry Kelly.

"Hello, Jerry. How are you doing today?" It was an open ended question, encompassing the chief's physical health, psychological well being and the status of the police investigation. The chief stuck to the basics.

"We've got some promising leads. We believe that our recent homicide victims were involved, possibly the robbers themselves."

Sir George needed more specifics. "Do you believe one of our employees is a participant in these events?"

"We haven't ruled out that possibility, Sir George, and, in that vein, Roni Menendez has been freed from the murder investigation and can return undercover the day after tomorrow."

"Thank you, Jerry. I will make certain that she returns without questions or harassment," the hotel owner acknowledged.

The chief had shared as much as was prudent. "We appreciate your cooperation, Sir George." And he hung up.

Chapter XXXI

So far, the 'Hide Shannon' campaign had been a success. The media had been unable to find who was housing her. Some guessed that she was being put up by the hotel and all knew their security was legendary. There were plenty of other stories besides the pretty masseuse, and the reporters were talking to police, forensics, and anyone who knew the deceased. The identification of the victims had sent media types all over Olde Bonita, interviewing the extended family of Louis Gonzales, ex-teachers, and probation officers. Dale Aduino became an instant celebrity. There were reporters parked outside Bonita Grease and Go. They wanted him to tell them all about the beautiful Shannon Scott. His inability to give them significant details about her and their relationship was interpreted as chivalry rather than ignorance. Finally his boss blew up, demanding the news hounds buy tires or get an oil change, otherwise he was going to call the cops or fire Dale, whichever impulse last grabbed him. Scared now, Dale went back to his lube pit.

There was new speculation that the homicide victims had been the parking lot robbers and that the case was nearing a conclusion. Not much was known about the other dead man. Jack Burdine was not a local, they knew, but there were rumors that he was from the West Coast and had a rap sheet. A check of California records by some industrious scribes confirmed the early conjecture and that opened up a whole new direction of inquiry. There were reports then of California gangs, the threats of criminals arriving from other venues, and other provocative pieces.

The biggest shift in town was the reduction of alarm among the wealthy at the Hotel Sherill. The hope was that they were no longer at the same level of previous risk. Now that the hysteria had diminished, as well as the strength of the media blitz, the elite went on about their leisurely business. Without a crisis at the big hotel, there was much less to discuss. Soon the top one percent of the upper class would be as insulated from pain as before the crimes took place. Guests again began to use the concierge desk to plan dinner dates away from the hotel. Yeti's, Virginia's, and even La Rive Gauche began again to get crowded with Sherill referrals. Things were returning to normal among the rich at the area's most exclusive hotel.

Richard felt the drop in pressure. Guests were using him to leave the grounds for fun. The staff had banded together to protect Shannon, enjoying the game of evading the TV stations while helping one of their own. Of course, the ostensible overriding principal was saving the Hotel Sherill from further embarrassment. Their noble employer, who helped them rub shoulders with the uber-rich, allowed them to catch a whiff of what it would be like to be economically emancipated without the hope of ever getting there. That, however, did not in any way minimize the pride felt by the upper level staff, the Spa women, the concierges, and the bell hops. These most visible employees knew how important their performances were in the creation of superlative expectations and the delivery on those promises. This had been the substance of their orientations, and the tips verified their importance in the myth of ambience, providing all guests 'particular pleasures!'

Roni was not quite so inspired as she prepared to return to the depths of the Hotel Sherill. She'd tried to ease Mrs. Gonzales' visit to the morgue, but there was no way to stifle the shock of seeing her eldest son on the cold stainless steel slab. The woman had cried out at the damaged shell that was once her child. It had to be done and Roni knew of no other police officer that would have gone that extra mile. Going back to the laundry was, at the least, a less traumatic use of her time, but hard work is hard work, and ninety degree heat and humidity frizzed her hair.

Katina was glad to have her back, and to be once more not the least and lowest of the laundry maids. Mrs. Marin was eager to let the young team go it alone so she could choose the less rigorous of the maids' jobs, like counting towels. Mr. was still bewildered by the latitude allowed this ignorant new employee. On the positive side, he had, in the past, been able to manipulate these 'just off the boat' staff, threatening them, getting an occasional kickback, and best of all, having sex with them. He would somehow find out if they had relatives with sketchy citizenship credentials, and then say that he would turn them in if they failed to give in to his primitive desires. His ace-in-the-hole, naturally, was the threat of termination. Roni was very attractive, very shy, and very vulnerable. Best of all, she had trouble communicating with people, even in her native tongue. He would humiliate her, he thought, and she would know her place.

The days were getting longer, the outside temperatures rising. Even the Gulf of Mexico had reached eighty degrees, on its way to ninety by June. There was no way the laundry room was going to become comfortable. Roni tried to maintain her focus, listening and watching, but the work was conspiring to diminish her acuity. On break, she wanted to close her eyes and sleep. Her mantra became "How do they do it? How do they do it?"

At lunch, she saw the front end staff clustering around Shannon and the ladies from the Spa. Roni recognized the pretty one from the news stories and their crime reports. There appeared to be plenty of support for this unlikely "witness." She heard Mrs. Marin scoff at the attention Shannon was getting. "If it had been one of us, no one would have wanted to take our picture!"

After lunch, Roni went outside to get some fresh air. She stayed upwind from Katina who was having her last smoke of the work day. Roni saw Dan's cruiser parked outside the administration building. She was a little envious at that moment, wanting so much to be with him and Sean, going over personnel records in air-conditioned comfort.

Sean and Dan had been at it for about two hours. Most of what they had reviewed looked complete enough, no gaps in chronology or questionable recommendations. Sean was antsy. "The chief said we should try and talk to anyone who we thought might be able to give us more answers than the first interviews, right?"

Dan had his head in a folder. "Yeah, right. That's what he said."

Sean grabbed his notebook. "Okay, if you need me, I'll be at the Spa. There are a couple more questions I need to ask." And he was out of the door, before Dan could think of a logical reason for that not to happen.

Sean was happy to be in the hotel's latest facility. The Spa elevator was glass-lined and looked out to a palm filled atrium as he rode to the fourth floor and into the massage wing. There was some kind of eastern music being piped through the speakers, and he could smell something exotic in the cool air.

He was able to locate Susan who found a small room and ushered the most recent hired employee through the door. Sean was as mesmerized by Shannon's beauty as he had been at their first meeting. She was less shy this time, looking directly into his eyes, transfixing him with her blue crystals.

"Thank you for meeting with me again, Miss Scott. There are just a few more questions."

"Certainly, Sergeant. I am happy to cooperate. Anything I can do to help."

Sean felt a surge of desire and affection for this beautiful girl who had just said that she would do anything to please him. He resolved to extend this ecstasy for as long as he could think of questions. He checked his notes. "Miss Scott…" But she interrupted him.

"Please call me Shannon, Sergeant. I feel more comfortable that way."

"Beautiful stranger, I sure don't want make you feel uncomfortable," Sean was thinking, but what he said was, "Certainly, Shannon." He looked down again at the blur on his pages, afraid to stare too much at this vision of loveliness. "You said before that you and the other women here socialize with the hotel's front end staff. Is that a correct summary?"

Shannon lowered her gaze. "Yes, Sergeant."

He waited for a longer explanation but none came. "Do you all talk about the robberies?"

"Yes, we've talked about them. Most of us don't think that they're related to any employees here."

"You said 'most.' Does anyone suspect an in-house person?"

"Some do now, Sergeant," she said quietly.

"Why at this particular time?", using that significant word that he had come to know pretty well by now.

"You know. Because of the murders. Those two men."

"Could you be more specific?", he prodded.

Shannon seemed reluctant to expand on the speculation, but continued, "A few of the girls think that the men were killed because they might have given away the name of a third robber, or a gang."

"What about the concierges? Do any of them suspect a hotel person?", knowing he was zeroing in on a tender spot.

She blushed then. "Well, you know. They're the ones who make the reservations for everything."

Shannon was flustered, but seemed to have no trouble defending her lover. "Richard is just worried about me and the hotel's reputation."

"What do you mean, Shannon?"

"After we found the bodies, he helped me stay away from the reporters."

"How'd he do that?", he asked.

"Well, he called Susan, and she gave me a bedroom, and they get me to work and back so the media can't find me."

"And what was that about being worried about the hotel?" He was on full scale alert, now.

She sat up, proud to explain Richard's dedication. "He takes his job very seriously. Richard is kind of their leader. He certainly wants no bad publicity to hurt the hotel's reputation."

Sean slid one in sideways. "So, if people thought that a concierge was the one planning the robberies, it would hurt the hotel's reputation?"

She didn't catch the question's implication. "That's right, Sergeant. It would *not* be good for the hotel, if people couldn't trust the concierges."

He tried it from another direction. "But if one of the front end staff was involved, how would Richard know? Wouldn't he be in the dark about it?"

Shannon's brow furrowed. "Hmm. I guess you're right. There'd be no way he would know, unless..."

"Unless what, Shannon?" Sean found himself holding his breath. Was she going to give him up?

"Unless the person confessed to Richard, and Richard didn't want to report him to the police. But that's impossible."

"Why would that be impossible?", Sean asked.

She arranged her reply. "Because Richard is too responsible, that's why. He'd never protect someone who was stealing from the hotel. He's too honest. He cares about the hotel so much." She let that answer trail off.

Sean let it drop. He had some ideas that needed consultation. There were several certainties: Richard was a leader of a special group, on top of what happened among the concierges. He appeared conscientious, but he could have been as motivated by self-preservation as by job loyalty. Everything he did could have a double meaning.

Sean wanted to talk to Dan. There was not too much to gain here, except finding out more about this wonderful woman. "Have you been able to get some rest after Saturday night's discovery?"

"Yes, thank you, Sergeant. It's quiet at Susan's house. She makes sure that I get to bed on time."

"What about bad dreams?" Sean was thinking about Shannon at rest, arms akimbo, mouth parted, an erotic fantasy.

"I don't dream too much. We never really got a good look at the bodies. The police put up tape and kept us back. I was just cold and uncomfortable."

"I'm glad to hear you're not having flashbacks," he told her as he slid back his chair. "Thank you again, Shannon. The department wants you to know that we appreciate all your assistance, and we hope we didn't cause you any alarm."

She stood up and took his hand in her strong fingers. He was reluctant to let go, but released her when she began to step back. "No, Sergeant. You've been very kind and sweet."

He watched her go, admiring her white outfit, seeing her ears, tight to her head, under those blonde curls, with that long neck on square, athletic shoulders, and that perfume that wouldn't leave his nostrils... and those blue eyes. She had called him "sweet"! Sean shook himself, rotating his shoulders, getting rid of the stiffness the concentration created. He hoped the spell was broken. There was still so much work to be done.

Sir George felt as well as he had in weeks. The attorneys had presented a compensation package to the Espositos that had finally satisfied them. It included full retail price for the stolen earrings and a check for five hundred dollars. In exchange, the hotel received a written promise absolving the venerable resort from future claims and liabilities. This included a clause demanding that Gloria refrain from further bad-mouthing the facilities that were now providing her VIP accommodations for free. Getting that gag order signed was worth all the inflated damage claims.

Now, Sir George could get back to the job of making money, the old-fashioned hand over fist way. It would start with the annual Diamond Exposition. Every year, the Hotel Sherill hosted the expo, an extravagant end-of-the-season tribute to the fabulously wealthy visitors. Jewelry vendors arrived from all over the country to demonstrate their wares, offering their best gems and taking orders for custom pieces. It was a ten day affair, encompassing two weekends. There were cocktail parties hosted by the largest firms and, the grand finale, a costume ball the last Saturday in March.

Gloria Esposito had decided to stay through the gala, and had demanded that her husband use his two grand windfall to purchase her a suitable replacement for the stolen engagement present. Myra Frothingham was thinking of buying her husband another watch to replace his missing Patek-Philippe retirement gift. Everyone was giddy over what was promised to be the biggest show yet, one guaranteed to generate the buzz required to reunite only the top one-tenth of the one-percent, most wealthy, part-time Southwest Florida residents.

Chief Jerry Kelly had registered his reservations about the timing of this year's event. However, in the face of Sir

George's renewed confidence, and a tradition that resisted alterations, he was spitting into an institutionalized wind. The fact that the hotel was still participating in an ongoing theft and homicide investigation was something Sir George and the Board wished to forget. And if they could not forget it, the least the hotel could do was to conspire to avoid any and all references to some unfortunate events that now were to be described (if at all) as ancient history. They could not, and would not change the dates for the Exposition. The suspect robbers were dead, security was high, and nothing would go wrong. Bring on the bucks! As Sir George had willed it, so it would be done. Besides, if they had cancelled the show, the vendors would have gone straight to the Ritz, which had for years, been salivating over this prestigious money-maker.

Roni was wet and tired. She checked her watch: "Two hours left!" They'd brought the last heavy load to the laundry area. Katina snuck off for a cigarette leaving Roni to separate the dirty sheets and towels into two damp piles. The hall doors were open to attract the afternoon breezes off the Gulf, cooler than the air over the parking lots. The ceiling lights had been turned off to curtail their heat and she could see the brightness of the afternoon sun in the distance, toward the employee parking lot. Roni was in a fog, thinking of her surveillance, while doing the counting with a part of her brain too primitive for thought.

"Hey, Menendez!" She was awakened from her reverie.

"Senor Delgado!" And then, in Spanish: "What do you want?"

"*Venga aqui! yo le necisisto!*" ("Come with me! I need your help!") This was a direct order, needing no explanation, as he turned toward a door off the tunnel. Roni followed the boss, thinking that there was some manual labor that was somehow beneath his supervisory status. He opened the door, gesturing for her to come in to a dimly lit room. There were piles of dirty towels and sheets. Most were torn or in some disrepair. Roni thought, "This must be where they put the ripped bedding waiting to be fixed or thrown out. Maybe he wants me to help separate the inventory."

Again he called "Menendez," and she turned to see Juan Delgado unfastening his belt, as he gestured for her to join him on one of the mounds of bedding. It was clear to her that the boss was not used to his employees disregarding his orders.

"Why you dirty bastard!" she thought, "How many new immigrants have you sullied to preserve your manhood, such as it is... and what must they have thought about their 'opportunities' here in America, with sex as their only job security?" Roni had to be certain of the coercion.

Again in Spanish, she asked, "Senor Delgado, what is it you want me to do?"

"Venga aqui usted wetback pequeno, yo tengo algo mostrarie!" ("Come here, you little wetback! I have something to show you!") With this he dropped his pants, exposing his growing hardness. He gestured again for Roni to kneel and perform oral sex. She came toward him slowly, judging the angle that would be required for a takedown, if she needed to go that far.

"Come on, I haven't got all day." Then the clincher: *"Quiere usted mantener su trabajo?"* ("Do you want to keep your job?") *"Hay nadie protegerie aqui!"* ("There is no one to protect you here!")

It took Delgado a few seconds to adjust to Roni's transformation. She was talking to him in clear English.

"Mr. Delgado, my name is Corporal Menendez. I am a Naples Police officer, doing undercover work for the hotel. You are under arrest for sexual harassment and implied sexual assault." He tried to run while pulling up his pants at the same time. Mr. Macho was all too easy to tackle. Roni drove his face into the dirty towels as she kneeled into his back, pulling one of his arms to the rear.

"Sir, and I use that term loosely, don't move or I'll add resisting arrest and battery on a police officer." He lay quietly, breathing quickly, as Roni dialed 911 on her cell phone.

"Officer requesting assistance! I am in the basement corridor of the Hotel Sherill, facing the employee parking lot. There are officers on site needing notification of my location."

She spoke to her prisoner. "You're smart not to try anything more here today. And you have the right to remain silent," and Roni finished the Miranda litany.

Sean was the first one there, running through from the Spa exit to the tunnel. "Are you okay? What happened?"

Roni was calm. "Let's handcuff this sucker, and I'll tell you what went down." They heard more pounding of feet to see Dan sprinting the corridor toward them.

"What happened? Is anybody hurt?" She was suddenly tired and hugged Dan, as much to keep standing as for emotional support.

"I'm fine. This dirt-bag is my boss. Apparently, he believes he can have sex with all the new Hispanic maids. It seems as if he demands sex and then threatens them and their families before, during, and after the fact. Get him outta here before my partner comes back. We can have the Human Services director come up with an explanation until I am through being undercover, unless I'm now finished with this assignment."

Dan gave her another look. "Are you sure you're okay. We could relieve you out."

"No, I'm almost through with my shift anyway. Let's keep the charade on until the chief calls it off. Get going with my dear Senor Juan Delgado. Enjoy his company. He's a real sweetheart. I'll see you later at our office meeting."

The two men led the stunned soon-to-be-ex-supervisor away, toward the employee parking lot and a waiting cruiser. Roni went back to her laundry cart, leaning against it as she started to tremble. Katina returned, smelling of smoke, not even trying to apologize for taking so long outside. She walked to the front of the cart, looking back to nod the order that it was time for her work mate to begin pushing again.

Chapter XXXII

After her shift, Roni decided to go home first and take a shower. There was real and symbolic dirt requiring removal. Refreshed and in civilian clothes, she joined her partners in the chief's office for their planning session. They all stood when Roni came into the room. Jerry Kelly held out his hand to shake hers and lead her to one of the chairs.

"I'm really sorry you ran into a buzz saw this afternoon. It's my fault this happened."

Roni smiled tiredly, "Chief, don't worry. Nobody got hurt. No harm, no foul. If nothing else comes from this assignment, I'm feeling good removing an habitual offender from the bowels of that fancy place. He was real scum."

Dan was curious: "Can we hold this guy twenty-four hours before he lawyers up? Although, I doubt he's gonna want to broadcast what happened there today, anyway."

The chief agreed. "I don't think his release before trial will affect the undercover operation. I'll talk with Sir George and he can inform Human Resources to find a replacement for him. Sir George is all jazzed up for the Diamond Expo which I know you all know, starts this weekend, of all times."

Sean wanted to know, "Yeah, what is that? There's a buzz among the staff."

The chief groaned, "It's hard to believe, after all they've been through, but this is a yearly event. If you think about it, you'll remember that the newspaper is filled with stories on this every March and April. The cover for all the hoopla is charity. Some of the money generated goes to help local groups in need. The word 'some' may be taken a little as tongue in cheek."

Dan added, "And it marks the end of the season here?"

"That's right," the chief acknowledged. "It's the last chance to wear jewels and dress up. Dan, do you have your tuxedo cleaned?"

"My what??"

Roni brought them back to reality. "Before we change the subject from Mr. Molestation, there may be a number of female employees who have been assaulted by this perv. They will need the chance to file any relevant complaints to my charges."

The chief nodded. "You're right Roni. That will be just another memo for Sir George, unless you have another idea."

She was certain now. "As a matter of fact, I do. After we've finished the undercover, I'd like to speak to the maids and explain what happened and give them the chance to file charges on any unreported assaults. It's possible this could put this guy away for a long time, *and* get him on the sexual predator list. Forever."

The chief was on board. "Of course. You're absolutely right. The only thing on the hotel's side is that this latest flap probably won't hit the headlines until after the Expo is finished. God help us all."

Dan added, "So that's another reason to keep the undercover going? To protect Sir George?"

The chief could see the point. "Not the only reason, but a good one. If Roni doesn't think there's anything to discover down there, we could pull her out today. It comes down to what we should be doing now, which is to pool what we have and decide what to do next. Let's start with you, Roni."

"Good choice, Chief. I probably have the least to report. It's amazing how little contact the laundry maids have with the mainstream hotel. No wonder they don't care if we can speak English or get abused." She heard herself using the word 'we' as if she were already a part of the laundry maids. "There's real animosity. Maids against the more high profile staff which, maybe not coincidentally, are mostly white. Beyond that little profile in ethnic preferences, the maids don't know squat about the robberies. But, as I said before, the executive maids have the best opportunity to steal. My people, by and large, do *not* have access to the computers and the reservation lists."

"Thanks, Roni.", Chief Kelly said. Then, "Dan?"

The big Detective checked his notes. "I've been through most of the files on the concierges. I'm saving a couple to go over again. As for the reservation lists, eliminating the laundry maids leaves just about everybody else, and that's a huge list of possible subjects. If we have to narrow the number, my best guess would be to concentrate on the concierges, and remove them all from contention before we focus on another group."

It was Sean's turn. "The Spa girls are tight with the concierges. The woman that saw the bodies last Saturday goes with a concierge named Richard Smythe."

Dan sat up straighter in his seat.

Sean continued. "He seems to be calling the shots for some of the concierges, and the Spa girls respect his concern for Shannon. I mean, Miss Scott. He helped set up an elaborate plan to shield his girlfriend from the media and they all bought into it. Now, she's saying that Richard is doing all this because he cares for her, and he doesn't want the hotel to suffer from any more bad publicity. But I was thinking that, if he was involved, this employee loyalty bit would protect him, too."

Sean didn't tell them that nothing would make him feel better than to see this hotshot take a fall.

Dan was alert now. "This is one of the files I want to review. It seems to be short. There are no employment specifics beyond the last few years, all in the Naples area. He said he came from California, but there are no references for that part of his life, which for this guy, is most of it."

Roni wanted to know, "What does he look like?"

"Good looking, dark hair, six feet, not a pretty boy, but you could see how a young girl could get hooked."

She nodded. "I think I know who you're talking about. He sits with Sean's massage woman. And there's a shorter concierge, and a woman with dark hair, also attractive, who sits with them."

Sean added, "I think that older woman is Susan, the Spa supervisor. She's housing Sha... Miss Scott until the media frenzy slows down."

Dan thought out loud, "I know this may sound crazy, but when I talked to the California cop about Jack Burdine, he said the dead guy was connected to a known jewel thief out there."

The chief was curious. "Do you think this Richard could be the same man, the jewel perp?"

"That's the hard part," Dan admitted. "The sergeant didn't have a physical description, and the name was Dick Smathers."

"Sort of like the old TV show comedian?", the chief asked.

"One and the same. Dick Smathers, Richard Smythe. It might be a stretch, or it could be right on the money. This Burdine character was playing cops and robbers with the authorities. First he ratted out this Smathers guy to buy some time, but when the police raided the apartment, most of the jewels were gone, and the place had been swept clean. When they went to shake Jack's tree for more data, he was gone, and they lost him until he turned up dead, here."

The chief was encouraged by some of it. "Okay. We still have more work to do. Roni, you go back just to keep all appearances the same. You might learn something. You might not. But at least no one remarks about a sudden absence. I know you think the laundry maids are invisible, and that may be true, but let's not take that chance. Dan, you and Sean dig into the files that seem the most questionable and schedule the follow-up interviews. We're going to keep the expensive watch and not tell anyone that our killer may be a hotel employee. I don't want this guy to run before we have the goods on him. So tread softly, you three. Please?"

Sean didn't want to be alone with his Shannon fantasy. "Anybody for pizza? I'm buying."

The chief begged off. He had to call Sir George and tell him one of his supervisors was in jail. The other three drove to Guido's. Roni stayed in the car, letting the men go in and order.

Sean had enough beer and soda to go around at his house. Dan was driving and said no, but Roni was thirsty as well as exhausted. Sean fetched her a beer. The couple sat and looked at each other. Dan squeezed her arm.

"Can you stand it down there a little longer?"

Roni smiled at his concern. "I'm feeling better, knowing Delgado's gone, hopefully for a very long time. And I'll get the chance to do abuse intervention with the other maids. So what if there're no clues. I can still watch and listen."

Sean handed Roni a cold one and wondered, "Will we be playing good cop, bad cop on any of these guys?"

Dan shook his head. "Not until the very end and with a guard on the door. This person has been smart enough not to give anything away, and we'll need more than guesses to get a warrant for his place."

"How about a tail?" Sean was willing to keep the planning going at almost any cost. He wanted this guy!

Roni got up. "Thanks for the slice and brew, Sean, but I need my sleep to survive the dirty sheets brigade."

Dan stood too. "We've done enough for one day. That's a good idea to put someone on Richard's bumper. I'll talk to the chief about that tomorrow." They left Sean with thoughts of a beautiful masseuse.

Roni was quiet, head back on her seat. Dan was worried about her. "I can take you home and then give you a ride back to the office tomorrow morning."

She managed a grateful smile. "Thanks, sweetheart. I'd be a liability on the road tonight." When they got to her house, she slid across the seat and kissed him gently. "I'll be better after a good night's sleep."

He saw her walking slowly to the front door, waiting until the outside light went out before heading to his quiet house.

The whole town was getting behind the Diamond Expo. Rich people were coming from all over the state and were willing to spend. Wealthy Neapolitans were planning cocktail parties and arranging formal dinner outfits. The newspaper was highlighting the charitable giving, the donations miniscule compared to the wealth that was going to be on display. The hotel had hired more security teams to guard the jewelry. The staffs were all told that there would be extra work required, but the promise of big tips was enough to keep them all on task. The Spa was booked every hour of the day and into the evening. The beauty salon workers were buying orthotics to get them through the ordeal. Some guests would have a different hair style every night. Fox News had sent a team to highlight the activities of the arriving rich and famous patrons.

Richard took a chance. He had a feeling that his time at the hotel was running out. Stan Merrick decided to take a rare three day break. It would be his last chance for freedom before the exposition would require six consecutive fourteen-hour days. This gave Richard the opportunity to unlock the office and lift the master key to the VIP rooms' private safes. He sent the key overnight delivery and got it back, plus a duplicate, the next evening. All it had taken was five hundred bucks. He'd checked the cheapest locksmiths in and around Miami Beach, choosing the most marginal shop, a one man operation owned by a boozer on the brink of going under. For this guy, a few successful jobs could set the last transaction, the partnership sealed, the next bender financed.

When the front end supervisor returned from his too short reprieve, the master was in its proper spot and Richard was in business.

The news people forgot about Shannon. Louis Gonzales was a memory. Jack Burdine a footnote. All the talk was of diamonds and who would wear them and maybe buy them. Still, Richard advised Shannon to stay at Susan's for a little while longer. One night he even cooked for all four of them at her home. It was really very simple, just sautéed bay scallops in butter, virgin olive oil, white vermouth and scallions. He made a green salad with garlic paste and Greek dressing. The regular spaghetti was not too soft. He tossed the scallop mixture with the hot pasta and parmesan cheese and with the crusty garlic bread, they were ready. Susan and Barry were impressed and ate until they ached. Shannon was proud of her boyfriend's culinary talent. This gave Richard the chance to catch up on the gossip, getting the three of them to share what they had heard among the staff and guests. Susan was telling them that all the rooms and services were booked until the Expo's last day.

She added, "I even had to tell Gloria Esposito that she might lose her ten-thirty pedicure. I mean, how many mani-pedis in a row can one woman have, for God's sake? Myra Frothingham is bringing her whole family and they've booked all my nail technicians until noon. Dear Gloria started to make a stink. For some reason, she stopped and accepted an afternoon appointment. Thank you, somebody, whoever you might be," Susan said while looking up to the skies.

Barry had some info on that. "Mr. Merrick told me that they made her sign a letter saying she wouldn't be critical of the hotel. EVER!"

Susan laughed, but was intrigued. "Gloria Esposito agreed to that? OUR Gloria Esposito? She seems to love a good fight!"

Barry finished the thought: "She had to say she'd be good in order to get the reimbursement for the lost cash and jewelry."

Susan and Shannon both smiled with absolute understanding.

Richard was more curious about the investigation. "Anyone see any of the police around?"

This was Shannon's first chance to share her recent contact with Sergeant Sean Brady. "I got called back. He was still very nice."

Barry asked, "Why'd they want to talk with you again? Because of the bodies?"

"Yeah, you know. I was at that crime scene and stuff like that."

It was Richard's turn. "What stuff?"

She was trying to remember. "Actually, he wanted to know all about us, the Spa people and the front end staff. The sergeant was interested in our group, who went out with who, that kinda stuff."

Richard smiled confidently. "What'd you tell him about all of us?"

"I told him how hard everyone worked to keep me safe from the reporters and I said you were worried about the hotel's reputation."

"Who'd you say planned everything?" Richard could feel his heart starting to race.

Shannon punched him playfully in the arm. "Why, you and Susan, of course!" He pretended to hug her for the compliment, smiling at them, as he accepted the congratulations.

He was thinking: "SHIT! Thanks a lot, Shannon, for putting me in the middle of this mess, the mastermind behind the cover-up. Either they think I'm a prince or I could have something to hide." Instead, he just smiled at her. He was glad it was the weekend. He would need his sleep.

With the arrival of the first guests for the Expo, the hotel had hired extra valets to handle the cars clogging the front entrance. Luckily, these cops went home Friday night, not to return until Monday, or later Richard hoped.

Roni found it easier to get by, for the rest of the week. She resolved not to be a pushover and in a louder voice demanded to take turns pushing the cart. The other woman was surprised by this new assertiveness, but didn't complain. Roni was through taking shit that was not essential to her disguise.

She finally got the chance for a private chat with Sandra Barton, the Human Services director.

"And you say, he could get out of jail tomorrow?" She asked, "What if he comes back here?"

Roni had some cogent advice. "You need an order of protection and a picture to be given to your twenty-four hour security. I'll have the chief fax all the information to your CEO. You can get that picture out now. Don't wait for the paperwork. It's a done deal."

"Is there anything else?" Sandra Barton found this whole sexual harassment issue distasteful.

Roni wasn't finished. "I'd like to speak to the laundry staff about Mr. Delgado and my experience. If he thought I was a pushover, we're guessing that he's victimized others here. This doesn't have to happen until my assignment is over, but it'll be important that the women get the chance to add to the charges, if they have been assaulted."

The supervisor was having a problem seeing the need for all this trouble. "He's already been charged. Do we have to keep bringing this back up?"

Roni was not going to let this go. "If you need permission for me to talk with your maids, I'll have my chief consult with Sir George. I think your boss will want to avoid the chance that your department could be sued for not protecting its workers."

Roni was not going to waste any more time on someone who had trouble acknowledging the humanity of a whole class of workers. She went back to work in the sweaty, underbelly of the elite hotel.

Chapter XXXIII

Shannon thought Richard seemed a little distant, so she snuggled closer to his side of the sports car. "What d'you wanna do tonight?" He'd told her that he was tired of the noise at Pincher's and wanted a quieter place. Besides, the great singer wasn't there tonight.

"We could walk Fifth Avenue, grab something at Cheeburger Cheeburger." She took his arm and he was still reserved. They stopped into some of the art galleries. Richard seemed to like the exhibits from the Southwest.

Shannon was a little bored, wanting more excitement. "D'you wanna go dancing?"

He didn't feel like dancing or any other mindless thing. He wanted to plan his escape - the method that would cover the most miles in the least time, a speed and distance beyond any closing net, on the other side of danger. But, he couldn't leave her hanging. Someone might ask her why she was blue and upset at her boyfriend who was now acting so differently. It was too soon to let her go. "Sure," he said, surprising her. "Let's go to Swings!"

Shannon was embarrassed. This was the place the cracker had taken her. She certainly didn't want to be recognized, remembering that her exploits that night had been chronicled in all the papers. "Couldn't we go somewhere else? I'm afraid someone will say, 'there's that girl!'"

He could see her point. "I'm sorry. I should have remembered that. I guess it's because Swings is the only real nightclub. Let's check out Ft. Myers Beach. They might have a place where we could dance."

She wanted to change into something more elegant, if it was a place for older people. They drove slowly on her street. Shannon stayed down in her seat. Richard didn't see any strange cars, so they slid carefully into her driveway. She opened the front door quickly and they went inside, making sure to turn on a minimum of lights. Shannon changed quickly, and they were on their way in ten minutes. Richard was looking for any signs of reporters, but Pennsylvania Avenue was clear. When he finally turned right on Bonita Beach Road, he didn't notice the gray sedan move into the same lane, three cars behind them.

She enjoyed the ride, not trying to intrude on his solitude. He pointed to the remnants of the sunset to let Shannon know that he wasn't ignoring her. The Ft. Myers Beach main drag was crowded with cars and pedestrians. They went over the Matanzas Bridge, the Gulf behind them and the Estero River to their right. Richard saw some neon lights at a dockside restaurant, and took his next right, and a series of turns to an out of the way bistro, called La Bella.

The other car stayed on the bridge, the plain gray cruiser pulling over, a driver watching them through binoculars.

There was a small dance floor with about enough room for six couples in very close quarters. The jazz trio was running the gamut from the 1940's to current pop. They waited for a slow number, something called "Thou Swell" from the olden days. He held her gently and Shannon rested her head on his shoulder. There was something sad going on. She felt as if he was pulling away, not suddenly, as in an argument, but gradually, inexorably moving to a place she couldn't go. Shannon held Richard's shoulder more tightly. It didn't change what she was experiencing.

They stayed two hours, dancing and drinking. Shannon switched to seltzer. She wanted to stay focused on this man. She didn't want to flirt any more.

The cop on the bridge called in. "They're in a bar. Do I have to sit here all night?"

The answer was not helpful. "Stay put. If you think they'll return using the same route, maybe you better turn your car around so it's heading back where they came from."

By the time Richard brought Shannon to Susan's house it was one AM. The cop reported in at two saying he thought Richard would be staying the night.

There was not a lot of sympathy on the other end of the phone. "Go home. You have enough overtime."

The Diamond Exposition was in full swing by Monday afternoon. Most of the vendors had finished setting up by late Sunday, complete with their lighted display cases surrounding the immense Grande Salon. Jewelers were available to open the cases and hold the diamonds so that all the highlights were visible. There were Security personnel at all the exits. The first show was a Tuesday luncheon with wealthy locals arriving for cold finger sandwiches, petit fours, and champagne. Uniformed servers would announce which tables were to begin rotating the displays. On Wednesday there were two shows with models, one at lunch and the other during and after dinner. The tall elegant women paraded diamond necklaces, earrings, watches and ankle bracelets. Many wore complimentary furs donated by local merchants who were hoping for end of season sales. The gowns were also available for purchase. Everything was for sale, the drinks double their usual price. No one seemed to care.

Dan called Richard in for his second interview. "Good afternoon, Mr. Smythe.

"Good afternoon, Detective. Please call me Richard."

"Thank you for coming back again," the detective said.

"As if I had any choice," thought Richard.

"I just have a few more questions, if you don't mind."

"Certainly, Detective. Glad to help, if I can." Richard was determined to be the dedicated service professional, even to the point of compulsivity.

Dan continued. "I was talking to your supervisor, Mr. Merrick. He told me that the hotel vetted employees extensively, but he didn't remember much about your previous work record. Why do you think that was?"

Richard made a point of gathering his thoughts. In truth, he had rehearsed an answer to what he had guessed was a predictable question. "Well, Detective, I was hired to the front end staff from another hotel position. It was assumed, probably, that someone else had reviewed my file for the earlier job."

"That makes sense, Mr. Smythe, but Mrs. Barton from Human Services didn't have any more records on you, either."

"Maybe the reason for that," he had rehearsed, "is that my first job at the hotel was in the laundry division, and many of those employees haven't been in this country very long."

Dan was getting frustrated at this man's calm logic. "Why aren't there more references to your California work history?"

Richard projected sympathy for the detective that was cursed with asking routine questions and then flummoxed by receiving mundane answers. His response highlighted the complicity of the hotel's hiring process, and the laziness of the applicant. "I just filled out the application the way they wanted. The hotel was only interested in my recent work here in Naples. The restaurant jobs and my good recommendations showed that I did well in the service businesses."

"Did you tell them about your jobs on the West Coast?", Dan asked.

Richard pretended he wanted to help this policeman. "It was just more of the same thing. I've worked in a lot of restaurants, everything from dishwashing to sous chef. The job I liked the best was being a host, helping customers get the service they wanted. Those positions were no different than the ones I had here in the Naples area."

"Do you have any records of those jobs, old pay stubs, anything?

Richard indicated that he wanted to help. "I don't have much from the West Coast. I had a nasty breakup with a girl, and I just wanted to put some serious miles between her and me."

Dan tried to catch Mr. Slick in a lie. "What was her name, this girl you had the fight with?"

Richard hung his head, as if there was a chance he might cry. There was an audible sigh: "Sandra Jackson. She was a waitress at a place near the beach off Santa Monica Boulevard."

"Do you have her address or telephone number?"

Richard was willing to give as much useless information as this policeman wanted. He had old numbers and addresses at home, and knew they were no longer current. "I don't have them with me, Detective, but I could get them for you tomorrow. I haven't spoken to Sandy since before I left, and that was almost four years ago."

Dan was being stonewalled by an expert. He didn't want to scare this one off until there were more facts connecting the concierge to the crimes, hopefully enough for a search warrant. Richard was treating him almost as if Dan was a counselor, and was available to listen to all of the young man's tales of woe. The big cop was frustrated. If this guy was the mastermind, someone else might have to give him up, because this one was not implicating himself.

"Thank you, Richard. If you would get me that name we discussed and a list of your last three jobs in California it would be very helpful. We are trying to match the backgrounds of all the employees so we have a five year history for everyone."

"I understand, Detective. I'll try to find some of the documentation you're looking for. Please try to be patient if I have some trouble digging up this stuff. It's been quite a while since California."

"I understand completely, Richard. Thanks for your time today. Will you please send in the next employee?"

Richard smiled grandly, in the style of the consummate professional: "It would be my particular pleasure!"

Partially closing the conference room door, Richard saw that Marta was fidgeting in her chair. "Have fun. You're next!"

She gave him a strained smile, fighting her anxiety. She whispered to him, "Why are we talking again? I already had one interview."

Richard whispered back: "Don't worry, they're just going over old news. You'll be fine!" And he patted her on the back as she opened the door to go into the interrogation.

Richard's smile evaporated as he walked back to the front desk. "No doubt about it," he was thinking, "I'm on their list." Then: "I wonder if I have a tail?" Richard resolved to check through his rearview mirror the next time he was out and about. "If they had any hard evidence, I'd be in some kind of custody. They're still fishing, but finding the bodies means they've put more people on this and they're checking sources. My time here is short." He was not a happy man.

Marta was not being successful trying to hide her nervousness.

"Good afternoon, Mrs. Schultz. How are you today?", Detective Logan asked.

She tried to concentrate on how handsome he was, but his physicality intimidated her. "I guess I'm just a little nervous today, Sir."

"Why is that, Mrs. Schultz?"

"You know. This is a murder investigation now, not just robberies. I'm not used to things like this."

Dan tried to reassure her. "I'm sorry if this makes you uncomfortable. Truthfully, the only people who should be nervous are those who are involved in this criminal act."

"But surely you don't think that one of the employees could have been involved in any of this."

Dan was willing to share some of the general information. "Well, Mrs. Schulz, try to look at this from an outsider's perspective. There are robberies of hotel guests by two men. Then, two men are found murdered. There's some evidence that suggests that these two could have been the thieves. Why would anyone want to kill these two?"

She was shocked at the graphic presentation. "How could I possibly know why people are killed?"

Dan tried to calm her. "Pretend you're a cop and you're looking for a motive. What would be your guess?"

Marta was willing to try. "You say the two men could be the robbers, and someone killed them to... keep them quiet?"

Dan congratulated her. "That's good. Any other reasons?"

She sighed, thought to herself, "At least he's not saying I did it!" and answered his question. "Maybe the third person thought they kept too much of the money?"

He helped her put it together. "All right, Detective Schultz, let's keep going. You say these men were murdered to keep them quiet and maybe so that the killer could keep all the profits for himself. Is that right, Mrs. Policewoman?"

Marta blushed at the title, but accepted the challenge: "That's my guess, Detective."

He looked at her. "Why couldn't the third person work here? Many staff access the reservation lists. They know where guests are being sent to dinner. They know which restaurants have dark parking lots and they know that the guests are wealthy and not physically strong. Wouldn't a staff member be a good contact person?"

Marta wanted to defend her co-workers. "But we make good money here."

Dan was willing to accept the initial thrust. "The salaries may be good, but do you know if any of your co-workers have a gambling problem, or a drug habit, or a secret wife or mistress?"

Marta was flustered again. "Um... no. I mean, I don't think so. I don't really know."

Dan began again. "See, it's at least possible. For instance, how well do you know your fellow employees, the other concierges? Tell me about them, say, for example, Charles."

Marta thought that choice was not fair. "Charles works at night. I don't get the chance to talk to him very much, just when his shift overlaps mine."

"Maybe that wasn't a good choice. How about Barry?"

Marta smiled, up to the challenge. "Barry grew up in Estero, and he went to college at Florida Gulf Coast, and he lives in Golden Gate and he's dating Susan from the Spa." She grinned triumphantly.

Dan wasn't satisfied. "Anything else?"

"Well, he has an older married sister, and they have two kids. More?"

"Are you sure that's all you know about Barry?", he asked again.

She was thinking, "This is work! Maybe I'm not cut out to be a cop." Then she remembered more and said, "Let's see. He likes to watch basketball, and he plays soccer in a Saturday league, and his favorite beer is Corona."

Dan leaned back and applauded. "Excellent, Marta. That was quite a summary. And you didn't even get the chance to prepare."

Marta smiled at the compliment and thought, "This must be all he wants. I hope."

But Dan surprised her again. "What about Richard?"

What the heck; she was on a roll. "That's easy. I like Richard. He's the fastest of all the concierges. No one can do more things at once than Richard can."

"That's great. Richard can do a lot of things at once. Where did he grow up and go to school? Does he have any family?"

Marta was flustered. She really wasn't quite sure about that part. "I think he said he grew up in California. Or maybe it was New Mexico."

Dan kept the pressure on. "He couldn't grow up in two places. Was it New Mexico or California?"

"I-I'm not sure," she said out loud. "Maybe he was born in New Mexico and moved to California."

"And where did he go to school?"

Marta was trying to remember. They had talked together many times before, but not so much recently since he started to go out with Shannon and the Spa girls. Why couldn't she remember where he said he'd gone to school? Did they ever talk about his schooling? She had certainly told him all about her college experience, and falling for Mark, and getting pregnant for Heather, and the mess the house always was. "I don't know, Detective. Maybe I forgot."

"Okay." He'd try to pull up other memories from her. "What about his family, mother and father, brothers and sisters, first girlfriends, favorite vacation, best jobs in California?"

Marta shook her head. She couldn't remember any of his life. Is it possible he hadn't told her? Had she dominated the conversations so much, he didn't get the chance to share?

Dan sat back again. "You don't have to know everything about everybody. It's not a requirement for your job. But I guess you can see that it's possible to work with someone and not know a whole lot about their lives."

Then he took the pressure off. "And he's a person you work with every day, maybe have a beer with after work. What about the other employees, the executive maids, the bell hops, the valets, the limo drivers? They could have all sorts of problems that would make them vulnerable to money issues that might push them over the edge."

She could see his point. "I guess we don't always know a lot about our co-workers. But I could have sworn, I knew more than I was able to tell you. Richard is our fastest concierge."

Dan relieved her tension now. "You know more about your friends than you're giving yourself credit for. It sounds like an exciting place to work. You have a lot of responsibilities, Marta. It must be difficult to keep them all straight. All this and a family, too. That's quite an accomplishment."

She was grateful for the compliment. "It is hard, Detective, but I love what I do. We all do."

After she was gone, Dan closed his notebook. "No proof," he was thinking. "Richie Boy, you sure have played it close to the vest. Nobody knows shit about you, and I bet that's just the way you planned it. All we need is one piece of hard evidence and we can trash your place with a fine tooth comb."

Chapter XXXIV

The group of five were in a booth at Shula's. It was Richard's idea. He suggested they needed to wind down, away from the hustle of the hotel and the chaos of the tourists traps. There were surprisingly few patrons at the bar.

Barry had the answer. "Everybody is at the Sherill getting into Diamond Expo!"

"Not so!" Susan had another theory. "It's two for one day at Pincher's on the River!"

Shannon had her tired feet resting on Richard's lap. "But it's only Thursday. No way they'd do that until the weekend. And besides, John Friday isn't there tonight."

"Maybe the Season is almost over," was Richard's hopeful suggestion.

Marta didn't care. "I'd be satisfied sitting in the park, just to get the chance to not have to say 'particular pleasure' to a soul."

Susan poured a refill from the pitcher. "So, Captain, why did you drag us over here?"

Richard pretended to be taking a nap. "Was that you, Susan? You don't have to stay, if this is a waste of your valuable time. I think I hear Gloria Esposito calling for three appointments at once."

She clutched at his arm: "I didn't mean anything! Don't send me back there. Please, Sir. That woman will tear me apart."

He sat up, patting Susan's hand which was still holding his shirt. "You may stay, if you behave. I was just wondering how everyone was holding up, getting ready for the Expo, and having to sit through the police interviews."

Susan had a big smile on her face. "I've only had one, and that was after the first robbery."

Marta punched her arm. "You're so lucky. I thought I'd never get out of there."

Richard was naturally curious. "How so? I was only talking for ten minutes."

She tried to explain. "It was like he was playing a game. He asked me what I knew about all the concierges, Charles, Barry, and you. He told me to pretend I was a cop, and asked me if I could think of a motive for the murders of those poor men."

Richard wanted to know more. "Did he explain why he was doing that?"

She nodded. "I guess he was trying to get me to see why they were there in the water. He said there had to be a reason why those men died and that it might be connected to the robberies."

"Was it like a test?", Barry asked.

Marta nodded again. "Yes, he was testing me to see how much I knew about everyone I worked with. I couldn't say much about Charles, but I aced it with you, Barry." Then, looking at Richard, she added, "And I flunked with you."

"Really? How?", he casually asked.

"It seemed as if he asked a hundred questions about where you grew up and went to school, and your family, questions like that. I had a hard time coming up with what he wanted."

Richard let Marta off the hook. "He did the same thing with me, asking about you and Barry."

"Thank goodness. I thought that the Detective was just picking on me." Then Marta sat back and relaxed.

Shannon remembered her second interview with Sean. "Sergeant Brady was just like that. He wanted to know all about our group, and he asked a lot of questions about Richard, how long we'd been going out, how well I knew you. That kind of stuff."

Susan was angry. "It's like they're from People Magazine or The National Inquirer. I don't think what we do after work is any of their damn business."

Barry held up his fists: "They ain't gettin' nuttin' outta me!"

Richard was willing to laugh off the whole thing, copying Barry: "Let's Fughedaboudit! Who wants more beer?"

Susan was ready to party. "I'll buy the Buffalo wings!"

Marta looked at her watch. "Whoops! I am really late! Mark is going to kill me." She threw two dollars on the table and ran for the exit.

Richard pretended that it was possible to relax, to leave the work hysteria back at the hotel. He shifted to pull Shannon closer, providing all the comfort needed to shield her from the outside world. They ate and chatted, avoiding the police matter, concentrating on the crowds coming for the Diamond Exposition. This was Barry and Shannon's first expo and they wanted the insider details.

Susan was happy to give her side. "All the women get dressed up and wear their best jewelry. But first, they come to the Spa and get all buff, so they won't embarrass themselves in their strapless gowns."

Shannon was curious about the diamonds: "Do they have models for the expensive jewels?"

Richard had some information on that. "There are some models, but the real show is when selected guests are chosen to wear the most dramatic earrings, bracelets, and necklaces."

Barry asked, "How do they get picked?"

Richard laughed. "That's the easy part. Sir George selects the wealthiest women, the ones whose families have the most and stay the longest. That way, he makes sure that they'll return next year to keep their records intact."

Barry smiled and said, "I suppose that 'particular pleasure' eliminates our dear Gloria."

Shannon laughed but was still concerned. "How do the people protect the jewels?"

He had an answer for that one, too. "The hotel hires extra security. Guests get screened at the front door, and the guards walk them back to the VIP floor. "Then the guests lock the jewelry in the room safes until the next day."

"What happens at the end?" Shannon wanted to know.

Richard looked at Susan. "Do *you* want to tell her?"

Susan said, "Go ahead. You're on a roll."

Richard paused for dramatic effect. "On the last night, the masked ball takes place. The chosen few gather on the stage. The jeweler introduces the spectacular diamonds, and then the wealthy woman takes off her mask so that all can see how 'particularly pleasured' she is!"

Barry chimed in, "And that's it? That's the end of the show?"

Susan couldn't help herself. "Pretty much, *except,* sometimes the rich husband buys the necklace and gives it to her on stage!"

Barry scoffed. "They should call it the "Green With Envy Show!"

Susan laughed. "Particularly if it's an emerald!"

Shannon was shocked: "How much is all this jewelry worth?"

Richard looked at Susan and shrugged. "What was it last year? Fifteen to twenty million?"

She nodded. "Yup. I heard it's even more this year."

Richard let it drop then. He didn't want anyone to know that he had reviewed the publicity on the prospective itinerary detailing the specific pieces and what they were worth.

They didn't stay late. Everyone knew that tomorrow would require their best. Susan took Shannon with her.

Richard was on his cell when he pulled away from the restaurant's parking lot and drove to the prearranged meeting spot. As he started to park, he noticed a gray Crown Victoria duplicating the maneuver.

Using his cell phone, Richard called his buddy. "Eddie! Where are you?"

The trucker sounded excited. "I'm almost to you. I'm near the last exit on 75."

Richard needed more clarification. "When do you load?"

Eddie had a quick answer. "They said they could start this evening and finish tomorrow morning. It's just medical supplies, mostly scooters and motorized wheel chairs. They'll drive most of the vehicles on, and then stack the boxes in the top rack."

Richard had some changes. "Get your sleep in the afternoon. I think we may have to take off tomorrow night."

"Friday? I thought you said we would leave on Sunday, with less traffic."

"Alterations, Eddie. There's a tail on me right now."

"When did that start?", Eddie wanted to know.

"To tell the truth, I'm not sure. Maybe a couple of days ago."

"Okay, good buddy. Watch your back."

Richard signed off: "Ten-four!"

He drove to the exit, turned right, and then left on his own street. He went two more blocks before he saw the gray car continue around his corner, driving slowly, maintaining the four hundred yard separation. Richard had confirmed his own suspicion.

Chapter XXXV

Dan wanted to know, "What's he doing now?"

Ted Simmons was settling in. "Looks like he's there for the night. I drove the street to Vanderbilt, went around the block and came back. The lights are on and I can see the reflection from the TV."

"Hang in there. Gary will be there by eight. The subject should be leaving for work by eight-thirty."

Richard was not, in fact, in the living room watching television. He removed the false partition from the closet and began his inventory. The material on his bed represented three years of astute collecting. The jewelry was primarily small pieces of bracelets, earrings, and petite necklaces. There were a variety of watches, all gold. He had withdrawn most of his checking account, now in cash, letting the teller know, anecdotally, that he was buying a car privately, and the owner was a little paranoid about paper transfers. The three hundred remaining in the bank was proof that Richard would soon be replenishing the account. Richard was reasonably certain that his transactions last week had come before the start of his tail.

Roni had noticed the guards by the elevators at the end of her shift. She heard some of the workers talking about the Diamond Expo, and her own early morning phone discussions with Dan had prepared her for the increased security.

"Stan Merrick told me that they give some of the jewelry to the wealthiest society women to wear to the fashion shows and charity auctions," he told her.

Roni had wanted to know what happened next.

Dan told her. "The guards ride with them up to their rooms. They stay until the guests store the stuff in their room safes. Then, the next day the women take them out for the next round of appearances. At the end of the last dance, the guards gather all the loaned valuables, or the husbands buy it for their wives."

"And that's the Saturday night masked ball?"

Dan congratulated her: "See? You *do* hear things down there in the laundry room!"

She ignored the dig. "How are *you* doing on the record reviews?"

Dan tried to sound hopeful. "If you don't count the newcomers from Haiti and Mexico, the biggest data gap is with this guy Richard Smythe. We have a tail on him, waiting for a wrong move."

"Have you tried to rattle him?"

"He's a tough nut. Either he's completely innocent, or slick as hell. He's promised me that he'll bring me documentation by Monday, but I hate to wait any longer. I've got a bad feeling about this one. He might skip."

"What about a warrant?"

Dan agreed. "That's the missing piece on this investigation. All our interest is based on guesses, supposition, and circumstantial evidence. The chief is waiting for Judge Fogarty to come back from vacation. He's the only justice that would go for this presentation, so Monday is the earliest we can talk with him. After that, if we get it, we'll wait for Mr. Quick Concierge to come home from work and offer to clean his place for him from top to bottom. For free.

No maid charge. If he's cocky and dirty, we'll find something. In the meantime, we wait."

Roni was ready to talk about something much more important. "Where are you taking me to dinner, Detective Logan?"

He wanted to get far away from the hotel. "Want to take a drive first?"

"What do you have in mind? Motels are out, if that's what you're thinking."

"Oh, ye of little faith. I was thinking of the Rod and Gun Club in Everglades City."

She liked that idea. "You old romantic, you. We can watch the sun go down over the Baron River behind us with grouper on the table in front of us. Great choice. And we can get ice cream at that place near the air boats."

Dan was happy. "Let's get an early start. Can you change at work?"

She saw the sense in that. "I'll bring extra clothes with me. Will you pick me up at Tin City? We'll be that much closer to the Trail."

He stopped himself from repeating the Sherill mantra.

"Barry, I have an idea."

"You haven't disappointed me yet, Richard. Whassup?"

"This is for after the fashion show tomorrow. What would you think if three of us delivered champagne and the dessert cart to the women who get to wear the designer jewels. There could be a great tip in it for us."

"But the fashion show doesn't end until ten o'clock," Barry said.

Richard nodded. "That's the catch. It would mean we would pull a shift and a half. But think of the money. We could take the girls out after we finish. We might be rich men by then."

Barry was intrigued. "We could maybe really be able to afford to go some place fancy."

Richard slapped him on the shoulder. "Any place in town!" He grinned and added, "Except here. Unless, you want to come here - where they don't want us."

Barry shook his head. "Any place but here. By that time, I won't want to see the Sherill anytime soon. Who would be the third concierge?

"I think we can persuade Charles. He doesn't usually get the tips we do, and it's his shift, anyway."

"All right. You, me and Charles. How would it go down?" Barry was trying very hard to keep up.

"After the couples go to their rooms, we call and say that the hotel has a complimentary surprise for them, in honor of their selection as the diamond models."

"What if they say no?"

Richard was optimistic. "Would *you?* I think they'll be high on the excitement and will want to keep it going. We have to be ready with the carts, but it's possible that the three women and their husbands will retire at different times. They should know that this is just for them, not for any of the other VIP suites."

"What does Mr. Merrick think of the suggestion?" Barry wanted to cover his own rear.

"I haven't told him yet. I wanted to run it by you first. If *he* gets the credit, I hope he goes along with it. Win-win. He gets the boost and we get the money! Will you go with me and help me present this to him, please?" Richard felt he had Barry in his pocket now.

Barry was ready. "It's gonna help me with Susan, the chance to blow some serious change on her."

They knocked on the office door of the front end manager. Come in, gentlemen," Mr. Merrick announced. "What can I do for you?"

Barry rushed ahead. "Richard has an idea for the guests that are chosen to wear the fancy jewelry."

Richard kept it going, sharing the responsibility. "We thought it might be an innovation if the concierges delivered high end champagne and dessert to their rooms, after the fashion show and dinner."

Stan Merrick was cautious. "But there are three women honored. Who would be the third concierge?"

Barry spoke again. "We think that Charles would jump at the chance. He's been sort of out of our loop lately."

Richard continued. "The ladies would have just returned to their suites and put the jewelry in the room safes. What do they do then? It's over and they're a little depressed. They don't get the chance to wear the necklaces until the masked ball, a whole twenty-four hours away. They're just sitting there in their anticlimax mode when the phone rings and the hotel announces that it isn't over yet. They're going to get another congratulatory surprise!"

Mr. Merrick was in the process of taking over. "And the excitement continues, thanks to the staff from the front end, the men from the accommodating Concierge desk. Some of the desserts for Saturday night are already on ice. They would get first crack at a few of the Masked Ball creations."

Richard was ready to pass the baton. "That's a good idea, telling them that no one else yet had seen the sweets that were preserved for the next night."

The manager was seeing another accolade being placed in his growing personnel file, the one predicting his rapid rise to a Vice Presidency. "I'll call him right now No. I'll go up. No need for you two to come along. I'll get back to your desk later. It'll mean you both will have to work another four hours. Are you okay with that?"

"No problem," the two men said, in unison. They could have said the other phrase, but there were no patrons to impress.

Roni and Dan had their quiet time. Once past the Collier Boulevard intersection, the Tamiami Trail became just two lanes, a ribbon through the Everglades. They could see roosting cormorants and anhingas on the telephone wires. Alligators lined the west-facing banks, loading up on solar energy, mouths agape. In less than an hour they were at the turn-off to Everglades City. Roni pointed to some feral pigs digging near the canal's mangroves. They went over the bridge and could see fishing boats lined along the docks, next to piles of crab traps. The Rod and Gun Club was on the banks of the Baron River. It was an icon of the old hunting and fishing resorts that were the only reasons, back in the day, wealthy people would come to this tiny town on the edge of Everglades National Park. Inside, on the walls were the mummified monuments of past sporting largesse: trophy tarpon, wild boar, deer, otter, Florida panther, and many more species, all now in relative environmental peril. There was a dimly lit bar that was the kind of place where one could lose perspective on whether it was day or night. Most of the patrons chose to eat on the expansive screened lanai that gave a hundred feet of unobstructed views of the river, the six knot tidal flow, and another gorgeous Florida sunset.

They chose a table as far from the other patrons as the servers would allow.

"Seltzer with lime, please," Roni requested.

"Make that two," Dan replied, enjoying the view of the quiet waterway and his beautiful bride-to-be. "Three more weeks to go. Can you believe it? Are you ready?"

Roni frowned. "Don't remind me. We had to send the maids' gowns back."

"What? I thought that was a done deal."

"I ordered champagne beige and they sent silver. Other than that major flaw, they were perfect!"

Dan was sympathetic. By comparison the tuxedoes were easy. "I'm sorry. What's the turnaround time?"

She wasn't worried. "They have the sizes and we could be in business in ten days, but that still wasn't something that was supposed to go wrong."

"And your gown?" he asked.

"It's in my closet and that's all you're going to know about it. Plus, if I am going to fit into it, no dessert tonight."

The grilled grouper arrived juicy and golden brown. Roni ate all of hers and the salad but gave the hush puppies to Dan. The tide was running hard, bringing in the last boats that didn't need much more than idle speed to fly upriver. Two cruisers and a sailing catamaran tied up in front of the hotel, planning to eat and take advantage of the complimentary dockage. They both thought about the contrast between this peaceful place and the chaos waiting for them all too soon at the Hotel Sherill.

"What about our honeymoon here?", Dan thought out loud.

Roni was skeptical. "I was thinking about something a little less primitive. I am not a fisherperson. What do people do for fun around here?"

Dan looked out on the bucolic setting. "Well, take walks, go fishing, take the National Park boat tour, and go fishing. Oh, right. I already said that. They rent a boat and try chumming for trophy marine animals. Oops. Same thing. I'm beginning to see your point about the available recreational choices. But, who cares? Don't newlyweds just stay in bed the whole time?"

Roni was more realistic. "Sooner or later, big boy, they have to come up for some air, and that's when they explore the resort!"

He reached to squeeze her arm. "Will you promise to bring something back for me at the hotel?"

Roni laughed: "We'll *be together!* Checking out all the freebies. You will *not* be stuck in bed, in the dark, watching ESPN! Guaranteed!" Then in angry Spanish:

"Debes estar loco si piensas que voy a permirtivte quedarte en la cama durante nuestra luna de miel, haciendo el amor a un televisor!"

"If you insist," he replied sweetly. "I'll try to pay a wee bit of attention to you at that point in time."

Chapter XXXVI

Friday night could not come too soon for the Sherill staff. They had been wired all day, the excitement palpable. Susan and Shannon met their favorite concierges in the staff cafeteria.

"I'm happy that I brought two pairs of shoes to work today," Susan almost whined.

"Why so, Honey?" Barry asked.

Shannon supplied the answer. "She's been on her feet so long today, Susan's gone up a shoe size. So, by bringing another pair, the next size up, Susan's covered for the late afternoon into evening group."

Richard was congratulatory. "Very smart, Susan, but what are Barry and I supposed to do? Wear sandals?"

She had a quick response. "You could've brought another pair, too."

"Yeah sure," Barry scoffed. "The day I buy another pair is the day the first shoes wear out."

"Suit yourselves," Susan said, "And speaking of formal wear, are you both in tuxedos tonight?"

Richard chimed in. "Of course, but we've added a new twist."

Shannon was intrigued. "What could you add to a tuxedo? A top hat? No, wait. That goes with tails, doesn't it?"

"Not a bad guess. Actually, Charles, Barry and I are going to have Sherill aprons over our tuxes." He added in a lofty voice, *"We* are going to be serving Champagne and special desserts to the women who are chosen to wear the signature jewelry of our most famous Diamond Exposition!"

"Wow," said Susan, "I hope they're color coordinated."

"As a matter of fact," said Richard, "they're white, instead of gold, in deference to the dark blue tuxes."

"When are you all doing that?", Shannon asked.

Barry filled in the last part. "We think that everyone will be done by ten. Richard says that people know they need their sleep for the Masked Ball because that doesn't end until sometime Sunday morning. So we should be finished by ten-thirty. Right, Richard?"

Richard nodded, without comment.

Barry was glad for the short night. "We have a surprise for Saturday. We're supposed to get big tips Friday. At least we *hope* we will. We would be honored if you two would join us for a fancy dinner Saturday night."

Shannon was a little disappointed. "You mean we won't see you at all on Friday?"

Richard acted apologetic. "I'm going to be coming off a sixteen hour shift and I'm not as young as I used to be. I probably won't be good for anything or anybody. I don't know about Barry, but I'm going to be saving up for our big night on Saturday."

Susan poked Shannon, smiling and saying, "It'll do them good not to have us for an evening. We can go shopping for some new dresses. We'll be so hot they won't recognize us when they finally see us!"

Shannon smiled at the thought of getting gorgeous for Richard. "Okay. Just as long as you guys don't go out after your shift."

Richard was incredulous: "Are you kiddin' me? I'm just gonna be draggin' myself home, as it is. You don't have to worry. I'll be in bed, out like a light."

Roni felt the excitement too, but hers was measured more in heat and humidity. They had never delivered or returned more towels. "Don't these women know how to hang up anything?", she found herself thinking more than once. Katina was tired before noon. She'd been working harder lately, as her once reticent laundry partner was no longer doing more than half the work. Roni was experiencing the euphoria of a 'short timer', someone who wouldn't have to be doing this labor very much longer. She'd never been more grateful for her degree dependent career with her chances for advancement, as she knew this servitude would soon be just an unpleasant memory. They'd seen the Spa and Concierge group in the cafeteria. Roni noted the easy intimacy of the four. Nobody seemed worried or was acting in a covert fashion.

"If that dark haired man *is* our guy, he sure doesn't seem very concerned," she thought and wondered if Dan had been able to uncover any more evidence to help in the search warrant application. "Well, we'll know better on Monday."

They announced the winners at the noon fashion show. All the TV stations and print media were there to get the delicious details of the rich and famous. They said they were on site to report the totals gathered for the local charities, but the truth was that people liked to hear about the fabulously wealthy, both the local bigwigs and the celebrities from out of town as well.

Sir George was at the microphone: "It gives me great pleasure to announce this year's Diamond Expo's honorees to wear these beautiful necklaces. The Hotel Sherill is proud to introduce the first of our three designees: Kiera Cunningham. She is the wife of David Cunningham, CEO of Cunningham Industries of Jacksonville, Florida. Mrs. Cunningham will be wearing the Grace Diamond necklace, valued at four million dollars!" The jeweler came forward and placed the jewelry ceremoniously around the lucky winner's neck. There was loud applause and flashes from cameras close enough to get a likeness of the recipient and her temporary acquisition. The host continued, thanking everyone for their donations to the local foundations, asking their representatives to stand for recognition, as close to the wealthy as they were going to get, until next year. Sir George was dragging this out. All the winners were yearly visitors, some staying for weeks while reserving suites for friends and family.

"Our next honoree comes from Savannah, Georgia. Sylvia DeChamps. Her husband, Edward, owns the largest paper manufacturing company in the South." Sylvia was dramatically younger than her seventy-year-old spouse, appearing more like a daughter. She rose regally to receive her sparkling appendage, not reacting to the ripple of conjecture at the obvious age discrepancy.

Sir George continued: "Mrs. DeChamps will be displaying the Shamrock Emerald necklace, currently appraised at six million American dollars." He paused to let the commotion die down. "And the last Madame will be adorned by the Johannesburg Starburst, a spectacular multi-diamond necklace and earring set, here on loan from our friends in South Africa. It is valued at fifteen million, and that estimate may be going up as I speak. We at the Hotel Sherill are proud to present it to our forty-eight hour owner, Myra Frothingham! Her husband Albert is the retired president of Stamford Equities, and the heir of Stafford Frothingham, the late Ambassador to the Court of Saint James."

All the guests rose at that announcement, applauding, as the South African representative adjusted the clasps for the happy matron. Wait staff began to serve immediately. Sir George had told them that the room had to be ready for clearing at ten, if not before.

The three concierges met in the kitchen for their carts and aprons. The chef delegated the contents, giving strict instructions. "Two bottles each of our finest champagne. One for consumption now, the other for their suite refrigerator." Pointing to the desserts, he added, "These are cold enough, so they shouldn't melt as you serve. Please do not handle them. Use the silver forks. Pay attention. You do not want to get chocolate on your white gloves."

Charles wanted to know about the Champagne flutes and dishes. "Do we wait until they're finished, before we come back down?"

"No. After you have arranged the sweets on the plates and have poured the first glasses, you should excuse yourselves. You are not there to observe their eating habits."

"How long do we wait for our tips?" Barry sounded greedy.

The chef looked at his watch. "The three rooms have been alerted, as well as the elevator guards. They are expecting you. We assume the guests are arranging tips and will hand you cash, or an envelope. If they just say thank you, expect an envelope later. If the gratuity is not offered quickly, do not linger. Any questions?"

Richard could see that the hotel had bought into this perk, as it was in the tradition of going overboard. Sir George would make sure that it became part of the annual event. The men needed no more directions and headed for the service ride to the eighteenth floor, the VIP wing. The guards were grinning as they exited the elevator. One lifted a white napkin to peer at the array of goodies.

"All that for three couples?"

Richard was sympathetic. "If we have any left over, you're welcome to sample the tray on our way back, but we have to leave all the champagne. Sorry."

"That's okay. We can't drink on duty anyway, but that chocolate covered fruit sure looks good!"

The concierges separated to their specific assignments. Richard knocked at the door. He could hear Myra's excitement as she granted him permission to enter.

"Richard! So good of you to be the one to bring this wonderful tray."

"Please sit," he suggested, "and I will arrange the dishes." Richard presented a small white linen tablecloth, and spread it on the sitting room table. Then he excused himself to go to the entrance corridor to prepare the plates and decant the bottle. The Frothinghams heard the muffled pop of the champagne. Albert was getting impatient. Myra put her hand gently on his lap to stay seated, so as not to upset the orchestrated ambience. What they did not see was Richard opening the wall safe with the counterfeit master key, removing the necklace, and putting the jewelry in a small sack inside his pant leg. He replaced the missing item with one of his junk collection, bearing a small resemblance to the South African gems.

"Tah-dah!" Richard made a grand entrance, pushing the cart with the exposed desserts, equally distributed between two plates. First he served Mrs. Frothingham, and then her husband. As they were beginning their tastings, Richard poured the first of the two glasses, presenting them to the honored guests. He stepped back, as they took their first sips of the very dry, very expensive Champagne.

Myra took a deep drink, and then frowned at her husband. "Albert."

"Oh, yes," and he stood to hand the server an envelope. "Thank you, Richard," they said in unison.

"It was my particular pleasure," came the familiar response. He was out the door quickly, heading back to the service elevators, pushing his cart, minus the two magnums in silver buckets. Charles was already there. Barry had yet to emerge.

"I guess old Barry is laying it on pretty thick," Charles suggested.

"Or having to wait a long time for his tip," Richard added quietly. Just then they saw him, hustling around the corner.

"I thought old Mr. DeChamps would never go into his pocket! But you should see his wife in a night gown. She never put on her robe the whole time. She can't be much older than we are. She knows which side *her* bread is buttered on!"

The elevator guards were happy with the leftovers. Richard handed them napkins to keep the chocolate from spreading on their uniforms.

"This is really great!", they exulted, stuffing their mouths with a variety of the remaining goodies. "Don't you guys want some?"

Barry was thinking about the big dinner date tomorrow night. "We're supposed to keep these white gloves clean. You go ahead. They may throw the rest out."

"If you put it that way," and they each took another handful. "Thanks a lot. We really appreciate it. We never get perks like this."

"No problem," Richard responded, as the elevators closed for their ride back to the kitchen.

They opened their envelopes in the parking lot. Charles was exultant. "A hundred bucks! I never get tips like this. Thanks for including me on this deal."

Richard held his bill to the lamplight, as if to test its authenticity. "Same here, Charles. We couldn't have done it without you."

Barry was disappointed. "You score C-notes and I get a lousy fifty? I guess keeping young Mrs. DeChamps happy does cost a lot more!"

Richard was apologetic. Sorry, old man. I'll split the difference, so we both get seventy-five."

Now Barry was ashamed. "No, I was just kidding. You keep yours. It was your idea."

But Richard had his wallet out and handed Barry a twenty and a five. "Look, we were in this together. We'll combine the total for the dinner tomorrow night, anyway. Deal?"

Barry slapped Richard's upraised hand. "Deal, buddy. But I still owe ya."

"No you don't. It'll all even out some day."

Barry was happy with the added cash, the prospects of being able to pay for half of the dinner bill, and most especially impressing Susan, the older woman in his life.

"Do we have reservations?", he asked Richard.

"We have eight o'clock reservations at La Rive Gauche. They said there would be no more seatings at our table. We can take our time, running through the wine menu."

"How on earth did you wrangle that one?"

"It was partly because we're Sherill concierges. They know our names. It's also getting near the end of the season, so that helped, too." He didn't mention the fact that this restaurant had never quite recovered from the robbery in their secluded parking area.

"I don't care how you did it. No time limit at Rive Gauche will knock Susan's socks off."

"And that's probably not the least of her garments she'll toss at you!"

"And I owe it all to you, Richard. I am in your debt."

The men shook hands, got in their cars, and went home. Richard saw the tail and took his time getting back to his driveway.

"Where is he, and what's he doing?", Dan asked Ted Simmons.

"Dan, I tell you. He's home for the night. He got back at eleven, after a late shift at the hotel. The car's in the driveway and the TV is on. This guy is Mr. Predictable."

Dan was irritated. Nothing this concierge did altered a routine. "Ted, stay on the house until your shift is finished. Who has Saturday?"

"Gary. He has the rest of the weekend days."

"And you have the nights?"

"Yup. That's lucky me. Until Monday. Love that time and a half! Thanks for requesting me. I really don't mind this gig at all."

Dan smiled and said, "My particular pleasure." But then he got serious. "No offense, Ted, but we hope you're off nights very soon. Right after we get the warrant to toss his house."

"And that's Monday?"

Dan was hopeful. "Judge Fogarty should cave, and we get the chance to find out if this guy has something to hide."

Chapter XXXVII

Richard added the Johannesburg Starburst to his collection and put six days of clothes in the bag. He set the timers and exited the rear window of his bedroom. He cut through some back yards and worked his way to the Tamiami Trail. He walked to the east end of the prearranged plaza and stood in an alley between a furniture store and a men's clothing store. It was eleven-thirty PM when the eighteen-wheeler came in the south entrance and hugged the perimeter as it eased along the dark stores. Eddie was doing five miles per hour when he heard the bang on the passenger side door. He eased the big rig to a crawl as Richard opened the door and threw his bag in the bunk.

"Keep rollin, good buddy. Time to log some miles!"

Eddie was wide awake. "And howdy-do to you, too. And thank you, Mr. Absent! What have you been doin' in this godforsaken town?"

Richard slapped his arm. "Didn't I say I appreciate the lift? Maybe this will convince you that our friendship has a financial base." He opened the bag and lifted out the diamond necklace.

"Holy-Mother-Of-Blue-Blazes! Is that as many karats as I hope it is?" Eddie was having a hard time keeping his eyes on the road at that moment.

Richard's smile was even. "Pay attention to your driving, if you please, kind sir. And yup. More karats than either of us has ever seen." Richard put the jewels back in the bag and settled down, moving the seat back so he couldn't be seen above the window. "How are the Sarah and the kids?"

Eddie became the proud father. "We're lucky that there are three thousand miles for you to become acquainted with the exploits of our gifted children. Let's just say that there's a contest between whether they play pro ball, or get Rhodes scholarships."

Richard whistled. "We *do* have a lot to talk about!" They turned out of the plaza heading for the I-75 entrance, heading north toward Gainesville.

Myra Frothingham had never felt better. She'd been chosen to wear the premier necklace and would be recognized last at the Masked Ball. "Isn't it wonderful, Albert? We're finally getting our due, here at the hotel."

He was not as euphoric. "I just hope you don't think I'm going to buy you that thing!"

"Aren't you?"

He snorted. "Are you out of your mind? That's a museum piece. Some day it'll be worth fifty million!"

She didn't see his point. "Right. So why not buy it now, at the bargain price?"

He was finished with the nonsense. "We can visit it every year, on our anniversary," was his sarcastic response. "I'm not going to bid on an icon that every thief in the Western Hemisphere wants to steal!"

When Gary drove up, Ted was more than ready to go home. "I've never had a tougher time trying to stay awake than for this guy. He goes to work, comes home, and goes to bed. I get him when he sleeps."

Gary was sympathetic. "I don't know how you do it. For me, he goes to work and comes home, and sometimes he goes on a date. You at least get the chance to see the looker at the other woman's house."

"Big deal!", Ted answers. "She gets out of his car and goes in the house. Sometimes he goes with her. More often he just goes home. I get five seconds of gorgeous and eight hours of porch lights!"

"All right. So we both have dull jobs, but the pay is good." Gary admitted. "What do you have for me this morning?"

Ted started his car. "He came home, watched TV, and went to bed. It's like 'Groundhog Day' all over again. I could phone you his routine from my house."

Gary was tired already. "Then you would lose your overtime. Go home, and leave me to my boredom."

Shannon and Susan shopped until they dropped. "They better appreciate our new dresses", Susan said laughing. Shannon had chosen a lime green linen suit she hoped would make her look more mature. Susan liked her off the shoulder, purple cocktail dress.

"I've never been to La Rive Gauche, have you?" Shannon had heard of the restaurant, now more famous because of the robbery, but it had always been way out of her league.

Susan had eaten there once. "I was asked out by a Spa guest. I wasn't supposed to date a patron, but he was so cute, and he had that French accent."

Shannon wanted to know what happened.

"He said that Naples had no good restaurants, but when I mentioned La Rive Gauche, he pretended he needed me to find the place for him."

"And then?"

"It turned out that 'Mr. Frra-aw-nsh' was just a spoiled Momma's boy, out for a good time before he had to go back to France. He kept telling me how rich his parents were, and that he was going to inherit their estates and wineries. And all he needed to keep me in his memory bank, was to get in my American pants!"

"What did you do?"

"I helped him rack up a bill only a credit card could love, and when he drove me home, I kissed my finger, put it on his nose, and never looked back."

"Did he get mad?" Shannon was giggling.

"Who cares? He was a phony who thought I was a pushover hick. He made me so mad." Susan changed the subject. "I love your suit. And so will Richard."

"You think so?"

"You look adorable in it. Of course he'll love it."

"I don't want to look adorable," Shannon said quietly. "I want to look like a woman."

Susan was concerned. "Why do you say that?"

Shannon was close to tears when she replied, "Richard is so mature, and he's almost ten years older than me. I'm afraid that he'll find someone more like him."

Susan wasn't so sure about that. "Maybe he likes you because you help him feel younger, more energetic, more full of life."

That made Shannon feel better. She would show him tonight that she could handle herself in a swanky restaurant, the kind of place the Sherill's guests frequented.

Dan called the tail. "What's going on today, Gary?"

"Funny you should ask, Detective. He got up at eight, at least the lights went on in the kitchen, and so far, he's stayed home. "

"Is that normal for this guy?" Dan was a little curious.

"Hard to say. This is my first weekend on surveillance. Maybe he got all tired last night because of the late shift."

"What about his girlfriend?" Dan could feel his curiosity increasing.

"You mean the 'looker'? My guess is that he'll go out with her tonight." Gary tried to sound alert.

"All right. Stay on him. We don't want him to skip before we get the search warrant."

"Ten-four, Dan."

Barry was the first at Susan's house. He whistled when he saw the women twirl in their new outfits. "Wait til Richard sees you two. He may have to get his eyeballs realigned."

Susan was happy to get another chance at the French restaurant. "We haven't eaten all day. I'm famished."

Shannon's suit was not too tight. "I'll eat anything, but not snails."

Susan finally brought out some crackers. "Do you want a drink, Honey?"

He checked his watch. "It's quarter to eight. Not like Richard to take his time. I'll have that beer."

Susan wasn't worried. "It's called being fashionably late. You said we had the table for the whole night. There's no need for him to be here early."

Shannon took a cracker and some cheese. "Do you think he meant that we were to meet him at the restaurant?"

Barry tried Richard's cell. There was only the message: "This is Richard. I am obviously unable to answer the phone. Please leave a message and I will turn over heaven and earth to get back to you."

What Barry did not know was that his friend's cell phone was now at the bottom of the Caloosahatchee River joining hundreds of other unwanted, traceable electronic devices. Richard had tossed it from his passenger window at midnight before climbing into Eddie's bunk, just before they reached the Lee-County border.

Myra Frothingham had chosen her gown, and the mask. She was to be a harlequin, all blacks and whites, the mask covered with sparkling glass, to mimic the diamonds in her necklace. George had decided against his first tux and chose his more traditional model. He, too, had a reflective mask. She went to the safe to retrieve her short-term prize. The earrings looked right, but there was something wrong about the necklace. For some strange reason, it looked cheap.

"Albert, can you come here a minute, please?"

He squinted at the glass jewelry. "That doesn't look like your necklace, Myra. Where did you put it?"

Anger was better than fear. "In the SAFE, you NINNY!"

"Then where is it, Myra? This looks like it came from a toy store! Are you sure it's not in the closet?"

"I *couldn't* have mislaid it. Oh, please. I know I put in the safe after the dinner party."

Albert refused to believe she hadn't made a mistake. "Let's look around before anyone calls Sir George. I don't want to be embarrassed when you find it in the bureau." He started to rummage through her lingerie.

"Albert, stop! It's gone! I'm calling Sir George!"

Chapter XXXVIII

The police had taped the room and dusted the safe. Dan and Sean contacted the concierges. Charles was at home and they reached Barry on his cell phone.

"Richard is supposed to be with us at a restaurant. He's not answering his cell phone. Something is wrong! Could you check with the hospitals and see if he's been in an accident, please?", Barry begged the policemen.

Dan called his surveillance officer, Ted. "Where is he now?"

Ted sounded bored. "He hasn't left the house. The car is in the driveway. There are lights on and I can see the reflection from the TV. It's just like the movie. He's home alone!"

"Don't go anywhere! We're coming with backup!", Dan warned.

"Backup for what? I told you. He's watching television." Ted Simmons felt like he was in left field.

"I'll explain when we get there," was Dan's short answer.

They had police behind the house when Dan rang the front doorbell. There was no response but everyone could hear the television. He knocked again and then they broke in, guns drawn. The place looked lived in. There was food in the refrigerator and dishes in the sink. They dusted for prints and searched all the rooms and the garage. Dan found some junk jewelry in a bag. He told Sean, "This must be some of the stash he used to fool Mrs. Frothingham."

Sean was angry. "I guess we won't need that warrant."

Dan wanted to make sure. "We'll get it anyway. Let's cover all our bases on this one. I don't think our dear Richard will be coming back, if he's left with the necklace. Who knows if he had other stolen items. This piece alone they say is worth over ten million, if they disassemble the stones."

"And intact?", Sean asked.

"A lot more than that. But the point is it's so recognizable, the jewelers are guessing the thieves have no choice but to break it down. They all know what it looks like."

There were no comatose hospital victims that night. Dan met Charles at the young man's residence.

"When did Richard ask you to help with the serving?"

"Actually, he suggested me, but Mr. Merrick was the one who assigned me to the job."

"And you all went to different rooms?"

"That's right, Detective. We each had a separate suite. I had the Cunninghams in 1804."

"How long did it take to finish the serving?" Charles instinctively looked at his watch and was embarrassed:

"I think it just took ten minutes. No more than that."

"Was Richard different on the way back down?", the detective asked the concierge.

"No. He was the same, before and after. We were all a little excited to see which one of us got the biggest tip."

Sean went to Susan's house and interviewed the shocked inhabitants. Barry had stayed there after the disappointed group had returned from the restaurant, sans Richard. Sergeant Brady could see that Shannon had been crying. The other two appeared in shock.

Susan kept repeating, "There must be some mistake. Richard can't be involved."

Sean was going over similar ground as Dan had. "And you say, serving the jewelry winners was Richard's idea?"

"That's right, Sergeant," Barry answered, sounding a little croaky. "He thought it would help highlight the luxury components."

"Were there other reasons for this perk?"

"I guess he was thinking that it would reinforce the event's reputation in the community. And give the hotel a more positive position."

"What about the chance to get a big tip?"

"Well, sure. We all thought that we could get a good pay-off. At least, we hoped so."

"What was the take?"

"Charles and Richard both got one hundred dollar bills and my envelope had a fifty. But Richard offered to split the difference and he gave me twenty-five. We were supposed to use the money to help pay for dinner tonight at La Rive Gauche."

Sean added the postscript. "But Richard never showed. Did he call?"

Shannon started to cry all over again. The officer wanted to hold her and say that she deserved better than this, but he still had a job to do. "Did Richard ever say he was going on vacation? Leaving town for any reason?"

They all shook their heads no.

Shannon had no real information. "We talked about our free time when the season ended, but it was all things we would do around Naples."

Sean looked at the others. "Were there any discussions of favorite places to go? Like, for example, New Mexico or California?"

Shannon made eye contact with her friends. "He never said anything about those vacation spots, did he?" Susan and Barry shook their heads in agreement. And bewilderment.

Susan supported her roommate. "He wanted to be successful here, and he was."

Barry chimed in. "Richard was the fastest concierge. Nobody was even close! I'm sure people have already told you that."

Sean had heard that rep, but now all they could be sure of was that Richard could have made one of the quicker exits from town.

Richard's picture was faxed to all the terminals. Police were interviewing agents at the International airport and bus depots. The Naples and smaller hubs were checked for charters and puddle jumpers to Key West and Fort Lauderdale. No one had seen a tall, dark haired man in any of the transportation centers, including any of the cruise lines. The toll takers on Alligator Alley didn't remember a driver or passenger of his description. To cover the waterfront, both day catamarans to Key West were surveyed and had not seen him, either.

"Where are we now?" The sun was shining, and he heard Eddie fire up the big rig.

"Gulfport, Mississippi, good buddy. It's a beeootiful, sunny day!"

Richard squinted as the driver swung away from the bright light and the truck stop, heading west again on Interstate 10.

"I know a great diner five miles up, a lot better than this joint, and their bathroom is a two-holer."

Richard had slept well. "Good enough for me, old friend."

The compartment behind the driver's bunk was a little cramped, but there was ventilation and an adequate pillow. Anyone curious enough to climb up to the window would have seen just one sleeping occupant, as Richard was invisible.

Chapter XXXIX

Dan called California. "Good morning, Sergeant Avila. Dan Logan from Naples, Florida. It's still morning there, isn't it?"

"Yup, still morning and we're back in the sunshine! You have some news for me. I hope?"

"Yes, I do. But not all of it is good. We have an I.D. on our criminal, a suspected jewel thief and possible murderer. Rick Weber, with a grand theft record from California. He's been in our area for a little over three years."

"Where is he now?", the sergeant inquired.

"Flown the coop, I'm afraid. He had an eighteen hour head start between the theft and discovery, and none of the hubs has a record of his departure."

The sergeant had his web site up. "I've got his sheet here and the guy fits our profile. My guess is that he and your victim did some time together. It wouldn't take too long to verify that."

Dan had use for the data. "Could you send me your information, real and anecdotal, please? And I'll give you our crime scene reports and investigation summary. It's just possible he's heading your way."

Sergeant Avila was hopeful. "We would love to sweat this guy, for both our robbery and that missing service revolver. Any cold case we clear is a load off our minds, and my old partner has never lived it down." There was nothing more to say except, "Thanks for the new info, Detective. We'll see if this swallow comes back to Capistrano!"

"Ditto, Sergeant. Good luck! And if you're ever out this way, let's look each other up. Let's hope we owe it to ourselves. And call me Dan."

Sir George was not happy. The event insurance from Lloyd's, shared by the hotel and the jewelry merchants, would cover the losses, but next year's premiums would be through the roof. Restoring the Hotel's reputation was another matter. He knew that the Ritz and the other high end hotels would be offering to host the next Diamond Expo, suggesting that they could provide much better security than that delivered by the unfortunate (and, sadly aging) Hotel Sherill. Stan Merrick was sweating into his chair while the CEO reviewed the missing concierge's personnel folder. "Merrick, I don't see any background checks on Mr. Smythe. Tell me why you didn't follow protocol for hiring front end staff, of *all* people?"

The supervisor's dry mouth made it difficult to speak. "I'm not sure. We had a concierge get sick and Richard jumped in. You know, the seamless service thing, I guess. "

"Okay, I get the dropped ball connection, but after he was installed, why not do the background check then?" Sir George wasn't going to let Stan off the hook quite that easily. At least not yet.

Now the stammering began. "I, I -- we were in the holidays, beginning of the season, and we were so busy, and he was doing such a great job, and…" Then Stan tried to pass the buck to save his own hide. "Besides, he was already a hotel employee. Wasn't he already checked out?"

Sir George made a note in the record and looked up. "You're right on that one, Stan. There should have been more diligence at the beginning." There was a pause: "But it says here that his initial position was in the laundry, and you and I know those staff rarely get the chance to mingle with our guests and their property. Our front people have the highest profile and responsibility. You should have looked at this guy more closely."

Mr. Merrick was relatively speechless, but his mind was spinning. "What went wrong?", he wondered to himself. He had anticipated that the next sit down with the CEO would have been to consider a Vice Presidency, but this one was turning into a blood bath. Finding his voice, the stammering continued. "He, umm, he was the fastest concierge. No one could service more guests at once."

Sir George was not impressed: "Apparently your fastest concierge used that speed for personal gain, rather than the reputation of this hotel! Our records indicate the increase in reported losses for valuables came not long after "Quick Richard" became your latest, non-check hire!"

The supervisor was speechless.

The Coast Guard got a call for a partially submerged "Hazard-To-Navigation." It was an old seventeen foot Carolina skiff, found off Chokoloskee near the Everglades National Park. The boat was registered to the now deceased Louis Gonzales. The manufacturer would have been happy to know that the installed floatation foam had kept the boat off the bottom, but nonetheless in harm's way. Holed, and running out of gas aiming toward the Yucatan, the craft had succumbed to the prevailing currents, bringing her back, and in the general direction of the Florida Keys. There was nothing of an evidentiary nature left on board.

It was ten PM, and they were coming into El Paso. "The truck stop is just ahead and we'll bunk until morning."

Richard was looking for the shoehorn to help extricate his tired butt from the front seat. "I am so ready for a shower. How could you stand riding with me for the last four hundred miles?"

"I had the window open," Eddie answered, smiling. "And I had to smell myself, so your filthy hide was irrelevant. I have an extra towel. Take my shampoo. There's soap in their bathroom."

Richard was gratified to find the empty men's room, not wanting, if possible, to leave any cross-country imprint.

Chief Kelly had scheduled a courtesy call to the Hotel Sherill. The investigation was primarily over so he and Roni arrived in civilian dress, so as not to further offend the very delicate ambience. They rode the guest elevator to the fifteenth floor. Roni felt strangely liberated telling her boss, "I've never been on fifteen. We rode the service elevator, express, to the VIP suites on top."

He asked, "Are you glad to be out of here?"

She smiled with relief. "It's a joy not to have to push that laundry cart in this heat. I still feel badly for some of the working conditions here. Those poor unsuspecting women."

The assistant ushered them into the teak lined office. The chief began formally with the introductions. "You remember Corporal Veronica Menendez, our undercover officer here." They shook hands.

"Thank you for assisting us, Corporal." Sir George gestured toward a tray table. "Can I offer you some coffee, tea, lemonade? I assume Champagne is out."

Jerry Kelly nodded in agreement. "We may be out of uniform, but we're still on duty. I thought we would review the progress of the case and share our conclusions."

Roni made a point of filling a crystal glass. She saw floating fruit, and it looked fresh squeezed. The chief took some iced tea.

Sir George began. "I would like to thank you both for coming over and maintaining a degree of anonymity. I take it you have not been able to locate our missing concierge?"

Chief Kelly opened his folder. "The theft was reported at six-thirty PM, on Saturday. We assume the transfer took place the preceding night, around ten-thirty PM, while your concierge, Richard Smythe, as he was known here, was serving the Frothinghams. That gave the suspect an approximate fourteen hour escape window, between the alarm and his alleged Naples exit. The safe was opened with a master key which we expect was a forged duplicate. We can tell you now that your ex-employee was using an assumed name. His real identity is Richard, or Rick, Weber. He's a known California felon. He had violated probation there, but was not otherwise a fugitive from justice."

The CEO was curious. "Was he your murderer?"

The chief nodded. "He is our only suspect. There is no direct evidence linking him to the deaths of the two robbers, but if he had fed them the reservation data, there was an obvious motive to keep it quiet."

Sir George interrupted. "The Hotel would also like to thank you for returning Mr. Frothingham's watch. Apparently, it had as much sentimental value as its high price tag." He sighed. "If there was a silver lining to any of this, finding that particular belonging and giving it back helped two of our guests feel a little less violated. The other benefit for us is the expectation that our losses from thefts will diminish dramatically, now that Mr. Smythe/Weber has left our hen house. We think the police involvement could have pressured him to leave us more quickly than he might have wanted. For that breakthrough," at this point Sir George looked from one to the other, "we at the Hotel Sherill are in your debt." The distinguished chief executive, to the surprise of the chief and Roni, made a half bow from his chair.

This gave the chief an opportunity. "Obviously, we were just doing our jobs. First, Corporal Menendez wanted to offer something. Roni?"

"Thanks Chief. This concerns Mr. Delgado and his sexual assault on me."

Sir George coughed. "Why, uh, yes, Corporal. We want to especially thank you for bringing that, ah, unfortunate matter to our attention. We are well rid of that scoundrel!"

With or without interruptions, Roni was going to have her say. "I believe that the laundry supervisor has a history of assaulting his workers, particularly those who have arrived recently and who are English language impaired. He came on to me, expecting little fight, and threatened me with the loss of employment here. When I presented this to your human resources boss, she seemed to want to keep it under the rug. That's why I asked to speak with you." She wanted to finish without more input. "I would like to talk to the other laundry maids and ask them how many have been pressured for sex by Mr. Delgado. If we get more complaints, this guy will go away for a long time and may be placed on the sexual predator list, meaning he will be monitored for the rest of his punitive life."

Roni waited, while Sir George gathered his thoughts.

"I am surprised by Mrs. Barton's response. Of course you can address those afflicted staff. I do have some concerns. You are aware of the cumulative, negative publicity that has evolved from the robberies. The Board and I wish to stem this onslaught of criticism, and would be grateful for any insights as to how we could, as they say, 'stop the bleeding' of the media feeding frenzy."

Now it was the chief's turn to do some thinking. He looked at Roni and gave a little shrug, to let her know that this was not to minimize her efforts. "If Corporal Menendez is successful talking to the maids, we will have enough proof to more than make our case against Mr. Delgado. Given the preponderance of evidence, his attorney will want to make a plea bargain. To avoid negative publicity against his client, and to minimize a sentence, the lawyer could accept both the plea and a change of venue. This would effectively move the case to another jurisdiction, taking it out of the public eye."

Chief Kelly turned to Roni. "I'm not talking about this guy walking. With the multiple counts, he will still get a stiff sentence. Just not the max. Get me?"

Roni understood. "He doesn't have to max out, as long as he's seen as a multiple offender and gets the label forever."

The chief continued, this time to the hotel magnate. "Even if the judge doesn't grant the change of venue, the plea bargain will take it out of a jury trial and out of the reporters' notebooks."

Sir George was seeing some light at the end of what had been a very long dark tunnel.

"We would be very grateful to see this end for us without any more bombshells. What could I do to demonstrate our thanks for all your assistance?"

At this, the chief exhibited a dry grin. "Of course, we can't accept any remuneration for doing our civic duty. However, Corporal Menendez has been having difficulty finding a place to hold her wedding and, if I'm not mistaken, the big event is just about three weeks away. Is that right, Roni?"

Now she was really blushing, totally blindsided by this revelation of their planning problems. "But we do have a place, Chief! Don't you remember, Domen--"

He stopped her. "Officer Menendez has been so busy with her police work, going undercover, that sort of thing, that her wedding has sort of have been put on the back burner, so to speak. I guess you would understand the competition for space, when people haven't yet seen the last of the season."

Sir George could see perfectly, and the chance to turn the tables on the publicity people was suddenly a wonderful opportunity. "We don't have to mention that Ms. Menendez was here undercover, do we?"

The chief was quick to relieve the hotel from further scrutiny. "Certainly not. Corporal Menendez would just be another beautiful bride who just happens to be a successful police officer. Her fiancé was one of our investigators working here, interviewing your employees for the last few weeks. Detective Dan Logan."

Roni's head was on a swivel, reacting to the machinations going on between the two leaders. "Now wait a minute! We can't affor--!"

This time it was Sir George's turn to interrupt. "We do a variety of giving to the community. The last thing, I think, was that Easter egg hunt on the beach. We opened that to our employees' kids. If I remember correctly, they ran a piece in the Naples Daily News. We are in a position to offer a sunset wedding on the beach for two local police officers, complete with a reception to follow in one of the side rooms for… when was that date?"

Roni's head was spinning. "April 26th, but we don't nee---"

"What is your budget for the event?", Sir George asked.

"It's four thousand, but we are--"

"PERFECT!" was his reply. "There will probably be at least two other weddings scheduled for the afternoon and evening, but with a hundred yards of sequestered beach and ten auxiliary rooms, we can more than accommodate the addition. Please schedule a meeting with our event coordinator and you can go over the details. I will inform her to expect your call. Now, is there anything else? I have another meeting in five minutes with the vice president of personnel." He was opening the door, ushering them out, his business completed.

The chief was grinning from ear to ear and Roni was in shock. She turned to him in the hall, her eyes huge. "Did I just hear what I think I heard?"

"Let's stop early in Phoenix. Wouldn't you like to stretch your legs?" Richard was lifting his feet from the floor. "If I don't walk soon they'll fall off, and you can carry me the rest of the way."

The eighteen-wheeler pulled in to one of the largest truck stops Richard had seen, and parked on the outside of nearly one hundred big rigs. It was twilight and some of the drivers, anticipating early departures, had already fallen asleep. The two men walked the outside perimeter near a wire mesh fence.

"We could make a long run and get to San Diego tomorrow," Eddie suggested.

Richard wondered if that was necessary. "Is there a need to rush? What if we stopped early, and had some daylight for maneuvering once we got there."

Eddie was agreeable. "That'll work. We can overnight in Ocotillo. I didn't know what kind of hurry you'd be in."

Richard didn't want to push the envelope so late in the plan. "If you have some flex in your delivery schedule, I'd just as soon come into San Diego with some daylight left."

"Okay with me. It'll give us more time to discuss my children's futures," Eddie quipped.

"Wait a minute. We already have them through medical school. What's left?"

"Are you kidding? Wait until we get to the part where they start their own hedge funds."

Richard laughed. "I get it now. This is just before they tell you that they'll be taking care of Sarah and you for the rest of your lives."

Eddie nodded. "Now we're on the same wavelength. We have come full circle -- their births to my decrepitude!"

They split up then, each one entering the big cafeteria separately, sitting at different tables, pictures of solitary truckers. Later Richard took another shower and got back to the truck, looking to see if anyone would be watching as he entered from the passenger side.

Eddie had moved the partition to let his friend enter the secluded rear bunk. "Don't snore tonight, buddy. I need my sleep!"

Richard feigned astonishment. "Me? Last night, I didn't know if the truck next door had a muffler problem or whether you swallowed chicken feathers!"

Eddie moved the cover to hide Richard. "No one ever complained about my sleeping before, so I know it's you." Behind, the plastic wall he heard Richard snicker, "Our first fight!"

Shannon had no desire to go home. It had been a week since the big mess at the hotel, and she was just going through the motions. "Would you mind if I stayed a little while longer? I don't think I can be alone just yet."

Susan was more than sympathetic. "I *want* you to stay. The reporters need more time to realize you're not going to talk to anyone. We can still sneak you in and out of work so they'll get the message that chasing you is a waste of time. Besides, I kind of like having a younger sister."

Shannon almost smiled.

The press briefing had helped. The chief and Sir George had met with all the media in a room just off the Grande Salon at the hotel. Sir George had provided the famous Sherill buffet, complete with wine and an open bar.

Later, Barry had told the ladies that staff had never seen so much alcohol consumed at one time. "And it wasn't even one PM yet!"

In the aftermath of that restorative bacchanal, the reporters had treated the old hotel with some charity, describing the events as "unfortunate" and "unprecedented" while pointing out to their print and TV audiences that the Sherill had instituted some changes in their personnel and had added high tech security equipment that made future breaches very unlikely. The robbery had been attributed to a now-absent fugitive, an ex-concierge, and that same man was a "person of interest" in the murders of the parking lot snatch-and-grabbers. Sir George had told the public that his facility was now cleansed of its bad apples. From this point on everyone could go forward, assured that the Hotel Sherill was still the hospitality leader of Southwest Florida.

"We have to go to the party house," Roni announced.

"Why?" Dan was resisting, not really liking the place. "Didn't we already leave a deposit?"

"That's the reason we're going. I need to pick up that money and I need you there, in case Mr. Domenici gives me a hard time."

Roni was trying hard not to smile. Her fiancé was confused, not totally out of line with being a husband-to-be, but this didn't make sense.

"Wait a minute. If we get the deposit back, we lose the place."

She pretended to be throwing caution to the winds. "Who cares, you never really liked it there, anyway. Admit it."

Now he was in the middle. "Well, actually, I guess it could have been nicer, but we were running out of choices."

Roni was triumphant. "See, I was right. You hated that room!"

Dan was approaching disorientation. "Aren't we getting married soon? And don't we need a wedding site?"

She was having trouble holding it in. "I'll explain in the car. Let's go now. We'll ride in your cruiser."

He took off his hat and mopped his brow, not looking at her.

Roni was bouncing on her seat. "Promise me you won't drive off the road?"

He turned in her direction, surprised to see her radiant smile. "Okay, what do you have up your sleeve? Something is screwy here."

"We have a new location for our wedding," she beamed.

"What are you talking about? What new place?"

She leaned over and kissed him on the cheek. "We're going to say our vows on the beach."

"The *beach?* What beach? Where?"

"Why, at the Hotel Sherill, of course. Where else?"

He pulled over in a driveway and looked at her. "Huh? The Hotel Sherill? Are you nuts, woman? We can't afford that place. We didn't even price them, they cost so much. We only have four thousand dollars! Did you forget that little detail?"

She let him sputter until he was out of breath and then calmly gave him the new nuptial arrangements. "Sir George told the chief and me that they have a huge beach and can handle two or three weddings at once. And they have more than enough private rooms, so there won't be a problem."

"But we can't afford them, honey."

"Sir George assured me that he can give us a wedding there that fits our budget."

"Wait a minute. Is this charity? You know we can't accept anything like that."

Roni was going to defend Sir George's decision to her grave. *"No me prolema en esto, tipo grande. Nade en demsiadas hojas sucias para perder esta oportunidad!"*

"HUH?"

"He is the *boss*, Dan, with control of discretionary funds. And he can decide who and what gets the gravy! Our wedding is going to be part of his gravy, but we have to invite him to the festivities. I said he could come. Is that all right sweetheart?"

Dan sat and thought for what seemed an endless minute. He turned in the seat and grabbed his fiancée. "Let's go get our money back!"

Sergeant Brady had to make another visit.

Susan looked out her kitchen window. "It's that policeman that came to the Spa. I can tell him that you are too sick for any more questions."

Shannon came from the bathroom, drying her short, blonde curls. "No," she said in a tired voice: "I might as well get this over with. How much worse could it get?"

Sean rang the bell, and the older woman let him in. Susan whispered, "Please take it easy on her. She's had a rough time."

Shannon was sitting at the kitchen table. Sean took the opposite chair. "I'm sorry to take more of your time, uh, Shannon."

"That's okay, Sergeant. I don't have many tears left."

"Last time, you asked me to call you Shannon. So I'm Sean, okay?"

"All right, -- Sean."

"This will not take too long, Shannon. First of all, we wanted you to know that you will not have to put up with any more interviews. The department has cleared you of all involvement. You are what we call an innocent bystander."

Shannon felt a hint of relief, both for the end of the investigation as well as her involvement with a fugitive. "Thank you, Ser.. Sean. That does make me feel a little better. I didn't know when it was ever going to end."

"We understand that you've been through an ordeal and would like to know if you are getting any help. We have a Victims Assistance program and there are counselors who could come to your house."

Shannon could see that the young man appeared to be sincerely interested in her well being. "How long could I get that counseling? Right now, I have my friends. But I'm worried what it'll be like when I go home."

He was glad that she willing to ask for help. "This offer remains open. If and when you want them, they will come to you." He had another question. "Have you been bothered by the media? Have they stalked you?"

She was surprised that he was worried about that. "We haven't had much trouble from them. Ever since Sir George's news conference, they seem to have gone away."

He had another solution. "If you believe that anyone is following you, we can provide an escort, or advise the person that he could be charged with harassment."

"You would do that?" Shannon was feeling more at ease, now.

"Certainly. Our jobs are to serve and protect. We... I want you to know that with all the publicity on the lost jewels, we... I didn't want you to think that we had forgotten your help in our investigation."

"So this is sort of like a 'Thank you?'"

He smiled at her. She liked his smile.

"Yes, Shannon, in a way, this is showing you our gratitude for what you have been through, and how hard you tried to be a cooperative citizen." He was laying it on thick, trying to prolong the contact. "I want you to have my card. I've written my cell phone on the back and you can see the office number. Please call me if you need to talk about anything. I promise I will try to help."

Shannon took the card. She was impressed by the obvious effort. "Thank you, Sean, for coming over."

He rose from his chair and she stood to take his hand. Shannon could see that he was taller, and had bright blue eyes. She liked how his uniform fit, accentuating his broad shoulders and narrow hips. He could smell her shampoo, and wanted to kiss her until she was happy again. Instead, he squeezed her hand and backed out the door. Sean knew he would call her again.

Susan came back in the kitchen. Shannon watched him get in the patrol car and drive away.

"He likes you."

Shannon turned and arched her back: "What are you talking about?"

"He likes you. He thinks you're special."

Shannon looked out the window again. "He was just doing his job."

Susan snorted. "Do you think the police visit every person associated with a crime after their work is over?"

Shannon didn't reply, but somewhere deep inside her, a hidden smile marked the beginning of some healing.

"Thanks for the lift, Eddie. You were a lifesaver."

The driver opened his envelope. "Wow! This is way too much!"

Richard patted his friend on the shoulder. "No, it isn't. Not when you think how much college tuitions have gone up."

Eddie blew into the envelope. "You're right! Where's the rest of it?"

The passenger smiled. "You'll be getting supplements regularly, but below the IRS horizons."

"My kids will leave cookies and milk for you every Christmas, Santa. Where are you meeting your guy? Have I seen him before?", Eddie inquired.

Richard had a wry smile. "You'll never meet him. I don't want you to know anything that might get you in trouble. When you next hear from me, I'll have a new name and birth date, so don't throw that mail in the trash."

The cab pulled up. Eddie pretended to be wiping his eyes. "Don't forget us, Santa. Have a good life."

Richard hugged his friend. "Kiss Sarah and the kids."

"I will, oh generous one. Until next time."

Richard was waving goodbye to Eddie as the cab pulled away. *"Buenos Dios. Broadway para Apoyar la Avenida, por favor."*

Roni was surprised to meet a new director of Human Resources. "Where is Sandra Barton?"

"She is no longer with the Hotel," was the cryptic response. "My name is Marisa Dowling. Mr. Sherill gave me the background. You wish to speak with the laundry maids. I will call their new supervisor. He is outside. Mr. Merrick, can you come in now, please?"

A harried looking man entered the office. Marisa Dowling wasted few words.

"Corporal Menendez is ready to interview your staff. Please assemble them in that small conference room off the corridor."

"You mean that space next to the linen repair area?", he asked in an embarrassed voice.

The woman spoke more gently. "Yes, Stan. You'll soon know all the nooks and crannies down here. It just takes a little time."

Roni walked with him down the dark sweaty hall. "Thank you for helping me this morning."

She had trouble understanding the grumbled response. It sounded a little like: "It would be my particular pleasure."